TOGETHER

WE

CAUGHT

FIRE

Also by Eva V. Gibson

Where Secrets Lie

TOGETHER

WE

CAUGHT

FIRE

Eva V. Gibson

SIMON & SCHUSTER BFYR

New York   London   Toronto   Sydney   New Delhi

SIMON & SCHUSTER BFYR

An imprint of Simon & Schuster Children's Publishing Division

1230 Avenue of the Americas, New York, New York 10020

Text © 2020 by Eva Gibson

Cover photograph of metallic string © 2020 by Ines Seidel

Cover photograph of couple © 2020 by garetsworkshop/Shutterstock

Cover photographs of paper and string by iStock/kev303, ksushsh, and martijnmulder

Cover design by Laura Eckes © 2020 by Simon & Schuster, Inc., inspired by "Woven Story" by Ines Seidel

For information about special discounts for bulk purchases, please contact Simon & Schuster Special Sales at 1-866-506-1949 or business@simonandschuster.com.

The Simon & Schuster Speakers Bureau can bring authors to your live event. For more information or to book an event, contact the Simon & Schuster Speakers Bureau at 1-866-248-3049 or visit our website at www.simonspeakers.com.

Also available in a hardcover edition

Interior design by Laura Eckes

The text for this book was set in Perpetua Std.

Manufactured in the United States of America

First SIMON & SCHUSTER BFYR paperback edition March 2021

2 4 6 8 10 9 7 5 3 1

The Library of Congress has cataloged the hardcover edition as follows:

Names: Gibson, Eva V., author.

Title: Together we caught fire / by Eva V. Gibson.

Description: First Simon Pulse hardcover edition. | New York : Simon Pulse, 2020. | Summary: Eighteen-year-old Lane, still dealing with her mother's suicide when she was five, must now adjust to her father's remarriage to Skye, making Lane's long-term, unrequited crush, Grey, her stepbrother.

Identifiers: LCCN 2019006486 (print) | LCCN 2019009187 (eBook) |

ISBN 9781534450219 (hardcover) | ISBN 9781534450233 (eBook)

Subjects: | CYAC: Stepfamilies—Fiction. | Dating (Social customs)—Fiction. | Love—Fiction. | Grief—Fiction. | Family life—North Carolina—Asheville—Fiction. | Asheville (N.C.)—Fiction.

Classification: LCC PZ7.G339274 (eBook) | LCC PZ7.G339274 Tog 2020 (print) |

DDC [Fic]—dc23

LC record available at https://lccn.loc.gov/2019006486

ISBN 9781534450226 (pbk)

For Cora

THIS STORY CONTAINS content that might be troubling to some readers, including, but not limited to, depictions of and references to death, suicide, cutting and self-harm, vivid nightmare imagery, substance abuse, homelessness, childhood trauma, and PTSD. Please be mindful of these and other possible triggers, and seek assistance if needed from the resources on page 347.

❧

TOGETHER

WE

CAUGHT

FIRE

1

THE WIND CLAWED AT MY LIMBS, DELVED MIST-HEAVY
fingers through my hair as it tried its best to pull me through the
open window. We'd lost ourselves in the twists of trees and shadows along the Blue Ridge Parkway, leaving the lights of downtown
Asheville far behind. Grey sat rigid in the driver's seat, clenched
and flexed his fingers on the steering wheel in nervous bursts as
the ancient Forester lumbered around the turns—a steady, reliable contrast to the idea unfolding inside it.

"No way. Absolutely not."

"What better way to get acquainted than to risk our lives
together?" Connor's eyes were lit in the glow of the dash lights
over a bright, sharp smile. "Lane. Laaaaane, come on. How else
will we establish trust?"

"I'm sure we'll think of something," I deadpanned. "Maybe
once you've known me longer than a week."

"Fair enough." He leaned between the front seats, zeroed in
on my antsy stepbrother. "Grey?"

"Dude, this is just a bad idea. The statistics alone—"

"Yeah, I get it. I don't need your academia. Sadie . . ." Connor turned to his sister, found himself face-to-face with a death glare she'd almost definitely learned from him. He fell back to the seat beside me with a shrug. "Know what? I won't bother asking."

"I am not riding on the roof of a moving car, Connor Hall, and you should know better than to even think it up. This is not how you and I were raised."

"I know. Isn't it great?"

He didn't climb out the window, not exactly—just slid his upper body through the space, fingers tight around the assist handle, leaned out backward as far as he could. He was all frayed hems and unbound laughter. His chain-and-leather wrist cuff caught the moonlight, winked at me from the shadows.

"Oh Lord, I don't like this." Sadie twisted around in the passenger seat, made a grab for her brother's ankle. He kicked her hand away. "Lane, honey, help him. Get him back in here."

"Like he'll listen to me?"

"Well, grab his arms, or something. He's about to go all over the road."

I undid my seat belt and scooted into his vacant seat, rose onto my knees to the left of his, ignoring the plaintive buzzing in my jacket pocket. Jeremy's bravado had apparently crumbled all the way to fucking dust in the few hours since I'd reiterated my desire to remain single for an undetermined stretch of eternity. A text or two on the heels of *that* talk was to be expected, but holy shit.

My tap on Connor's wrist did nothing; my insistent tug on his sleeve did less, and then I was caught—his hand closed around my biceps and dragged me through the window, pulling until my hips hit the doorframe. My shriek was a thin, useless thing, lost in the rush of night around us. Swept away along with his answering laugh.

"What are you *doing*??" I yelped. "Get back in there." He shook his head and leaned out farther—dangerously, heart-stoppingly farther. His grin formed words that never reached my ears. "What?"

He repeated himself, let go of my arm long enough to gesture at the sky.

"Look. Up."

Nothing about those instructions resembled a good plan. I did it anyway. I twisted my torso, clutched Connor's sleeve with one hand and the roof rack with the other. Tipped my head backward in a mimic of his.

We fell into the stars.

They funneled out of the darkness and seeped into my senses, overlapping and infinite, distant and impossibly close. The wind blew my hair across my tearing eyes, turned the sky to a moonlit blur of shadow and sound. My hand ached with the force of my grip, every joint threatening to pull apart. Every nerve poised to unravel.

Sadie's frantic taps on my knee pulled me back to earth. I snagged the shoulder of Connor's jacket and dragged him back into the car, where we landed in a breathless, dizzy heap.

"Not a bad view, huh, Lane?"

"Wild," I gasped. "We totally should get on the roof."

"Now you're talking. Sadie, tell your boy to slow it down till we're settled, then when I give the signal, give it all he's got."

"You're just a big old mess, Connor." Sadie shook her head, scowling at Connor over the back of her seat. "Both of you are way too much for me."

"You know you love this mess," he cackled. "Don't even act like you don't."

He snaked back out the window, leaned out again, shaking off my grip; Grey's foot pressed heavy on the gas pedal, as Sadie's apprehensive squawks slithered into my ears. I stretched out on the seat, tipped my head back, returned my eyes to the sky. Sought a second glimpse of Connor's view, from a significantly safer place.

We parked at an overlook, though there was nothing to see but deep, vast darkness, mountain shadows spackled with the twinkle of far-off cities. I drifted out of reach of the headlights, leaned against the guardrail as Grey cranked the music loud, and Connor cranked it louder. Sadie tugged at her brother's arms, begging him to dance even as he playfully smacked her hands away.

"Hey." Grey's drawl brushed my ear, rode the chills down my arms and back. I looked up and lost my way, drawn to him with that familiar sickening swoosh. A pitiful tide, held fast in the grip of the moon. "I'm glad you came out tonight."

"Oh. Thank you. Sorry for—I mean, I know Skye made you—"

"Elaine." That name, falling softly from his mouth. He was the only one who'd even think to use it. "Mom has nothing to do with it. We—*I* want you here, or you wouldn't be here. You're my sister now, right?" His grin faltered into uncertainty. "It still sounds weird, I know. But it's true."

"I guess it is." And it was—one week and counting, legally speaking, it was true. Horribly, unfairly, devastatingly true.

"You heard their vows. We're in this together. Always."

"Where is everybody?" Sadie's twang blew past me and circled Grey, tugging his eyes from mine. She'd paused her solo dance party long enough to realize the rest of us had disappeared. "Grey? Baby, where'd you go? I can't see one single blessed thing out here."

"Coming, babe." He darted past me, and it took everything I had to blink back the burn as he swooped away and into the wash of headlights, caught Sadie around the waist, lifting her off her feet to spin with him.

Together. Always.

How many years had I waited, hoping to hear those words from him? How many more years would I spend sending habitual smiles across tables and rooms, through gritted, aching teeth? How many nights would I lie awake, listening through the thin wall of my bedroom for the sleep-jagged edge of his breath? This boy, so long unreachable—the core of everything I'd wanted, mangled and reassembled into a cosmic joke.

One week into eternity, and I wanted to cry every time it crossed my mind. Because that's a healthy and productive method of problem-solving.

Admittedly better than my usual methods, though—all good-looking and nice and boring and replaceable—all attempts to feel *something*, for literally any attractive, age-appropriate guy who was not Grey McIntyre. All of whom lay in ruins behind me—stitches dropped from the end of the needle. Tiny holes, ruining the finished piece.

God. I should absolutely never be a life coach, in any form.

Connor emerged from the night, a jigsaw of edges and shadows, startling his sister. She shrieked, then giggled, clinging to Grey.

"Oh, there you are." She craned her neck, squinted past the headlights. "Where's Lane? Lane? Are you out there?"

"I'm here," I called, bolstered by my calm, tremor-free voice. Proud of my straight, solid spine and dry eyes, and the way my feet didn't hesitate to carry me forward over Grey's footprints. "I'm right here."

Sadie. All spark plugs and Southern charm, laughter bursting from her throat and sliding like a dropped skirt off her cello-curved hips. The alphabet threw us together year after year, from grade school all the way to seventeen, and it was weird how I hadn't really known her before now, when I'd spent my life sitting either next to or right behind her: Hall, just ahead of Jamison. Sunburst, just ahead of shade. Sadie is the girl you feel guilty for resenting, even when she's wrapped around the boy you love. The girl who, when that boy officially introduces you as his new stepsister, hugs you right there in the hallway, vocally covets your vintage Docs and begs you to crochet her a scarf exactly like the one you're wearing, only in pink. Admires your hair, the straight, dark brown monotony that's made it to your hips without seeing a salon, much less followed hers in a trip around the color spectrum that ended in bright lavender and turquoise slashes, peeking out from the naturally blond top layer. All those things of mine so un-Sadie somehow made enviable through her enthusiastic eyes.

As for Connor—well, I'd never actually met him before, but I knew him. Everyone knew Connor Hall, former lifelong anchor of the youth group set. Everyone knew he'd been exiled from his family at sixteen, disappeared from school and life, devastated his parents and more than a few good Christian girls when he came out. Everyone knew he'd faded into the streets of Asheville, emerged years later as a furious collection of hollows and angles before moving into his boyfriend's riverfront warehouse-turned-studio, where he wrested art from metal and fire and knives. Connor, once as healthy and solid as his little sister, now gone to bone. Now skeleton and sinew, bound with bitter thread, his messy hair and eyebrow ring and pretty, troublesome mouth the antithesis to the scrubbed-wholesome gleam of the boy he'd been.

I'd always recognized them best as the kids from the television, before—the Hall siblings and their bowed heads, combed shiny for the public-access cameras. Numbed to their father's brimstone shouts and flailing arms. Sadie and Connor. Two stubborn ends of the same short stick.

And Grey.

There was a reason I tied myself to no one—there was a reason I focused on schoolwork, stayed busy with our stall at the farmers' market, threw myself into knitting more inventory at the first hint of a spare moment. Sweet, book-smart, oblivious Grey. He'd occupied my heart for years, long before he'd occupied the bedroom next to mine.

Seriously. Kill me.

Sadie turned her focus back to the music, let her head drop back onto Grey's shoulder as she swayed them both to the beat. They moved together, pressed close, cheek to cheek and all the way down. Her hand was a fluttering wild thing beckoning us closer as they danced our way, Grey's promise ring a violet glint on her finger. Amethyst, of all the options on the face of the earth—the stone of Saint Valentine. The symbol of fidelity and commitment and deep spiritual connection. His smile lit the world, slipped a sharp shard of glass through the soft space below my sternum.

"Not your thing either, huh?"

The voice appeared at my side, out of nowhere. I looked up into Connor's smirk.

"Not in any sense," I sighed. "Unless I'm very drunk."

"Right there with you. It's hilarious, though, huh? My funda-mentalist baby sister, all but engaged to your wizard brother. An end-to-end clusterfuck in the making."

"He's Wiccan, not a 'wizard.' And he's *not* my brother."

"He's the poor man's Harry Potter. Their kids will fuck some-thing up—break a dish, set fire to the curtains—and won't know whether to wave their wands or pray to Jesus."

My head ached with the images conjured by his words: a sweet-faced, chubby girl, all rosy cheeks and striking green eyes, surrounded by shards of crockery; a boy, Grey in miniature with Sadie's chin, clutching a matchbook in dimpled, guilty hands. The endgame of everything they were: together. In love. Com-mitted against all odds since freshman year, despite the initial blowback—the brainy pagan and the busty preacher's daughter, a joke on a silver platter for the boys who'd spent our early years drawing devil horns on his notebooks. Who'd called her prissy and frigid, and every mean version of fat, until they finally caught on she didn't care. The same boys who now couldn't help but look as she swung past, stepping on their girlfriends' slender shadows to wrap herself in Grey's open arms.

It wasn't fair.

I was too distraught to stifle a yelp as my phone buzzed *again*—for the first time, I realized, since I'd gone out the car window. We must have hit a dead zone on the mountain-side, or maybe Jeremy had taken a dinner break. Either way, judging from the string of missed calls and the renewed cascade of bullshit texts overlapping on the already full screen, he appeared to have picked up his tantrum right where he'd left off.

Answer the phone, Lane.

I knew you'd do this.

ANSWER ME, YOU UNGRATEFUL BITCH

"I think the word you're looking for is 'unsubscribe.'"

I blinked up at Connor. He peered over my shoulder, eyebrows lifting as a collection of similarly caustic messages assaulted my phone.

"Yeah, it's this guy I used to know from school. He's got his feelings all in a bunch."

"Boyfriend?"

"God no. Summer thing. End of summer, really."

"And yet here we are on the cusp of fall. Which, I take it, is the problem?" He nodded knowingly at my sigh. "He's not giving you shit at school, is he?"

"No. He graduated last year. He shopped at our booth a couple months ago, and—well, behold the results of that chance reunion."

He watched my thumbs fly across the screen, as Jeremy's onslaught continued to vindicate my life choices. For once.

Jeremy, I said I was fine being friends if you could be cool about it, but it appears you're not. So.

I KNEW you'd do this. Everyone knows how you are—they FUCKING WARNED ME. I KNEW IT.

You KNEW it because I TOLD you. I told you from day one this would never be a long-term thing, and you said it was fine. Lie much? Or are you just in denial?

You think you're hot shit, don't you. Think someone like you can do better than me? YOU CAN'T. NO ONE WILL LOVE YOU LIKE THIS EVER AGAIN.

Huh. Sounds like I'll really be missing out.

Fuck you. FUCK YOU, LANE. Fucking BITCH. #SLUT

Nice hashtag, asshole. Bye.

WAIT. I'M SORRY. PLEASE DON'T DO THIS

Already done, guy. So very, VERY done.

LANE PLEASE I LOVE YOU

Obviously. #Blocked

"Ah, high school." Connor shook his head. "Why burn a bridge when you can carpet-bomb a whole fucking village?"

"He was nice enough at one point, believe it or not," I sighed, shoving my mercifully silenced phone back in my pocket. "Most of them are."

"Wow. So 'abusive dick' is your usual type?"

"I don't really have a type."

His answer was a muttered blur, losing itself in the shadows as my gaze wandered back to Grey. Sadie's arms wrapped him like holiday ribbon, her laughter ringing loud and long and genuine. His answering smile was winter sunlight, white-bright and blinding, a match for hers, and it was no mystery at all, really. Of course he loved the girl behind that gleam of constant, unbound joy. What boy craved the threat of rain over a brilliant, cloudless sky?

Not Grey McIntyre. Not the boy who danced closer all at once, whose hand snaked out and snagged my wrist, dragging me into their sway. Not the boy who caught my waist and stole my breath, whirled and spun me inches from his grin, then reached past me to thread his fingers through Sadie's as she shimmied closer. They enfolded and surrounded me, hugged me between them. My heart strained and cracked, fat at the seams with sorrow and laughter and a crazed, futile flare of hope.

We spun together, or the world spun around us, or maybe both and it didn't matter. His breath was warm on my neck, his low laugh a flame sliding over the curve of my ear. His hands were around my wrists, puppeting my arms to mirror

Sadie's. His scent was a drug; his touch, an infection.

I looked to Connor, but he had moved to the edge of the light, an enviably safe distance from us. His profile flared orange as he lit a joint in his cupped hands, held his smoke and blew it into the sky, then glanced our way. My eyes slid shut against the drum-heavy blur of the night, and when I opened them, he was there, smirk in place, fingers closing around my sleeve.

"Oh, there you are! You have to dance, honey. I'm so—" Sadie's eyes and exclamations lit up the world, then narrowed as she sniffed the air. "Are you smoking *marijuana*? Connor Hall, you know better than to—"

"Fuck off, Sadie," he said, earning a smack on the shoulder. "I need to borrow Lane. That cool, Lane?"

"Of course," I said, eyeing his too-wide gaze. "I'll just be a minute, okay, Sadie?"

"Fine." She flung her arms around me, squeezed me tight, winding threads of guilt around my heart. "I'm so glad you came with us tonight, Lane. Get back to me as soon as you can, okay?"

I followed Connor to the edge of the overlook and waited as he stretched and yawned, scratched his jaw, took another hit. Watched him compulsively push his golden-brown hair behind his ear, trying and failing to make it stay put.

Why I hadn't thrown myself over the guardrail by that point was a fucking riddle.

"So. Was there really something?" No response. Not even a shrug. "Connor."

"What? Oh. No, that was bullshit. You looked miserable as hell. Figured I'd give you a hand." The corner of his mouth lifted, a half-curved commiseration with a wicked, sideways twist. "But while you're here . . ."

I leaned toward him, took a long, deep hit off the proffered joint. Escaped into a lungful of smoke. He chuckled at the resulting cough, took another pointless swipe at his hair as I turned away, seeking Grey. Finding him on the cusp of the night, reaching once more for Sadie. Letting his silhouette melt into hers.

They spun together, out of the headlights' reach, and they were lost to us.

THE BATHROOM OF OUR OLD HOUSE WAS ENTIRELY white: white tile, white sink, white toilet. White walls and cabinets. Even the fixtures were vintage white porcelain, individual taps labeled HOT and COLD. My mom loved that bathroom. She hung white linens on the bars, and framed black-and-white French postcards on the walls. She kept it spotless and shiny and smelling like tea roses.

I like to think she'd have been furious with herself to see the mess she made.

I'd loved that bathroom too, because she did——afterward, not so much. Dad had all but gone broke moving us out of that house as fast as he could, but life is nothing if not a shitshow of everything you'd rather forget entirely, so it makes sense that I get to see it over and over again, for what appears to be the rest of my natural life.

The dream is always different, in tiny, varied ways——I never know, for instance, which Lane I'll be. Most nights I'm Present-Day Lane, but sometimes I'm five years old again, closer to the ground, closer to her. My voice is higher, shrill and uncomprehending as I call for her, as I did in life—to my knowledge, the first and last time she failed to answer my cries.

So, yeah. Not much sleep happening on a regular basis in Lane's world.

Blood itself wasn't the problem. Cuts, now, those were a different story—the parting of skin beneath steel, blood or no blood, never failed to fuck me up. Blades against skin, even shaving accidents, left me grasping for control, gasping for air. So dinner prep was always fun, but blood on its own wasn't *horrible*.

Which was fortunate, since I happened to be cursed with the most agonizing menstrual periods on the face of the earth.

It was almost a parody: cramps that rendered me horizontal for hours at a time. Migraines that knocked me on my ass. Nausea that devolved to vomiting that devolved to me lying on the bathroom floor in tears, begging random entities for relief, stomach yearning for sustenance that only made things worse. Did it suck? Yes. Did it ruin several consecutive days of every month, like clockwork? Absolutely. But I was used to it. It was part of my routine.

So I didn't even consider the far-reaching implications of a shared bathroom until I was slumped on the floor at six a.m. a mere two weeks into the new living arrangement. Moaning into the bathmat with a bile-sour mouth, as Grey McIntyre's voice sounded at me from the hallway.

"Elaine? Are you—oh, shit. Mom? MOM??"

His footsteps went pounding all over the house in a frantic

search for Skye, and my agonized groan rose to a thin, tiny wail as I realized exactly what was about to transpire.

There was no stopping it. It was already set in motion, and it spooled out just how I knew it would: Skye took one look at me, sent Grey to put the teakettle on to boil, and set to work sponging my wan face with a cold, damp washcloth.

"Are you okay, Elaine? Did you eat the wrong thing?" She lowered her voice, glancing over her shoulder at the door. "Do you think you might be pregnant?"

"God, no," I croaked, fighting off another wave of nausea. "Just that time of the month. The usual fun and games."

"Yikes. Have you seen someone for this?"

"Long time ago. It happened to my mother too. Endometriosis. Apparently, though, I'm too young for that, and this is all in my head."

"That doesn't sound right at all. Were you diagnosed?"

"Not officially. My doctor says it's just bad PMS, and we should wait on testing until I'm older. I guess for now I'm supposed to just suck it up and deal."

"Ugh, you poor thing. Sounds like you're in the market for a new doctor."

"Yeah, he's generally useless. But hey, if this ends up killing me like it did her, maybe that means I won't actually be dead, right? It'll all be in my head, and my body can carry on as usual. So that's an upside."

"Oh, Elaine."

"Sorry. That was a bad——" I auto-swallowed a surge of acid, and immediately wished I hadn't. It burned all the way back down. "It screwed up her fertility, and then with what happened to my brother——I'm sorry. I shouldn't say these things. Something is very wrong with me. You can go if you want."

"Honey, stop. I know about her difficulties, and her death. We all process these things differently. If a bit of dark humor does the trick, you shouldn't hold back. Did he at least give you anything to treat your symptoms?"

"They put me on the Pill. But it only helps sometimes."

"Well, sometimes is better than not at all. And it's good to have access to reliable birth control at your age, in any case. Greyson, there you are."

I squeezed my eyes shut at the sound of his name, gathered the strength to reach over and paw at the toilet handle until it flushed. It was bad enough the whole room stank of my vomit; all I needed now was him standing there staring at it while his mother ruminated on my birth control. Jesus fucking Christ.

"Is she okay? I have some Pepto under the sink, if she needs it." His voice was small, thick with concern. It pierced my heart, that sweet, protective instinct of his——the reason I'd fallen for him all those years ago. He was still so ready to help, so eager to take care of me and temper my pain. He was still so good.

"She'll be fine. When the water's ready, I need you to brew some ginger tea, and add a few drops of my guelder rose extract. Oh, and plug the heating pad in by her bed, would you, honey? Thank you."

Dead silence. I couldn't look at him—that my face was already back in the toilet, dry heaving at the water, was a mere technicality. He knew. He'd lived with Skye long enough to know what guelder rose and all that other shit was for. She'd probably sat him down and explained it, nurturing his empathy concerning the biological path into womanhood, or however she'd phrase a horrible thing like that.

Kill. Me.

He was gone by the time I pulled my head out of the bowl, but Skye remained on the floor beside me. She wiped my face again, helped me twist my sweat-damp hair into a braid. Rubbed a hand in small, soothing circles over my back.

"You don't have to stay," I told her. "I'm used to dealing with this alone."

She didn't speak, just smiled and settled in beside me until Grey crept back like a shamed dog, bearing a steaming mug and refusing to make eye contact. She stayed as he scurried away again, and as I drank the tea and puked it back up, and then she brought me another cup. Once my stomach settled, she helped me into bed and tucked me in with the heating pad.

It wasn't until I heard her on the phone calling me in sick to school, taking care of even that small detail, that it really sank in: She *didn't* have to stay with me. She didn't have to care. But she did anyway.

It was more than my own mother had done, in the end.

I let myself sink beneath the weight of that thought, let it close over my head like graveyard dirt. Let Skye's voice carry me softly back to sleep.

3

I PREFERRED LIFE IN SMALL, ORDERED DOSES—AN unmuddled bento box, with little to no overlap. Less chance that way of one issue bleeding into the rest. Less chance of losing myself in the resulting chaos, or stumbling over a random sharpened edge.

I wasn't interested in edges. Hadn't been since I was five years old and found my mother.

Annie. My mother. Beautiful and gentle, wild-eyed and mad. She'd slipped into nothing on the rhythm of her own heart, chasing my stillborn brother into whatever lay beyond a pulse.

Her face in my mirror. Her chair at the table, nearly thirteen years empty, suddenly occupied by her antithesis.

Skye. She was the brightest version of her name—cheerful and airy and endless, a gathering place for the softest springtime clouds. The new, constant light in my father's eyes, blending so perfectly into our tiny world—her shawl on the coatrack; her cherry-red rain boots by the door; the sweet sigh of her lilac shampoo—as if a tornado had whirled through and set her gently in her place, scattered her belongings through the rooms, filled every empty corner with her laughter.

Smashed her son down alongside her, staining my world in Grey.

My Greyson. My Greyson who was not mine at all, actually— nothing but a trick I'd played on myself in eighth-grade Advanced Biology class: the smiling nerd deposited at my lab station on dissection day, when our respective partners chose to take the F rather than slice their way to hell through a sedated yet still-living frog. Grey McIntyre, green-eyed and focused, his hands casual on the scalpel where mine shook. Laying open that frog belly with a single, careful swipe, pinning back the skin flaps, making short work of the peritoneum membrane. Brushing a gloved fingertip over the exposed heart. Taking my hand without a word and pressing my finger to the impossibly tiny pulse.

I felt it all the way up my arm: a frantic staccato, so rapid it was almost a shudder. My throat seized; I jerked away, stumbling over his foot. He regained his balance on the stool, caught me against his chest, his own strong heartbeat thumping against my back—once, twice—before he righted us both, and it may as well have been me pinned open on that tray, paralyzed by a blur of scalpels-turned-knives and splattered bathroom tiles. Choked by the stench of bleach and blood.

"Steady," he'd whispered, guiding me to my stool and turning back to the frog. He'd handed that thing in forty minutes later, perfectly dismantled and bearing both our names. His parting smile was shy and shiny with braces as he waved goodbye, fading into the stream of our classmates. I followed at a careful distance, losing myself instantly and completely in a way I'd never known I could.

I'd seen him everywhere after that—four years of Grey's voice weaving its way into my ears over the general hallway clamor. Four years of watching his hair grow into a cinnamon mop, sideburns filling in around his sharpening cheekbones and jaw. Watching his arms slide around interchangeable girls, his hands moving over interchangeable waists and hips until they'd landed on Sadie. Nearly four years, and not another word between us, which was fine by me—he was safer as an idea, untouchable and perfect. Perfectly satisfactory, in a way even he couldn't ruin.

Until the night Dad took me to a rare dinner out to meet his Skye, his unexpected second shot at life. Took me to dinner to meet her son, who blinked at me over our automatic handshake.

"Skye, this is my daughter, Elaine." Poor Dad. So shy and nervous. So happy. Skye's infectious smile shone bright; her hands reached for mine, without hesitation.

"Oh, Elaine. Oh, I'm so, so thrilled to finally meet you. This is my son, Greyson."

"Grey," he said, at the same time I said "Lane." And everyone laughed, and we four began our transition into one before I'd realized what was happening—what had *already* happened. An engagement, to be exact, admittedly sudden after only a month, but met with genuine, if somewhat shocked, enthusiasm.

Enthusiasm that, on my part, gave way to dawning realization, then panic and horror and denial.

That dinner, oh my God. The longest meal of my life, filled with Skye's laughter, and Dad's moony grin, and Grey's every last little thing. Grey McIntyre: longtime occupant of my heart's most vulnerable nook, hopeful and buoyed in the chair next to mine. The only boy I'd ever loved.

My future brother.

Kill me. Seriously.

"It just never connected," he'd said. "Mom has been all 'Rob Jamison' this, and 'Rob's daughter, Elaine' that for weeks, but my brain never linked him to you. You prefer Lane, right? That's what you're called?"

"By everyone except Dad." My laugh was cheerful, my voice a bright, teasing lie, and holy shit, did I deserve an award statue. He hadn't even known my real name. "He's talked about Skye as well, but obviously I never connected Miller to McIntyre."

"Yeah, she kept her name when she married my dad—which made it easy, since she didn't have to bother changing it back." He studied me, biting into his own grin. The braces were long gone, the smile a sideways, dimpled thing. "Would it be okay if I call you Elaine? I think it suits you."

"Only if I get to call you Greyson."

"Whatever you want—apparently, we'll be family, soon enough." His smile stretched even farther. "Crazy, isn't it? I've always wanted a sister."

I'd clamped down on my agony and smiled through that thought, and through the goddamn endless dinner, and the domino fall of everything that followed. I smiled at the handfasting ceremony a mere week later, just the four of us and an ordained friend of Skye's, on the last day of summer vacation. I smiled as Grey recited his own blessing over our parents' joined hands, though I was the odd one out—the lone agnostic, hovering at the edge of their pagan rituals—and as they moved into my house that same afternoon, as I helped him carry his things from his cramped apartment to the bedroom next to mine. My smile stayed on through another eternal dinner out, through the car ride back home, only faltering as we stepped into our shared living room.

I smiled until it hurt too much to do anything else. And Grey and me, who'd spent years as nothing more than hallway nods and a single moment shared over a dying amphibian—we were thrown together all at once, bound in the weirdest version of forever.

It all happened so fast.

The first day of our senior year, watching him eat a bowl of homemade granola with chia seeds at my kitchen table.

The ride to school, punctuated by the first of many detours to feed his Starbucks vice.

The parking and walking into school together.

The official introduction to Sadie and her sweet-scented hugs, her sincerity and enthusiasm and endless, overbearing kindness.

His new role in the family business, redesigning our website and working alongside me at the farmers' market, selling Dad's organic soaps and lotions, my hand-knit items and crocheted jewelry and lace—effectively rendering my weekend booth shifts a little less lonely and a lot more secretly anticipated. Schedules were readjusted; nerves slightly unwound. Life was a new, vibrant thing, louder and sweeter and richer in all ways, even as it tore me up from the inside out.

And so we began.

4

DAD SMIRKED ACROSS THE TABLE AT THE SOUR PINCH of my mouth. This batch of kombucha had turned out better than his last one, but that bar wasn't exactly the highest.

"Drink up, Elaine. It's good for your—"

"—digestion. I know. It's still disgusting."

"You'll live." His chuckle rolled out ahead of yet another thunderclap.

Rain slashed at the windows and splashed along the gutters, but the basement was warm and dry, pungent with incense, lined with shelf after shelf of supplies—jars of dried herbs, flower petals, and essential oils; containers of lye; vats of coconut oil and olive oil, shea butter and beeswax; bin after bin of yarn and notions; stacks of packaging and shipping supplies. The "business" side of our business, awaiting us in neatly ordered rows. It was rote work, and time-consuming, and it wasn't ever going to make us rich. But it made us happy. After so much misery, that was more than enough.

It used to be a regular thing, working together. I'd sit across from him and knit while he made supply lists, filled custom orders, balanced the bank account. We'd package product over cups of tea and rare batches of homemade oatmeal cookies. Sometimes we'd chat, or watch a movie on his laptop. Sometimes he'd put on a playlist of cheesy pop songs, and we'd sing along until we were laughing too hard to breathe. I'd gotten older, though; gotten busier with school and boys. Gotten old enough for my own shifts at the market, leaving him to handle the back-end tasks. The shift in routine wasn't personal—it just *was*.

But today I'd run out of yarn mid-project, gone rummaging through my fiber stash, found him hauling one of several bins of product down from the kitchen; we'd settled at the table without a word, and gotten to work. Grey was out with Sadie, and Skye had picked up an extra shift at her job, so there we were: me, Dad, and a shit-ton of freshly cured soap.

It was soothing and repetitive, our routine: I wrapped the bars in waxy paper, sealed them with our label, and passed the finished product to Dad, who wound decorative twine in bright loops around their middles—red for peppermint, purple for lavender, green for tea tree, pink for rose. The colors trailed from his fingertips, wrapped like vines around the slender phalanges, lay in bright hanks alongside the graceful ridges of his knuckles. Those hands, larger, paler versions of mine, that never failed to pry beauty from the scraps of his world.

"We haven't talked in a while," he began, eyes on the table, fingers suddenly fidgety with the twine. "Keeping busy?"

"Yeah, you know. Lots going on."

"Seeing anyone special? Boyfriend material?"

"What? Oh. Um, no. Like I said, I've been busy." It was a weird question, a step outside our usual conversational stratosphere. Like I was going to bring a hookup home to meet my dad.

"Oh, sure, sure. No doubt. School's okay, then?"

"Sure," I hedged. "Dad, are *you* okay? You're being—"

"Weird. I know. I just need to make sure you're fine. With this."

The words burst out of him all at once. I eyed him over the jumble of our work space, waiting for something other than ellipses. Took in the tension in his arms, the squint of his hazel eyes; his pale lashes and strawberry-blond hair, the same chin-length Cobain cut he'd worn since the early nineties, now slashed with gray. The curl of twine, pulled tight around his purpling fingertip.

Talking with my father was like reaching into a bag of Scrabble tiles, searching for that one missing letter. Coming up, every time, with a handful of question marks that didn't belong in the game.

"With the soap?"

"Jesus. No, not with the soap, Elaine. With Skye. With me."

I had to bite back a smile. Dad had spent the time since my mother's death focused on perfecting his craft, on running the business. On being a father. And he was good at it—all of it. But more than once, I'd wondered how long it would take him to grow weary of perpetual solitude.

Right around thirteen years, that's how long. Better late than never.

"I'm fine, Dad. I'm happy for both—for all of us."

His relief was tangible, raw enough to make me wince.

"Thank you. Thank you, Elaine. I'm so glad this is working out. Skye adores you, she truly does. And Greyson—you two seem to be doing well. Getting along. Bonding."

Yeah. About that.

"We get along fine. He's nice."

"Oh, he's definitely a Nice Guy," Dad chuckled. I could hear the capital letters, even without his air quotes. "Just ask his mama. But really, he's a good kid. He's polite, and kind; he excels in school. He follows the rules, no questions asked. He even sat me down to assure me he'd keep the door open, when you two are alone in a room. Which was awkward, I have to admit."

"He *what*?" My stomach hitched, sending up a splash of kombucha. It wasn't any better the second time around, nor was it much worse. *"Why?"*

"He wants to avoid a double standard," he said cheerfully as I died inside, over and over. "Sadie's mother requires her visits with Greyson to be supervised. Skye wants to respect that, so they have an understanding—she won't hover, as long as they don't shut themselves away. An 'open door policy,' if you will." He chuckled again and rolled his eyes, delighting in his Dad Joke. "As if that's a concern with you."

"Right."

Dad's forehead creased at the catch in my voice. I pressed

my toes together beneath the table, kept my face still as possible beneath his unblinking stare. If so much as a trickle of my thoughts leaked into his reality, our new family would implode.

"Elaine," he said, "Skye and I—this must have—look. I know it was sudden. I know that. And it can't be easy, having a boy you hardly know living here out of—"

"It's fine," I managed. As if he had a clue in hell how *uneasy* this was. "Whatever makes you happy."

"It's *your* happiness that matters." He coughed into his sleeve, finally blinked down at the half-tied twine, still wound around his fingers. "It matters to me. It mattered to your mother. She'd have wanted—"

"She got what she wanted."

It flew out on its own dark wings, beat its way past my teeth. Sunk its talons deep.

I didn't spend much time dwelling on spirituality in general, much less the concept of an afterlife. Dad himself waffled on the specifics of his beliefs—sometimes he pondered reincarnation, or transmigration; sometimes he went on about astral planes, and the post-conscious bliss and punishments of our own creation. He'd declared more than once that death was the end—that the cycle of human life ended in oblivion and a natural return to the earth. But now I watched his jaw clench and his grip falter; watched the knot fly apart as he met my eyes, and my mother was surely in the room, real as she'd ever been in life. Perched like an owl between us, impossible to ever really bury.

"I promise you. She didn't."

"Then that makes two of us." I finished wrapping the last bar of soap, secured it with the sticker, creaseless and dead center. Perfect every time. I slid out of my chair and headed for the stairs, head down. "Done."

"I love you."

I stopped in the doorway, straightened my spine. Unclenched my teeth, until my grimace became a smile. Let it soften my cheeks and light my eyes before I turned to face him. His own smile trembled at the corners, pleading for forgiveness. Wanting so badly to mirror mine.

"It's okay, Dad. Really."

"I love you," he said again. "Above anyone or anything. Never doubt that."

It wasn't fair, blaming him for any of this. We'd been two for so long, it was easy to forget we'd once been three—really, very nearly four. Far too easy to forget the way he'd broken and fallen beside me.

But he'd pulled himself up. He'd rearranged the world for me; he'd tried and failed, over and over, but never ever failed to try. He'd lost everything else, but he'd never stopped.

And now we were four again, and he was my dad. There was nothing to forgive.

"I know you do."

I left him there, still smiling, surrounded by everything we'd made.

5

"OKAY, SO WHICH WAY IS UP, AGAIN?"

Grey's words drifted out on an easy laugh as he knelt in the grass beside me. His hands were full of flower bulbs and all but lost in Dad's spare gardening gloves, arms dirty to the elbows, face covered in sweat and sunshine. So adorable it hurt to look at him.

I had to laugh in return at his unabashed cluelessness. He fumbled the bulbs like a juggling clown, deliberately clumsy. My reply was a casual, neutral thing, as if I wasn't living the dream in my own backyard: planting flowers with Grey McIntyre on a beautiful autumn afternoon, the day after my eighteenth birthday. The sweetest, most unexpected gift I could imagine.

"It doesn't matter which way is up, because this space is for tulips," I said. "Those are daffodils—upside-down daffodils. Looks like I'll have to keep an eye on you out here."

"Someone has to."

He grinned, tossing his head in a fruitless effort to flip the hair out of his face. I wanted to push it back for him, drag my fingers against his scalp until he couldn't help but moan. I wanted that so badly. Instead, I tucked a straggling lock of my own hair behind my ear, pretended I hadn't noticed the way his eyes had strayed to my lips as I answered. Pretended even harder that the flush in my cheeks and sweat pooling at my throat were the fault of the sun.

One month and two days. It had been one month and two days exactly since he'd moved in, and I'd spent most of those days on guard, every thought edged with his presence. The little things were what stood out, the ways we fell into our new life. Things you'd never think about until faced with them every day: his toothbrush resting on the bathroom vanity; his bottle of aftershave smack in the middle of the medicine cabinet, a sentry standing guard over my tweezers and face lotion; his smudge-stick smoke drifting under my bedroom door. His socks tangled with mine in a load of laundry. His scent tangled with mine in the lining of my bedspread.

It was so perfect in its own way, finally having him all to myself. Our parents had left for the market early that morning, leaving us to sleep off the previous night's festivities; when I'd finally stumbled into the kitchen, Grey had the table decked out with Skye's Tree of Life tea set, folded cloth napkins, and a platter of sliced fruit arranged in the shape of a smiley face, birthday candle stuck right in the orange-segment nose. It was just the kind of thing Sadie would love—as if he'd laid the table for her pleasure, assuming the catch-all sentiment would work across the feminine spectrum. It was a sweet, simple gesture, matching up with everything I knew about him; it was a single-minded assumption that hit me like a boot in the softest part of my belly.

Still, he'd done this thing for me. He'd tried to please *me*, in his own way, and if it was a shade too cute for my preferences, I wasn't about to complain. So, when he'd offered during that breakfast to help with the gardening, I'd damn well taken him up on it without hesitation.

Weird as it was to have him suddenly in my house, Grey was as at home in the outdoors as if he'd sprouted from the earth on his own. He unearthed and rearranged the rocks in the decorative border, tackled the weeding and tilling without complaint, pausing to bless the soil in the flowerbeds, ensuring strength and abundance. It was an afternoon of sunshine and soft, safe words. It was an afternoon spent in wanting, in ways that went far beyond the flesh.

"There you are, baby. You forgot all about me, didn't you?"

Her voice reached us before she did—lovely Sadie, in a pink silk blouse. Cotton candy threaded through with glitter, and Grey was smiling before he even looked up.

"How could I ever forget you, babe? Give me two seconds to clean up, and we can go."

I kept my eyes on the dirt as he scrambled to his feet, only heard the kiss he gave her on his way to the house. She had her lip gloss in hand when I looked up, was already squinting into her compact as she repaired the damage. Her eyes slid over to mine, glimmering above an impish smile that belonged on her brother's face.

"How are you feeling? Hopefully not too hungover?"

It returned in flashes: my birthday celebration. The official lifting of my already lax curfew—a long-promised acknowledgment of my legal adulthood—immediately followed by Dad's meek request that I continue to text him my post-midnight locations, purely for his peace of mind. Me and Grey and Sadie and Connor, eating too much cake and piling into Grey's car, taking the curves of the Blue Ridge Parkway far too fast, until we reached that same overlook. Shotgunning cans of PBR and laughing until I choked, then dancing with Sadie on the roof of the Forester while poor, sober designated driver Grey yelled at us to get down before we dented it. The three of them singing "Happy Birthday," crowding around me in a staggering group hug that ended with me lying on the pavement with my head in Grey's lap, legs hooked over Connor's prone form. Getting stoned with Connor while Grey and Sadie argued and made up and made out against the hatchback. Leaning far over the guardrail, eyes wide and full of night, the wind rushing cold across my cheeks, dizzy with laughter and starlight and the open, endless sky.

"Tired, but not too bad," I answered her. "Grey wouldn't let me sleep last night until I had water and tea and Advil. You?"

"Oh, I'm fine. Connor's in rough shape, though. He said to tell you happy birthday weekend, but not to expect a text or anything until his soul returns to his body. And he's pretty sure you have his stash . . . though I'm perfectly happy to tell him you have no idea what he's talking about."

"I don't *think* I have it, but I'll double-check my bag. Give me one second. I'm almost done here."

She checked her lip gloss once more, flicking away a minuscule smear, as I poked one last bulb into the flowerbed and cleaned the spade and garden claw.

"You have the prettiest skin," she said after a moment. "I can't tan to save my life."

"It's a delicate balance. A minute too long in the sun, and my mom's Greek glow becomes a mess of Dad's freckles." I stood and stretched, arching my back. "My DNA needs to pick a team."

"Silly. You're lucky, Connor and I burn red if we so much as step outside. We—oh."

"Everything okay?" I lowered my arms and pulled off my gloves, shook the tingles out of my hands as her brow furrowed.

"Fine, honey. I—has Grey been out here with you all day?"

"Since about two. I needed to get these bulbs in the ground before the weather changes, and he offered to help."

"That's nice," she said, distracted. "And I take it this is your usual bulb-planting outfit?"

"This?" I gave myself a cursory glance. My cami top was plain, pilled cotton, a solid dark blue stained darker with sweat. My low-rise khakis were a baggy disaster, worn and ripped, cinched with a canvas army belt and rolled halfway up my dirty shins. "Yeah, I know—I'm a mess. These pants are probably on their last legs."

"It's not the pants," she bit out, ignoring my dumb joke. "I don't want to overstep, honey, but . . . you seem to have forgotten your bra today. Now that my future husband lives in this house, shouldn't you try to keep yourself decent?"

I had to fight to hide the devastation those words brought down on my head; I had to fight hard, and I almost lost. Only anger steadied my expression between defiance and annoyance, kept it from sliding into misery. Only pride allowed me to square my shoulders and lock my eyes with hers.

"Wow. Mind your own business much?"

"Bless your heart, I'm not *insulting* you. You're so pretty and thin, and it'd be one thing if he was your actual blood family, but come on—*you* know how boys are."

She gave me a sly, sideways look, as if our respective encounters with boys were comparable in any sense. As if the cami's built-in shelf panel wasn't more than enough to contain what little I had. Unlike the strained buttonholes of her own thin blouse.

"'How boys are' is not my problem, Sadie. I'll wear whatever the fuck I want—and maybe *you* can stop checking out my rack."

"*What??* I am NOT checking out your—you're taking all this the wrong way, Lane. I never said—"

"I heard you just fine. And not for nothing, but I've certainly never had any complaints on it before."

Something darker than the Sadie I knew crept across her face, casting a dangerous shadow.

"Oh, believe me—I'm *well* aware how few complaints you get. *Everyone* is well aware of *that*."

Her meaning crawled over my skin on a thousand sharpened feet, as my brain reached for every mean thing I'd ever heard said regarding Sadie Hall—and it was quite a long list. I was so close to unleashing. So close to ripping her apart from the heels up, until she looked how I felt.

"Speaking of minding your own business." I turned my back and knelt in the dirt, stuffed the gloves and tools and the rest of the bulbs into my canvas bag. By the time I faced her again, my eyes were dry, dark as blacktop and twice as hard. "Looks like I'm done here. If you want to wait inside for Grey, follow me."

Even her footsteps on the flagstone path were wary, though they drowned out my angry stride without trying. It was ridiculously hard to stomp away in Crocs. I kicked those off on the doormat and led her through the kitchen to the living room, waving her to the couch. She caught my wrist, though, clasped my hand in both of hers.

"Lane. Lane, I'm so sorry. I am. I don't care about any of that, you know? You're the best friend I have, and I just love you to death, no matter what anyone says."

"Well, thanks, Sadie. How noble of you."

"Honey, don't. I didn't mean to hurt you, I swear. I know you're not trying to—well, I know you wouldn't do those things with Grey."

Her words ate at my insides. I believed her, when she said she hadn't meant to hurt me. Sadie's lack of filter was a well-known thing—which was why I also believed I was, in fact, her best friend. The list of contenders for that role wasn't the longest.

She was wrong, though. I *would* do those things. I would do every one of those things, to him and with him and for him, and it would be everything I'd wanted since I began doing those things at all. It wasn't personal—it wasn't even an attack. Sadie herself was incidental. Whatever claim she had on Grey, he'd lived in my heart before she'd even bothered to learn his name. Whatever happened, I'd loved him first.

Still, he wasn't mine. That was that.

I wasn't about to steal away someone's boyfriend just because my living situation had fucked itself sideways. I was pathetic, but not to *that* degree. Besides, however much I wanted him, I'd never actually done anything about it—it was way too late in the game to start humming that sad tune. Sadie was my friend, and she loved Grey, and if she thought I was bad based on rumors, none of which even skimmed the surface of my secret thirst— well. She just had no idea.

So, I let her hug me, heedless of my defeated spine and sweaty, dirt-streaked skin. I let her lose herself in absolution, so I wouldn't have to answer. Even a nod of agreement would have been a lie.

"Let's forget it, okay?" She released me with a gloss-sticky peck on the cheek. "Go take a bubble bath, have some cake. Treat yourself. We'll talk more later."

And I might have done just that, had I not needed a clean towel from the load waiting in the dryer. I might have made it all the way into said bubble bath without further incident, remained blissfully unaware forever of the fiasco occurring in the laundry room.

I couldn't help dragging my eyes over the line of his neck and the dip of his spine, the curve that led into the waistband of his jeans. Couldn't help but stare, even as my cheeks burst into flame.

My stepbrother, wet-haired and shirtless, shower mist still beading his bare shoulders. Frozen in mid-motion, the most delicate contents of my delicate laundry cycle spilling from his hands, and why. Why was my life such a ridiculous fucking punch line.

"Greyson—what are you *doing*?"

His head snapped around, then volleyed back and forth between the bra and me, as if his brain had stalled and had yet to sputter back to life. Why was he still holding it? What was he thinking, letting his fingers tangle in the things I wore closest to my skin—he should have dropped it the second he made contact, not held it up to the fucking light, as if he had to ascertain exactly what it was before deciding to put it back.

"Sorry. Sorry, sorry," he mumbled. "I came in here to get my shirt, and I figured I'd switch the clothes to the dryer, and—"

"It doesn't *go* in the dryer. The dryer will ruin it." I practically tore it from his grip. It was my good stuff too—one of the lacy ones I wore on dates, because why would it be anything else? "What is wrong with you?"

"I didn't know. I was trying to help." He steeled himself and faced me, furiously quiet, hyperaware of Sadie's proximity. His wild, wide eyes swept over me, kindling on open flame. "I promise you, I didn't mean to touch your—your—look, I'm sorry. I am. It won't happen again."

He retreated to his room and slammed the door, and I locked myself in the bathroom, stripped off my filthy clothes, drowned myself in a shower that smelled too much like him and utterly snuffed out the sunshine glow of our afternoon. By the time I emerged, they were gone, and only after a thorough search of the house—only after I confirmed that I was, indeed, completely alone—did I let myself break. Only then did I curl into a miserable ball beneath my quilt, and cry until I choked.

I have good news and bad news, Connor. Which do you want first? It's Lane, btw.

I know it's you. Both at once.

I have your stash and will return it ASAP. However, it may be slightly depleted.

Goddamn it, Lane. I GUESS I forgive you. Since it's your birthday and all. ☺

Sorry. It's been kind of a day. How's your hangover?

I'll live. You okay? Need to talk?

No, I'm good. Thanks anyway.

No problem.

"Are you serious, Elaine? What the hell is your deal?"

I'd spent the evening holed up in my room, fully intent on never coming out again—a plan that would have worked fine had Grey not barged in a scant few minutes after his return, startling my fingers mid-text. His face was a flushed, humiliated nightmare.

"I said I was sorry," he yelled from the doorway. "You don't have to be a bitch and drag it out like this."

"What are you talking about? I'm not dragging anything out."

"Then why," he seethed, "is your shit hanging all over the bathroom? I wasn't *trying* to mess with it, you know. You don't have to turn it into a joke."

"It's not a *joke*. That's where I hang it to dry, you jerk. It's where I've always hung it."

I scrambled off my bed and pushed past him to the bathroom, yanking my things off the shower curtain rod and wall hooks. I stormed back to my room, and there he was, arms crossed, like a goddamn hall monitor. He stepped aside to let me pass at the same moment I made a flustered lunge in the same direction. We ended up in a clumsy side-to-side shuffle, silent and huffy and avoiding each other's eyes. He stilled me with a hand on my hip, stepped deliberately past me. Disappeared into his own room and slammed the door behind him.

I slunk into my room, curled up under my quilt, and stared at the wall through stinging eyes. I could hear Grey moving around his room——the tread of his feet on the hardwood, the groan of a loose floorboard. The sharp aroma of burning sage as he smudged the negative energy from his room, because Wiccan passive aggression is definitely a thing. The click of his nightstand lamp and squeak of his mattress, as he settled into his own bed. The creak of the bed frame, frustrated and restless, then suddenly regular. Deliberate.

The air hitched in my throat; my hip sang where he'd touched me, the memory of palm on bone bursting hot and cold across my cheeks. I shifted closer, pressed my ear to the wall. Heard the careful, rhythmic tell of bedsprings, heard his breath catch and shudder. Heard a name ride out low on the echo of his sigh.

My name. And not Elaine——not the softer, girlish family version, wrapped in innocent context——Lane.

My clenched hand flew to my mouth, barely trapping the splash of sound that surged from my throat. My skin simmered; my veins were kerosene, aching for the touch of a match. Everything hung on that word——our lives and family, present and future; the seconds before and after it left his mouth ran together like gooseflesh melting smooth in the sun, and this wasn't my fault——he'd found me on his own, plunged blind into dark, brackish depths, dredged me from the groundwater so we surfaced together. Never stopped to think if we should breathe in open air.

It was only a wall. A wall and a door and a hundred thousand miles. It would be so easy to leave my bed and slip into his——just a few simple steps between our rooms—the literal turn of a corner. Instead, I unleashed my thoughts, let them run loose in a way I hadn't since before he'd moved in. Let my eyes slide closed and my hand slide lower, let it become his in a sudden rush of heat. Instead, I turned away from the wall, stifled my own gasps in the pillow before I upended everything—before I pushed through those miles and found him, crossed every line, undid every lie I'd lived since he'd become my brother.

Before I set fire to everything between us, letting it spark and scorch and devour us both, until there was nothing left in the world to burn.

MY LEAST FAVORITE VERSION OF THE DREAM WAS THE
one with the puzzle pieces. My mother was two-dimensional,
a flat card-stock version of herself. Still dead, of course; still
sprawled in blood and staring at nothing, but punched out in jigsaw segments, scattered and unassembled and smooth. Until they
began to rise.

One by one, they swelled and formed, bursting into shape
like popcorn. They trembled, fit themselves together, clicked
into place until she was whole again. Until her eyes flew open,
and her head snapped sideways to catch me, as I tried to run. I
never could run, though, because I had no feet. I never could
run, because I stumbled on the stumps of my ankles, fell to the
floor beside her. Landed shoulder to shoulder, eye to eye, shark-
toothed grin to terrified scream, and I could see them: the slither
just beneath her skin. The worms, eating her from the inside out.

I woke up when I rolled into the wall.

As bad as every version was, that one stuck to me in shards,
lingered long after the others faded. It was never about going

back to sleep at that point; it was only about escaping. Slowing my heartbeat long enough to scuttle down the hallway, as far from my bed as I could get.

I pushed the nightmare aside, focused on replacing it with the now-week-old memory of my name, the way it had shuddered its way off his tongue, cracking fault lines into fissures beneath our feet. Since that night, Grey and I had called a truce—if a truce can, in fact, be defined as two people referencing an event in neither word nor look nor deed. He chatted easily through meals and car rides, smiled across the distance between us, as if he could erase the laundry room incident with every flash of teeth. Not that I'd blank out on that mess anytime soon. I certainly couldn't forget the things I'd heard, that night and nearly every night since, or how my mind and body responded every time. How I put my ear to that darkened wall and wished, waiting for him to give in. I scavenged for those crumbs—pressed them to my lips, licked them from my fingers. Fed on his sounds and hoped they'd sate me, even as they only woke my need.

I didn't want to ignore them, even though I knew I should. I didn't want to forget.

I moved around the dark kitchen, grabbed a mug and a tea bag, filled the kettle and put it to boil, then leaned against the sink, staring out the window at the backyard. The moon dipped into the trees, turned the world to slate. I focused on the sky, shaking off the worst of the shivers.

"You too, huh?"

His voice curled out of the darkness, tugging me around to

face his bedhead and moonlit eyes. My breath hitched on the corner of his sleepy smile.

"Greyson. What are you doing awake?"

"Chronic insomnia. Had it since my dad left."

"You don't sleep? Like, ever?"

"No, I sleep. It's more a matter of settling my brain. Once I'm out, I usually stay out—it's the getting there that's tough." He shrugged and smiled again, and my God, but he was pretty. "You?"

"I have nightmares some nights. Most nights. Sleep-wake, sleep-wake, every few hours."

"That's actually not too far removed from the body's natural sleep cycle," he said. "Small periods of unconsciousness, punctuated by wakefulness. It was a fairly normal pattern, prior to the invention of the electric light. Creativity is thought to be at peak levels during the time between first and second sleeps."

"That sounds better in theory than it actually is." The kettle skittered on the burner. I turned and caught it, right before the whistle. "Want some tea?"

"Sure." He padded across the kitchen, recoiled at the sight of my mug. "Thanks, but I drink actual tea. Not that mass-produced bag-on-a-string shit."

"Well, aren't you fancy." I giggled as he grabbed the tea bag and lobbed it at the trash can, plucked a loose tea canister and a set of infusers from the cabinet. "Oh my God. Please tell me that's not a Death Star infuser."

"Of course it's a Death Star infuser. Go. Sit."

I sat at the table as he brewed our tea, watched the shadows dart over his hands and up his forearms. He'd been a skinny kid, with braces and knobby knees. Pants cinched tight at the waist, shirts billowing into space off a coat-hanger frame. Now his T-shirt strained around broad, solid shoulders. Now he was standing in my kitchen that was also his kitchen, making us cups of tea at three in the morning. He turned and caught me staring, smiled at me through the curls of steam. Moonlight caught in his messy hair, winked off the pewter pentacle around his neck. Both of us were bed-rumpled, both in pajamas, and it was far, far too easy to wear down the edge of a wish until it blurred into a delusion.

"Have you studied Jung?"

"What?" I blinked my way out of those thoughts, hoping none of them showed in my eyes. "I don't think I've heard of . . . that."

"Him, not 'that.' Carl Jung, the psychoanalyst." He set my tea in front of me and slid into the next chair, dragging the infuser chain in circles over the rim of his mug. "The objective and sub-jective methods of dream interpretation—objects and people in dreams representing themselves specifically, versus those same things representing aspects of your subconscious. I have some books on his theories, if you're interested."

"Oh. I'll pass, actually. Literally the last thing I need is to pick apart my dreams."

"Are you sure? It might help you figure out some of the deeper meanings, or where they're rooted in your mind."

"Thanks, but they're all about my mom being dead, so I think it's pretty cut-and-dried."

"Oh. I'm sorry." He was so earnest and sweet, sitting there in his pajamas, lisping around his retainer and trying to think of ways to help me. I wanted to kiss him. I wanted those fingers dug into my hips, wanted the texture of his unshaven face against my cheek and jaw and neck. "Well, I hope the tea does the trick. You keep drinking that bagged shit. No wonder you can't sleep."

"Right. *That's* the reason I can't close my eyes for more than an hour at a time—commercial tea bags."

"Whatever. I think—whoa, careful. Heh—looks like the good stuff *is* wasted on you."

I'd absently pulled the Death Star all the way out of the still-steaming tea. It dripped and pooled, and ran off the edge of the table.

"See? You should have left me alone with my shitty tea bag. Saved us both some trouble." I wrinkled my nose as a drop splashed on my knee. "Ow. Cleanup time."

"I've got it, Elaine."

"No, it's my mess. Sit down."

"No, *you* sit down."

He was teasing me, blocking my way to the sink. I pushed past him, and he grabbed me by the waist, swung me back toward the table. I spun him by the shoulders and slipped beneath his arm, breathless with a childish, giddy hope. His laughter was hushed, his hands strong around my wrists as we stumbled toward the counter. He grabbed the dishtowel, then stopped cold, stumbling over his own feet. I looked up and caught his eye, in time to watch his world slip and shatter.

I saw it happen. I saw it in the clench of his fingers around the towel, the tremble of his lips around a sharp breath. His eyes moved over me, changing as they went, shifting low to my hips and back up again, lingering. I stood straight and lowered my chin, hardly daring to look.

The moonlight poured in the window, washed me in a silver-blue gleam. It stained my arms and hands and body, shot straight through my thin pajama top, and lit me like a star. I might as well have been topless.

A soft, pitiful noise worked its way up from my lungs. Chills broke across my skin like snowmelt, freezing, then slicing, dripping from scalp to neck to spine to soles. My eyes leaped up in time to catch his slipping over my shoulder, off the curve of my collarbone. They reached into me and burned and burned, and undid something in my chest.

"Grey—"

"Sorry."

The word flew from his mouth in pieces. He was already headed for the door, still clutching the towel. Still stammering apologies over his shoulder as he disappeared.

7

"OKAY. SO, I DON'T KNOW WHO ALL'S GOING TO BE here? But be prepared. Every now and then, some real freaky people show up."

We sat in Sadie's car, parked but still buckled in, staring through the windshield at the warehouse. It was a low, squat thing, stretching its way across a gravel lot in right angles of brick and metal. One of many holdouts from the historic Industrial District, located just far enough from the bright bustle of revived, gentrified studios and shops of the River Arts District to reap none of the proximal benefits.

Grey had, unsurprisingly, declined the invitation; he hadn't exactly sought out my company in the four days since our little nighttime tea party had literally gone tits up, which made day-to-day life more than a tad unbearable. Nothing like having the boy you love literally bolt from the room the second you walk in. Nothing like checking around every doorway and corner to make you feel like an intruder in your very own home.

Plus, he'd clearly told Sadie just a bit less than not a goddamn thing. Not that I was aching to take up that particular mantle on his behalf, but the memory of that night scraped my conscience raw. She was my friend, and she trusted me—and yet, she'd been perfectly comfortable shaming me for my gardening attire, unprompted. Even though what had happened in the kitchen was a genuine accident, I had no doubt she'd find a way to throw every scrap of blame at my feet. And in the end, she was Grey's girlfriend, not mine; far be it from me to dictate the boundaries of their intimate communication.

So I played along—I mirrored her smiles and giggles, listened in a guilt-edged haze as she babbled through our lunch period about her brother's art, and when I'd remarked that I'd never seen a metalsmith at work before, she'd nearly lost her mind right there in the cafeteria. She'd texted Connor before I could stop her, informing him of our impending afternoon visit. He'd sent back a neutral *That's fine*, which left me at once excited and unsure, nervous to intrude, yet secretly dying to see the fabled warehouse.

"So it's *not* a studio?" I asked her, eyeing the selection of badly parked cars in the lot.

"More like a co-op. A workshop, for artists who don't have their own creative space. There's no storefront or gallery, nothing like that—oh, and it's not open to the public. Paul doesn't care for tourists. Or retail customers. People in general, really."

"Who's Paul?"

"He owns the warehouse. Or his parents do, anyway. He's the

one who brought my brother here in the first place, gave him a place to live. Taught him his trade."

"And they really let just anyone in here? Isn't there a screening process?"

"Yes—if a person has one hundred and fifty dollars to hand to my brother, that's the screening process. It gets them free run of the space for a week, anytime between noon and two a.m. They can use the easels and tools and stuff, but if they want to use the finite materials, like paint or clay or whatever, they have to buy them directly from Connor or Paul. But anyway," she continued, "those are the rules. If someone makes trouble in here, Connor will ban them for life on the spot. If they act creepy, they get banned. If they break something and don't replace it, or get caught stealing? Banned. Don't worry—if I see anyone looking sketchy, I'll tap you three times on the left shoulder, like this."

"Ow. Maybe not so hard, okay? Anyway, how bad could they be?"

"You never can tell. He's only had to ban, like, four people, though. That I know of. We should be fine."

We left those ominous parting words hanging in the car, and let ourselves in.

The warehouse was equal parts cool and scary, the perfect place to suddenly find yourself trapped and panting, running through the twists and turns and rooms in search of a nonexistent exit. The front room was a cavernous open space, with spotless concrete floors and industrial ceiling fixtures, rows of shelving and supplies lined up along the exposed brick walls. Sadie didn't bat an eye as she led me through a scatter of occupied easels to a hallway, pointing out different rooms as we passed: pottery and ceramics. Beading and lapidary. Woodworking. Fiber arts—a riotous rainbow of yarns and fabrics she had to drag me past.

We found Connor in the metal room, mired in art, soldering iron in hand. He bent over his worktable, not even acknowledging us until he'd set the iron to the side, straightened and stretched, pushed his safety goggles to the top of his head.

"Hey. Didn't expect to see you two so soon." He stretched again and glanced at me, lifting his chin to indicate the hallway. "So? What do you think?"

"It's amazing. A whole room for yarn? A spinning wheel? You're lucky I even made it back here."

"You're into fiber?"

"Connor, that's pretty much all I'm into. All the handmade items in my dad's inventory? These are the hands."

"Really?" He pulled the goggles off and faced me, eyebrows raised in approval. "Do you spin?"

"I've never had the chance to learn."

"I'll teach you. Once I'm done in here, we can whip up a skein or ten."

"But first you need to show her how *you* work," Sadie butted in. "Let Lane see the process, start to finish."

Connor rolled his eyes.

"Ah yes, 'the process.' And let me guess, Sadie—you want me to demonstrate the process by making you . . . ?"

"Bangles. Please? Pretty please?"

"Okay, okay, I'll make you *a* bangle. Singular. Settle down."

That was a pointless thing to ask of Sadie, but she did at least fall silent. Not that her chatter would have made much difference—Connor went hyperfocused once more, as he measured and cut a length of thick, half-round silver wire, pounded texture into it, and filed the edges smooth before dropping it into a Crock-Pot labeled NONFERROUS.

"It needs to hang out in there before I can shape and solder it," he explained to me. "But, Sadie, I want to do a wire wrap on this, string a few stones on. I can leave it plain, if you want, but—"

"No way. I love it when you go all nutty on my jewelry. Now make one for Lane."

"Oh no," I said, instantly awkward. "You don't have to make me anything."

"Of course he will. Won't you, Connor?"

"Sure. It's no problem. Let me grab some more wire, and—" He went quiet, studying me with his head to one side, one finger pressed to his chin. He reached over and took my hand, turned it palm up next to his, comparing the insides of our wrists.

"I think . . ." He trailed off, bit his lip, and squinted at our arms. "Not silver. Not with your undertones. And not a bangle. Hold on a second."

He dropped my arm and beelined back to the shelves, pulled

down about six bins and started going through them, lip still caught in his teeth. I sent a quizzical glance at Sadie, but she was grinning, nodding her head, bouncing on her tiptoes as Connor headed back to us at a fast walk, laid a square of copper sheet metal on the table. He took my hand and placed it on the copper, bent so close his hair nearly brushed my fingers.

"Perfect. Hold still."

There wasn't a force in the universe strong enough to budge me as he measured my wrist, then hunched over his sketchbook. I stood there, staring, until he turned his focus back to the copper, marked his measurements, and went to work on it with a set of shears.

"I'm doing a foldform cuff for you, instead of a bangle," he said. "I won't finish it today, but I have a design idea that's fucking brilliant."

"You don't have to do this, Connor. I mean, I appreciate it, but—"

"Lane, it's happening. You don't have to take it, but no way am I *not* making this, now that I've envisioned it. It'll be amazing, as long as you don't mind—ow." He jerked his finger away and stuck it in his mouth. "Hand me that Kleenex box, will you, Sadie?"

The edges of the world went dark, shrank to a cave to a tunnel to a slit, and all I saw was the blood edging the freshly shorn copper—fat crimson drops streaking to a smear, as Connor absently rubbed them with the side of his fist. And then my head went bad, and there were two Connors. Then none, as my eyes slid closed, the world listing gently to the side.

"Lane? Oh Lord. Connor, where's the stool? Lane, sit here, honey. Head down."

Someone's hands were on me, one to my forehead, the other on the back of my neck. Another hand held my shoulder, another my hip.

"I don't know what's wrong. She's been fine all day." Sadie's voice threaded through the fog. "Should I call Grey? Or an ambulance? Lane, can you hear me? Do you need a doctor?"

I shook my head, forcing myself back to lucidity, opened my eyes to Sadie's flushed, frightened face.

"No, no doctor. I'll be okay. I have"—I paused, breathing through a wave of nausea—"sort of a problem. With cuts and knives, and stuff."

"Oh my word, honey, and I went and brought you *here*?"

"Way to go, Sadie," Connor sighed. "I don't make my living on cuts and knives, or anything."

"Shut up, Connor. Lane, are you okay? Why didn't you say something?"

"I didn't know this would happen. I'll be fine." I swiveled on the stool to face Connor. Sadie slid into view beside him, hand still hovering near my shoulder. "My mom killed herself when I was five. I found her. Seeing people get cut still fucks me up."

They blinked at me, two sets of the same wide eyes over frozen, parted lips. It had been ages since I'd had to see that look.

When I'd returned to kindergarten after the funeral, my teacher had taken me aside and made it abundantly goddamn clear that the details of my absence should be left at the classroom door. The number of people I'd subsequently told fit on one hand's worth of fingers, with room to spare. Not that *that* little tale surfaced often in conversation; it was the kind of thing most people tripped on or scuttled around, before desperately tackling a change of topic. Which, honestly, was fine with me.

Connor recovered first.

"Shit, that's awful," he muttered, dragging a hand through his thicket of hair. "I'm sorry, Lane. I didn't know."

"It's not your fault. It just means I have a thing about sharp edges. And blood. Really only when one results in the other, but still." My eyes darted between them, a single concern bobbing to the surface of my infinite supply. "Could we maybe not mention this to Grey? Like, in any capacity? I don't want him bringing it up at home. Getting my dad all worried, stuff like that."

"Absolutely, honey." Sadie's reply was immediate and sincere. "We won't say a word, will we, Connor?"

"I don't mention much to Grey in general. It stays in this room until Lane says otherwise."

"Thanks." It was easier than I expected, returning his smile. "Are *you* okay?"

"Me?" He looked genuinely confused, until I nodded to his hand, redirecting the focus along with his gaze. "What, this? This is nothing. I don't even need a Band-Aid. Do *you* need anything?"

When I shook my head, Connor sat back and studied me, stared at the shears, then at his fingertip. At the remaining smudge, dark against the copper gleam.

"Well, if you're hanging out in here, blades and blood are unavoidable. And . . . to paraphrase . . . the best way around a problem is to go right the fuck on through it. So—yeah. Let's fix it."

He pushed aside the shears and selected something from the worktable drawer—something long and silver, shiny and sharp. My insides turned to acid.

"When I moved in here," he said, setting it down between us, "Paul had a pet tarantula. Scared the shit out of me, but I had to live with it, so I'd carry it around on my shoulder. To desensitize me."

"Ohhhkaaaay. Did it work?"

"It worked in the sense that I no longer fear that particular tarantula. Just as you will no longer fear this brand-new, super-sharp X-Acto blade, once you cut me with it."

His words took root, seethed and sprouted, choked my automatic laugh with whip-strong vines of panic.

"No. No *way*. *Cut* you?" My lungs closed off, vision wobbling at the edges once again. "You think I can hurt you like that, and be okay with it?"

"You won't hurt me. Look at my hands." He stretched them toward me—they were fine-boned but strong, rough with calluses, threaded with scars. "I work with knives every single day.

Do you know how many times I've bled? Go on. I trust you."

"This is not about trust. I can't."

"Yes, you can. Do it."

"Connor, I literally can't. I—"

"Do it."

His voice went dark and alpha; his eyes burned through me and out the other side. He was the Connor Hall of rumor—he was the warehouse itself, dark and labyrinthine and halfway to crumbled. Brimming with strange people and stranger creations.

Someone else's arm reached for the knife. Someone else's fingers gripped the handle, turned the blade. Took hold of his left hand, drawing it closer.

"That's it," he said, low. "Steady."

When I was nine, Dad took me to a swimming hole in Pisgah National Forest—a long-anticipated day trip, cut short when I slipped and went under, got myself stuck in a waterfall. Not behind the curtain, but beneath the falls itself, trapped and blind and clawing, unable to breathe without choking. That single word from Connor put me right back between water and rock. Right back between two very different heartbeats.

"What did you say?"

"Keep your hands steady. You can do this, Lane. You're in control."

I touched the knife tip to the pad of his thumb, paused, looked up. He hadn't blinked. He hadn't even flinched. And he didn't flinch in the next second, when I bore down, dragged it across. Felt the flesh give beneath the blade.

It was over in less than a breath, about the same amount of time it took for me to break.

He never took his eyes off mine even as my hand revolted. The knife clattered to the table, scattered drops of his blood across the surface. His good hand reached for one of mine, gripping it tightly as I wept.

"That was perfect. I'm proud of you."

"You're *proud* of me? What the fuck, Connor. You're deranged."

"Lane, look at me. I'm fine. It's barely a scratch."

"But I made it *happen*." I practically tore the top off the Kleenex box as I grabbed a wad of tissues, squeezed them hard as I could around his thumb. The pressure only made it worse. "Oh God. I made you bleed. I'm so sorry."

"Yes, you made me bleed. You did this, and look—you're still on your feet. You're already stronger than you were this morning. And now, you're going to fix me."

I stared at him, gasping around my sobs as he gently pulled his hand from my tissue grip and laid it, palm up, between us. The cut was already clotting, the bleeding slowing to a trickle. He pulled a small first aid kit from the drawer, set it between us, and looked at me. Waited.

Connor was quiet as I cleaned up my mess, soaked cotton balls bright red, fumbled with gauze and iodine and medical tape. He was quiet when I broke down again, and as he cleaned his blood off my fingertips and closed his bandaged hand over both of mine, holding them still until my tears dried up and my tremors subsided.

And Sadie, for once, was also quiet. So quiet, I'd forgotten she was even there until her voice drifted over from across the table.

"You guys," she said, breathless as me but twice as calm. "I mean, I love y'all to death and all, but seriously? Y'all are a special kind of crazy."

8

"COME IN."

His voice scurried up my back on chilly feet, burst between my shoulder blades, and trickled down my arms as I pushed open his bedroom door, my chin held high in what I hoped would play as confidence. I'd been standing in the hallway for a solid two minutes, working up the nerve to knock; things had been awkward enough between us without me scuttling along the baseboards like a shamed rat at the first hint of necessary interaction.

I hadn't been in the room since it became his. It was surreal—a space in my house, once used for storage, that I'd never thought twice about entering—that space now overflowed with Grey McIntyre: his constellation bedspread and *Star Wars* posters, and teetering stacks of comic books; a book of matches on a stoneware plate, half-hidden by a burnt smudge stick. Sadie's senior portrait framed on his nightstand, her smile reflected over and over in the pictures tacked to his walls and stuck in the edges of his mirror. The dried boutonniere he'd worn to Homecoming. A worn, stuffed bear, with a frayed-stitched nose that broke my heart, peering from the lowest corner of his bookshelf.

Grey sat cross-legged in the middle of his bed, two different textbooks and his laptop open in front of him. A fan of handwritten notes covered the lower half of the mattress. A bread-crumb-strewn plate and crumpled napkin perched on the pillow next to an empty microwave-popcorn bag. He grinned at me over the mess, made eye contact for the first time since that night in the kitchen, and if that grin was a shade too hectic, I wasn't one to judge. My own eyes slid away and then back again, and I matched him, tooth by overcompensating tooth. To stand there in his bedroom after everything that had and hadn't happened stirred a storm of memories and trepidation; I forced my posture into neutral, determined not to cringe, or stammer, or shuffle around like an asshole. This was my territory—this was my home. It would be fine. I could do this.

"Oh. I didn't—sorry. I'm sorry. I don't want to interrupt." Real nice, Lane. So much for that.

"It's no problem. What did you need?"

"Dad left us a grocery list. Are you up for a Trader Joe's run before dinner? It can wait, if you're busy. Or I could go myself, if you don't mind me driving your car."

"I could use a break, actually, before I pass out all over these equations." He slid off his bed and stretched. My eyes ate up the lines of his arms. "I'll drop you off and hang out at Starbucks until you're done. Sound good to you?"

"That sounds perfect." I turned my face away, swinging my

hair forward to hide the heat in my cheeks. "Have you been studying all this time? It's been hours."

"Yep. The 4.0 won't earn itself."

"Seriously?" I peeked out at him, expecting the smugness, catching him instead with a bashful grin that rushed warm around my heart. "Wow. I knew you were smart, but—"

"I'm ambitious. If it was just about being smart, I wouldn't have to work so hard."

"Still, that's awesome. Any big, ambitious plans for the 4.0?"

"Yeah." It was his turn to drop his head. "Duke."

"Duke? As in, Duke University? Are you kidding me?"

"It's my dream school. I'm sending my early-decision application in November. But—" He broke off and started fiddling with his pentacle, tucking it inside his shirt, then pulling it out again. Tracing the five-point pattern with the tip of his finger as he slipped into his Converse. "Do me a favor, will you? Don't mention this to anyone else. Not now."

"Oh. Okay, but—doesn't Skye know? Or Sadie?"

He wouldn't look at me. Something strange and apprehensive slithered between my shoulder blades.

"Greyson? What's wrong?"

"It's nothing. I don't want everyone making a big deal about it, in case I'm rejected." He raised his head and leveled me with a shy, hopeful smile, an anvil dropped from the top of the clouds. "I'd rather keep it quiet for now. Just between us."

It was a full-body shiver, those words. A mist of water over sun-warm skin, shocking and cooling, jolting me awake. Did I mean so much to him already, that he'd trust me with something this big? Or was it that I didn't mean enough to matter?

My father was a magnet for secrets—people stopped him in the market, or the library, or at one of the many shops that stocked our products. Told him all sorts of random shit, from illnesses to divorce, love affairs, and joyous news—unsolicited words that swelled and bubbled, demanding release at the first sign of a friendly face. Dad ate it up with a goddamn spoon, reveled in being an emotional dumping ground for strangers and friends alike. A personality trait he'd decidedly failed to pass on to his child.

But this was Grey. This was a dream he'd spent years nurturing—a hope so fragile and sacred even Sadie didn't know, yet he'd shared it with me.

In this one tiny way, he'd chosen me.

My answering smile formed softly, wiped the worry from his wary eyes. They held mine right to the edge of just enough before shifting back to his hands.

"Consider it our secret," I said, filling the following silence.

"I knew I could count on you." He stood and walked toward me, playfully bumped my shoulder with his on his way to the door. Sent a glow from his grin to the tips of my fingers. "Let's go."

* * *

I browsed the aisles in a fog, mind stumbling over thoughts of Grey. He'd been quiet on the drive, and though he claimed it was study fatigue, he'd barely looked at me when he dropped me off. The thrill of a thing told in confidence warred with the unease of that same thing kept from Sadie. She was my friend, his girlfriend—or future wife, or almost-fiancée, or whatever label she chose on any given day—yet here we were, adding another secret to the ever-growing collection between us. Seeing as West Asheville hadn't yet been reduced to literal burning rubble, I was pretty sure he still hadn't told her about the whole I-accidentally-saw-Lane's-rack incident either. But I'd made him a promise regarding Duke—it wasn't my news to share, and that was that. Still, the knowledge hung sour on the edge of my tongue.

"Hey there, Lane."

So weird, how my Sadie-centric guilt seemed to summon her brother from the very ether. I smiled as he approached, raising an eyebrow at his companion: the boyfriend, I assumed, big and broad and long-legged, with dreads to his waist and large, solid hands. He carried their shopping basket over one forearm and texted while walking, unconcerned by his surroundings. At the sound of my name, though, he looked up, interest flitting across his face.

"Ohhhhh shit. This is Lane? This is *the* Lane? Lord. I'm not sure whether to run away screaming or give you a big old hug."

"That's . . . interesting?" I blinked at his enormous grin and hyper eyes, a lovely brown just a shade lighter than his skin. "I feel like I should take the hug, but I'm not sure who you are."

"That's Paul." Connor shook his head. "Paul was very impressed by your recent wielding of my X-Acto."

"Damn straight I was," Paul said, smirking as I cringed at the week-old memory. "What are you doing after this? Oh, come back with us. Please."

"Are you sure? I don't want to get in the way."

"Like I'd even be talking to you if I thought you would."

"Well, when you put it that way." I couldn't help but smile at his excited squeal. "I need to text Grey, though. He's waiting for me at the Starbucks."

"Grey? Sadie's Grey?" He turned to Connor. "Why would Grey be waiting for her at the Starbucks?"

"He's my stepbrother." The word formed heavy in my mouth, a rough-cut stone too big to swallow. Paul looked back and forth between Connor and me, phone hanging forgotten from his hand.

"*Oh.* That means y'all two will be—oh, that's *hilarious.*"

"What's hilarious?" I furrowed my brow at Connor, who shrugged, clearly unaffected.

"You'll learn to take Paul with a grain of salt. And a grain of every other damn thing. So." He leaned past me and snagged a box of crackers off the shelf. "We'll be another fifteen minutes or so, if you're coming back with us."

"*If* she's coming back with us, he says." Paul set his basket down smack in the middle of the aisle and swept me up in a bear hug, groceries and all. He smelled like candy canes and sawdust. "'If' is not even a negotiable thing, Laney."

"Fifteen minutes, then?" I laughed as he set me back on my feet.

"Fifteen. You and your future stepbrother-in-law can finish up the food shopping, while I go drink myself some more of those little coffee samples. They got that pumpkin-flavored shit out today."

He sauntered off, abandoning the basket. Connor retrieved it and continued along the aisle. I trailed behind him, texted Grey my change of plans, turned Paul's words over in my mind. Returned again and again to a single phrase.

"Is that really what we'll be to each other?" I asked, standing idle as Connor picked through the bin of apples. "Stepsiblings-in-law. How does all that work?"

"Not really sure. I'll be brother-in-law to your stepbrother, but I don't know if that makes you and me family, legally or otherwise. Could just be semantics." He shrugged, added three pears to his basket, and headed for the checkout lane. "Anyway, that's assuming they go through with their 'wedding' in the first place. Otherwise, it's a moot question."

His casual words were a fist to the throat. I made myself breathe as we paid for our groceries, waited until we were outside on the curb and he'd texted Paul before I spoke.

"Why did you say that?"

"Say what?"

"About Sadie and Grey. 'Assuming' they go through with the wedding. Are they having problems?"

"Not that I'm aware, but come on—they're in high school. Sadie's not even legal. I'm sure they think 'true love' will triumph, but I doubt they've considered the reality."

"Wow." My smile crept out, in spite of itself. "Glass-half-full much?"

"More like near-empty. But come on—can *you* picture settling down forever, the day after graduation?"

"God, no. I don't do relationships at all, if I can help it."

"Oh, really? What *do* you do?"

"Distractions." I watched my meaning settle over his face. Winced as it lit his eyes and tugged a laugh from his throat. "Wow. That sounded far less horrible in my head."

"Trust me, those stones are not mine to throw." His phone buzzed. He dug it out and checked it, rolling his eyes as he showed me the screen.

New snack display. Get comfortable.

"Aaaand speaking of stones, a potential conquest has officially been spotted. So we might be here awhile."

I blinked at him, caught off guard. "And you're okay with this?"

"Does it matter if I am or not? Paul will be Paul. He enjoys the single life, regardless of our timetable."

"Oh." Apparently, Connor and Paul were no longer the happy couple they'd been when they moved in together. "So your place is basically a bachelor pad?"

"You could say that. We share a room, but we respect each other's space. The boundaries go both ways."

"I guess. But it doesn't bother you?"

"No. Why should it?" He dismissed my frown with a wave of his hand. "I'm a little more open-minded than my sister, obviously. Not that she can say a goddamn word to me, when her own alleged fiancé hasn't been past second base."

"*Connor.*" My eyes nearly left their sockets. "Oh my God. Speculate much?"

"Speculate whatever. Sadie's True Love Waits thing is hardly a secret."

I gazed past him at nothing, distracted. Fighting down the sultry thrill building in my belly. They'd been together for years, but apparently, never once *been* together—how was that even possible? And how much had his restraint factored into our interactions? For all I knew, my moonlit body was the most he'd ever seen.

"I wouldn't know," I finally said, once I trusted myself to speak. "We don't exactly discuss Grey's celibacy goals around the dinner table."

"I doubt it was his idea. My sister, now—she's all about God's plan. No shacking up, no college, no job. Just get married and start ejecting babies, as a righteous woman should. Defer to the man of the house, at all costs."

"Gross. You're about to get smacked."

"*I* don't agree with that bullshit—it's how we were raised to be. I was groomed for head-of-household, believe it or not."

"Yeah, not so much."

"Right? I mean, if it's what she really wants, I'll support it. I'm even making their wedding rings. But she could do so much more—go away to college. Volunteer. Do missionary work. Join the Peace Corps. Stuff I'd have been happy to do myself, instead of starving."

"What? Instead of—oh."

I'd never heard him talk about that time in his life. Most rumors painted him as a renegade—the out-and-proud boy who'd cast off his oppressive upbringing to live on his own terms. The image of him scrounging for nonexistent food didn't match up with the legend of Connor Hall.

His words fit, though. They fit the knobs of his wrists, the honed edge of his jaw. Lurked in the smudges of his angry eyes, and in the hollows beneath his too-sharp cheekbones as he buttoned his jacket against the post-sunset chill.

We fell silent after that. He texted Paul again, sat on the curb, rummaged in his grocery bag for a granola bar. I watched him from the corner of my eye, wondering what else he'd planned to say to me, before I'd turned to stone.

9

THE WAREHOUSE WAS DIFFERENT AT NIGHT, THE EXTERIOR washed in sudden floodlights that sparked to life at the approach of Paul's car. He'd banished Connor to the back seat, insisted I ride shotgun, and the two of them had immediately started giving each other endless amounts of shit. By the time we pulled into the warehouse lot, I was laughing too hard to breathe.

The change in their demeanor was instantaneous as we walked inside—both spines straightened, both sets of shoulders squared. Both smiles flipped as they flanked me and bulldozed down the hallway, scanning each room for any sign of disarray or shady behavior. The place was calm, though, the artists quiet and hard at work.

Their living space was enormous, a shadowy expanse of concrete and brick and scattered wood shavings. A half-carved sculpture dominated what was clearly Paul's side; a low, padded stool stood beside it, next to a wheeled cart loaded with tools and bins. His bed was large and cozy-looking, covered in pillows and a zebra-print spread. A set of metal shelves bracketed the bed, each stacked to capacity with carvings and statues, trinkets and blown-glass sculptures. A mini fridge and a small safe squatted beneath a glass-topped table, on which rested a laptop and speaker system, a Keurig brewer, and a high-end work lamp. Two rolling garment racks, hung to capacity with clothes grouped by color, stretched along the wall. Everything was spread out and comfortable and casually pretty.

The other side of the room, Connor's side, smacked of austerity—the involuntary kind that sprouts from need rather than want. A plain drafting table and metal stool. A dilapidated, folded-out futon, messy with blankets and mismatched throw pillows. A wooden crate, overflowing with paperbacks. A small wheeled cart that held his bathroom caddy and a coffeepot, an electric hot pot and an oversize mug. The stacks of plastic bins that held his clothing, half-covered by a tired canvas tarp. A smaller plastic bin filled with ramen packets, granola bars, and loose pouches of instant oatmeal. All of it scrunched and stacked and starkly visible from where I stood, reluctant to encroach upon the side of the room he'd once shared. Something wrenched in me at the sight—a surge of pity for a boy whose whole life fit into a warehouse corner. A boy who considered a corner an improvement over what he'd had.

They divided and stored their groceries as I edged into the room, unsure where to put my feet. Nervous for no reason, clumsy out of nowhere—I nearly fell over my own grocery tote bags, which Connor had set just inside the doorway.

"Is there a bathroom I could use?" My voice was a small echo that drew both their gazes.

"Nah," Paul drawled, stretching languidly across his bed. "You can pee out back by the river's edge, like everyone else. Unless you think you're too good for the way we live."

"The bathroom is the next door down to your right." Connor sat cross-legged on his futon, grinned at my hesitant blink. "It's minuscule, but it's indoors. Grain of salt, right, Paul?"

"Y'all know you love me." Paul threw me a wink. "Go on, girl. Don't leave the seat down."

The word "minuscule" was a generous descriptor—my bedroom closet boasted more floor space. There was no tub or shower, just a toilet and a pedestal sink, and enough room to stand in front of each. A toilet brush and plunger skulked in the corner behind a tiny wastebasket. One wall was a floor-to-ceiling abstract mural of black, blue, and purple paint, a weird contrast to the olive green of the floor tiles and graffiti-laden industrial gray of the other walls. There was a mirror above the sink and a wall-mounted soap dispenser, but no medicine cabinet or shelving or other storage space. A roll of paper towels sat on the lid of the toilet tank next to a spray bottle. The seat was up, of course, but the toilet itself was surprisingly clean, and I saw why as soon as I sat down. A metal picture frame that screamed Connor's handwork hung on the door, a handwritten list secured behind the glass:

ALL USING THIS BATHROOM MUST ADHERE TO THE FOLLOWING:

* Close the door. No one needs to see your business.
* Flush the toilet. I don't care about your water conservationist environmental bullshit. Flush. The. Toilet.
* Wash your nasty hands with the soap provided.
* Spray and wipe the toilet and sink with the cleaning supplies provided. Clean up your mess, and throw your trash in the damn can, not the toilet.
* Leave the toilet seat UP. Because I said so, that's why.
* Turn off the light. If my electric bill goes up, I'll take the bulb out of the socket myself, so help me.
* If you need toilet paper for your house and can't be bothered to buy it from the motherfucking store, you can buy it from Paul for $100 a roll. Convenience has a price, and that price in here is $100. If you

STEAL MY TOILET PAPER, I WILL END YOU.

* FEEL FREE TO ADD TO THE GRAFFITI
WALLS IN HERE, BUT DON'T DEFACE THE
MURAL, AND DO NOT DRAW, WRITE, OR
OTHERWISE MARK ON THE WALLS OUTSIDE
THIS BATHROOM. THAT SHIT WILL RESULT
IN AN AUTOMATIC LIFETIME BAN.

* ANYONE CAUGHT NOT ADHERING TO THE
ABOVE WILL BE ASKED TO LEAVE AND USE
THE BATHROOM IN YOUR OWN GODDAMN
HOUSE.

I was still giggling when I returned to their room. Both of them were absorbed in their respective sketchbooks, their faces identically focused and intense. Paul's tongue poked out the corner of his mouth; Connor's lower lip was anchored between his teeth.

"There you are," Connor said, looking up from his sketchbook as I closed the door. "Sorry about the lack of seating options—we're not too fancy around here."

"This is fine. This is great, actually. I'd kill for a setup like this."

He smirked at that, bumping my shoulder with his as I settled next to him on the futon. "You just want a turn on that spinning wheel. Don't lie."

"You spin?" Paul poked his head up, interest sparked. "She spins?"

"Not yet. I plan on teaching her once I dig out that wool, but we didn't get the chance last time, because my hand got the shit cut out of it by this one girl."

"Shut *up*," I moaned, returning his playful shove. "You're the worst, Connor."

"So I'm told. But yeah, Lane's a fiber artist."

"I knit and crochet. Scarves and hats, mostly." I ducked behind my hair to dodge Paul's approving grin. "My stuff sells, but I don't think anyone sees me as an *artist*. Not the way you guys are artists."

"Whatever with all that," Paul scoffed. "Art is art. Envision, attempt, create. And then, hopefully fucking profit. If you make money off your work, you're ahead of most of the folks who hang out here."

"And some of the folks who live here," Connor sighed. "This month, at least. So, speaking of living here . . ."

"Please. When I tire of your indentured servitude, I'll let you know. Find you a nice girl. Toss her some bribe money to take you off my hands."

"Girl?"

The word leaped out of my mouth, my brain loping along half a mile behind it. I blinked back and forth between their quizzical glances.

"Assuming there exists one who can deal with his bullshit," Paul said, "so odds are I'm stuck with him for life."

"But—" I turned to Connor. "A *girl*?"

"Yeah? Why is that—" Connor went silent all at once, then red, and then a gasp and a high-pitched cackle burst out of Paul and shrieked their way across the room. Connor's hands hit his face, and his back hit the mattress, sending a jolt through the futon. "Jesus. No. Oh my God, Lane, I'm not gay."

"You're—what? You're *not*? But I thought you two—" My head swiveled between him and Paul, who had tipped over and was hanging halfway off his own bed, literally screaming with laughter. "You and Paul—"

"'Him and Paul' not a goddamn thing," Paul bellowed. "Hard pass on the 'him and Paul,' if it's all the same to you."

"Yeah, definitely not so much." Connor sat up and rubbed his eyes, fixed them solidly on the floor between his feet. "Lane, I think we need to back up a few steps. Where, exactly, did you hear this?"

"From everyone. I mean, they said—" I blew out a frustrated breath, refocused my thoughts into coherent words. "Your youth group friends went around to the whole school with it. Years ago, back when you got exiled. They said that's the reason you left home."

"Wow. That makes sense, I guess, in a fucked-up way— explains why every last one of those so-called friends forgot my name overnight."

"Wait—are you saying they made it up? Why? That actually *doesn't* make sense."

"Punishment, Lane. The prize sheep ghosted the flock—can't have that, or the other kids might start thinking for themselves. I'm just surprised this shit didn't make it back to me sooner."

"What the fuck." I stared at his barely perturbed face, shook my head at his casual shrug. "Seriously, that's the worst they could do—say you like guys? Like that's even a bad thing?"

"That congregation is wall-to-wall bigots stacked on assholes, and yes—to them it *is* the worst, if their endgame was to shut me out for good. Looks like it worked."

Paul's laughter trailed into silence. A self-conscious heat swarmed up my neck, danced its way over my cheeks. Stupid. So, so stupid.

"I am so sorry, Connor. I am." When he didn't answer, I plowed on, raking my hands through my hair, working it into a mess of tangles. "I'm sorry that happened to you, and I'm sorry I never knew, or thought to question it. I know how much shit goes around that school, and—"

"Whoa, careful." His hand stilled mine, and he leaned closer, all business, unwinding a snarl of hair from my fingers. "It's fine, Lane. 'Gay' isn't an insult in my world."

"Of course it's not," I muttered, looking everywhere but at him. My gaze leaped over Paul, then returned. He watched us silently, head to one side. "Sorry, Paul."

"Sorry? I'm not bothered by those bitches. Anyway, the look on his face when you broke the news? That was the funniest shit I've seen in ages." He glanced at his phone, then rolled off the bed, grabbed his car keys off the glass tabletop. "I need to go shower. You guys coming?"

"To the shower? With you?" I peered at him, but he seemed perfectly serious. "Um."

"To the gym," Connor said. He tucked the now-smooth length of hair behind my ear and sat back, satisfied. "No shower here, as you might have noticed. You go on, Paul. I'll head over in the morning."

"Damn right you will. Go early, do some squats. Keep that ass looking how you know I like it." Paul cracked up at himself, waving off Connor's raised middle finger. "You need a ride, Laney?"

"Oh. No, Grey is expecting my text. But if I'm in your way, Connor . . ."

"Well, I *was* planning to finally make my move on Paul, but the moment appears to have passed."

"Like I even would with you," Paul sniffed. "*You* take him, Laney—get this boy set up at your place and out of my hair, and you can *have* that spinning wheel."

"Oh, okay," I scoffed. "I'm sure my dad won't mind that at all."

"Yeah, because your dad's the problem." Connor slid toward me and leaned in, sending a whisper into my ear. *"Elaine."*

"Shut up." I jerked backward, everything burning in my cheeks. His face was bright and flushed, mouth pulled into an impish smirk. "It is *not* like that. It's—fuck. *Fuck.* Connor, I swear—"

"Sure it's not. Like he wouldn't if he thought he could." He shook his head at my glare, settling back on the futon. "What? He's a good kid, but come on—he's no saint. And neither are you."

We stared at each other. His words reached through my skin,

flicked at the raw hollow behind my heart where I'd buried so many things I'd tried to ignore regarding Grey—things Connor casually dropped between us like innards on a butcher's block, gross and disposable. Unavoidable.

I lowered my eyes, focused on the white-knuckle clench of my fingers. Bit down on my tongue to still the tremble of my chin.

"I don't want to talk about it. And you shouldn't either."

"That's fine." He leaned backward and reached behind me, snagged his sketchbook from a fold in the blankets. "It's above my pay grade, anyway."

"Meaning?"

"Lane, you're pining for my sister's boyfriend. Even if he weren't your brother, that's some high school drama that'll do its thing without my input."

"He's not my brother," I hissed. "And I am not *pining.*"

"Oh, look at *this* mess." Paul leaned against the doorframe, grinning at me with all his teeth. Enjoying himself way too much to leave. "The lady doth protest, right?"

"Don't you start," I snarled, face catching fire as they both fully lost their shit. I glowered at Connor as he doubled over, laughing too hard to breathe. "Wow. Thanks for your support, asshole."

"I'm sorry," he howled. "It's just so fucked up. Your life. Your poor life."

I didn't bother arguing with that one.

Paul cackled his way out the door as I slid off the futon and rummaged through my bag, seeking the needles and skein attached to my current hat-in-progress. Might as well get some work done while stewing in said ridiculous life.

Connor's laughter slowed to gasps, then trailed to chuckles, as he bent over the sketchbook. The hush was sudden and obvious; the only sounds were the rustling of pages, the scratch of his pencil, his quiet breathing. I stood there with my yarn, unsure where to sit. Wondering if it was too late to chase down Paul and dive into his car, peel out of the parking lot in a hot-cold cloud of adrenaline and skin-crawling shame. Why did every visit to the warehouse seem to culminate in an excruciating silence? This was even more awkward than the dead-mom conversation.

"I should go." He didn't respond. I swallowed hard, voice catching in my throat with a tiny click. "Connor."

"What?"

I'd startled him out of his trance. He blinked at me through a stray lock of hair, then swiped at it until it settled behind his ear with the rest, and I was back in the metal room, blade poised, voice caught in the spaces between each impossible breath. The last time his eyes looked like that, things had ended in blood. An eternal pause hung between us, as if the awkward moment in the Trader Joe's parking lot had sniffed out our trail, followed us and found us, engulfed us once more in its thickening silence.

"Don't." My voice was little more than a whisper. "Don't look at me like that."

"I wasn't looking at you at all, until you said my name. But I'll stop, if it bothers you." He tilted his head to the side, considering, then let his eyes slide from mine to the floor, and all the way back up. The corner of his mouth curled into a slow, wicked smirk. "Hmm. Or should I look at you more often?"

"God, will you not?" I glared at him, cheeks sparking and flaring all over again as he refocused on his work, not bothering to stifle a laugh. "What's so funny?"

"Nothing. Just, eye contact wasn't a problem when I was gay." He made a show of peeping through his hair, ducking back behind it when he glimpsed my scowl. "Ah, shit. Busted."

"Oh, fuck off."

He burst out laughing, deflecting the flying skein. It bounced off his arm and landed behind him on the futon. I gave him a halfhearted scowl, wishing it was possible to fade a blush by sheer force of will.

"Okay, Connor, you made your point. Any chance we could never speak of this again?"

"Hell no. This is forever our thing."

"But you won't——" Even thinking the words made me cringe, but I forced them out. I had to. "You won't speak of——anything—— to anyone else either, right? Please?"

"Wait——what exactly are you asking me to hide?" His eyes darkened; his mouth pulled into something just short of a snarl. "I was borderline joking earlier, but if he's messing around on Sadie——"

"No, God——nothing like that. It's not about her——it goes so far back, way before them, but I would never——" I stumbled over my own protests, pressed my palms over my eyes to block his judgment. He was going to tell Sadie. He'd tell her, and she'd rip the world off its hinges, and I would deserve every last bit of the resulting fallout. "I'm the worst and I know it, okay? But it's all on me—he hasn't done anything. He doesn't even know."

The silence that followed was damn near eternal, building and buzzing in my quaking limbs. His sudden laugh, when it happened, nearly sent me out of my skin.

"Lane, if you can maybe locate your chill, that would be great. So, you have a crush—so what. As long as my sister isn't getting screwed over, I honestly don't give a shit."

"You—don't?" I peeked out through my fingers. Connor gazed at me, unblinking, mouth quirked, eyes in neutral. "So you won't tell them?"

"Like I'd do that to you." His conspiratorial wink sent a sharp burst of relief through my bones. He shook his head at my sigh and gestured to the space beside him. "Jesus, you're a mess. Sit down, knock out some rows. Grab something to read or whatever, and calm the fuck down before you pass out."

"Are you absolutely sure, Connor? If I'm in your way—"

"Never stopped you before."

"You're such an asshole." I climbed onto the futon and retrieved my yarn, stretched out beside him on my stomach. Leaned against his knee, determined to bulldoze my way back to normal. "I'll show you 'in the way.' Move over."

He grinned at the fading flush of my cheeks and resumed work on his sketch, shifting sideways. Making room for me.

10

MY EYES STRAYED AROUND THE LIVING ROOM, MIND blank, vision bleary. When I'd settled on the floor next to Sadie for an afternoon of studying, I'd drastically underestimated the definition of the word as it applied to Grey McIntyre. He'd been fused to the couch for literally hours, hunched over his work, hammering on his laptop and muttering equations under his breath. It was exhausting just being in the same room.

I set aside my homework and stretched out on my stomach, braced my hands, pushed up into a full plank. From there I lowered into chaturanga, moved into up dog, then down dog, and from that into child's pose. I leaned into the stretch, focused on my breath, letting my spine lengthen and my muscles melt. I'd spent several predawn hours that morning curled into a fetal post-nightmare ball; the ache still lingered, right down to my bones.

"I always wanted to try yoga."

Sadie's voice disrupted my meditation. She watched me pointedly, head to one side, then turned back to her book. My eyes leaped sideways, catching Grey's——they were wide and hectic, occupied with my limbs. Too late, he started, blinked back to his laptop, stared a hole through the goddamn screen. Guilt bloomed bright across his cheekbones as I looked to Sadie, then him, and back again. She was lovely and serene, once again absorbed in the page.

It had to be an accident——a random glance that meandered past its own intention. Hell, he'd barely looked at me since that night in our kitchen, and now he was damn near craning his neck past his future whatever's head. I'd stretched without thinking; a habit, formed over years of practice, and what the fuck was I supposed to do about that——should I check myself forever now? Retool my wardrobe and my posture, and my whole goddamn existence, in case the interloper in my house yielded unto temptation, or what-ever the fuck phrase somehow transformed his faults into mine? What the hell was with his sudden, reckless stares?

"You should come to the studio with me some weekend," I squawked at Sadie, wincing at the cheerful blare of my voice. "I've been slacking hard since school started."

"Oh, I don't think so. It's not really in line with my belief system."

"The classes I take focus more on the physical elements of the practice," I reassured her. "Stretches, poses, controlled breathing. There are definitely people who embrace the spiritual aspects, but how far you get into that is up to you."

"Try it, babe," Grey said, twirling a lock of her hair through his fingers. "Make it a girls' day out. Come by after, show off those little stretchy pants."

"Oh stop," she giggled, delighted blush visible even beneath her makeup. "I'll take a girls' spa day over a workout, thank you. A massage and a mani-pedi. Maybe a nice makeover."

"You, Sadie Hall, are gorgeous just how you are."

Her giggling intensified as he leaned over, kissing a trail from her cheek to her lips. I let my forehead drop back down, much preferring the shoe-and-foot funk of the carpet to the visual of him latching himself to her face, so suddenly focused on his one and only love. So blatantly signaling his *true* intentions, regardless of where his eyes preferred to wander when she wasn't looking.

Kill me.

"It's a good idea, though," she said when they resurfaced. "A makeover day. Oh, Lane, we so have to do that."

"We so do not. Though thanks for the implication that I need a makeover, Sadie. God."

"Don't be ridiculous, honey, you're lovely—but they're so much fun. I can do your face and nails right now, actually. Like a trial run. Please?"

"Whatever." I sat up and stretched one final time, set to work unraveling my mussed braid. Much easier to let her have her way, seeing as I barely gave a shit. "Nails only, though. A glittery face is not a thing for me."

"I have a matte palette, if you don't want glitter." Sadie's eyes gleamed as she dug in her bag. Grey chuckled and shook his head, directed his smirk back at his screen as I covered my face with one hand, waving her away with the other. "Oh, fine. Nails it is. I only have pink, so that's what you're getting."

"Like I expected anything else."

I had to hand it to Sadie—she was all about outdoing herself at every turn. The girl pulled a full manicure set out of that bag, along with about eighty bottles of nail polish—strengthener, base coat, topcoat, and, of course, every shade of pink under the goddamn sun. Twenty minutes later, my toenails were a creamy carnation, Grey's homework was done, and his patience was hanging by its very last thread.

"This is going to take all night," he sighed as Sadie started on my hands. "Meanwhile, my stomach is physically digesting itself."

"We'll grab dinner as soon as I'm done with Lane," she reassured him. "Go get a snack. It won't be long."

"I would love to go get a snack. Getting a snack, in theory, is my very favorite thing. If only Elaine hadn't left my fucking snacks all the way across town."

"And a day later, you're still bitching," I retorted, rolling my eyes. "I said I was sorry, okay? I'll make a special trip to the warehouse tomorrow, just for you."

"Fuck tomorrow, I'll drive you over right now. Get your shoes on. I'm starving."

"Don't you move, Lane. Your toes are still wet." Sadie finished buffing my thumbnail and picked up the polish. "Why in the world were you at Connor's with Grey's snacks?"

"I ran into him and Paul at the store. They invited me back, and I left one of my—don't you give me that look, Greyson. It happens."

"Oh, I'm so glad you met Paul," Sadie squealed. "He's such a sweetheart, isn't he? And he has the most wonderful laugh in the world."

"Yeah, I heard it." My face combusted all over again at the memory. "It made quite the appearance when he found out I thought he used to date your brother. Really gave the moment that special something."

"Wait, what? You thought *Connor* was——" Grey's laugh was sudden and sharp, and just a shade too loud. "Are you high?"

"Apparently? Everyone at school said he was—and if it's true, that's totally fine, but I guess no one thought to double-check with him."

"Oh, that." Sadie waved off the rest of my rambling. "When Connor left home, some kids from church went around spreading lies—everybody whispering, saying he liked boys, and he'd betrayed Christ. That anyone who accepted him would burn in Hell at his side. It was awful."

"The fuck?" Grey slid off the couch and settled beside her. "What is wrong with people?"

"I wish I could tell you. I know what Daddy preaches—I know how ugly they can get—but I don't believe they speak for God. I can't. The Lord I love would never turn away His children. Not even the sinners."

"It's not a sin in the first place," he answered, eyes on her downcast face. "You know that."

"I know——and either way, it's not for me to judge. The world needs all the joy it can get, these days." She was quiet for a moment, her mouth a sad, pink quirk. "I love my brother. You know I do. But sometimes I really miss him."

"Babe, you see him, like, ten times a week."

"I don't mean like *that*——I miss who he was before. When we were kids. He never would tell me what happened to him, all that time he was homeless, but I know it was bad. It changed him."

"Unsurprising," I said flatly. "Not to be a bitch, but your family threw him out like garbage. I'm sure he did what he had to."

"Whatever that was, Lane, it's not his fault. Believe me, when it comes to my parents, we all do what we have to." She blew gently on my ring finger, eyes fixed on her handiwork. "By the time I met you, Grey, Connor had been gone a year, and no one talked about him at all anymore, rumors or otherwise. Anyway, you know him better than they did. You know the truth."

"But Elaine was clueless up until yesterday." Grey's side-eye swung my way, the edge in his voice sawing its way across my spine. "What did he do, hit on you?"

"Baby? Why would you say *that*?"

He blinked away from me, as if caught off guard by the reminder of Sadie. She'd paused in her task, brush poised over my finger. Stared at him when he took a little too long to answer.

"Just surprised he hasn't," he finally mumbled. "She's been all over him since day one—practically chased him down."

"I have *not*," I sputtered, brain spinning recklessly backward, sifting through the images of the past month. Freezing frame after damning, relevant frame: me stretched out beside Connor on the futon. Lying on the pavement at the overlook, drunk and laughing, legs tangled with his. Leaning out the window of a goddamn moving car, fingers sunk into his sleeve like claws. All that without even counting secrets and conversations and inside jokes—like the picture of the missing groceries and about eight cry/laugh emojis Connor had texted me the night before, followed by the selfie of him smirking into the camera, clearly simulating direct eye contact. Not to mention the joint grocery shopping itself, like we were some old domestic couple, or the whole mess that led to cleaning his blood and my tears off both our hands. All utterly without motive prior to our weird little reverse-coming-out party, but oh dear God, Grey had way too much of a point. Jesus *Christ*. "Did we not just establish I thought he liked guys?"

"Rumors, honey," Sadie snickered. "Like I said."

"It wasn't like that, anyway. Paul was ripping on him for some-thing, and I said—oh, it's a long story. But he's never hit on me, and I obviously never tried to hit on *him*." I shook my hair off my face and sat up straight. Zeroed in on Grey until he met my eyes. "And in case you were unaware, Greyson? I do *not* 'chase' guys."

He answered my glare with skeptical brows, sending a guilty jolt from skull to sacrum. His fading blush crept right back to red when I refused to blink——I sure as fuck wasn't the one feasting my eyes on stepsibling ass scant moments before, and we both knew it.

"Really," he finally droned, as if the whole issue existed, but only on a plane far beneath his notice. "Why's that?"

"*She* doesn't need to, baby——if a boy is interested, he'll let her know." Sadie smirked at my hand, dragged a final swipe of pink down the center of my pinkie nail. "*If.*"

"What the hell does *that* mean?" I snapped. Her answering laugh was light but raw, like music——the kind that winds its way in, rooting into your bones. Her lips parted, then closed over a breath, gulping back her follow-up thoughts.

"It doesn't mean a thing, Lane. Hand me that topcoat, will you? Your toes are just about set."

I passed her the bottle, cheeks burning, eyes fixed on the way her lips curved into a glossy smile. The way they barely quivered at his nearly silent sigh.

SEEKING OUT GREY'S SMILE IN THE SCHOOL HALLWAYS had been a staple of my daily routine for years—it was sweet and frequent, one of my favorite sights in the world. It was still the strangest thing, to see it aimed at me.

"Ready to go?"

"Very." I closed my locker, adjusted my messenger bag strap across my body as we fell into step side by side, headed for the parking lot. "This day has dragged like a dead limb."

"Tell me about it. Are you up for a Starbucks run? Mom texted me—they're going out tonight, so we're on our own. I thought we could grab coffee and some sushi, have a Netflix binge. If that works for you."

A weird thrill of anticipation crept over my skin, threaded over my scalp and down my back. Coffee and sushi and Netflix. A dimly lit living room, in an otherwise empty house. A perfect date night. A perfect storm of pitiful wishful thinking.

Nothing real would come of it, of course. I'd walked that road before, knew the exact number of steps that led to its typical, anticipated end. With Grey, however, the path would always end at a big brick wall, ideal for banging my head against until the end of time. We'd eat our food and watch our show. He'd shut himself in his room to study, or read his daily tarot or some shit, while I busted out my yarn and needles alone on the couch, just like any other night.

He'd been trying so hard to pretend the lines we'd crossed were tiny hiccups in a larger waking dream, all of which could be redrawn by deliberate, platonic interactions. Like if we made it through a whole season of *Riverdale* without accidentally spooning, everything would return to normal. It was almost sad, how desperately he wanted to be my brother.

Still. I'd take what I could get.

"Yes. Yes, to all of that." I faced him, forgetting to steel my face. Watched him start, then falter at the sudden intensity of my focus. "Grey, I—"

"Grey! Greyson McIntyre!" Sadie was an IMAX version of herself, careening toward us, tackling Grey against his car. I heard the air leave his lungs in a long sigh, felt myself deflate as well, toppling right off the pathetic bliss cloud I'd been primed to ride straight into the sun.

"Hello to you, too," he said when they came up for air. "Everything okay?"

"Everything is perfect. Connor texted me. He wants us to come over and look at his designs."

"Designs? For what?"

"Baby, our rings! Our wedding rings!"

Something strange flitted across Grey's face, a momentary

glitch eclipsed almost immediately by a smile that seared the edge of my heart.

"Really? Awesome. I'll drop Elaine off at home and meet you at the warehouse."

"Oh, Lane's invited too. Something about yarn."

"Sounds great," I said, shark-toothed smiling. Happy as could be about tagging along to watch them select their fucking wedding rings. What better way to spend a day?

I hid behind my hair as she bounced away to her own car, focused on my seat belt as Grey slid behind the wheel. Focused on repressing the tremble in my fingers. The Forester smelled like warm, worn cotton, sage smoke, and our shared bar of shower soap. The sharp, sweet hint of Sadie's cherry lip gloss.

Grey's mood only brightened as he pulled away from the Starbucks drive-through, passing me one of the drinks. The pumpkin spice waft hit me before I even got it to my mouth. He was already recoiling from a mouthful of my Americano.

"Yeah, that's mine, Greyson."

"I noticed. Sorry."

He switched cups carefully, balancing the latte on his knee as he drove. I pressed my lips against the rim where his had been, tasted the ghost of his tongue. The closest I'd get to a kiss. Quite the fitting nightcap to that imaginary date we'd almost had.

Sadie's car was parked askew in the nearly empty warehouse lot. We found her in the front room, sweeping the floor as Connor arranged easels and stools against the far wall. She shrieked when she saw us and flung the broom aside, launched herself at Grey—an incoming missile of flying hair and loud, smacking kisses.

"Holy fuck, Sadie." Connor set the broom in a corner and joined us, brushing his hands on his jeans. "It's been how long since you saw him? An entire twenty minutes?"

"Excuse me for wanting to properly greet my future husband, Mr. Snarlybutt. Can we see the sketches now? Can we?"

"Only if you lower the volume. People are trying to—oh, you've got to be joking. Oh, hell no." Connor was suddenly gone, striding toward the door and the four guys who'd walked through it—none much older than us, all rangy, all in various stages of unkempt. He stopped in front of the scraggliest one: a dangerously thin blond, wild-eyed and twitchy, his cheek a constellation of open sores. "The fuck you think the word 'banned' means, dude? Was I somehow unclear?"

"What, I can't even hang out? You were serious about that?"

"Damn right I was. Out."

The shortest guy, who I vaguely recognized as one of the painters, stepped between them.

"Come on, man, Aiden's cool. I'll vouch, okay?"

"Oh really, Bukowski? Last time you vouched for that junkie piece of shit, he got about a grand's worth of my tools halfway across the parking lot. He's done here. Bring him around again, and you're done too."

"Whatever," Aiden drawled. "Fuck you, Hall."

"Fuck me, huh?" Connor shouldered past Bukowski and grabbed Aiden's collar, hauled him through the doorway until he stumbled off the step. "Get your ass out, and don't come back. If I see you anywhere near this place again, I'll slit your fucking throat."

He slammed the door shut, turned his back on the rest of the group, and strolled toward us, flipping his hair out of his face. "WHO WANTS TO MAKE SOME YARN?"

"Dude." Grey's stunned face looked like mine felt. "What the hell was that?"

"That," Connor said, "is what happens when a grown man fails to both comprehend and follow simple instructions." His eyes swept over us, landed square on mine. "How about that spinning wheel, Lane? You ready to see how it's done?"

"Rings first," Sadie butted in. "Once you guys get on that wheel, me and Grey'll be sitting around for hours waiting on you. Show us your ideas, and we can at least take our time picking out favorites."

"Come on, then."

He led us down the hallway to the metalworking room, Sadie falling into step beside him while Grey followed a few paces behind. I trailed after, jacked up on a blend of my own adrenaline and the mellowed rage that continued to waft off Connor as we watched him dart back and forth between the shelves and his worktable. He was a wilder, brighter version of himself, only intensifying as he shifted into creative mode, and his smile wouldn't have been so unsettling if he'd just gone ahead and blinked at some point.

"You." He spun on his heel and aimed his finger at Grey. "I need your ring size."

"Oh. I don't know. I don't wear rings."

"That's cool, I have a sizer." He regarded Grey, head to one side. Took in the gun-shy stare, the involuntary curl of his fingers. "You're okay with me doing these, right? You seem a little off."

"I'm fine. A little unsettled, maybe."

"Don't worry about that guy," Connor said, clearly missing that it wasn't Aiden who'd bothered Grey. "You're on board with this, then?"

"Of course he is," Sadie answered. "Hold out your hand, baby."

Connor sized Grey's ring finger, jotted down numbers in his sketchbook, and flipped through several pages, explaining his various ideas. Sadie and Grey huddled together, her head on his shoulder, his hand tucked in the back pocket of her jeans.

"Can you believe we're doing this?" Sadie's voice was a shadow of her normal twang—low and hushed, almost reverent. "Our wedding rings."

"Wild, isn't it?" He looked up from the sketches, fixed his eyes on her glow. "You're sure you don't want something traditional? You know I can't afford a diamond right now, but in a few years . . ."

"Oh, I don't need anything like that. I don't even care what it looks like, as long as you're the one who gives it to me."

"I love you, Sadie."

"Oh, Grey."

Their words skewered me one by one. I turned my back on them, swiped at my phone with frenzied fingers. Accidentally tweeted the letter *H* by itself on our business account, then deleted it before the whole of the internet realized what a fucking mess I was. Couldn't have that.

"On that note." Connor left his sketchbook on the worktable and sailed past, pointing to his eyes and then to mine, winking at my automatic grimace. "You. Me. Yarn."

I tucked my phone away, casting one last glance over my shoulder. Grey's hand cupped the back of Sadie's neck. Hers were caught in his hair. Their kiss was deep and intimate, as if they were already alone. As if they were already married.

Something hot and horrible rose in my throat, bitter as bile. Bitter as the taste of his mouth on my coffee cup.

12

CONNOR'S BACK WAS A FAST-MOVING SMEAR THROUGH my stinging eyes. I followed him through the warehouse to the fiber room, breathed my way back to calm as he pulled a bag of wool and two sets of hand cards out of the supply cabinet. We settled in next to the spinning wheel, where he walked me through the steps of carding, and soon we were working in sync, the rhythm soothing the snarl in my gut. Before long, my resulting rolags looked just as good, if not better than, his.

"Hey. You okay?" he asked out of nowhere, about half an hour into a surprisingly comfortable silence.

"I'm fine," I chirped, tossing another finished rolag into the basket. "Clearly kicking all kinds of ass on this carding thing, so not sure why you'd ask."

"Just checking in. When I invited you along, I didn't think of how that might be awkward, considering—well. Their whole teen-wedding, eternal-partnership thing, versus things you asked me not to mention. Kind of surprised you showed up at all."

So this conversation—this verbal acknowledgment of my

pathetic heartspace—this was a thing happening in real time. This was me, doubling down on the busywork, barbed-wire smile fixed in place, and I'd die on the spot before letting it slip even an inch.

"That's their business, Connor. I'm just here to hang out and make some art."

"Got it. So, since that's a nonissue, I want to clear something else up." He ducked his head, reloading his card. I paused, attention caught by the downturn of his voice. "I feel bad you had to see me flip my shit on that guy, but this is far from his first offense. Trust me when I say he doesn't really respond to polite requests."

"I get it. It sounded like you had your reasons."

"Well, yeah. I mean, he's a thief. He fucked with one of the doors, tried to break in. Tried to swipe some equipment. Like he could just sell beads or metal shears or what have you on the street, or trade it—who knows what he was thinking. That shit ruins your head. I never messed with anything hard like that, but a lot of kids I knew did. A lot."

"Messed with what, exactly?"

His glance was bewildered rather than derisive. As if he got that I was clueless, but couldn't believe it was to such a staggering degree.

"Meth, Lane. Could you really not tell?"

"I wasn't sure. I don't know any meth heads."

"No, you wouldn't. And you should keep it that way." He

sighed. "Look, I'm not judging him for that—you reach a certain point, you'll do anything to make it all stop. I did fourteen months on the street, and——"

"Fourteen *months*?" I slacked on the carding, and he shot me a small frown, motioned with his chin to pick up the pace. "Connor. You were just a kid."

"Barely sixteen. So I get why it's a thing, but I can't have it in here."

I didn't have many memories of Connor from before. He was Sadie Hall's Big Brother—a vague blend of pressed khakis and clean-cut hair, polo collars buttoned to the top beneath that wide, white-toothed smile. Head bowed low in prayer around the school flagpole, until the day that same circle formed smaller, other hands linking through the space where he'd stood.

I let my eyes move over him, took in the cords of his forearms, the line of his shoulders and neck and jaw. Rearranged the shards of that scrubbed, mundane memory until they formed the riddle before me: the lean, unhinged boy whose hands knew the precise moment a blade went from sharp to blunt. A boy who'd bled to make me stronger. How could I know if what remained was real, or how much of it was due to the months he'd spent malnourished and sick, sleeping on filth when he'd felt safe enough to sleep at all? How had a boy who'd been clothed and fed and pampered since birth survived that corner of the world?

I didn't realize I'd voiced my last thought until he answered.

"Total honesty? I almost didn't. I was damn near the end of my rope when I met Paul. He let me crash here because the shelter was full and there was a fucking snowstorm approaching. I'm alive because he helped me, and I'll do whatever it takes to keep this place safe."

I know I looked ridiculous—wide-eyed and horrified, mouth stumbling over all the wrong words. He glanced up, then looked away, as if he hadn't realized the magnitude of his story until he saw it reflected in my face.

"Hey. This is only context now, okay? I'm off the street, and I'm safe and fed, and I'm an *artiste*. So it's not all bad." He nodded at my nervous, tapping fingers; his smirk was a deflection, a change of subject disguised as a challenge. "Slowing down, Jamison? Should we get this wheel spinning, or do you need a break?"

"I'm fine, *Hall*. Do *you* need a break?"

"No way. You feed me the wool, and I'll show you how it's done."

We let the wheel talk for us after that, settled into the synchronicity of his feet and my hands. Connor leaned over his work, brow furrowed, lips pursed. Picked a snag of wool loose from the spindle, pushed the hair out of his eyes and behind his ears. It swung back down immediately. He growled at that, then shot a sneer in the direction of my giggle.

"Don't look at me like that, *Lane*."

"Like I can see your face behind that mess," I huffed. My mistake regarding Connor Hall was assuming he'd eventually let the whole eye-contact thing drop. "Once we're done here, I'll knit you up a nice headband. Pink, so Sadie can borrow it."

"Hey, if you made it, I'd take it." He leaned closer, squinting at the crocheted necklace sparkling at my throat. "Is that one of yours?"

"One of my best sellers."

"May I?" At my nod, he lifted one of the delicate strands, ran it between his fingers, admired the faceted stones and tiny, even stitches. "Gorgeous."

"It's simple, once you know the basics."

"I can do simple." He let it drop and raised his eyes to mine, hopeful, sweetly hesitant. "Teach me?"

"Of course, but—weird much? You can spin, but you can't crochet?"

"Paul taught me to use all the tools in the space, in case anyone needs help. Spinning's easy—doesn't mean I know what to do with the end result."

We abandoned the wheel in favor of one of the many works-in-progress stashed in my bag. I sat beside his stool, demonstrated a few fast stitches, showed him how to maneuver the hook with his right hand and feed the fiber with his left. He tried. He did try, I'll give him that.

"How am I ruining this, Lane? You made it look easy."

"It *is* easy. Hold it like—no, like this. Here." I shifted to my knees and leaned across him, repositioned his grip, and placed my hands over his, winding the thread over both our fingers. As I guided him through a stitch, then another, I felt his fingers draw up more thread, then adjust to match the rhythm of mine. "Keep the tension in your left hand, hook with your right. Like this. See?"

"All I see is miles of your hair," he said. I leaned sideways as he tried to peer over my shoulder, and my head collided with his face. "Ow. Wait, I think I'm stuck. And—yep. So are you."

"Our hands are literally tied together?" The stitch slackened, threatening to slide off the hook as my grip faltered. Connor tugged it tighter. "Unwind the thread off your pinkie."

"I can't. It's knotted up on itself. No, don't drop the stitch, Lane. Focus." He redoubled his efforts, wincing as the loop cut deeper into his skin. "Ah, shit. I can still smith with nine fingers, right?"

I couldn't help it. My laughter rang out, dragging his words into a loud echo that rattled us both as I managed to finish and secure the stitch.

"Okay, it's solid," I finally said. "Now hold still, or we'll have to live like this forever."

"I can do that."

His voice snagged my laugh from the air and wrung it out. I froze for an instant, then ducked my head, and I focused, all right. Focused on picking the knot loose, and on the way his fingers lined up with mine as I unwound the thread, bit by careful bit. Every tendon and scar, every scratch and vein; the slender outlines of his bones; the press of his leather cuff against my wrist. The press of his chin, lowering to rest on my shoulder, an instant before the last knot gave. Connor took my left hand in his, turned it over for inspection. Massaged the angry grooves on my knuckle.

"I think you'll recover," he joked, and it was the perfect opening to let the moment pass with an answering chuckle, had said chuckle not regretfully been lodged in my throat. His fingers paused on mine. "Lane? Everything okay?"

The half-done necklace fell from my grip, slid down my lap to the floor. My hand flexed beneath his, then turned so we were palm to palm, pressed together. Waiting.

I felt him lean against me, tentative, my back to his chest. Felt his cheek graze mine, then again, and then our hands were clasping, fingers linking, our breath drawing in unison from the same small space, as my face turned toward his.

"Sadie, we talked about this." The sudden snap of Grey's voice was a blade across my throat. "I feel like you never *listen* to me."

"I am, baby—but you're not listening to *me*. Communication isn't a one-way street."

"You say you're listening, but you're not *hearing* me. When I said—"

"Aaaand, there they go." Connor dropped my hand, stood and stretched, shook out his hands, cracked his knuckles. Kept his back to me. I stayed on my knees, fighting silently for air. Trying so hard to claw past what had almost happened. "I told Sadie to stop bringing him by here if they can't keep it down. People are trying to work."

"Oh. That reminds me." I rummaged through my bag, took

way too long to unearth my wallet. "I don't have it all on me, but I can give you the rest on Friday. Thanks for letting me do my thing."

"What's this?"

"Sadie told me you charge for using the space. I've been hogging the room all afternoon and will probably be back tomorrow. So."

"Sadie!" When the argument didn't even pause, he took a breath and made himself heard. "SADIE."

Silence, then footsteps, then her head poked through the door. *"WHAT?"*

"Did you tell Lane I was charging her for wheel time?"

"I most certainly did not, and *you* most certainly *shall* not. She's not one of your tenants, Connor."

"I wasn't *going to*. What I was *wondering*, is why she's in here waving money at me, saying you told her she'd need it."

"I told her you charge *people*, not that you'd charge her. Lane." They aimed identical stubborn glares my way. "You're my future sister-in-law. You're not paying my brother to use a wheel that's just sitting there anyway. Now, if you'll excuse me, I was in the middle of a discussion."

"Yeah, keep that shit down, while you're at it," Connor said. "You sound exactly like Mom."

She stuck her tongue out at him, unruffled, and flounced away, leaving me with only one Hall side-eye scorching its way through my head.

"Don't look at me like that," I said, tucking the cash into my pocket. "I'm trying to respect your setup."

"My 'setup'? I thought you came here to 'hang out and make some art.'"

"That's what we're doing, right? I'm using this wheel same as anyone would——I can at least pay my share. And don't tell me you don't need the money, Connor."

"Not enough to bum it off my friends." He shook his head. "If a rental space is all this is to you, I might as well go on back to the metal room."

"If you'd rather be in there, don't let me keep you."

My words leaped over the spinning wheel and seized him by the throat. I wrapped a loop of the finished yarn around my sore finger, pulled it tight. Willed myself not to fly apart.

"That's not what I meant." Connor's eyes left mine first, too slow to hide a flare of pain. "I didn't ask you here so I could get paid. What kind of person do you think I am?"

Where to start with that one? He was an artist. A preacher's son. A street kid. He was my friend. He'd listened to me and made me laugh, pulled me through a window into a star-scattered sky. He'd taught me the finer points of yarn spinning after threatening to slit some guy's throat, then held my hand in a way I hadn't known I wanted. And speaking of unanswerable things, what was *that* about? That moment, begun by me, broken by the voice of my stepbrother——my unaware, unrequited love, arguing with his alleged other half. What the hell was I *doing*?

"What you said," I began, "about being stuck with me. You need to know that I don't—"

"It was a joke, Lane."

"Well. *I* knew that." Everything caught on the burn behind my eyes. I unwound the yarn, massaging my numbed, purple fingertip, reaching for feeling. Reaching for anything. How the fuck had he thought, even for a second, that words like that could make me smile? "Let's just finish this skein, okay? I need to get home."

He sat back down at the wheel without comment, face turned away from me, and started working the treadles. I knelt at his side and fed him the rolags, quiet and shaking. His sigh was a small, weak thing, soft and sad and nearly silent. It cut me just the same.

Our work morphed into a distraction of its own. I focused on breathing through the cut-and-dried specifics of turning wool to yarn, as if I couldn't feel the stress radiating from Connor's arms and shoulders, or see how the clipped precision of his usually confident hands mirrored my own irregular motions.

After almost twenty minutes spent wedged into that weirdly specific pocket of hell, I was ready to shed my human form and slither out through the ventilation shaft, if that's what it took to escape. When Grey passed by the doorway without stopping, motioning for me to follow, I dropped the skein I'd been winding and stood, wobbly on nervous legs.

"Thanks for the spinning lesson." I stared at Connor's down-cast profile, waiting for him to answer. When that didn't happen,

I sighed, stepped around him, and headed for the suddenly blurry door. "Guess I'll see you."

"Lane."

A swell of regret engulfed my heart, dark and warm and overwhelming. I blinked away a strange prickle of tears and turned to face him as he stood, took in his hunched shoulders and downcast gaze, and how many times was I going to almost fucking cry today before just giving in and letting loose?

"Yes?"

"I'm sorry. Look—this wasn't some plot to, like, lure you in with the spinning wheel, okay?"

"Plot? I don't—wait, do you mean the . . . crochet thing?" I cringed, guilt flaring red across my cheekbones. I'd let the whole wedding ring mess get in my head, steered the afternoon off its perfectly productive path, and run it straight into the goddamn brambles. Now he felt like a creep, when all he'd wanted was to learn a skill. "Connor, that one's on me."

"It's not really 'on' anyone. But it won't be an issue again. You're safe here."

"I never thought I wasn't. Besides," I muttered, catching his eye, "it takes more than a spinning lesson, you know. I'd need to negotiate for at least half the finished yarn."

He almost kept a straight face, to his eternal credit. A snort escaped through his nose, though, followed by an echo of my own laughter as I closed the distance between us and pulled him into a hug. I felt him start, then settle, then return it, felt the tension drain from his arms as they wrapped around me. I leaned into him, resting my cheek against the conundrum of jutting bone and soft, worn flannel.

"I'm sorry too," I whispered into his shoulder. "About the money thing. I wasn't trying to imply—"

"I know. I'm weird about that stuff sometimes." He pulled away and swiped the hair from his eyes, let his hand drift down to fiddle with his leather cuff. "Think we can get past this? Not really a fan of losing friends over silly shit."

"Same."

His gaze locked on mine for an instant, then darted away—like he'd been going in for the direct-eye-contact stunt, and thankfully, pulled up short at the last second. Things were awkward enough without shoehorning *that* joke through the middle of our truce.

"Elaine." Grey's voice reached around the doorframe, followed by his head. "You ready?"

"Coming, Greyson."

I followed him out, looking back as I reached the hallway. Connor nodded at my wave, tossed me a sideways smile as he squatted by the spinning wheel and started gathering stray scraps of wool. I turned away, leaving him to clean up the last of our mess.

13

THINGS WERE GETTING OUT OF HAND. I'D BEEN FIGHTING cramps and gastro issues all morning, determined not to broadcast my goddamn menstrual woes to all and sundry; after a while, I'd concluded it was easier to banish myself from the actual house than continue smiling through eight kinds of misery. Easier to disappear than ask for help.

I was curled up on the porch swing by myself, on my second hour of thunderstorm watching, when Grey burst out the door, phone glued to his ear, yammering at light speed—the rational end of the conversation, if Sadie's muffled howls were any indication.

I reached for my phone and pulled up Connor's number. Since that little snafu the previous week, when I'd offered him money right after we'd almost made out—and really, there was no way to spin that one into anything not utterly horrendous— our friendship had realigned itself to normalcy. United in the ever-futile quest for peace in the presence of our respective siblings.

Connor, it's Lane.

I know who it is. Your number is stored in my phone.

Whatever. Are you with Sadie right now?

Unfortunately. First one to get them off the phone wins?

Ready set go

"Well, I'm sorry, Sadie, I don't think I *would've* missed that section, if I'd spent the time studying instead of watching *Supernatural*." I jumped at Grey's overloud snarl and tried to shush him, but he waved me off, absently settling next to me on the swing. "No. No, I don't. Look, babe, I don't think—no, I'm not minimizing your efforts, I'm—I do. I respect you, I swear. Yes, I like watching with you too, but I'm trying to maintain a 4.0, and I—"

"Oh, for the love of—give me the phone, Greyson." He leaned away from me, but I yanked it out of his hand and put it to my ear. "Sadie, he'll call you later."

I disconnected her inane babble and set the phone on the side table, out of Grey's reach. He gaped at me, stuttering over the dregs of his unvented anger.

"The fuck did you do that for? I was talking to my girlfriend."

"You were yelling at your girlfriend. Yelling about something that should barely be a discussion, much less a fight."

My phone buzzed.

Nicely done. You're awesome.

I glanced at Grey. He was red and scowling, gaze darkening in sync with the sky as I typed an answer.

Pretty sure you're the only one who thinks so right now, Connor.

"You had no right," he snarled. "You don't know our business."

"Everyone knows your business, Grey. You yell it up and down the block, and why? Why *her?*"

"'Why *her?*'" His eyes narrowed, voice stopping just short of a warning. "What does *that* mean?"

"You're just always fighting," I backpedaled, choking down the rest of my outburst. "Seriously, you're barely the same species. Everyone says so."

"'Everyone' knows shit. How's Connor, by the way—gay? Not gay? Because *everyone* said—"

"Okay, past tense much? That was years ago."

"But it's still happening—then it was him liking guys, and now it's me and my secret satanic lifestyle, or my mother, the crazy witch. Or you, being a sl—" He bit the word in half, the two remaining letters flaring an even darker red across his face. "*You* know what they say. And as to 'why' Sadie? We got paired up to read a scene in drama class, freshman year. It was forever, right from the start." His faraway smile slit me down the middle. "Yeah, she's a firecracker, but 'forever' means sticking around. Working things out, instead of moving on at the first hint of conflict."

"Well. Obviously you haven't done *that*."

"Dude, what is your fucking problem?"

"I'm not the one getting my ass chewed daily by my 'fire-cracker,' Greyson. So who's the one with the problem, really?"

"I'd rather have a firecracker than an ice queen. Trust me, Elaine—if Sadie were as cold as you, I'd have slit my wrists ages ago."

His words slammed through me, a fist in each eye. A third, right down the middle of my heart.

"Fuck *you*." My voice cracked and broke, crumbled shrill around a dry, barking sob. "I can't believe you'd *say* that to me, after—God."

"After what? What are you even talking about?"

"My mother, you asshole. What is *wrong* with you?"

"What?" His head snapped up, eyes seeking mine for a scrap of a joke. "Mom told me your mother died, but—"

"Suicide."

And I didn't say anything after that, because the words got lost in a surge of orange-juice acid and partially digested pancakes. I bolted from the swing and made it to the railing in time to unleash the whole mess into the yard. Rainwater dripped from the gutter, sliding through my hair, running like snowmelt over the back of my neck. It was no more than I deserved, assuming it was safe to eat a normal meal even four days into my cycle. How many times would my skin melt to blisters before I gave up reaching into flames?

"'Suicide,' not 'died,'" I spat as I turned to face him, swiping my sleeve across my mouth. Bile, rain, tears—it didn't matter. Everything lingered. "Cut her arms open in the kitchen, then had her own little parade to the bathroom. Left a perfect little trail for me to follow, just like Hansel and Gretel—only blood, not bread crumbs."

I watched his eyes change, saw them blink and blank, then widen in tandem with his listing mouth, and it was so ironic, how I hadn't even gotten into the real dirt—how she'd danced a razor down the softest part of her arm, buried its gleam in the crook of her elbow. Swallowed Clorox to make it stick, then bled to death on that bright, clean floor, slumped against the edge of the white claw-foot tub. I looked away, stared past him in the silence that followed, loopy and light-headed—a sideshow act, performing outside my own skin. Thirteen years, and I'd never said it all out loud. Not like that.

Grey should be thanking me, really, for letting him off with the sanitized version.

"Are you serious?" His voice went shrill around the question mark. "You *found* her like that?"

"Yeah, it's funny how you hear the word 'trauma' as a kid, but you never really *get* it until you're trying to physically push your mom's blood back into her open veins. Really throws a wrench in your whole ice-queen theory, huh?"

"What? My whole——oh, fuck. Oh *God*. I *said* that. I literally just——" The swing jounced as he pushed to his feet, took the porch in two long strides to the railing. The rain reached past the awning and tapped his knuckles; his fingers clenched white on the peeling paint. Staring down at my rain-muddled puke, because things could always, always get worse.

"I'm sorry, Elaine. I am so, so sorry. I'm such a *dick*."

"You really didn't know? Sadie didn't tell you?"

"Sadie? No, not a word——I swear to you, with everything I am, I had no idea. And it was a fucked-up thing to say, either way. I don't think that about you, not really. I——"

"No. You're right. I *am* that way——I shut everyone out, and I——" A tear escaped, and I all but smacked it off my cheek. Another took its place, then a third, and then I bent forward, pressing my fingers to my eyes. It was such bullshit. Since the end of my long-ago stint in therapy, where I'd done more listening than speaking, I'd practically perfected dodging the dead-mom talk; now, between the X-Acto incident and this garbage dump of an afternoon, here I was, having it for the second time in less than a month.

Sadie had kept quiet, though. That tiny truth——that she'd honored a promise I'd admittedly expected her to break——stung on its own, in a way I barely understood.

I felt his arm around my shoulders, leading me to the swing; felt a shudder spark deep in my bones as he sat beside me, fingers moving over my hair. It was so hard to remember I shouldn't love him.

"God, this is pathetic," I sniffed. "You can go if you want."

"I'm not going anywhere." His voice was so close. His hands slid down my arms, closed over my clenched fists, and held on tight. "It'll be okay. I promise."

"It won't."

The words broke from me out of nowhere, and I broke with them. And not from nowhere at all, really—from a canyon I thought I'd long ago restored to placid desert. It had been there all along, though, a soft, treacherous path, ready to cave at the hint of footsteps.

I don't know how long we huddled like that—me bent double, eyes pressed to our intertwined fingers; his cheek resting on my back, arms warm around me. Eventually, he pulled me out of my hunch, keeping me close, holding me against the same heartbeat that had turned a small, kind gesture into the center of my world.

"Was it the same thing with the frog?" he whispered, hesitant. "The dissection, back in lab?"

"You remember that?"

"Of course I remember—you freaked out. It's the kind of thing that tends to stick. Was it because of your mom?"

"Yep. Sure was."

"Fuck. You stayed, though. Why'd you stay?" His breath was

soft on my hair, smoothing its way over all my edges. "Hey. You can talk to me, okay? I get how it feels, you know—to lose a parent. Not in the same way, but still. You can trust me, Elaine."

I sighed. My name in his mouth always shook something loose deep within my body, and I wanted to trust him. I wanted so badly to trust my heart in the cup of his hands—to know he'd be as precise and delicate with mine as he'd been with that frog's. To forget how those hands were what exposed it in the first place.

"I didn't think about it. It was just another lab day, and then they brought out the frogs and the blades, and—well, then it wasn't. But it's okay—you took care of me. And here you are now, taking care of me. Still."

A horrible, barbed silence snaked from those words, spooling around us and yanking tight. I disentangled myself, moving carefully from the soft cadence of his heartbeat and slow, even breathing to the chill of empty, Greyless air. The swing squeaked as we both sat up, shoulder to shoulder, eyes fixed straight ahead.

"Still feeling sick?" he asked.

"Not really."

"So, you're okay?"

"Not really."

His low laugh sent a shiver across my skin. My head turned automatically toward that smile, and he must have been reaching to smooth a tear from my cheek, maybe tuck a strand of hair behind my ear. I don't think he meant to catch his thumb on the corner of my mouth. I don't think he meant for our noses to collide, or for us to draw the same sharp breath from the space between our faces. I know he never meant to hook his eyes into mine and hold them far beyond the line between us as we were, and all my secret thoughts of him.

He didn't mean to do any of those things. They happened anyway.

And I went ahead and let my eyelids close, like the fucking idiot I am.

The swing practically jerked off its chains, he stood up so fast. I kept my eyes shut through the jolt, squeezed them against the horrid, awkward mess. *This* wasn't what I wanted from him— not his earnest ministrations, or his pity cuddles, and goddamn sure not some bullshit accidental kiss that would annihilate our literal world, and how. How did I manage to ruin so many things.

"It's really raining," he blurted. "We should probably go inside."

Grey was all proper manners and fussy old grannies on the way inside, holding open the screen door, helping me over the threshold like I was incapable of forward motion. He settled me on one end of the couch, spread Skye's rainbow afghan over my legs, then hovered, twisting his fingers in his shirt.

"Do you need anything?" he hedged. "I can make some tea. Mom has this really good blend for relaxation. Would that help? Because I—"

"I'm fine. Thanks anyway."

"Yeah. Good. Okay." He slid onto the couch, leaving a coun- try mile of cushion between us. The TV remote lay on the coffee table, but neither of us moved to pick it up. Instead, we fixated on the dark screen, the air ringing with unsaid thoughts. I couldn't look at him.

"Hey," he said after a hideous stretch of time. "I don't know what happened out there, but it won't—it *can't* happen again. I'm with Sadie. You get that, don't you? I love *her*. I don't know if you've ever been in love, or pledged yourself to someone else, but that's where I am—in my head and my heart. I need to know you understand."

I wanted to puke again. I wanted to scream at him and slap his face, kiss him until the world burned down. Dare him to ever call me cold again, once everything we'd known was ash.

"Wow. Okay," I finally spat. "Like I'm over here all day, just yearning after Sadie's leftovers? Assumptions much?"

"I'm not assuming anything. Just making sure we both agree on, like, proximity, you know? Boundaries."

"Awesome—boundaries are my favorite. And if all else fails, there's always the whole slit-wrists thing to fall back on."

"Holy shit. Elaine, that's not funny. Look, I know we weren't friends before, and I know there's been some weird . . ." He trailed off, wisely choosing not to list the many and varied weird incidents. "But this is how it has to be, from now on—this is how it *is*. We need to put this behind us and be a family. Together. Always."

The syllables burst open and scattered, souring the air. Family: its own brand of *f*-word. Worse from his lips than any four-letter version on earth. His eyes were bright and desperate, begging me to agree.

It broke me in two, that desperation; split me down the middle of compassion and resentment. That promise of him and me, stuck in the wrong sort of forever.

"Yes, Greyson. Together. Always."

Those words—our parents' wedding vows, drifting out in a half whisper. He stared at me, helpless, then finally turned his face away, pulled his hands through the mess of his hair. Forced a neutral smile and reached for the remote, choosing safety over reality. Choosing the me he wanted over the me he knew—the me who'd carved my shape into every corner of his world.

Grey and I were good at lies, if nothing else. We lied to each other with those separate couch cushions and unsaid words. We lied with the deliberate distance between our bodies. We didn't speak. He texted Sadie, fingers brisk and efficient on the screen, while I stared out the window, barely breathing.

We lied and we lied and we lied.

14

OCTOBER ENDED IN A DRIZZLE, FROSTLESS AND SOGGY and beautifully bleak. The sky outside my bedroom window was a silvery thing, streaked and striated, shifting to night. Less gloomy than Sadie's expression by far.

"I just don't know about all this, Lane. Tell me again, *exactly*, what's involved?"

I fumbled with my earrings, met her eyes in the vanity mirror. She sat on my bed with her back against the wall, brow scrunched, pout in place. Screams and chain saws drifted through the door, followed by laughter: Connor and Grey, immersed in their second viewing of *Army of Darkness* as they waited for us.

We'd spent the afternoon carving jack-o'-lanterns, each doing our worst to a huge, fleshy pumpkin, each yielding decidedly different results. Connor's was beautiful insanity, a twisted human face rendered free-form in intricate, shrieking detail; Grey's was just as meticulous, but he'd used a template, never missed a line, traced and scooped and carved until it looked exactly how he wanted. Sadie went for simple, classic whimsy: bold triangles for eyes and nose, a smiling mouth with three stubby teeth. I'd gone in with no plan beyond a vague idea of creepy, and ended up with a ridiculous, half-realized mess. I'd placed it on the porch anyway, slightly behind the others, wondering why I'd even tried. At least no one had gotten cut.

"It's nothing shady," I reassured Sadie, working a tangle from my hair. "Just a Samhain gathering."

"Sow-win," she repeated, her twang butchering the hell out of the poor word. "And it's, like, a Halloween party for dead people? Not demons?"

"What? No. It's a cross-quarter day on the pagan calendar— the midpoint between the equinox and the solstice."

"Lord, honey, I don't know what any of that means."

"It's not a catch-all—what the rituals 'mean' to someone, specifically, depends on the practitioner. In the very simplest terms, Samhain is a celebration of the harvest and the summer's end, and an honoring of those gone before." I eyed her in the mirror, dropped my voice to a teasing, spooky whisper. "Some say it's when the spirits are at their most active in the living world. What better time to summon a soul from the very grave?"

"Wait—like a séance? We're summoning *ghosts*? Grey never said—"

"Jesus. No, Sadie, we're not summoning ghosts. People do believe, though—in their connection to the earth, and the elements, and everything beyond. Paying tribute to the ancestors and celebrating the dark season is part of all that. Think of it like praying, from a different perspective."

"It is *not* the same as praying, Lane."

"Isn't it?" I shifted my gaze back to my own reflection, ignoring her huff. "Look, this is Greyson's religion, not mine—all questions should be directed at him, his mom, or my dad."

"You don't practice? I thought y'all were, like, all in it as a family." She sighed as I shook my head. "You and my brother are just alike. He won't believe in anything anymore."

"I'm not an atheist—before my mom died, my parents agreed to let me choose my own path, but I've never felt pulled to any one particular way over another. If I'm going to pray, I need it to feel real. It needs to be the perfect fit."

"That makes sense. Grey says prayer, to him, is a language not of the tongue, but of the heart. Sounds like you feel the same."

"How do you not know all of this by now?" I said, turning to face her. Grey was far from the most fervent practitioner I'd ever met, but his paganism was hardly breaking news. "His rituals, his holidays—has he really kept you out of it all this time?"

"Oh, honey, I never asked. He's tried to explain some of his basic beliefs, and invited me to gatherings in the past, but this is the first time I've agreed to go." She pulled her hair forward over her shoulder, working her fingers absently through the colors. "He and I don't really talk about that stuff as much as we should—just between us, I'd rather not hear about it at all. But I guess I need to learn what I can if he plans to bring it into our marriage."

"Right." It was a bitter fight, keeping the anguish out of that one syllable. I pretended to retie my bootlace, ducked my head in time to hide the twist of my mouth.

It was hard sometimes—really, really hard—not to resent that girl. Not to burn with the shame of that resentment, down to the very last drop of my blood.

"I don't get why you guys are in such a hurry for all that," I continued, voice barely skirting the edge of bitterness. "There's so much you both could *do*."

"What's the point in waiting? A life with him is all I want. It's all I've ever wanted."

I almost believed her. Surely she'd said those words often enough since she learned to speak—over and over, until they tasted sweet as her smile. Surely she'd never *tried* to want more than what she thought was her only option. It was there, though: a spark of doubt, tiny as the twitch of her lips. Bright as the twists of turquoise peeking through her thick, blond curls.

"Anyway. We'll see, I guess." She shooed away the thought, then jumped up and delved into her tote bag with a grin. "But tonight I'm being nice, and nonjudgmental, and going to this witchy gathering thing, even though it'll probably get me in trouble with God. And since I'm doing this to make you and your darling stepbrother happy, *you* are going to let me do *this*. I'm telling you, it'll change your life."

"Get that thing away from my face." I tried to dodge around her. She blocked the door and advanced on me, eyes brimming with glee. "Sadie, I'm serious. No."

"Please, Lane. *Pleeeeeease.* You're so pretty—all you need is a little color. The eyes and cheeks, and maybe a nice red lip. Come *on.*"

Twenty minutes. Twenty solid minutes of my life was the price I paid to indulge her as she lined and shaded and blended and enhanced. And when she finally pronounced me done, I was tense and skeptical, yet strangely buoyed. Maybe she was right. My mood had been all over the place since Grey moved in— maybe I did need a little boost.

"I knew it. You're perfect. You're an absolute vision." She steered me toward my vanity. "Behold."

My eyes were ashes and soot, my cheekbones a gold-dust gleam. My crooked upper lip was foreign, filled in and darkened and weird. I was Sadie's version of an ideal Lane— striking and elegant and utterly gorgeous. Absolutely nothing like me.

I pulled away without a word and headed straight for the bathroom, ignoring her squeaks of concern. Locked the door behind me, before I came undone.

"You okay, honey?" Sadie asked when I emerged ten minutes later, scrubbed back to the basics of skin and stoicism. "Aw, you didn't like it? I thought it looked amazing."

"It's not really my thing, I guess. And it itched." I smoothed down the front of my cardigan, adjusted my mother's silver pentacle charm against my throat, some small, sad part of me wishing for that connection—the spiritual certainty that bound my parents, linking them even in death. Wishing I could believe she was just past my fingertips, poised to slip through that thinning veil and find me. "Let's go get those boys."

"This place seems very far from any other place."

Sadie's nerves were showing. She was trying, I'll give her that, but as the familiar city streets became lightless country roads, her enthusiasm gave way to apprehension. She sat bunched in the passenger seat, unusually quiet.

"Settle down, sis," Connor said from my right. "I'm pretty sure your witch boy won't actually let the coven sacrifice you when it comes down to it. I mean, they'll have to rush around to find another virgin at the last minute, but we do need a fourth for the demon summoning, so there's that."

"That is *not funny*, Connor. Grey, do you *promise* me there are no demons?"

"Of course there aren't demons, babe." Grey rested a hand on her knee, adjusting his grip on the wheel. "If you're really uncomfortable with this, I'll take you home. It's not a problem."

"No. I'm okay." She took a deep breath and beamed at him with all her might. "I want to be there with you."

Connor's skeptical eyebrows were visible even in the shadows, but he didn't contradict her. Instead, he sat back and turned to me, gesturing at my pentacle.

"Is this your thing too?"

"My parents'. This charm was my mother's. Dad still practices, but I was raised secular. He doesn't believe in the indoctrination of children."

"I like him already."

"Don't you get above your raising, Connor Hall." Sadie glared at him over the seat and reached back to swat his leg. "You were born in the church and saved in the church, washed clean by the Blood of Christ, and just because you strayed doesn't mean He's abandoned you. I really think—"

"I *defected* from the church, Sadie Hall. I *escaped* what passed as my raising, especially that 'washed in the blood' shit. And I—hold on a second." He leaned toward me, thumb extended, took a swipe at my face. "What the fuck, Lane? Are you wearing glitter?"

"Oh. I might be. Not by choice, though."

"Goddamn it, Sadie, you really had to, didn't you? You're like a little kid with a box of crayons and a big white wall."

"It was the new Urban Decay palette, excuse you very much, and she was lovely. Absolutely glam."

"I'm sure she was," Grey said, badly stifling a laugh. "Must have really set off her knitting needles."

That one was a backhand to the soul. He and Sadie laughed, both lighthearted and teasing, neither meaning to wound. Neither aware of the hole in my gut, filling slowly with shame and ice and a hot rush of blood. Connor blinked at them, then sat back and shook his head.

"Wow. Fuck you, too, dude."

"Oh hush, Connor," Sadie giggled. "He didn't mean it like that. Anyway, you should have seen her. I'll admit the glitter was a bit much, but the smoky eye looked amazing."

She turned in her seat and tried to catch my eye. I stared at the back of Grey's head.

"Honey, we're just teasing you. You're totally pretty without it, I promise. I only wear so much because I don't like a plain, boring face, you know? I like lots of color. But you——" She shut up abruptly, jogged to silence by Connor's knee thumping the back of her seat.

"Elaine." I met Grey's worried eyes in the mirror, drawn, despite myself, to his voice. "I didn't mean——"

"Forget it, Greyson. Just drive."

I shifted my eyes away from his, swiped my sleeve over my cheekbone. It came back clean.

We managed to reach our destination without further shrieking, park in a sea of cars, and follow a torch-marked trail through the woods to a tree-ringed clearing, lit orange by several small, scattered bonfires. Costumed children sailed in circles around the flames, some tailed by nervous guardians; most, free-range. Quite a few adults had dressed up as well—the number of people garbed in full fae was ridiculous, even for a pagan gathering. There were, however, plenty of neon glow sticks and commercial Halloween disguises mixed in with the street clothes and the antlers and the DIY wings.

It took me a moment to spot my dad, whose formal ceremonial

robes blended right on in with the crowd. He and Skye stood apart from the other, larger clusters of people, hands joined, heads swiveling. Looking for us with that earnest, heartbreakingly parental air, which forever disregarded legality and self-sufficiency.

Skye spotted us and flitted over, gathered Grey and me together in a simultaneous hug. She was earth and flame all over, robed in moss-green silk and burgundy velvet, hair twined into a single, hip-length braid. Her eyes, when she drew back, glimmered brighter than the moonstone setting in her circlet.

"We have a few moments before the main event," she breathed. "I'd like to cast our own circle first, if you two agree."

My answering nod left a smile on her face that spread to Dad's as he joined us, squeezing my arm in quiet thanks.

The four of us linked hands and Skye called the corners, led our family in the prayer she and Dad practiced together, then fell silent while he honored my mother. We closed our tiny circle in time to join the large one forming in the center of the glade—dozens of people, hand in hand, linked around the biggest bonfire. Grey's hand was warm in mine, his grip sure and solid and confusing. He only tightened his hold when my own fingers slackened, answering my questioning glance with a small, private smile that pried its way under my skin.

Sadie and Connor hung back at the edge of the woods, apart from the circle but clearly visible from where we stood. For all his earlier demonic banter, Connor was on his best behavior—he stayed quiet, clasped his hands behind his back, kept his head respectfully bowed as the ceremony commenced. Meanwhile, the wild card that was Sadie stayed glued to her brother, as if afraid she'd be suddenly set upon, strapped to a broomstick, and launched into the sky. She managed to keep it together during the opening prayer and community rites, didn't actually shit her pants at the chanting or songs, but afterward, when a small group of nearby women formed their own circle, called the corners, and began their own specific invocation, she dropped Connor's arm and retreated, walking backward until she slipped on the soggy grass and landed on her butt with a little yelp. Connor was immediately at her side, whispering in her ear, tussling back and forth with her before giving up on reasoning and flat out dragging her to her feet, yanking her along behind him as he stalked away.

Grey and I shared a panicked glance and followed them, abandoning the circle and the clearing and our parents as the drizzle turned to steady rain. The Hall siblings had already disappeared onto the trail; we had to run to catch up. As soon as she heard our footsteps, Sadie stopped in her tracks, breaking Connor's grip and turning on Grey, every ounce of her fury a blast in his face.

"You listen to me, Grey McIntyre, and listen good. If you want a life with me, you *will* rethink your entire approach to salvation. I've tolerated our differences up till now, but this is the line that can't be crossed. I will *not* have this witchcraft business in our marital home."

She turned on her heel and headed for the car, face damp with a film of mist and rage tears. Grey matched her, step for step.

"Hold the fuck up. Did you just tell me I'm not allowed to practice my *religion* under my own roof? Is that really what you said?"

"That's exactly what I said. This is *blasphemy.* It's nothing but a path to the Devil himself, and you need to—"

"I 'need to' not a single goddamn thing, Sadie. This is how I grew up. This defines *my* family, as much as your fundamentalist shit defines yours."

"Don't you call it 'shit.' You don't have the first *clue*—"

I slowed my steps as their pace increased. Their snarls reached backward, rising and falling, growing louder when we reached the parking area. No chance of losing track of those two in the deep, dark forest, that was for sure.

"Is there any way we can pretend we're not with them?" I muttered. Connor's sigh spooled from the shadows to my left.

"If only." He winced at Sadie's twang, rising on cue as we piled into the car. "Come back with me, hang out at the warehouse. You don't want to be the third wheel when they escalate."

"You don't mind? I don't want to be in your way, but . . ."

"Fuck that, Lane, it's absolutely fine. I won't even make you cut me this time."

"Fuck *you.* That was horrible."

"It was a shared moment. Just get out with me when the car stops."

And that's what happened. They bickered all the way back to Asheville, barely pausing for breath. I practically dove out of the back seat as soon as Grey hit the brake; only the sound of both doors closing alerted him to the fact that I'd left the car at all.

"What are you doing, Elaine?"

"Going with Connor. I think you guys could use some time alone."

"She'll be fine, Grey," Sadie snapped, focused his scowl back her way. "I am nowhere near done with this conversation, in case you were unaware."

"And here I was, thinking I'd actually get a moment's peace at some point in my entire life." He caught my eyes in the side mirror. "Text me if you need a ride."

They careened out of the lot, Sadie's reply trailing out the window in a cloud of bitchy mist. Connor shook his head and looked at me, and then we doubled over laughing, leaning against each other like a couple of drunks.

"Can you picture them still doing this shit in twenty years?" he wheezed. "I nearly strangled them both."

"If you ever need an alibi, let me know." I glanced at the warehouse, all rough edges and silent angles, blackout curtains drawn and dark. "Is everyone out?"

"Out? Lane, it's just after midnight on a rainy Saturday. You've never seen this place busy until now."

He yanked upward on the handle and slid the door sideways, opening his world to me.

15

CONNOR HAD BY NO MEANS USED THE WORD "BUSY" IN a hyperbolic sense. The warehouse hummed with activity, overflowed with people and smells and intensely focused scowls. Five of the easels were occupied, each artist wielding a different medium, each looking a hairbreadth from total insanity. The beadwork room sparkled with nimble hands and scattered stones. The fiber room was a mess—a woman crouched in a sea of yarn and fabric, winding two skeins into a single length around her bent arm, while a pale, sweat-stained man worked the spinning wheel like Rumpelstiltskin's bitch. Metal screeched on metal. Chisels met wood. The air reeked of fixative and sawdust and the sting of turpentine. No one even looked up as Connor led me through the chaos to the living space, past the crates and materials and the hum of the wheel.

Paul waved at us from his footstool, then refocused his energy into coaxing life from a block of wood almost as tall as me. I shed my coat, pulled off my muddy boots, and perched cross-legged on the futon, accepting the hand towel Connor tossed my way.

He settled next to me, blotting rain from his hair and face as I watched Paul work, mesmerized by the lines that emerged like magic with every tap of his chisel.

"He's great, isn't he?"

I turned toward the voice and met Connor's grin, returned the nudge of his shoulder with my own.

"Incredible. How do people learn to do that?"

"Skin-clawing obsession, coupled with years of practice. Here, check it out." He sat forward and shrugged out of his shirt. "My parents used to call me their little angel. I'm sure this isn't quite what they had in mind . . . but then again, neither am I."

His back was a canvas. Skeletal wings sprouted from his shoulder blades—scraps of shredded, ragged skin, strung and hung on a mosaic of bones. Rendered in such perfect detail, they threatened to launch him into sudden flight. A finger appeared on the line of a phalanx, brushed over the curve of a scapula—my finger, bold against his skin.

"Oh my God, this is beautiful. And Paul drew it?"

"He did. Talent like that can't be taught. Mmmm." His head rolled to the side, shoulders flexing at the drag of my fingernail. "Keep doing that."

"Oh. Are you sure?"

"Very."

"Okay." I continued sketching over every joint and shadow, forced normal-sounding words out around the catch of my breath.

What the fuck, Lane. "I remember you from back then, you know."

"You remember me? Shit. I'm afraid to ask."

"Vaguely. You were that church kid from the public-access channel. Had that Hall family accent: 'Y'all should come out to our youth group.' Et cetera."

"The 'y'all's and the youth group. Christ." His laugh was low and soft, ending in a sigh. "In reality, that family was done with me the moment I said 'atheist.' My father had me out the door within the hour—haven't seen him since."

"I'm sorry." I stilled my fingers, pressed my palm against the space between his shoulder blades. "You don't have to talk about it."

"Doesn't bother me. The road here sucked, but it made me tough in a way they'll never understand. Made me learn how to prioritize, and go without. Taught me to fight. This"—he reached over his shoulder and tapped the tattoo—"is my way of owning who I am: not the me they wanted, but the me they got. So, do me a favor and forget Church Kid existed, huh? He was about as real as these wings."

"Should I be worried about Sadie?" I hedged. "She seems happy enough, but—"

"It's not as bad for her. She's a true believer—one of them, in a way I'll never be. Plus, if she leaves, they lose face in the church, and they lose their control, so she gets away with the wild hair, and the attitude, and the whole pagan boyfriend thing."

Right. That. The evening returned in bits and pieces—Grey's

hand, strong around mine; Sadie's smile in my mirror, juxtaposed over her later, rain-streaked fury; Connor's face, furrowed and focused, as he carved his pumpkin; his hair and mouth, wet with raindrops; his ink-lined spine, warm and steady beneath my palm.

He turned to face me, lips quirking as I gazed back, every one of those thoughts buzzing through me in a hornet-sting swarm, and why. Why was I such an utter car crash.

"Don't look at me like that, Lane."

It was a challenge, not a request—a dare, demanding the opposite of everything it had meant to us before. I tried to stare him down. I failed so hard.

"Don't you look at *me*," I breathed.

"Is there a better view in this place?"

"Depends on what you're trying to see, Connor."

"Okay. I can't. I simply can*not*, for even one more second of my life." Paul's outburst yanked us back into the warehouse. We watched, wordlessly, as he stowed his chisel and made a beeline for the door. It swung shut behind him, then opened again, just enough to admit his leer. "I love you, Laney, but not enough to sit here and watch you eye-fuck my boy straight on into November."

The door slammed on his cackle, sucking the air, and my will to live, right out of the room. My eyes slid closed, tried their best to dissolve into my skull, so I'd never again have to look another human in the face. Maybe, if I stayed perfectly still, the world would do me a favor and cease to be.

"He has quite a way with words, huh?"

So. Connor still sitting there, existing beside me——flame and stardust, caught in the fabric of space——that was still a thing. Fuck. I steeled myself, cracked a lid, and peeked sideways; he was staring at the place where Paul had been, smirk gone weary with resignation.

"Connor, I swear, I wasn't——"

"Yeah." He turned to me, and it was every near miss and broken glance. Every time we'd almost touched, seething in the space between us. "Are we still doing the total honesty thing?"

"God. I——don't know. I don't know what we're doing."

"I know I'm not the McIntyre type." He took my hand and ran his thumb over my knuckles, as if tracing an invisible thread mark. "But you've been on my mind. Ever since that day."

"Mine too. I mean——" I swallowed the end of that blunder, floundering for something more coherent. Something safer. As if the thought of his scars against my skin hadn't already knocked Grey to the edge of the world. "You're my friend. If we let this happen——what would it be? What would *we* be?"

"It's your call. We could be nothing, or everything. A one-night thing, or the start of something more, or——"

"There is no 'more' for me," I snapped. "I told you, I don't do relationships."

"I remember." He gave me a wicked smile, wild and lovely as the shiver it sent across my shoulders. "You do distractions."

His words swept the wind from my lungs. He'd listened a

bit too closely that day in the parking lot, kept that detail stored at the ready, even all these weeks later. Threw it back my way, waiting to see if I'd bite.

"I also mind my business, Connor."

"Fair enough." The smile re-formed into half a smirk, pursed and pensive. My eyes dropped to our hands, still twined together on my knee, as he spoke. "Look, Lane, I know you have your feelings, and your reasons and all, but honestly? That kid couldn't handle you even if he was free to try."

"And you think you could?"

"That's a question that goes both ways." His thumb left a trail of sparks along my cheekbone. "How badly do you want it answered?"

I searched his face, seeking and finding that steady, reassuring familiarity. Connor knew my issues; he wouldn't expect a commitment. He wouldn't pout, or get jealous, or any dumb shit like that, so what did it matter if we carved a slightly skewed facet into our friendship?

It wouldn't have to change a thing.

So, I let my eyelids drop and my eyebrow quirk, let the corners of my lips tilt upward, slow and sultry. Let myself trip on the answering curve of his mouth as I leaned in.

It wasn't a kiss so much as an ignition——the sun lost behind the moon, the white-hot melt of flame and silver. It was the world flipped sideways, tilting us into chaos.

It was working. Grey was far away, finally fading. Finally stumbling off the edge of my thoughts.

"Hey." The word was a gasp, raw in the airless space between us. "You're okay with this, right? We don't have to—"

"Connor."

"Yeah?"

"Don't stop."

His answer trailed off to a low, wordless hum around the edges of my lips—a hum that turned to a growl as I rose to my knees, dragged my fingers through his hair. Descended upon him.

Shoved Grey McIntyre into oblivion.

I barely noticed the buzz of the warehouse, or the creak of the mattress beneath our shifting weight; didn't notice anything beyond Connor's hands moving over my jaw, through my hair, down my neck, pausing at the top button of my cardigan. I drew away, caught his eyes. Slid that button free, and then the next, and then I was on my back.

It wasn't even a question. There was no more doubt or hesitation, not in the drag of my fingers across his shoulders, or in the way he breathed against me as the world fell in splinters around us. And yes, it was a distraction, offered and accepted; it did begin, and end, as nothing. But as we lay together on his shitty futon—as he drew back to look at me, somewhere between a kiss and half a ragged breath—in that instant, for me, it was that much closer to everything.

In that moment, he was all I saw.

16

WE SAT CLOSE TOGETHER ON THE WAREHOUSE STEPS, just out of reach of the rain. It was well after three a.m., so when I'd finally texted Grey—Come get me whenever you wake up. No rush—I'd fully expected to wait out the night on that futon. His almost instant reply, Still awake, on my way, sent a surprising flare of disappointment through my belly.

"You can go crash if you need to," I said as Connor stifled his third yawn in as many minutes.

"I'll sleep after you go. Actually, I think I'll make coffee, and maybe some art. I'm suddenly feeling inspired."

"Shut up."

He laughed, pushing to his feet and pulling me with him as the Forester ambled toward us. We faced each other in the sudden glow of the floodlights, breath turning to haze in the air. He tucked my hair behind my ear, wiped a stray raindrop from my cheekbone.

"Lane. Tonight was . . ."

"It was, wasn't it?"

"It so was. Can I text you later?"

"You'd better." He smiled at that, and leaned in, and I let him kiss me, slow and deep and obvious. "Bye, Connor."

He headed inside as I dropped into the passenger seat. Grey stared at me, then at the warehouse, then gunned the engine in reverse, careened out of the parking lot, and blew through a stop sign before speaking.

"Tell me you didn't actually sleep with him."

"Wow. So is the boundary thing canceled in general, or just on your end?" His huff got lost in my short, dark laugh. "How about you let me know when Sadie finally gives it up, and *then* we'll trade stories. It'll be a whole family-bonding experience."

"What the fuck, dude. I can't believe this. Even someone like you wouldn't—"

He bit down on that one, exhaling the rest of it through his nose as my head swung slowly around to face him. Something flared inside, stung by the backhand of his existence.

"Someone like *me*? Finish that sentence, Grey McIntyre. I fucking dare you."

"You know that's not what I meant."

"Like if you keep saying that, I might believe you." I fixed my eyes on his profile, hating the habitual flicker of longing in my chest. I wanted to flatten his soul. "Guess we can officially put that whole gay rumor to bed, huh? So to speak?"

"Stop it, Elaine. Just—forget it."

I winced at the squeak of the windshield wipers as he smacked them to a too-high setting, slapped his hand back to grip the wheel, and what the fuck was he so mad about, anyway? What right did he have to even look at me with those furious, guilt-rimmed eyes?

The ride home was a silent, seething mess. I was out of the car and on the porch, digging for my house key before he even shut off the engine. The trick-or-treat candy bowl was empty, the jack-o'-lantern candles misshapen stubs in the shadows of our four faces. The carved edges curled inward, dry and dead.

I opened the door to a living room tinged with shadows and silence, yanked off my boots, and padded to the kitchen. I prepped the coffeepot and set the drip cycle for seven a.m., dreading the first whiff of morning. Grey and I were scheduled to open the market booth bright and early, regardless of how pissed we were at each other.

His disgruntled steps sounded on the kitchen tile, stopping right behind my back.

"I'm sorry," he said. "I was out of line, and your point about boundaries has been noted. But I still want to say that you dating Connor is a bad idea."

"Who said I was 'dating' him, Greyson?"

I couldn't help but smile at the sheer volume of his silence, broken by the buzz of my phone.

Total Honesty Mode?

I snickered at Connor's timing and replied, ignoring the huff at my back.

Sure, why not?

Miss you already.

"Well, isn't that sweet."

My elbow bumped his chest, he was that close.

"Mind your own fucking business, Grey. Last warning." I focused on my phone, let him see I was sending another text while blocking the screen from his view.

Miss you, too.

Everything okay?

Everything's fine. Just dealing w/ stepbrother bullshit right now.

Tell Grey hi from me, and also to go fuck himself.

Total Honesty Mode: Way ahead of you.

Damn right you are. Goodnight, Lane. I wish you'd stayed.

Me too. Goodnight.

"Connor says hi, and that you should fuck yourself." I set my phone on the counter and turned to meet Grey's eyes, reaching for the slow thrill that particular shade of green had sparked in my heart for years. Nothing. "I'm going to go ahead and second that."

"Whatever." He spun on his heel and headed for the door. "Excuse me for caring."

"I'm not sure why you do."

That stopped him dead in his tracks. He started to speak, then swallowed the words and shook his head.

"Yeah. I'm not really sure either."

A thousand replies gathered behind my lips, ready to explode all over him, but I bit them back. He stood there for another moment, my silence building between us, finally prodding him toward the doorway. I turned back to the counter, braced my hands against the cold surface. Pressed away the tremble in my fingers before it infected the rest of my world.

The scant few hours spent barely sleeping did nothing to boost my mood. Morning found Grey huddled at the table, looking like eight flavors of hell. The kitchen reeked of coffee and eucalyptus oil, undercut by burnt sage—his smudge stick again, clearly not quite doing the job, if his exoskeleton of negative energy was any indication.

"Is Skye okay?"

"What?" He squinted at me through bloodshot eyes. "She's still asleep, I think. Why?"

"The eucalyptus."

"Oh. That's me. Migraine."

"Oh. Well, at least take some real medicine. Your mom's great, but we both know that aromatherapy shit doesn't touch a migraine."

"Whatever, Elaine. Let's just go."

I glared at him and he returned it, I'll give him that. He glared right back, pathetic as it was. But he could barely keep his eyes open.

"Yeah, whatever, Greyson. Whatever."

The drive in didn't net an improvement—if anything, Grey's attitude only got worse. By mid-shift, I'd banished him to the folding chair with his fourth cup of ineffective coffee, taken his mood and turned it back on him. My own head throbbed from lack of sleep, my muscles ached, and I was right on the brink of my period; I was having absolutely none of his bullshit that fine November morning, and matched him snarl for snarl, until we could hardly look at each other.

I didn't see Sadie until she was practically in the booth with us. Her hair glowed as she bounced over for a hug, then swooped in on Grey, hovering and cooing and coddling, apparently over the whole Samhain versus Jesus debate from the night before. Connor followed in her wake, quiet, his confident half smile tempered by hesitant eyes.

Something broke loose in my chest at the sight of him—

something odd, which lit me up. We stood there grinning at each other, trying not to grin at each other, trying not to let those grins dissolve into laughter. I reached for his hand, remembering halfway there that I'd never deliberately held it before—outside of utterly fucked-up situations, of course, like that time we'd literally knotted ourselves together, or when he made me cut through it with his art knife. He closed the distance, however, and linked his fingers with mine.

"I promised myself I wouldn't make this weird," he finally said. "Or, you know. Awkward."

"Really. Fail much?" I giggled at his weary sigh. "Get over here."

His arms were warm, his kiss sweet and appropriate, cut short by Sadie's gleeful, inevitable shriek.

"What?!? What is *this*? Connor Hall, why didn't you tell me something happened with Lane?"

Well. This was awkward.

"Did you want me to, like, text you during?" he answered her as we broke apart. "Consider this your official notification."

"Is it why you had her go home with you last night?" She clapped a hand over her mouth, a shitty attempt to mask a gasp. "Have you been *secretly dating* this whole time??"

"What? No!" I almost laughed at her crestfallen pout. "Why would we keep it a secret?"

"Neither of us have time for your weird head games, Sadie," Connor sighed. "I asked her over as a favor last night, to help her escape your bullshit. And then Paul said—"

"Oh, don't drag Paul into this. It would have been so romantic, is all. So *clandestine*. Like, if part of your plan was to act like you're *just friends*, and then——"

"We didn't plan it," I cut in, "but it happened. And here we are."

"Oh. My. Word." Her face was a supernova, bright around the biggest smile. "This is perfect! We can double-date! What are you doing tonight?"

My eyes strayed behind her, found Grey standing there, silent and staring and blank. He turned away from us and began messing around with the display, stacking bars and rearranging bottles on the tabletop. I looked away, attempted to discreetly wipe my mouth on the shoulder of my shirt. Double date, my ass.

"Okay, calm down." Connor rubbed a hand over his eyes, as if the act would blot out his sister. "This is literally hours old."

"And we're not a couple," I added over Sadie's protests. "We're friends, but——"

"But? But nothing." She gestured to the way we stood: his arm curled around my shoulder, mine crossed over his waist. My thumb unconsciously hooked through his belt loop, fingers resting on his hip bone. "Lane Jamison, this is *not* how we touch our friends."

I couldn't help echoing the laughter that burst from Connor, spilling over both of us like sunshine. She was miffed to the point of cute——goody-goody Sadie, hands fisted on her hips, chin up, feathers ruffled. A little mother hen, pecking at our unrepentant toes.

"We're friends," he repeated. "We're involved, but not committed. Nothing complicated."

"So you're not officially together?" Her face scrunched into a pout at our simultaneous headshakes. "Well. I guess if you're happy, I'm happy. I'll have to work a little harder to convince you you're destined to be, but I don't mind. We can start with dinner tonight, just the two of you. I'll make a reservation."

"Or maybe you could mind your own business for once." Connor released me, ran his fingers through his hair and over his face, swatted at the hand Sadie jammed in his jacket pocket as she rummaged for his phone. At least she wasn't mad. "Not that I have a hope in hell that'll actually happen, but it doesn't hurt to put it out there."

"I'm sorry, honey, what? I wasn't listening. Does seven o'clock sound good? I know you're on duty tomorrow, but this is a special occasion."

"Goddamn it, Sadie."

My eyes cut to Grey, catching the corner of his sullen gaze as he abandoned the display and started poking around in the cash register.

"Everything okay, Greyson? You seem tense."

"Sorry if my mood's not great," he sneered. "When I offered you a ride *last night*, I didn't realize I was actually offering you a ride *this morning*."

"Holy shit, really? You *told* me to text you. How are you still mad about that?"

"I don't sleep enough as it is, Elaine. I don't appreciate what little I get being derailed by your conquests."

I blinked at the surge of venom in his voice. This was more than the migraine, or his precious sleep schedule——this was territorial. Was it some form of misplaced family protectiveness? Would he be throwing the same fit over any random guy, or was he upset I'd been with Connor in particular? Was he actually *jealous?*

And was he seriously doing this in front of Sadie?

My eyes crept over to her, waiting for the glitter-crusted rage tsunami to crash right down on our heads. She was preoccupied, trying over Connor's protests to add God knows what to his phone calendar.

"You hadn't even gone to bed yet, Grey. Anyway, I never told you to wait up." I turned back his way, caught the heat off his glare. Let it reach inside and spark and flame, until mine was a match. "But if it bothers you so much, next time I'll just stay over."

He was so close to smug at the beginning of that sentence. The smugness had even manifested on his face in a tiny, shitty smirk, all geared up for what he thought would be acquiescence on my part——maybe even an apology. Once my words hit the air, that smirk twisted into something crooked and dismayed beneath eyes swirling with contradictions; shifting between pain and shame, anger and confusion. I clenched my teeth around an outburst, choked back a bitter surge of guilt.

"Oh, *next* time?" he drawled. "Really? Wasn't aware there'd be one of *those*."

"Wasn't aware that was a *problem*."

"Oh, leave him alone, honey," Sadie interjected, pressing Connor's buzzing phone back into his defeated hand. He turned away from us, stepped outside the booth to take the call. "He's got that migraine, poor thing. Baby, why don't you take a break? You'll feel better after some lunch."

At Grey's reluctant nod, she tugged him off the stool, so I could take his place. I knew without looking that every bill in the register was lined even with the others, all faceup, all bottom-edge left. If he was really agitated, the coins would be stacked level with the tray partition. I opened the drawer, and sure enough.

Something ancient and sorrowful squeezed around my heart, a familiar hand fingerpicking my veins until they wept. That he could reach past my fury so easily with one unconscious tell; that he could still summon such poignant longing—that had to mean something. There had to be more to this than my own exquisite ache.

I raised my head and turned to him, followed his path: always in Sadie's footsteps, always even. Always, almost a perfect match.

She practically skipped out of the booth, beelining for the cider vendor. Grey trailed a beat back, his hand in hers, his eyes on mine. His gaze was a black hole, threatening to eat her light.

17

THE NIGHT GALLOPED IN ON AUTUMNAL HOOVES, LEFT its chill on the bridge of my nose as we climbed into darkness. Asheville lurked at our backs, eyed the four of us through the cloud of sage smoke rushing out the Forester's open windows as we snaked toward our usual Parkway overlook. A smudge stick smoldered in the ashtray, and Sadie chattered away in the front seat; neither was potent enough to cleanse the car of tension. Grey's mood had been set to low-grade bitch since the Samhain gathering.

Six days. An entire timeline built around my stepbrother's shitty attitude, measured and marked in the regular pause of his footsteps outside my bedroom door. Nearly a solid week spent catching his eyes across every empty space, catching the heat off his skin when he stood too close—which was everywhere he stood, in every room of our house. So sudden, the way our world had turned to flame. So wrong, how I couldn't help but let us burn.

Connor's phone trilled in his pocket. He retrieved it and checked his texts, returned my smile across the gloom of the

back seat—yet another empty space, this one flaring and sparking every time his eyes found mine.

Once we'd successfully dodged Sadie's attempts to arrange a
formal date, I'd expected our friendship status quo to continue
unchanged. Not that I'd been up for anything more vigorous than
hand-holding since our brief hello at the market—my period had
shown up early, commandeered my body that very afternoon,
right before the end of my shift. Grey had had no choice but to
sack up and run the booth, migraine notwithstanding. In any
case, after about eighty years spent drowning in the memory
of my night with Connor, picking apart every possible thing he
might say when I saw him next, I figured it was safest to assume
the whole thing had been a one-off, that we'd checked each other
off our respective lists and would never speak of it again.

After the worst of the vomiting had passed, I'd returned to
the warehouse, prepared for business as usual: gossiping with
Paul, working on our projects. Discussing yarn, and metal, and
other art-based topics. I was not prepared for the tiny, monu-
mental changes in our interactions—the anti-nausea lozenges
that appeared in my project bag after that first day. The way I
didn't hesitate to apply my limited knowledge of acupressure to
his work-tired hands, or the way he leaned against my shoulder
as we sat side by side. And I really wasn't prepared for the charge
in the air; for the thrill of a simple glance; the press of his fingers
on my hip bones as he massaged a cramp out of my lower back,
thumbs slowly working the ache from my muscles, lips hovering

a breath from my neck. The way he deliberately held back, turning every moment into a tease.

He hadn't tried to take things further. We hadn't even kissed. It was maddening.

"Anyone I know?" I asked, nodding to the pileup of emoji-laden notifications on his screen.

"Paul, locking up on his way out of town. I'm on watch until Sunday night."

"By yourself?"

"All alone." He sent a reply and set his phone aside. "Unless you want to keep me company. Maybe pick up where we left off, if you're feeling better."

"Oh." My teeth caught the edge of my grin as his hand found mine. "I don't know. Maybe."

"Open invitation, whenever you're ready. Tonight. Tomorrow night." He lifted our hands together, brushed his lips across my knuckles, leaving a warm glow on the back of my neck. "Any night you want."

"We have to work tomorrow."

Grey's voice plucked me out of the moment, grating my nerves, piercing my heart. I met his glare in the rearview mirror, resenting the habitual double beat of my pulse.

"Whatever, Greyson. Eavesdrop much?"

"Just save the hookup shit for later, okay? I don't need that in my car."

It was a glitch in the already thrumming atmosphere. I held

his gaze until he had to look away, let his words fuel my mounting anger. Sadie's head turned slowly toward him, then back to the window. Her profile stalled in neutral, a wary question she didn't want answered edging her reflection.

Connor, of course, had no such qualms. His laugh was a chemical burn, harsh and caustic. Sure to scar.

"This conversation is the most action this car has ever seen," he scoffed, waving away a curl of sage smoke. "Which is not really surprising—it smells like Stove Top stuffing, for fuck's sake."

"Connor," Sadie muttered, still frozen in place. "Be nice."

"It's just sad, is all—a rugged off-roader like this, and he still drives it like a little old lady. Won't even let me ride on the roof." He leaned between the front seats, aimed a smirk directly at Grey's stony profile. "And we damn sure know he's never even *seen* this back seat."

Grey didn't bother slowing—just fishtailed to the shoulder and slammed on the brakes. Practically hanged himself on the seat belt as he twisted to hiss in Connor's face.

"You want action? Go on then, man. Get up there."

Sadie's gasp sucked away what little air was left in the car. Connor stared at him for a stunned split second, and then he was out the window and out of sight in a thump of boot soles on steel. A scuffle, a thud; then his voice reached down to us from above.

"Ready."

"All right, then. Here we go."

Grey's low mutter, aimed at the steering column, snapped me out of my shock.

"Ready nothing, Greyson. Don't you dare move this car an inch until he's back inside it."

"You think he'll just climb down if I ask real nice, huh? Since when do I get a say in the shit he pulls? Since when does anyone?"

"Oh, stop it, both of you. This is ridiculous." Sadie stuck her head out the window, aiming an impatient, mother-hen cluck at the roof. "Connor Hall, you come back inside here, right now."

"Fuck off, Sadie!" Connor yelled. "Let's go, *Greyson*. Show us what you got."

The sun had set hours ago. The closest streetlight was miles behind us. The moon lurked on the far side of the mountain. We had the headlights, the dash lights, the faraway stars. Nothing more. Plenty by far to illuminate the teeth-grinding clench of Grey's jaw.

"Fuck him. He wants to play?" He slammed a fist against the ceiling. "HOLD TIGHT, BITCH."

Sadie's shriek blew through the car and out the window as his foot hit the floor. The Forester's back end swung out, rattling over branches and underbrush as we leaped off the shoulder and around the curve of the road, breakneck and sloppy, way too fast. Connor's boots beat on the roof, spurring my stepbrother on in a flurry of profane rage and another answering ceiling punch. I'd seen flashes of Grey's temper before, witnessed plenty of his sulks and snarls and assorted shitty moods, but I'd never seen him like this. His eyes were wide and furious in the rearview, face a twisted, fearsome blaze. He was a fucking stranger.

I pawed at my seat belt latch, shrugged off the strap, and leaned between the bucket seats, heart pounding, fingers numb.

"Grey, stop the car."

Grey's head turned toward me, so close his breath grazed my cheek—his gaze was a cut power line, live and lethal. It arced and sparked, zapped a current along the curve of my spine. Burst into flame as it locked with mine.

"How's this for 'action,' huh? See? No hands." He laughed off my panic, blocked my frantic grab for the wheel with one of his outstretched arms. "What? Everything's cool here, *Lane*. He wanted a rush—he's got one. You'll thank me later, I'm sure."

The Forester groaned around another curve, and I gave up on logic and on him. I scrambled across the back seat and pulled myself up and out the window. I braced my butt and thighs against the ledge and my legs against the door, clung to the roof rack as I slithered into open air.

Connor lay flat on his back, hands locked on one rack bar, feet planted against the other. Mouth stretched in a howl that broke and scattered and flew away. He ignored my shouts, my tugs on his jacket; he doubled his grip, drew breath, loosed another yell into the wind. I chickened out, withdrew back into the car as the tires left rubber around another turn.

Sadie was a silent cluster of nerves, shrinking against the passenger window. The rearview gleamed with the ugly curl of

Grey's mouth. His hands were back on the wheel, at least, but it didn't matter. I was done with his bullshit passive aggression and his weird attempts to strong-arm my behavior—like he really expected me to seek his approval before getting laid. Like he had the right to even say a word.

I was so very, very done.

"How's it going out there, Elaine? Is he having fun yet?"

"Pull over. Now."

"Can't. I am but a vessel—a cog in the machine." He shook his head, steered us around another curve. "Talk to the puppet master, not the string."

"Greyson, I swear to God—"

"Shut up, okay? This was his idea. He—FUCK."

It came out of nowhere. Or, rather, it rose up over the lip of the mountain slope, leaped across the road, cantered past us, and continued up in an untouched flash of hooves and antlers. It missed us by less than a foot.

Grey jerked the wheel and the Forester obeyed, swerved left, squealed and shuddered. Slammed me hard into his seat, then pitched me onto the back seat floor, knocked the thoughts from my head and the wind from my lungs. Sadie's scream blasted through the car, and I scrambled up in time to watch Connor slide down the windshield, roll sideways off the slope of the hood, and disappear.

18

"OH GOD. GOD. FUCK. SADIE? BABE, ARE YOU OKAY? Elaine? Fuck. *Fuck*."

The Forester shambled to a stop on the wrong side of the road, cozied right up against the goddamn guardrail. The world was a vast, bottomless cavern, seething with Grey's rambling and Sadie's tears and the steady nighttime buzz of the trees. Broken by a wild shriek of laughter from the shadows at our backs.

Sadie was out of the car before I even made it off the floor. I climbed past the panting, barely coherent husk of my stepbrother and went straight for the window, pulled myself halfway out as Connor loped into view, breathless and disheveled. His grin stretched all the way back to Asheville. Sadie tackled him in a flurry of howls and hysteria, nearly sending them both over the guardrail.

"I'm okay," I heard him say through her wails. "Sadie, I'm okay."

Connor caught my eyes over his sister's head. He broke from her and flew to me, an icy wind reaching to wrap around the moon. He caught me by the waist, dragged me out the window, and spun me off my feet.

"God," he gasped. "That was—"

"That was what? Amazing? Fun?" I shoved him off me, sent him stumbling, then rushed in and tackled him, running us both into the Forester's bumper. "Never again, Connor. You could be dead right now."

"But I'm not. I'm fine."

I tightened my grip on his jacket, felt the night roll off him in waves. His hand was knotted in my hair; his heart threatened to pound through both our chests.

Grey staggered out of the car, stammering over every apology on earth. I pulled away from Connor and turned on my step-brother. His anxious face bloomed to fear as I advanced on him.

"Greyson. You—"

"I'm sorry, Elaine. Connor. I'm so sorry. I—"

"Sorry? You're *sorry*?" Connor rushed forward, catching Grey off guard and off his feet, swinging him around the same way he'd done to me. "That was awesome, McIntyre. No idea you had it in you."

"Had it in me? If I'd been going any faster—God. I'm so sorry, man, I swear, I—what are you doing?" Grey threw off Connor's arms, stumbling backward as Connor swooped in again. "Dude, get off me."

"Grey, baby, let's just go home," Sadie sniffled. "Connor, get in the car. Please?"

"You need to do this, *baby*, no joke. Sadie, you're driving back. Your boy is riding on the roof with me."

Grey's face was a wreck of guilt and fury as he dodged another hug.

"The fuck is wrong with you? Leave me alone."

"No backing out. It'll blow. Your. Mind."

The headlock was a bad idea; the accompanying hair ruffle the final nail, smashed right down into the coffin. Connor was taller, but Grey was broader, big and solid and already rattled past reason.

Connor dodged the first shove, but not the second.

It sent him reeling sideways, snapped his laughter into jagged bits. The glee drained from his eyes, making way for something darker.

"Really." He tilted his head, took in Grey's stance and steady, heaving breaths, my shaking legs and wild-eyed stare. The shocked, silent statue of Sadie, face covered by her tear-damp hands. "Really?"

"Let's go."

He started forward. Connor closed the distance, a smile like spilled ink spreading across his face. They advanced on each other, slow, then faster, then ran into me as I threw myself between them.

"Back up, Greyson."

"Get out of my way."

"And if I don't?" I stared him down until he blinked. "Back up. Now."

I spun away from him, stalked over to Connor, who had already sauntered into the shadows. He leaned cross-armed against the rear bumper, the unconcerned eye of a storm. Dropped an actual wink as I approached.

"Really, Connor? Really? God. I don't even know what to say to you right now."

"I'm not the problem here." He indicated over my shoulder at the air horn that was Sadie, finally unfrozen, absolutely unloading on Grey. "His territorial big brother shit? It's only cute if you ignore its sketchy roots."

"It doesn't have sketchy roots."

"Lane, it has a whole sketchy ecosystem—and the really sad part is, he thinks none of us can see it. Look, I didn't start this, but if he wants a fight, I can damn sure guarantee I'll finish it. I'll raze his world to the fucking ground."

I left him chuckling against the car, his words burning hot in my cheeks. My anger and feet and heart carried me to Grey. Sadie's eyes found mine, darted immediately away as he turned to me, desperate with earnest, frantic regret.

"Time to go, Greyson."

"Elaine, I am so sorry. Can we just forget it? The overlook's up ahead, and—"

"Sure, because what we need is you and Connor getting wrecked and losing your inhibitions. Honestly, I could do without looking at either one of you right now. But this"—I swung my arm wide, gestured to Connor and the car, and our vast, star-specked surroundings—"is too much. This won't—it *can't* happen again."

I watched the words pummel him, like raindrops on a long-ago porch swing. Watched them yank a different near miss from the murk of his memory. His mouth drooped; his eyes were broken things, murky with defeat and regret, and some elusive, deep-lurking sorrow I couldn't quite place.

His voice, when he found it, was small and defeated. Meek as Sadie on the public-access feed.

"I'm sorry. I've been off-balance all day, and then he laughed at me, and I just snapped—I don't know what I was doing, but this isn't me. And when I think how this could have ended—"

"You *should* think about that," I snarled, "because it could have ended with Connor dead in the road. All because you 'just snapped.'"

"I know. I know, and it makes me sick." The breath clattered out of him in fragmented gasps; he actually clutched at his head, a near parody of tragic lament. It would have been ridiculous, if he hadn't been so clearly on the verge of breaking. "I can't do this anymore. I can't let myself get so mad that I—Elaine, how can I fix this? Tell me what you want from me." Oh, where to start with that one.

"I want off this mountain. Think you can make that happen without running us all into a fucking tree?"

I swallowed the lump in my throat as I turned away. Connor was already in the car, leaning casually against the door. I avoided his eyes and his grin, his peace offering of an outstretched hand as I slid in beside him.

Sadie yelled at Grey all the way back to the warehouse. No surprise there.

Connor turned to me as the car slowed to a stop, gave me the up-and-down sweep beneath an artfully raised eyebrow.

"So, total honesty—are we doing the telepathy thing now? Or did I already fuck this up beyond repair?" He sighed at my stony profile, climbed out of the back seat, then leaned over and offered me a hand. "At least walk me to the door?"

I don't know why I went. Maybe to escape World Wars Three through Seventeen, still unspooling in the front seat. Maybe to untangle myself from the foreign, too-sticky web forming around us all. But I seethed my way into open air, let Connor steer me into the shadows just to the side of the warehouse door, where his smirk faced off against my gritted teeth.

"You're mad." The smirk opened into a laugh at my answering huff. "You're so pissed at me right now. Don't even act like you're not."

"Don't you look at me like that, Connor. None of this is funny."

"You're right, it's not. But if I don't laugh . . ." He trailed off, smile re-spun from starlight into shade. "You know, you're cute when you're all riled up."

"Shut up."

"You are. You're gorgeous." He leaned in slowly, brushed his lips over the edge of my scowl. Followed my gasp and swallowed it whole, kissed it into a sigh. Pulled back and let our eyes collide. His hands were in my jacket, running slowly over my waist, and nothing I knew or didn't know about him mattered when he looked at me like that. "Still furious?"

"Yes."

"Tell me to fuck off, then. I'll go inside right now. You can let good old Greyson take you home, and you can text me later, if you feel like it. Or not. Or, you could stay."

I let him walk me backward until my skin met bricks. Let his chest and belly and hips mold to mine, lean and solid, everything hard all the way down, and my anger wasn't fading, but morphing, turning—burning hot and vicious, giving way to a burst of desire. That gaze, both a question and its own inevitable answer. That mouth, meeting mine once more, then drawing back just far enough to form the shape of the word, silent and slow.

Stay.

Grey's voice followed his footsteps, rough and short and sharp with gravel. A good distraction would be just the thing to drown him out.

"Elaine? Look, no offense, but I'm done. If you're coming home tonight—"

"It's okay, Greyson," I said, holding Connor's eyes, and who knew pure flame could burn dark as any midnight sky? "I'm not."

19

THINGS BETWEEN SADIE AND ME HAD TIPTOED STEADILY along the edge of weird since the car surfing incident. She'd stormed into the warehouse without knocking the morning after, launched into a preplanned lecture about recklessness and road safety, and Connor's responsibilities as a conscientious and respectful passenger. Her startled squawk and subsequent dash for the door, when she realized what she'd interrupted, was almost worth the awkwardness that followed. We'd spent the two weeks since then decidedly not discussing our involvement with each other's respective brothers. My mistake was answering her Friday night GIRLS' DAY TOMORROW??? text with a non-committal Sure, sounds good, and assuming she'd follow up with a concrete suggestion.

So, when she'd popped up in head-to-toe lululemon at eight a.m. Saturday, battering-ram smile crashing through the kitchen door, I was unprepared to join her in the morning yoga class she insisted was my idea. Not that I put up more than a feeble protest. Once Sadie hooked her teeth into a plan of action, it was easier just to go along.

I had to hand it to her, though——she went all the way in. She drove us downtown, all but skipped to the studio, and rolled her mat out right next to mine, keeping pace with me through all the basic poses. She'd tapped out on the inversions, and teetered and stumbled through tree pose, but hung in there until the end of class. Afterward, we burst into the crisp autumn morning, winded and sweaty, her cheeks as pink as her leggings.

"Lord, honey," she drawled as we ambled up Biltmore Avenue. "If that wasn't ten pounds of ouch in a five-pound bag. My legs feel like they could fall off any minute."

"You did fine. No one expects perfection in there."

"I spent half the class worrying I'd tip right over and get stuck on my back, like a turtle in a shell. It *was* a good workout, though." She stretched her arms above her head, swung her mat strap to the other shoulder. "And now I'm starving."

The bustle of Pack Square loomed ahead, promising coffee and comfort, and the breakfast I'd skipped in favor of sun salutations. I turned to ask Sadie where she wanted to eat, and spoke, instead, to empty air. She was gone.

I scanned the square, crowded as always with tourists and locals, hipsters and hippies, street performers and clusters of weary, homeless teens. The bright flash of Sadie's hair caught my eye as she sprinted across the street against the light, leaving me to wait for the signal. By the time I caught up to her, she was surrounded by people and beaming at one of the street musicians—a young, rangy guy with more piercings than teeth, whose tattooed hand she clasped in both her own.

"It *has* been a while, hasn't it?" I heard her say as I slowed to a stop. "My friend and I were about to get our caffeine fix. Can I get you a cup?"

"Sounds great. Hold on, I got some change."

He reached into his guitar case, but she shook her head.

"Put that away, honey. It's no trouble at all. We'll get all y'all something warm."

I nodded, mostly to myself, clenched the handle of my bag until my fingers ached. Sadie took a quick head count, waving off another half dozen offers of money. Shame flared in my chest, spread outward to my fidgety limbs as I watched her dig a packet of tissues from the depths of her glittery duffel bag and press them into the hand of a raw-nosed girl with runny, red-rimmed eyes—a girl I'd have carefully walked past, if I'd been on my own. It was so natural for Sadie, that simple gesture. That glimmer of goodness, brighter than any shade in her collection of palettes.

Why her, I'd shrilled at Grey, as if I hadn't watched her shine countless times. As if it wasn't perfectly clear why anyone would be drawn to the glow of her heart.

I looked around the group, zeroed in on a guy who huddled against the wall behind me, elbows resting on his drawn-up knees. He was a mangled wisp, dirty and tattered and high as shit. Vaguely familiar. The hood of his jacket listed off his blond head; he'd pulled the sleeves down over hands that worked non-stop, like trapped rodents, beneath the threadbare fabric. A finger crept out of his sleeve, absently scratched at an abscess on his chin. It must have been a nice chin, once, on a face that had probably been handsome, before his skin had gone to rot. He squinted up at me as I squatted in front of him, fixing my face into what at least felt like a grin.

"Hey, you want anything? Coffee?"

"Sure." He coughed into his sleeve, blinked around a flicker of lucidity as our eyes met. "You around here much?"

"Oh. Not really. I mean, I have school and stuff, so—well." So spoke Lane Jamison, orator for the ages. God. "Have we met?"

"Nah. Just feels like I've seen you, I guess. Or, maybe not." His mouth trembled at the edges, stilled for an instant in a smile that bit the edges of my heart. "But coffee's always good."

"Sit tight, then." As if he'd been on the verge of sprinting off.

I walked away from him on numb legs, eyes stinging, stomach a hollow, quaking pit. Not that I was great with strangers even under stellar circumstances, but this was worse—this was Lane caught off guard, staring down a wormhole into Connor's former life. I felt like melting into a wall, slipping down into a sidewalk crack—anything to ensure I no longer had to look that life in the face, hear the rattle of its inhale, or smell its sour, broken flesh.

Sadie waited at the crosswalk, beckoning for me to hurry before we missed the light. I followed her down the block and into a bright, crowded café, breathed my heartbeat back to normal as Sadie ordered a dozen cups of dark roast and a shitload of muffins. It wasn't until the barista turned away to run her debit card that I finally found my voice.

"So, are those kids Connor's friends? From before?"

"They're *my* friends. Our church did homeless outreach, when I was little." A turquoise curl escaped from her bun as she bent over the counter, signed the enormous tab without flinching. "Daddy cut that program after—well. A few years back. Anyway, I picked it back up on my own last year, once I got my car."

"By yourself? Isn't that—" I didn't actually say the word "dangerous," but she heard me anyway.

"I'm not naive, Lane. I volunteer at the shelter, and if I see the people I meet there on the street—like just now—I try to help where I can. It's not much, and I know I can't save everyone, but every little bit matters. It's the least anyone can do."

We shuffled across the café, hands loaded with trays and bags. I pushed open the door with my butt, got stuck holding it for four other people before impatience overrode manners. Sadie smiled as I finally joined her on the sidewalk, flinching at a sudden chilly breeze. The receipt flew off her tray and danced ahead of us, as if eager to lead the way.

"Do we need to go after that? For taxes?" I frowned at her quizzical blink. "Your parents don't write it off?"

"My parents? Oh Lord, they don't know about this. If they ask about the bill, I'll tell them I treated you and Grey, but I doubt they'll even notice."

We slowed at the crosswalk, waited for the light to change.

A car blew by, lifting the ends of my hair. I eyed her profile over the steaming cups, wondered at her dedication to this secret, thankless task. It wasn't about spreading the gospel or earning points with Jesus; it wasn't about filial duty, or guilt, or even her brother. It was nothing more than simple kindness. It was Sadie.

"Sadie, are you——" I swallowed the end of that thought, rearranged it, tried again. "You're okay, right?"

"I'm fine—better off than these poor kids, anyway." She indicated her friends with a tilt of her head. The traffic drew to a stop, and we stepped off the curb together, moving toward their eager smiles. "You know me, Lane. I have everything I need."

We huddled together that night beneath the silent moon, passing a fifth of Fireball carefully back and forth with mittened hands. We'd swathed ourselves in scarves and hats, burrowed under our own coats, and Connor's coat, and one of Paul's blankets. Our breath blew out in short wisps, turned every word to a curl of mist.

I'd spent most of the evening beneath the crook of Connor's arm, Sadie slipping along beside us through the oil slick of white-boy dreads and vegan sweat, patchouli and weed, and that sharp, earthy, oddly specific scent of beer spilled on batik cloth. Connor overdid it on the Fireball, then succumbed to it all at once, hadn't even argued when we bundled him onto the futon and left him to sleep it off. Grey had skipped the party, assumedly to cleave himself unto his calculus textbook.

"You're sure he'll be okay?" I asked for the third time, staring at my silent phone. She giggled and nudged me with her shoulder, nipped at the Fireball like it was candy. Typical Sadie—she wouldn't even say the *f*-word, but good luck getting a turn with a bottle once she got her hands on it.

"You really like him, don't you?"

"Well, yeah. I wouldn't be here if I didn't."

"I know, but I feel like there's more between you two than you're telling me. Women's intuition." She leaned in and dropped her voice to a whisper, as if we weren't alone on the roof of a soundproofed warehouse in the dead of night. Her breath was sharp, warm cinnamon against my ear. "*Plus*, I wanted to look at the rings again, so I peeked in the sketchbook. I mean, it's gross 'cause he's my brother, but *wow*."

"Meaning?" I watched her mischievous grin falter, then ebb, then give way entirely as she cringed, hiding her face against her knees.

Realization dropped over me like a net. I pried her arm away from her head, seeking confirmation in the guilty pinch of her face. Yep. There it was.

"Oh my God. Tell me you're joking, Sadie. Please."

"I figured you—ohhhhh crap. Connor might actually kill me for real, this time."

"What am I wearing?" She shook her head, and I let her go,

pressing my hands against my eyes. Spreading my fingers wide, to hide as much of my face as possible.

"Oh, don't be mad, Lane. The worst one only has, like, a side-boob. Half a sideboob. That's all."

"No. Stop. You did not just say 'sideboob' to me in this context."

"Really, it's not indecent. You should see how you look to him. He's going to fall in love with you someday, I can feel it."

I was just sober enough to bite back my answer—just lucid enough to refrain from detailing all the ways in which my nights with Connor didn't count as love. How her brother's hands scorched their way across my skin over and over; how the lines of his hips canceled out her boyfriend's eyes, smeared them down to a sullen, seawater muddle. Kept them at bay for another day, or hour even—another blissful, blank moment, during which I could pretend I wasn't an utter mess.

"Yeah, I can really tell," I said. "It was especially clear that one time he had me slice his thumb all the way down to the bone. Very romantic."

"Wow. You don't understand him at all, do you?" She squinted at a glint of whiskey on the back of her hand, then licked it off. "Helping you be strong is how he shows you he cares. That's his *thing*. Me and my parents. Your fear of knives. Sabine and her anxiety, and her codependency, and—"

"Who's Sabine—one of the painters? Or one of the fucking meth heads?" The answer, horrible and obvious, reared suddenly in my gut. "Oh, dear God. You are not serious."

"This really isn't a good night for me," she sighed, resignedly passing me the Fireball. "Kinda figured you'd have heard all about her by now."

"I have decidedly *not* heard about her, actually. At all."

"Well. I guess there's not *that* much to tell. She used to live here too, and then they broke up, and she kept on living here for, like, months. Just as roommates, he said. So."

I chewed on that one for a moment, oddly perturbed. The specifics of our friends-with-benefits thing had barely been broached since that first encounter, much less renegotiated. Though I'd visited daily and stayed overnight more than once since that first night, most of our time together had been benefit-free—hours spent on the spinning wheel, then in the metal room, him soldering and snipping and shaping while my knitting needles flew through the new skeins. Doing homework or chatting with Paul, while Connor hunched over his sketchbook, focused and furrowed. Falling asleep on the futon, waking hours later to a dark room and the second-skin weight of his sleeping arms.

Some of those nights, however, the sketchbook stayed closed. Some mornings we woke to each other, and I wouldn't get home until late afternoon, where I'd have to scramble through homework and chores while dodging Grey's surly glares and muttered asides regarding my nonexistent curfew. And not that I'd been qualified to recite chastity pledges alongside Sadie, but before Connor I'd never actually spent the night with a boy. And he, at nineteen, had already cohabitated—with this Sabine, who for all I knew was in the warehouse that very moment, laughing and twirling through the rooms they'd shared. Catching the specter of her lingering scent on my side of his bed.

"My" side. As if I had a claim on Connor, or his space, or any of his stuff. Not fucking likely.

"That's weird, though, isn't it?" Sadie said, swiping the bottle from my absent hand. "Falling in love, sharing your life, and then—nothing? How does that even work?"

"Well, it *didn't* work. She's gone. If they really loved each other, she'd still be around."

"I suppose. Or maybe it *was* real, but they couldn't make it stick." She took another swig of Fireball and held it in her mouth, savoring it before swallowing. "I like you with my brother, Lane. He needs a sweet girl—someone stable, to settle him down."

That one was worth a raised eyebrow at the very least, but she wasn't grinning or giggling, or even looking my way. She stared into the darkness beyond the floodlights, tapping the bottle rim against her teeth.

"And *I'm* the best option for that? Sadie. Please."

"Compared to the others? You're the first girl he's been with who lives in a house. His situation didn't exactly allow for normal relationships."

A flicker of guilt stung in my throat as I pictured Connor, rewound him to the kid he'd been—pictured his trusting eyes and the soft, needy underbelly he'd doubtless revealed to all the wrong people. That kid, seeking love and solace in any sideways smile.

And Sadie wanted me to strike that balance for him. Me, who couldn't regulate my own post-nightmare pulse, let alone soothe the blare of Connor Hall.

It made no sense. Was that the end goal of love, when it all came down to it—to shred your feet over the crushed-glass misery of another's chosen path? Did a person only become his or her best self on the back of someone else?

God. Whoever ended up with me was well and truly fucked.

"He might want to look elsewhere," I muttered. The front door opened directly beneath us, ejecting a gaggle of Paul's friends. They stumbled away in a swirl of laughter and unimportance. "I'm known for being neither sweet nor stable."

"Well, I think you work together—always thought you would. Connor has his baggage, but he's got a good heart. And he's definitely into you. And . . . not otherwise spoken for."

Her words froze the air between us, settled and solidified and turned my lungs to ice. I couldn't look at her.

She looked at me, though—deliberately turned her head and stared, waiting for my cracks to show. Waiting to prod until they ripped wide open.

"You're my friend," she continued, as if an eon hadn't passed, "but he's my blood. So if this is a passing phase, all I ask is that you tell him now, before it goes too far."

"Sadie." My words were low and even, steadier by far than my quaking insides. "I know you mean well, but you have no idea what you're talking about."

"I know he's worth more than just a fling, Lane. I do know that."

"That's not how it is," I began. "Connor and I—"

"And as for Sabine," she continued, as if I hadn't spoken, "it can't have been real, or how could they stand it? Being that close to someone you love, knowing you couldn't be together. It must be devastating."

"It's not an issue. He's not in love with me."

"Not yet, no. But soon." The words came out flat and weary, anything but a question, and for a single breathless beat, I had no idea which "he" she meant. "How could anyone help but love you."

20

HIS HANDS CAUGHT ME RIGHT BEFORE THE WORST OF it, dragged me, shrieking, from a bloodbath of skin and veins and splintered bone.

"Lane? Lane, look at me."

I blinked through bleary eyes, taking in the brick walls and blocks of wood, the blown-glass art, Paul's empty bed. Connor shifted his hold on me as I sagged, easing me back onto the pillows. The party had been far from over when I'd collapsed beside his unconscious form; now the warehouse loomed around us, a cavern of shadows and stillness. His drafting table OttLite was on, his work scattered across the surface, abandoned in his haste to wake me.

I'd known it was a risk, dreaming in a strange place—knew she'd always find me, wherever I closed my eyes. Still, some tiny, optimistic part of me had hoped for a reprieve. Hoped that Connor's presence would act as a barrier between sleep and sorrow. Guess not.

I drew a rasping breath, gathering the shards of my voice.

"Sorry. Sorry, sorry. I'm okay. I am."

"I know. It was just a dream." He crawled up beside me anyway and leaned against the wall, wrapped me in the blanket, then in his arms. "Go back to sleep."

"Oh. No, that's not happening anytime soon. You can keep working—I'm fine."

"I know you are." But he didn't move. "Is this a regular thing?"

"Since I was five."

He fell silent, catching the meaning in the timeline. His breath moved slow and warm against my temple; his heart beat strong against my back, twisted its way into my lungs. Triggered a confusing, too-familiar ache that didn't belong anywhere near the moment. My head turned and tipped toward him, forehead pressing against his cheek, and it wasn't so bad at all, letting someone hold me up.

"How long was I asleep, Connor?"

"No idea." I felt his smile against the bridge of my nose. "I woke up, and everyone was gone but you. Did Sadie get home okay?"

"Grey picked her up. She left me her keys. . . . I can get going if you need me to. I didn't mean to sleep so long."

"Stay. If you want."

My bones ached with the weight of his words. I looked up and met his eyes, found my reflection, and so much more. He was so close to that edge—less than a step between safe and sorry. I couldn't unsee it. I didn't want to.

"I will. A little longer, anyway."

"As long as you like. Lane." He tucked my hair behind my ear, tipped forward slowly until our foreheads met. "You look so sad."

"I'm sorry. It's not you. I don't know what it is, really. It's—"

"It's everything," he whispered, "and nothing. All at once."

He caught the tear before it reached my cheek, smoothing it beneath my eye. He wasn't quick enough to catch the one that followed, though; after that, he stopped trying. Too many words trembled on my tongue, all far beyond our boundaries. All aching to finally be said.

Instead, the dream snuck past them and fell into the world— how the bathroom itself changes slightly, from night to night—how the mirror breaks, sometimes a webbed crack, sometimes a single line. Maybe the light bulbs are gone, or the linens askew on the racks; maybe they're in the sink or hung on the tub's edge, so the ends brush the floor. How my mother sprawls on the tiles, mirroring reality, legs crooked at the knee, arms open. Veins open. Head to one side, staring up at me through sightless eyes—except, some nights, she's different, too.

Sometimes she walks.

Sometimes she stands in the tub, partially hidden by the shower curtain. Sometimes she hangs from the rod, spins in slow circles, arms twisting around each other like the chains of a swing until they run out of length and reverse, unspooling faster and faster, and her bones break the other way, with a squeal like rusty hinges. Sometimes she's smiling, sometimes she's crying. Sometimes her mouth parts and unleashes a sorrowful banshee wail, sends it riding out on a wash of blood.

Sometimes she opens her eyes and they look like mine.

I poured all that into the air between us——every hideous detail, every bit of anguish. Every drop of fear and horror. And when those words ran out, Connor was still there, one hand gripped in both of mine, the other cupping the back of my head.

"I'm so sorry," he said. "No one should have to dream those things."

"Bad as they are, the reality was worse. I'd take bad dreams forever if it meant I could truly forget that day."

I shuddered and leaned into him, my cheek finding the hollow between his shoulder and collarbone as he hunched around me, holding his arm in front of us. Pushing up his sleeve as he spoke, revealing his cuff.

"This is the very first piece I made when I moved in here. And this"——he unsnapped it, tossed it aside, turned his hand palm up——"is why I made it."

His wrist was a nocturnal thing, soft and pallid from lack of sun. Smooth from rubbing raw and healing over countless times until it learned to love the constant slide of leather. Bisected from the palm on down——three inches of raised, pale scar tissue, flanked by the starburst ghosts of stitches.

"Oh my God. What is this?"

"Rock bottom. I was in a bad place, for a long time. I'd been sick for a month, couldn't keep a job. I was out of money, out of food. No place to stay. No one would help me."

"Not even Sadie?"

"Sadie was fourteen when they kicked me out. I didn't see her again until she learned to drive and tracked me down here. So yeah, when I say I was alone . . . well, even she doesn't know about this scar." His arm tightened around me; his chin tucked itself against my shoulder. His voice was calm and unperturbed, so casual it cut my heart.

"I'm sorry. I don't mean to bring all this back for you, Connor. I shouldn't have——"

"Stop. I want you to know. If I can come back from my worst, Lane, you can get through this. You're stronger than I ever was. And when everything falls apart, know at least one person would be devastated if you let it take you down too."

I know he felt my breath catch, felt it restart again, shudder from my body in a wash of chills. I pulled away, just enough to slide around and see him. His eyes were raw, his face ragged along the seams of his usual blasé mask. This boy, who wore so many, and wore them all so well; who hadn't hesitated to reach for me, even as he risked himself against my jagged edges.

He's going to fall in love with you someday.

Sadie's words, slurred and swoony, wrapped in cinnamon. Seething with truth.

This was bad.

Too many boys had gotten attached and proclaimed their love——a Whitman's Sampler of Jeremys, trying in vain to coax reciprocations from my reluctant throat. But they didn't really love *me*—they loved my face, sure. They loved my body, my long hair, my lips and arms and legs wrapped around them—they loved that plenty, until they realized it was all they got, and then came the pouts and the glares. Then came the tears. As if they hadn't been plenty enthusiastic at the idea of no-strings sex before they found themselves entangled in it. As if they'd ever come within a country mile of the girl I really was.

What I had with Connor, though, was an intricate thing—a tapestry of chemistry and affection, friendship and respect. An unfamiliar sort of string, wound tight around my heart. It wasn't that dreamy, unmistakable certainty. It wasn't love.

But it was something. And what was wrong with me, that I stood so ready to snuff it out? It damn sure was more than could be cobbled together from the scraps of hopefuls past. It was more than an imagined touch through a literal wall.

It was inexplicable. The words knotted around my thoughts and each other and the unaccustomed twists of my tongue as I closed the distance between us, reached for his hands, pressed my lips against his scars—first the one I gave him, then the one he gave himself. Covered his mouth with my own to block any hint of reply.

The breath left his body as I let mine speak for us both. Let my skin whisper everything I couldn't say.

21

I FOUND MY FATHER IN THE KITCHEN, STANDING VERY close to his new bride. Her hands were lost in his, wrapped around the wooden spoon they dragged in slow circles through a simmering pot. She was wreathed in steamy swirls of lavender and rosemary, focused beyond what the task required. He watched her furrowed face like it was the green light on the end of a goddamn dock, his mouth stretched into a grin that conjured all the eye rolls in my inventory.

"Lotion?" I chirped.

"Infusion." Dad took a step back, moving the pot to a cool burner. "An infusion that, yes, will be blended into lotion, bottled, and delivered by night's end."

He turned to me, taking in my boots and infinity scarf, the hurried way I moved around the kitchen, grabbing granola bars and packs of raw almonds, dried fruit, and my Brita bottle. The water at the warehouse was potable, but just barely—I'd asked Paul if they had a filtration system, and he'd given me a look that was less an answer than a dismissal. Better safe than sorry.

"Heading out, Elaine?"

"Sadie's on her way over. We'll be at the warehouse, barring a change of plans."

"Don't leave the county without telling me. That's all I ask." He glanced at Skye, whose eyebrows had achieved flight over eyes loaded with intention. "Can we sit for a moment before you go? It's been a while since our last chat."

Fuck. They stood there wearing matching smiles, both emanating guilt-tinged camaraderie. Both perfectly aware that "chats" with Elaine had taken a back seat to everything else eons before their wedding day. My father, reaching for me through too many years. Long past the point where I could consider reaching back.

"Sure, we can chat." I sat at the table, eyes fixed warily on their earnest, hopeful faces as they followed suit. "What's up?"

"Nothing is 'up,' per se. That is to say, there's nothing untoward looming, to my limited knowledge. You've never given me a reason to mistrust you, and at this point, my feelings are incidental—'you have your way. I have my way. As for the right way, the correct way, and the only way, it does not exist.'"

"Nietzsche, Dad? Really?" Fucking philosophy majors.

"It works for my purpose, okay? What I'm saying is, you're legally an adult now, Elaine, and I respect that. I'm quite aware you grew up long ago." He was quiet for a moment, composure betrayed by the up-and-down scurry of his Adam's apple. "What I mean to say is—"

"Rob. May I?" Skye squeezed Dad's hand, and he nodded, choked by his own unsaid words. He looked at the table, eyes fluttering, mouth working. Jee. Zus. "Elaine, honey, we wanted to talk to you about Connor Hall."

"Okay."

They waited expectantly. I waited, silent and stone cold, not about to give them a single goddamn detail not preceded by a question. Skye picked up on that fast enough.

"We don't want to overstep, sweetheart. This is your home—you'll always be safe and respected in this space, and can tell us as much or as little as you feel comfortable sharing. Healthy boundaries and open communication are essential in any relationship, familial or romantic, committed or not. If you and Connor are getting serious, we should probably discuss—"

"He's not trying to convert you, is he?" Dad's outburst startled even Skye. "That church his father runs—it's a complete warping of the New Testament, crafted to benefit the patriarchal agenda of its leaders and utterly devoid of the true message of the man they call their Christ. It's disgusting, and if I find out he's trying to brainwash you, I'll—"

"Holy living—Dad, stop. Believe me, that is not the case."

"Are you absolutely sure? They have a very subtle, very insidious recruitment method. Your brother has seen it firsthand in his relationship, and I firmly believe he's only held strong in his own faith so far because that same inherent misogyny doesn't allow poor Sadie to make demands of him."

"Huh. Has anyone told Sadie that, or—?"

"It's a tragedy, really." Skye shook her head. "That sweet girl, looking to Greyson as her ultimate authority, as if he'd ever dream of exploiting another human being. We don't want to see you led down that same path by your own boyfriend."

"I appreciate that, but it's not an issue. Connor is an atheist and a feminist, and completely estranged from his parents. And he's not my boyfriend, anyway."

Their relief was a burst of elation. They actually fell back into their chairs.

"An atheist. That's wonderful, Elaine," my father sighed. "You have no clue how worried I've been over this." He stood and turned back to the stove, wet a dishtowel, and started wiping down the splattered surface. "Have a good night, and don't worry about work tomorrow. Take the day off. Have some fun."

"And see if you can't convince Greyson to have some fun too," Skye said, reaching over to pat my hand. "I wish he'd take a page from your book, to tell you the truth. He seems more repressed than usual."

I had to chomp the inside of my cheek. If only she knew.

"I'll talk to him if the subject comes up. Or tell him to talk to you."

"Thank you, sweetie. Robby, honey, let me do that. You get the shea butter and coconut oil, and we'll finish up this batch."

They were back in their bubble, and I was racing down the hall, desperate to get to my bedroom before the laughter poured out of me like rain. Conversion. Patriarchal agendas. Robby, for fuck's fucking sake. It was all too much.

"What's so funny?"

Grey's voice snaked past me before I could close the door. I collapsed on the bed, giggling into my cupped hands as he followed me in.

"Our parents. They just sat me down for their version of The Talk."

"They what? What did they say?"

"Not much. It was all about Connor, and boundaries, and respecting my secularism. The patriarchy. You know them. Skye is actually more worried about your repression, so unless you have a spare half hour, I'd steer clear of the kitchen."

"What the fuck. *My* repression? That's just . . ." His voice was the opposite of amused, his face a sudden burst of color. I covered my mouth, choked down my remaining mirth. "This family is so goddamn messed up. I'm the problem, yet they're fine with *you*?"

"Why wouldn't they be fine with me? I'm not doing anything wrong."

"Aside from your little warehouse sleepovers? Oh, nothing. I guess you worked out a payment plan for your art space after all."

It was a knife in the back, blade dipped in his most bitter thoughts. His mouth twisted, gaped around a flash of fear and regret, as if surprised those words had made it past his lips.

"Get out of here, Greyson."

"I didn't mean that. I didn't. I—"

I leaped off the bed and started toward him, but he stood his ground, a wall of fire and frustration blocking my doorway. Too intense, and far too close.

"Out. Now."

"No."

I blinked up at him, then shoved him backward, sucked the air from his lungs and the fight from his bones. Then again, and his hands flew to catch my wrists, but instead of blocking me, he drew me in, held my gaze, pressed my palms to the hammer of his heart. My own heart burst and shattered, re-formed and raged. He had no reason to look so wrecked; no right to draw me in with eyes that pleaded for forgiveness and understanding. Nothing made sense when he looked at me like that—not the drag of his thumbs over my pulse points, soft in contrast to his grip; not the chill that ripped down my back, or the sizzle of blood in my veins. How had we ever managed to breathe without the other? How had I thought we could end in anything but ruin?

I yanked my hands from his and pointed to the door behind him, too broken to hide the tears gathering at my lash line. Too furious to ever let them fall.

"GET. OUT."

"Elaine."

That was all I heard—my name, low and hard, the desperation leaking out around its edges. It said too much and not enough, and only the doorbell stopped his voice before it undid our lives with a rush of words.

The ten-minute drive to the warehouse was spent in a whirlpool of Sadie's chatter. She kept it up the whole time, I'll give her that; her upbeat monologue plowed right through my blistering silence and the barely checked ire Grey had settled into once he'd suppressed his angst. The lot was overflowing when we arrived, packed beyond capacity. Extra cars lined both sides of the road, forcing Sadie to maneuver into a faraway patch of curbside grass. She managed to park without incident, but that didn't stop Grey from cranking the bitch volume to its highest setting.

"Wow, this is a pain in the ass," he grouched, catching my eyes in the rearview. "Why didn't you tell us there was a party tonight?"

"I didn't know there was."

"So he doesn't even run these things by you? Nice."

"He doesn't need my permission, Greyson. What a concept, huh?"

"You two are so silly," Sadie broke in over Grey's splutters, "sniping at each other all the time, like me and *my* brother. I think it's really healthy—like you're becoming a real family."

I scoffed my way out of the car and was halfway to the warehouse before either of them had crossed the road. They caught up with me just inside the door, the three of us winding through the crowded front room. I turned to face them when we reached the hallway.

"See you guys later."

"So you're ditching us." Grey stopped in his tracks, and Sadie kept going, jerking to a stop when his arm ran out. "Should've known. Should've fucking known, huh?"

His voice drew both our gazes, two sets of eyes—hers, wide

and stricken; mine, a dark challenge. Grey glared back at me, ignoring Sadie.

"What is your problem, Greyson?"

"Why would I have a problem? Go ahead, go get your fix from——what is he, anyway? Sure as fuck not your boyfriend. Can you even call him your friend at this point?"

"Grey?" Sadie's words were small, her voice smaller. "What's wrong, baby?"

"Actually, know what?" he continued, as if she hadn't said a word. "I think you *should* go back there. Go ask *him* exactly what he thinks he is to you."

"He knows where he stands. You'd be amazed——sex and honesty aren't mutually exclusive." I cracked a small, mean smile as he faltered. "Not that you'd know anything about either."

"That's enough. Both of you."

Sadie's eyes darted between us, her mouth thinning down by the second as Grey's cheeks went from slashes of angry pink to a solid, deep, guilty red.

"We," she said, speaking to me but staring hard at him, "are going to go mingle. I'll come back and get y'all once *he* calms down."

"Take your time," I said. "Make sure you get that collar on him nice and tight."

"Excuse me?" Her face was a cavern of shock, wavering between comprehension and denial. Her mouth worked over a thousand unsaid things. Part of me wanted her to say them all——part of me was absolutely dying for her to unleash every-thing festering in our little trio. I raised my eyes over her head and met Grey's. I could bring him down with a word, and he knew it, and all at once, I'd had enough. It was so ridiculous, in that moment, to think he could've ever been more than a habit.

I'd spent years outside his orbit, gazing inward, the whole of the universe at my back. Now there he was facing me, finally wanting me. Hating me, for the way I writhed beneath his skin. His eyes were hard and angry, shot through with a fear that clawed at my throat. Like a kid caught with too many cookies, pathetic and trapped, so clueless it made me sick, and when Sadie turned to face him, they melted into sorrow. She stared, then stammered, then flinched away as he reached for her with peni-tent hands. I watched his silence devour them both, confessing everything she'd never wanted answered.

I watched them break, from a place beyond words.

I turned and walked away, half expecting one of her shrill admonishments to slap the back of my head, or one of his snarls to skitter after me and eat up my wake.

There was nothing from either but the loudest kind of silence.

CONNOR WAS EXACTLY WHERE I THOUGHT HE'D BE: IN the living space, at the drafting table, focused on his sketchbook. He looked up and smiled as I stalked toward him, blocked his greeting with a kiss that nearly knocked him off his stool. Let sensation overwhelm me; sighed away the memory of Grey's rage, and his insults, and his tortured, muddled eyes.

"Okay, then," Connor breathed, brushing the hair away from my flushed face when he finally drew back, his own hair wrecked by my searching fingers. "It's good to see you, too, Lane."

"Sorry. I might have gotten carried away."

"Yeah, not complaining. Something bothering you?"

"Nothing. Grey's in a mood." I pushed aside all thoughts of said mood, and everything it meant. Connor turned back to his sketchbook, hair falling forward to hide his face. "Sadie's out there dealing with him. She said she'll come get us after they mingle."

"Too many people are here if shit has reached mingling capac-ity," Paul yawned from his stool as I settled on the futon. "Laney, tell your boy to send his friends on home so I can get some peace."

"This wasn't my idea," Connor said, shooting a look at the door. "I thought that was *your* crowd."

"No. It isn't." Paul thumped his forehead against the sculpture. "If I catch the bitch responsible for putting these together every weekend, I swear to God."

"Right there with you. Once Sadie gets back here, I'll clear it out and shut down for the night."

Paul nodded in approval, rolling out of my line of sight. I sighed out the last of my nerves, stretched my legs, reached for my toes. Lifted my eyes to meet Connor's as he rose and walked toward me, holding my gaze. I tipped my face toward him, but he leaned past me, retrieved my knitting project from its paper grocery bag home beneath the futon, and tipped it into my lap; his follow-up kiss landed on my forehead. I smiled up at him, caught the edge of his answering grin as he resumed his work, and if that flutter in my chest even hinted at turning to butterflies, I'd rip it out with my own bare hands.

I flexed my fingers, picked up my needles, and let them set my rhythm. The blanket flowed over my crossed legs, warm and blue and ever growing.

"That's really coming along," Paul said after a bit. "Though I must say, every hour you spend on it is an hour you've spent here *not* wearing out my boy, so he may not be a fan."

"Ha, ha," I said, throwing a skein at Connor's chuckling back. It sailed past him, and he went after it, dropping it back in my lap on the heels of a wink. "It was your boy's idea in the first place. He even spun the yarn."

"The poor girl needs something to do when I'm obsessing over work," Connor said. "Oh, that reminds me, Lane. I have something for you."

"'Reminds' you," Paul scoffed. "Like you've had a single other damn thought for the past two days."

"For me?" I blinked at Connor's hesitant face, at the blush staining his cheekbones. The nervous fingers he ran through his hair. "It's early for Christmas, isn't it?"

"This isn't a Christmas present. Consider it an apology, since I managed to traumatize you during the creative process."

He reached into the shallow drawer of his drafting table and pulled out a bracelet, turned it over in his hands before offering it to me. I ran my fingers over the tarnished twists and folds, the intricate carvings, the inlay of tiny red sunstones—earth and fire, forged together in a flawless cuff. The memory rushed in and sucked me out to sea: the pale, blue-threaded underside of his wrist next to the darker lines of mine. A measuring tape and a sheet of copper. Blood-edged shears and a blood-edged blade, my hands trying and failing to close the wound I'd made in his.

"Oh my God." I slid it on, blown away by its weightless, perfect fit, the way it seemed to grow from my wrist. No boy—no person had ever given me such a gift. "Connor."

"Oh, thank Christ," Paul said, swiping a sheet of sandpaper around the base of his sculpture. "He's been all but soiling himself over that thing for weeks. If you didn't like it, he'd probably give up the trade for good."

Connor's smile was a living thing, shy and radiant, as he leaned in to kiss me over the pile of yarn. I set my needles aside and closed my eyes, breathed him, slid my fingers through his hair, and pulled him closer. Knocked the pencil from behind his ear and tugged the air from his lungs on a low hum.

It was a different sort of kiss than the one I'd given him in greeting. This one sparked from a sweeter burn and grew from there, snaking along the path of my pulse. This was as close as I'd been to something real—a wisp of longing, a thrill of anticipation. A thread of fear, woven tight around my throat.

Butterflies, for sure. Fuck.

"I love it," I whispered as he drew back. "Thank you."

"It's a pale imitation of its inspiration." His smile widened at my scoff. "No contest at all."

"The man and his muse," Paul cackled from his stool as Connor stood, retrieving his pencil from the floor. "Keep that up, Laney, and you'll get a matching cuff for the other wrist. Rings, necklaces, a fuckin' crown—anything you want. Shit, you're about to make me jealous."

"Hands off, Paul," I teased. "This one's mine."

Connor set his pencil on the table with audible finality. I caught him as he tackled me, sighing at the welcome weight of his body, the familiar way we fit. His words drifted into my ear, so soft they were nearly lost along the way.

"Am I?"

So wrong, to answer with a yes—risky to think, worse to voice. Impossible not to, when the endgame was that smile lowering to meet mine.

This was so very, very bad.

A collective whoop rang out from the front room, followed by yells and raucous laughter. Paul emerged from behind the sculpture, sneering at the closed door.

"And there's the cue to shut it down. This all-artists-welcome arrangement is officially on my last nerve."

"I'm on it."

Connor dropped a last hurried kiss on my mouth and rolled off the futon. I sat up slowly, straightened my sweater, finger-combed my hair forward to hide my flushed cheeks. Suddenly wished I could take back my words and my nods, and whatever the hell had possessed me to let the previous moment spool out unchecked, as if I could just *say* those things and think he'd let it slide. As if it wouldn't ruin us, to admit it might be true.

If I looked at him—if I let myself acknowledge his heart, or if he caught even a glimpse into the unsolved puzzle of mine—everything we were would unravel.

He moved around the room, collecting his dropped sketchbook and scattered pencils. I took a chance and slid off the futon, crept toward the door, wishing I were a little bit smaller. A lot more invisible would also do.

"Lane."

My name stopped me in my tracks. I forced my lips into a small, painful smile, turned to meet his eyes. They were wide and bright, slashed through with raw streaks of hope, and oh God, there it was. What had I done?

"Yes?"

"Everything okay?"

"It's fine. Just helping you find Sadie."

"And Grey." Paul rolled his stool slowly into view, then shoved off suddenly with his feet. He glided across the room, side-eye locked on mine, and drifted to a stop inches from the wall. "Your brother's out there too. Wouldn't want to forget about him."

"He's not my brother."

I left it at that. I turned my back on both of them and stepped into the hallway, immediately choked on a waft of chemicals and vomit. The bathroom door was halfway open, and the light was on, which meant someone—hopefully not Sadie—was either in there making their personal business public, or they'd made a mess of the place and wandered off. I held my breath and knocked. Nothing. The door opened wider at the second tap of my knuckles, and I stepped inside, almost tripped over somebody's outstretched boot. The spray bottle lay on the floor next to it, diluted bleach water dripping slowly from its cracked nozzle. My heartbeat doubled. I recoiled from the sharp, familiar stink, fighting back a strange scuttle of panic.

"Oh. Sorry. I—hey."

The guy slumped against the wall in front of the puke-spattered sink, chin-to-chest, legs askew, face hidden by greasy hanks of blond hair. Shirt and wall coated in what hadn't made it to the basin. Paul was going to be *pissed*.

"Dude, come on——at least get over the toilet. Are you okay?"

He shifted and moaned, head rolling to the side in a half-assed approximation of a nod. Close enough.

"All right, then. Let's get you up."

He heard me, at least. His head bobbed again, and he reached up, his hand all bones and scabs and chapped, stained fingers closing around mine, nail beds cracked and packed with grime, and what the hell was I doing. He was high off his ass, oddly familiar, and oh man, was he a mess. Skin like an old book binding, cracked and weathered. Mouth a decrepit graveyard of sores and rotten teeth. Eyes a scatter of burst blood vessels edging deep-space pupils. He was barely older than me.

I knew that face. I'd seen it on a street corner, shy and skittish, smiling at the promise of hot coffee. Seen it twisted in a sneer a million years ago, the day Connor taught me to spin yarn: Aiden, who broke locks and stole tools, got himself ousted from the fringes of the fringe. Who stretched out his shirtsleeves, to hide his shaking hands.

So weird, how life unravels people, weaving their loose ends into yours, thread by thread. This boy——this Aiden, who wasn't even supposed to *be* in the warehouse, let alone coating its interior in vomit; the world had juxtaposed us yet again, insistently and inexplicably, as if determined to make him stick. Damn if the third time wasn't the fucking charm.

I had a single goal: locate Sadie and Grey. I was fully justified to go do that, and let Paul scoop this kid off the floor and howl about the bathroom. Let Connor figure out the fastest, most efficient way to remove him from the warehouse without trailing muck all over the place. Let them scour puke off the wall and sink; maybe send Grey home for a spare smudge stick while they were at it, to cut the stench of soiled clothing and unwashed skin. This was their place—this wasn't my concern.

But that was the thing—this guy, Aiden? He wasn't *anyone's* concern. Hadn't been for a long, long time, from the look of him, and what the hell was *my* problem, that I could so casually wash my hands of a human being? What kind of shitty hypocrite was I to walk away, when I'd spent the past month wrapped around a boy who'd suffered the same indignities and indifference for so long?

The least I could do was help this person stand.

I actually couldn't, though. He was deadweight and limp limbs, way too heavy to lift. There was no way this would work without getting in close, wrapping my arms around his sick-damp torso. I wasn't sure I had that in me, good intentions or no—but I never had the chance to find out.

Aiden's eyes snapped open all at once, inches from mine. They skittered around the room, and there was no spark of recognition or any other thing, only haze; then a sudden flare of panic, and then nothing but whites and burst-vein red as he seized, limbs convulsing, neck locking. Hand crushing mine in a spastic, concrete vise.

The world caved in. I tripped on my own feet and fell hard, took the brunt of the floor in my left knee. Found myself on his level, eye to eye, and if I could just get him off the floor—get the blood flowing to his arms and legs—if I could help him find his footing, he'd take over from there. He'd walk it off. He'd be fine.

I tried. I doubled my grip and dug in my heels. Tried so hard to stand again and pull him with me, until my wrist popped, and my foot slipped, and I landed back on my knees, and what was I doing, I couldn't help him. I couldn't begin to unwreck this train.

"Get up. Get up, get up, oh God, stop. Please, please stop."

And he did. His tremors subsided, his head lifted, his eyes hooked on mine, and it wasn't any better, that stillness—it would never be better again. His scabbed lips parted around a wet gasp. His body curled in on itself, slumped like an unstuffed doll. Released its contents, breath and waste, and it was that same dank stench—that same filth, overwhelmed by eye-stinging bleach; the tiles hard beneath my knees; the flow of still-warm blood around my tiny, bare feet; her face, icy to the touch; his hand, rough and cooling, already changing around my fingers. How was this happening again? How had I doubled back to this place?

"No." The word was a whisper, building to a wail, filling and then spilling from my mouth. "No. No no no no no."

"Lane? What's going on?" Connor's voice reached me before he did. "Are you—*oh*. Oh God."

"Connor?" Sadie was a trill in the distance, tripping toward us in a slur of twang and unsteady footsteps. "Connor, what is it?"

"Sadie, stay back." He was close, then closer, prying my hand from the literal death grip. Catching me as I sagged against him, holding me tight to his pounding heart. "Get Paul. Tell him—oh God. Oh my God."

"Tell him what? Grey, baby, can you—where did you go? Connor, Grey was right here. I think he's—oh, Lane, there you are. What's happening?"

"Get back, I said!" Connor's voice ripped through me even as she defied him, weaving her way into the tiny room. Choking on her drink as she took in the sight at my feet.

The thing in the bathroom, slumped sideways, stuck between the sink and the wall—just a thing now, though at one time it had been a he. A pitiful scarecrow of a he, all jitters and sores and underfed limbs. I don't know if he'd known me at the end, recalled my eyes or my hair, or the nervous tilt of my chin, but it didn't matter. His eyes stared through me; his mouth listed open, as if poised to speak. As if he hadn't yet realized he'd never say another word.

Aiden. Another dead body on another bathroom floor.

And just like him, I couldn't make a sound.

Then Sadie found her voice, and her screams were more than loud enough to compensate.

23

BEFORE SADIE'S SHRIEK SHOOK OFF ITS OWN ECHO, Connor was moving. He hauled me to my feet and out of the bathroom, cut a rough furrow through the gathering onlookers, one arm curled around my shoulders. We broke through the crowd, and he picked up the pace, hustling me down the hall and through the front room, where he left me by the front door before disappearing back into the chaos.

I slid down the wall and into a ball, knees drawn up, hands splayed at my sides, braced against the cool, slightly gritty floor. It wasn't long at all before I registered Sadie's hysteria, a low wail looming closer, then bursting into the room ahead of her. She trailed behind Connor, who half carried, half dragged a stagger-ing Grey. It was all nothing to me; an underwater cacophony of noise, motion, and somewhat familiar voices.

I'm not sure how, but Connor got the three of us outside and all the way across the street to Sadie's car. He dug the keys out of her purse and deposited her in the shotgun seat, then stuffed Grey into the back along with my messenger bag. I braced myself against the trunk, streaming eyes darting over every crack in the world until they landed on the warehouse—it squatted blamelessly in the lot, still and silent, but was that a thump from inside? Was the door still firmly shut, or was it sliding sideways an inch at a time, slow beyond notice, and was that a pale, bloodshot eye peering through the tiny crack? Was it staring at me from a peeling face, pocked and crusted with pus? Were there fingers just beyond the eye, ready to lock themselves around my arms, or dig my teeth out one by one with dirty nails?

There had been no blood. Not on the floor or the walls or the body in that bathroom—*today's* bathroom, the most current in the now-pluralized list; only that knowledge kept me on my feet. I didn't see Connor standing there until I felt his hands—on my arms at first, then my shoulders, urgent, and finally cupping my face. Gentle all at once, thumbs brushing the tears off my cheekbones. His calluses rasped against my wet skin.

"Lane. Look at me."

His voice snared me, dragged me in, snapped my gaze to his. That same voice that once commanded me to cut, insisting I hurt him to help myself—now steeled and ready, braced for both our pain.

"Paul's calling 911," he said. "Get my sister out of here. Get yourself home safely."

"What about you? Come with me, Connor. Please. I need you."

"God. Lane, I——" He pressed his forehead to mine, squeezing

his eyes shut. "I have to deal with things here. You can do this. Be strong."

"I can't."

"You can. I love you."

His kiss blocked any possibility of a reply. I pulled him closer, clung to him, the words racing through my veins, welling beneath my eyelids. Then he broke away and was gone all at once. He bounded across the street without looking for traffic. Without looking back at me.

The warehouse swallowed him whole, and I was on my own.

I drove away from there on someone else's autopilot. Sadie was drunk and hyperventilating; Grey was drunker, facedown and moaning into the seat, and the fact that I was still somewhat functional and not yet fully catatonic rendered me the best driver by a margin so slim it barely existed.

I don't know how I got the car home in one piece. I do know Skye took one look at all of us as we staggered in the door and went into Emergency Mom Mode—that kettle was on the stove before I had my boots off. She was blending tea leaves and wetting dishcloths, helping me into a chair. Wiping Grey's flushed face as she would a child's, then rushing him to the bathroom when he started gagging. Holding Sadie against her shoulder as she sobbed out the events of the night.

I slouched in a kitchen chair and tried to ground myself—tried focused breathing, five different ways. Meditation. Sipping my tea. All the tricks I knew, all useless. Finally, I left the table and headed down the hall, ready to ball up forever under my quilt. Instead, I found Skye tiptoeing out of my bedroom, closing the door gently behind her.

"I put Sadie in your bed," she whispered, glancing over my shoulder at the bathroom, where her son stretched prone in front of the toilet. "I wasn't sure if they're sexually active. I didn't want to create a situation."

"Oh." God. Fucking kill me. "Um, no. It's fine if she stays with me. Thank you." I met her eyes, beyond grateful they held the compassion we needed, instead of judgment or rage. Speaking of which. "Her parents, though. I don't——"

"Oh, that's handled. I called her mother, told her you two were having a sleepover and Greyson was staying at a friend's house. I know how they are."

"Wow. You're being really great about all this, Skye."

"It's not that I approve of their behavior," she said, thoroughly failing at the whole stern-mom thing. "It's one thing to have a drink or two, and quite another to be irresponsible and sloppy. I'm glad you were sober, and able to get them home, but you can always call us. You and Greyson are adults now, but we won't—— well, we'll never *not* worry. This is just so horrible. That poor boy. You poor, poor kids."

The words overwhelmed me, as did her gentle hug. Both fed the gnawing in my chest.

"I need to get ahold of Connor," I wavered. "I need to see if he's okay."

"He can stay here tonight, if need be. I can pick him up." Grey came to life behind us, ejecting a stream of beer vomit onto the rug. "Oh, honey. Sit up, Greyson. Take aim."

I left her to haul him up and redirect his face to the toilet bowl. Sadie was out cold, so I crept through the house and slipped out the back door, sat on the steps overlooking the yard. The night was clear and still; the air nipped my face with frost-edged teeth. I pulled up Connor's number and started a text, fingers stuttering over all the wrong letters. Stumbling over the memory of our last kiss.

I shook the thought away, turned all focus on my breath, as if pranayama could counteract Connor's words, let alone his love. That moment yawned like a mouth around my heart, chewed through flesh and senses, left me weak. Left me shaking, in a way even his body never had.

Connor Hall was in love with me. And now I had to text him. Fuck.

Fine. It would be fine. He was a pragmatic kind of guy—he'd know better than to expect a hot take on his feelings less than an hour after he'd pulled my fingers from the clasp of a freshly deceased hand. He'd be cool about it regardless of how I'd fucked up before, what with all the kissing and sincerity, and other bad ideas, and I'd do exactly what I'd planned: I'd make sure he was okay. I'd pass along Skye's offer. I'd stonewall any attempt at

emotional discussion, and if it meant I had to camp in the goddamn backyard to avoid that little nighttime chat, so be it. Sadie
was in my bed, anyway—even if he did stay over, he'd likely
sleep on the couch.

I could do this. It would be all right.

I shook off the tremors and doubled my focus, finally managed
coherency on the fourth try.

It's Lane. Are you okay?

We'll be fine. Can't really talk now, cops are all over.
You made it home?

**Yes. You can stay here tonight. Skye says she'll pick
you up.**

Tell her thank you, but I can crash w/Paul at his
family's place. Don't know how long we'll be here.
Don't want anyone to wait up.

OK. Take care of yourself.

You too.

And that was it. I wiped my face and stowed my phone,
headed back inside, ambled aimlessly through the kitchen
and down the hall. Skye emerged from the bathroom with an

armful of towels and the rug, all wadded up and reeking of sick.

"Connor's staying with his roommate," I told her. "He said thank you for the offer, though."

"As long as he knows he's welcome here. Sweetie, could you go sit with Greyson? I'll be back to take over after I load the washer and check on Sadie. Oh, and I texted Rob—he's on his way home now. Shouldn't be long."

I nodded at her retreating back, zombied on past her to the bathroom. Grey emerged from the toilet, blinking at me through teary eyes as I slid down the wall to sit beside him. We were far too familiar with each other's puke.

"Oh. Hi, Elaine."

"Hi."

"That guy," he croaked, wiping his mouth on the back of his hand. "Was he—"

"Yeah, Greyson. He was."

"God. That's so fucked up. Did someone call the police?"

"Why do you think we ran out of there so fast? Connor practically shoved us in the car."

"Quick thinking. Good for him. The underage thing, and all that—nothing but trouble. Is this one of his?" He dragged his finger over the bracelet, eyelids drooping shut at my nod. "Pretty. Suits you."

"He made it for me."

"Inspiring. Inspirational. He gets you. Really sees you. Must be nice."

"He loves me." It was an exhale wrapped in a bone-weary

sigh, less a whisper than a ghost—the kind that haunts an already occupied space. The kind that clamors for human attention, waiting for acknowledgment to set it free.

If Grey heard me, he didn't react. Instead, he dry-heaved again, slumped against my shoulder. He was heavy and solid and warm, his hair silky on my cheek. It smelled familiar, a vague blend of his sweat and my own shampoo. His lips grazed my collarbone, jump-starting my pulse; my arms rose to circle him, but just barely—carefully, as if anything more would break us both. My name slid out on a half-formed mumble, sultry and sour against my neck. This was so very far from the way I'd once imagined holding him.

"I'm sorry," he moaned. "I am so. Sorry. I didn't mean those things I said to you. I didn't. I'm just so tired, like, just when I think I can deal—that I'm enough, and it'll be okay—then it all comes apart on the insides, and it's not fair. It's not. And I end up hurting everyone—hurting my Sadie—and I can't do this any—"

He gagged on his words and lunged for the bowl again, barely making it. I leaned against the wall and closed my eyes, too drained to translate his angst. Instead, I waited out his spasms, dismembering the evening in my mind. Placing each piece in a separate mental pocket.

I severed Aiden immediately from the rest, tucked that one far away, knowing, even then, he would never ever stay buried. Aiden, and his stare and his stench, the jut of his bones. His rotten teeth and sores and runny eyes. His threadbare sock, peeking through a hole in his boot. His dirty hand, tight around mine, then slack. Dead in my grip, long beyond help.

The memory undid everything else about that night—the horrible things Grey said to me; his attitude and drunkenness; the revolting mess to which he'd reduced himself. Sadie's proud spine, and her tears, and the barely there mask of her stern frown. Connor's hands and mouth and laughing eyes. His parting words, which should have sparked a surge of that gentle, floating contentment I'd felt when he'd gifted me the bracelet—that temporary cradle, upended all at once onto stone.

And holy shit, even if he'd always planned to tell me tonight— even if the bracelet had been the natural first step on a path to those words—his actual timing couldn't have been worse. Who declares his love on the heels of such a grisly scene? Connor Hall, that's who—a boy so damaged and cynical, it was a miracle he could stand to love at all, much less love a girl who picked sensation over feeling at every opportunity. Who'd gone ahead and walked the line between the two until she'd scuffed it right down into the dirt.

I'd loved Grey so long, I wasn't sure what the word looked like when pried apart from his name. Surely it was more than a desperate jumble of words, or a scorched-earth kiss. More than a whisper tucked between a car and a corpse.

It was probably a good thing I'd been too fucked up to answer.

24

SHE LAY IN THE BATHTUB, ONE EYE OPEN IN A HORRID wink. She'd pulled the stopper already, and I knew what would happen next, because I'd seen it endless times before: The blood would drain faster than gravity, faster than reality. It would disappear down the drain, and her toes would follow. Then her feet; her legs, bones cracking and warping, crushed into the shape of the pipes. All the way up, hips and waist and ribs and arms. Her mouth would open, and she'd scream herself bloody once more, restain the world in a wet, miserable shriek.

The bathroom door locked behind me again, not that I'd closed it. Not that she had either—she couldn't have, not from the bathtub. Her sobs echoed off the tile, distorted by the drip-drop of falling water. Not water at all, though—blood. My blood. My arms, opened to the elbows. My legs, soaked in the aftermath of cyclic pain. My reflection, shifting to hers, then back again; her mouth, shifting from laughter to screams until her voice ran out over my fingertips. Until the mirror burst into shards that pierced my eyes, and all I saw was red.

She knelt on the blood-soaked rug, her arms extended, reaching for me in a silent plea, and it was my mother. How could I not go to her? How could I pull away, even as her teeth bit and tore into my cheek, mangling the soft, defenseless flesh? Why couldn't I get away when she started in on my jaw, popped it loose, ripped it free, taking my tongue along and swallowing them both? Why couldn't I wake up, even when I saw her mouth unhinging, opening impossibly wide as she leaned in to consume me whole?

Those were the things that followed me through a day. Those things lurked beneath every automatic smile when I was called upon in class, or working or texting or spinning or breathing—a constant flow of tasks and motion. Anything to bury them deeper. Was there help enough for it in the world? Was there a magic pill or drink or bullet—some first step on a path leading safely out of my own mind?

It was no big trick to skip bedtime that first night, binge on Netflix and double-strength coffee. Knit a hat or two. Nothing I hadn't done before. Grey even wandered out and joined me on the couch, those eyes grazing my limbs, lingering on the length of my neck. Hanging a beat too long on my parted lips.

Grey. My earnest, anxious, well-meaning stepbrother, who hadn't looked me in the face since the night he'd lain drunk in my lap. Who hadn't gone a day without finding an excuse to touch me, no matter how minor: a nudge of his shoulder at the kitchen counter. His foot bumping my leg as he settled on the couch. Our fingers brushing as he passed me the remote or the throw blanket or a cup of tea. All minimal and neutral, almost accidental. All too deliberate to pass off as nothing. He'd been attentive and subdued, kind to me in little ways—fixing my coffee in the morning, picking up my slack on chores. Setting up study sessions in hopes of slowing my academic free fall, helping me stay afloat with extra-credit homework. Tiny peace offerings, absent of strings.

Not two months prior, the slightest nod from him would have left me reeling, senses heightened and helpless and hoping for more. Now I was as numb to him as I was to everything else. She engulfed the world, my mother—blotted out the sun itself, never mind the barely flickering flame of Grey.

So it went: the corpse of Annie Jamison, splitting every seam of night. Flung at my feet, over and over, by Aiden's stiff, dirty hands.

My mind was earthquake rubble, the world mixed and muddled, well beyond the boundaries of plain old fucked up. Everything bleeding into everything else.

There was an easy fix, of course—one solution, and one alone to refresh my body and realign my world: sleep. Natural. Simple. Unacceptable.

Sleeping felt like dying. So I stayed awake.

25

"'DYING / IS AN ART, LIKE EVERYTHING ELSE. / I DO IT
exceptionally well.'"

The words slipped out ragged, sanding the rasp from my throat as I paced back and forth between the metal room's work-table and supply shelves. It was a less than welcome place for that particular poem—not the room itself, but my weary mind, already brimming with stifled horrors.

Connor's voice wove into my whisper, picking up where I paused for breath. He spoke the next line without me.

"'I do it so it feels like hell.'"

I turned to catch the arch of his eyebrow peeking out the top of his safety goggles. His sleeves were rolled to the elbows; his hair, as always, at odds with the universe, and it didn't take more than a look to spark the air between us.

We hadn't kissed since that horrible night—a week and counting of accidental glances and unfinished sentences. I'd forced myself through the warehouse door the morning after the party, determined to cling to what I could of his world—the living space and the metal room, Paul and the spinning wheel and the constant creative buzz. I refused to let another trauma retool a place I loved into an etching of ruin. I'd face whatever waited. I'd been through worse.

But for all my bravado, I couldn't set foot in that bathroom, no matter how badly I needed to go. I couldn't even look at the door.

To his credit, Connor had played along without prompting, projecting a skewed, careful version of our pre-declaration dynamic. He sure as hell hadn't dealt any extra emotional confessions from the bottom of the deck, and what he'd said before was already primed for burial—he had yet to try recapturing what could have been a sacred moment. He hadn't let those words spool out a second time, or said anything else sweet, or romantic, or even remotely special. He hadn't made any of it real.

And here he was now, stealing poetry from my lips. Sending it back to me on a voice rough from too many quiet hours.

"Nice." My approval tugged a smile, real but guarded, from the edge of his mouth. "You know Plath?"

"Do I 'know Plath,' she asks. I'd be her modern incarnation, if I could write worth half a damn." His torch met the table with a soft clunk beside his unfinished work. "Interesting choice, though."

"I didn't choose it. It's for school."

"Got it. Need to talk?"

"No. I need to keep moving. I need—" A surge of whiskey splashed its way from my stomach to my mouth; I swallowed it without thinking, winced at the secondhand burn as it slid back down. Sleepless delirium with a chaser of Jack and Coke probably hadn't been the best idea, but since when had that stopped me. "God. I need it all to fade."

"What time is it? You're usually out by"—he squinted at his phone—"4:37 a.m. Christ, Lane. Why are you still awake?"

"You're still awake."

"I'm working. You're okay here, right? After—"

"I don't know. No. I'm not okay anywhere. I can't sleep."

It was pitiful how quickly the fatigue set in, as if it had been constrained only by the words themselves; locked-letter chains that shattered when they hit the air. I felt his eyes follow me as I drifted past, gathered myself into a perch on an unoccupied stool. Hid a desperate yawn behind the swing of my hair.

"Hey." Connor set aside his goggles and stretched, popping the tension out of his spine. "Come to bed. Get some rest. I can finish this tomorrow."

"No, I mean I *can't* sleep, Connor. I won't. I need to stay awake, at least until this feeling passes. If it passes." My eyes blinked and shuddered and realigned, slid over his brow and his bones. Caught and held steady on his worried mouth. "It's okay that I stay, right? If you need to work—"

"It's always 'okay.'" He stepped closer, slipped between my knees. Slid his hands in slow, careful arcs over my back as my arms rose to rest on his shoulders. The world doubled, then snapped back into hectic focus. "If you need me, work can wait."

My answer pulled up short at the edge of my breath, lingered long enough that I could have stopped it snaking through my teeth. It was a thought formed all wrong. It was the truest thing I knew, and the most confusing.

"I don't know what I need."

His slow smile dropped a curtain over eyes that never wavered, and if something in them flickered and faded, it was too small a thing to count.

"I do."

I let him consume me; let my mouth list open and my eyes fall shut, lost track of time and reason and my hold on existence. Connor's skin was warm, his hands solid, and what did it matter if love changed the angle of his arms? Would it be so bad, really, to feel its burn on his lips, or catch its sharp, sudden flavor beneath his tongue? Would it be so bad to never speak of it again?

His hands slid from my waist to my hips, then lower, and he was scooping me off the stool. He was turning and walking, taking me with him as I clung to his neck, breathed deep, filled my lungs with his clean, familiar scent. It was too easy to see him as a jumble of hollows and rage and delicate bones—to overlook the strength in his arms or the grip of those hands. The way they balanced my weight through the room, down the hallway, past the looming arch of the bathroom door.

The living space was dark and still, the mattress, thick with quilts and memories. All of it begged me to rest as he picked up the Plath where we'd left off, his whisper heavy with the lovely lilt of death. Maybe he was right——the words rolled dark and slow against my neck, an audible prequel to the follow-up drag of his mouth; my teeth caught the corner of my lower lip, and everything blazed at once, hot and bright as the burn of a star. Maybe this *was* exactly what I needed.

The poem slurred to a hiss, unfinished, as I pulled him off his feet. Pulled him into the slope of my body and the rise of my knees, as they fell open to graze the edges of the world. His face above mine, then, eyes hooded with needs of his own. Poised to bring us back to reality with his own pretty words, and I couldn't let him do this to me again. Not here. Not now.

"Lane, I——"

His voice crumbled to nothing against my mouth. My hands clawed through his hair, fisted against his scalp; his blistered their way down my body, our desire blending, then burning together, and yes——*this* was what I needed. Sensory obliteration. Silence.

"Don't let me fall asleep. Please."

He didn't.

Life lived at the edge of lucidity was hardest when I counted hours——in the beginning, when I still bothered to measure time. Everything after that was a stretch of existence, of measured breaths ending in a gasp, a cold sweat, and the flicker-fade of light at the edges of my eyes. The blip of my mother, in every reflective surface.

My mind was ellipses; my voice, the pause of a comma.

Soon enough my body rebelled, dropping me over and over into tiny craters of oblivion. I lost myself throughout the day, at school and work and home—those random, minuscule bursts of unconsciousness, eyes open but sightless. It was blinking without blinking, snapping back on jolts of adrenaline, sharp and sudden as falling in a dream. Nights were a pattern book of utter hell—a half hour here, an hour there—sometimes just enough to let my guard down; let the bolt fall off the door, leaving it ready to swing wide open at the faintest tap of her knuckles.

My yoga practice, already suffering the demands of our busiest market season, dropped off entirely—it was too relaxing, too close to rest, and I had to do what I had to do, and that was god-damn stay *awake*, until wakefulness itself became its own special nightmare.

It was a hand on the hot coils of the stove burner, the broken spiral branding the space between my thumb and wrist. An accident, I'd lied, as Skye broke fat stalks from the aloe plant, her worried eyes just short of suspicious.

It was my half-blue fingertips, wrapped too tight in a twist of yarn that knotted with itself and refused to break without the frantic tugs of my teeth.

It was bitten lips and cheeks, quiet fingernails scraped along the thin skin of my wrist. Swallows of blood from a ragged tongue. Tiny bursts of pain, designed to drag me back to the world.

It was familiar—the rolling boil of my approaching cycle. The ribs-to-knees cramps that started days before the bleeding. The distinctively different cramping of my stomach and intestines, opening acts for the mainstage event. The bottle of painkillers buried in the trash; the anticipation of an ash-and-lava landslide, guaranteed eye-opening pain, and maybe that would finally be enough. Maybe I'd actually eat for a change—stuff myself, even. See how much more my body could bring up, because I couldn't exactly puke in my sleep. It would keep me on edge, at the very least.

It was all those things in an unsettled blur. Feelings came and went in flashes, and it was hell; still, though, it wasn't all bad, because the lack of feeling is the lack of things. And things that don't exist can't hurt.

I hurt myself in other ways, and found them to be more than adequate.

26

MY PATTERN BOOK WAS GONE. IT WASN'T IN MY PURSE, or on Connor's rolling cart. It wasn't buried in the futon's perpetually messy blanket pile. I scrounged through the bottom of my messenger bag, fingers fumbling over the disarray of useless pens and knitting needles and a goddamn ball of yarn, all tangled up with a king's ransom of tampons, which were finally being put to use after a three-day stress delay that had me frantic over every possible outcome. Try keeping your eyes open around the clock after a dozen hours spent vomiting up chunks of your own soul. Then try doing that while still embracing the acid bath misery as preferable to the bloodless, ominous alternative. Girl power.

"It's not here. I can't find it. Every day of my life is a collection of things I need that I can't. Goddamn. Find." I upended the bag, spilled its contents onto the futon. Nothing. No pattern book, no scrap paper, no motherfucking phone charger, and why. Why was everything always so lost. "God*damn* it."

Connor paused in his sketching, concern tweaking the corners of his mouth.

"Hey. Everything okay?"

"No, everything is not okay. My notebook isn't in here, and my piece-of-shit phone is dead, and I can't. I can't make a supply list, Connor, and I need to make a fucking supply list."

"Jesus, calm down. There's a notebook in the metal room. Or, here—go ahead and use this."

I glared at the sketchbook he offered me, then redirected the glare his way, stuffing my things haphazardly back into the bag.

"I'll wait. Wouldn't want to stumble upon my sideboob. Or Sybil's sideboob, or whoever else's sideboob is in there."

That one soared out with unexpected wrath, freeing itself from a nest I'd tried so fucking hard not to build. I tossed my head and stared him down, ignoring the spread of heat across my chest—it wasn't my business. It never had been, and the number of fucks I had the right to give sat solidly in the negatives. Still, that the issue hadn't long ago burst into bitter flight was nothing short of miraculous.

"Pardon?" Connor withdrew, eyeing me carefully. "Lane, are you okay? Who's Sybil?"

"You know who Sybil is. *You* know."

"I actually don't. Paul." His voice was calm and unhurried, yet wary, pitched neutral in the way you'd communicate a plan of action when staring down a poised and rabid dog. "Do you know a Sybil?"

"I do not." Paul's head did the slow lean out from its usual place behind the sculpture-in-progress. "Can we back up to the sideboob part?"

"You'll have to ask your boy about that," I sneered. "Sadie told me he drew mine in his little book. *Why* he drew it is anybody's guess."

"What the fuck?" Connor blinked at me, genuinely bewildered. "I never did that. I drew you, but not your—here, take a look."

I took the book from his outstretched hand and flipped through it. Experimental sketches and lists of ideas. A series of steampunk animals, composed of gears and bolts and clockfaces. Strange furniture. Dozens of pages of jewelry designs, some marked with names and measurements and price quotes, some no more than half-formed ideas. Grey and Sadie's wedding ring extravaganza. And me.

Me in profile, me sleeping, me laughing, me knitting. Me gazing out the Forester window at a starry sky. Most clothed, some hinting at the lack of them—a bare shoulder; the line of my spine; the dip of my waist, smoothed into an exposed hip. The closest thing to a nude study was a profile sketch of me in his bed, propped on my elbows, smirking over my shoulder at him. I was naked but covered, swathed in a blanket from the hips down, everything above my rib cage hidden by the swoop of my hair and the angle of my arm. No sign of my breast. Not a hint of anything.

"I'm not finding sideboobs in here," I muttered, eyes darting to Connor, then Paul, then back again.

"Because there aren't any. Apparently, the word means something different to my sister."

"Oh. Well. I'm sorry I yelled about it, then. I'm not feeling very—" I swallowed hard against a surge of nausea. Tiny lights skittered along the edges of my vision. "Sorry about the Sybil thing too, I guess."

"Lane, I have no idea what you're talking about. I've never met a Sybil in my—" Comprehension and fatigue drifted together over his face, blending into a sigh. "Sabine. You mean Sabine."

"I do in fact mean that name, thank you very much." Way to make your outburst matter, Lane. Fuck, I was tired.

"Yeah. Thanks, Sadie." Connor left his stool and sat next to me, feet on the floor, leaning backward on his hands. A casual pose that contradicted every facet of his face. "It's no secret, okay? I'll tell you all about her, but I'm not sure why you care."

"I don't." The lie leaked out on the heels of an uneven breath. I swallowed and rubbed my eyes, redirected my words so they veered closer to the truth. "I mean, I don't need to hear about her. It's not an issue."

"Good, then we can drop it. Or if you're still dying to make your little list, I'll go get that paper, and you make me one of all the guys *you* used to fuck. How many sheets do you need?"

The words prickled over my scalp, ate a trail straight to the base of my spine as I swiveled to meet his glare. Paul melted silently out of sight.

"Really? Really, Connor? I can't even express how little that has to do with you."

"I'm aware. Just like Sabine has nothing to do with you." His eyes darkened. "But as long as we're on the subject, at least *Sabine* no longer lives with me."

"That's not the same thing." I floundered over the words, which only deepened his glare.

"You're right, it's a very different thing." His silence was pure restraint, lasting all of a breath before exploding into anger. "I hate it, Lane. I hate that he's all over your space, and I hate the way you look at him, and I fucking hate how he has a special name for you."

"What, 'Elaine'? It's my name, Connor. My *dad* calls me that."

"Yeah, well, I've never met your dad, aside from that two seconds on Halloween. You've never bothered to introduce us."

"I didn't know you wanted to be introduced. We agreed this wasn't that kind of relationship."

"It's not."

"Then why would you say what you said to me?"

The words burst out of me—poisoned marbles, spilling across the floor. We'd been dancing around that moment since it happened; it hung between us like smoke, stubborn and dark and hard to breathe.

"Okay, time to stretch my legs." Paul emerged once more from behind the sculpture, grabbed his jacket off the back of the chair. "This is out of my jurisdiction."

"Fuck. I'm sorry." I stood and caught his arm as he passed on his way to the door. "This is my fault. I'll go. You can—"

"Shut up, Laney. Go on, work it out." His giant arms tugged

me in, squeezed the fight from my bones as his head ducked to my ear. "He's a mess, but he's your mess if you want him. If you don't, you need to tell him. Now."

He left me standing there, afraid to turn and face the silence at my back. The headache spread from my temples, stampeded inward behind eyes that burned and itched and pleaded to close. I turned, braced for the glare, or the stonewall, or any variation of ocular weaponry native to Connor's arsenal.

Instead, I found him downcast. A vulnerability I'd never seen bloomed bright across his face, working its way into my bones.

"Why," I said, softer. "Why that moment, of all the moments in the world?"

"I know. I was never going to—but, Lane, it was all I knew to say." He raised his head, hesitant and hopeful, shredding me. "Loving you was the only thing that made sense."

"Oh." There it was again—that same warm thrill spinning through me, slipping along the current of his words. "What happened to keeping it casual?"

His eyes fell closed at the reminder of how we'd begun—the morning after, at the market, when we'd stood together and proclaimed ourselves nothing more complicated than friends.

"Is that still all this is for you?"

"No," I said, quiet. "It's more."

"Come here." He opened his arms, and I fell to my knees in front of him, leaned against the familiar angles of his chest. He hunched around me, cheekbone a hard ridge against my scalp, hands smoothing down the length of my hair. My fingers clenched his shirt reflexively; I forced them back to neutral. "Tell me what you want. Total honesty."

"I don't know what to say." I pulled back and searched his face, felt a burst of panic as I watched his walls go up, incrementally, at the sound of my guarded voice. Felt him fall away from me with every short, barely controlled breath. "Don't look at me like that, Connor. I wasn't expecting any of this."

"Neither was I—and I know I fucked up, letting myself feel these things. It's my problem, not yours." His jaw clenched, biting off the ends of the words. "Yet here we are."

"Hey. I'm only saying that—"

"No, you're right. You made your intentions clear from the first. And that's fine—that's fair. But it's too much."

He leaned back, unwound my arms from his body and stood, pulling away. Time slowed; I faltered, blinked through a disorienting glow as he crossed to his drafting table, as if about to start a fresh sketch. Instead, he leaned over, pressed his hands to the table surface, braced his shoulders against a sudden tremor.

I shifted to face him, gasping at the sudden dig of metal against my shin—one of his X-Acto knives, peeking from under the futon. I'd knelt on the handle. I scooped it up and stood, fiddling it absently between my fingers. A string of words fought its way to the surface, only to knot around itself and emerge backward and sideways and utterly wrong.

"Connor, when we first started this, I wasn't looking for

anything real. You know that. You said you were fine with it, you didn't care about the whole thing with Grey, but——"

"Don't you say his name. Don't you dare fucking say anything about him to me. Ever. Are we understood?"

"Excuse me? 'Are we *understood?*'" His words lit the fuse of my fury and blew it back across the room. "Should I tell you in person to fuck yourself, or do you prefer a text?"

"Goddamn it. Lane——"

"Stop. You do *not* get to say you love me, then speak to me like that. Do it again, and it'll be the last time you see my face. How's that for total honesty?"

I saw rather than heard him sigh, and even the soft rise and fall of his shoulders made me ache, nudging my anger downstream. Everything was so fucked up—if he turned around, we could at least try to dig our way through to something better. I'd tell him every thought I'd ever had, then I'd kiss him until the stars went dark. He'd never have reason to doubt me again, if he would simply turn and look at me.

Instead, he spoke, and ripped the world from beneath my feet.

"You should leave now."

"Connor, don't do this. Look at me. Please."

"Go."

And so I did. I grabbed my bag, turned and left, and that was it. Connor and Lane, barely a thing, ended before we'd really begun. The fallout of total honesty.

I was outside before I knew it, was halfway to the road when the car swerved in, lunging into a parking spot like a dying beast collapsing in its burrow. It ejected a bitter, furious mystery of wild hair and wilder eyes, and I almost didn't know her until we were toe-to-toe.

Sadie and I hadn't really talked since the morning after the party, when she'd woken, hungover, wrapped in my sheets. Neither she nor Grey had mentioned any change in their relationship status, and I'd figured she'd swept my part in that whole mess of a night briskly beneath her already lumpy rug. Now she stood before me in pieces, and I could barely think of a reason not to crumble right alongside her.

"Sadie? Are you okay?"

"Am I *okay*? Well, Lane Jamison, that is a very good question. Tell you what—why don't *you* go ahead and ask your fucking *brother* if I'm okay?"

Her eyes spit fire; her voice tore holes in my already threadbare facade.

"What the hell is your problem?"

"Lord Jesus, give me strength. Where should I even begin?" She gave me the once-over, took in my swollen eyes and clenched jaw, the stiff, cross-armed reticence of my stance. "What's *your* problem?"

I raised my chin and met her gaze, pain and anger clashing between us. "Why don't you go ahead and ask *your* fucking *brother*?"

I stormed past her, boots determined on the gravel, then the grass, then the road. To hell with it—the city wasn't that big. The warehouse lay square in one of the shittier parts, of course, but who even gave a fuck.

I was halfway to West Asheville before I realized I still had the X-Acto clenched in my sweaty hand. I shoved it in a side pocket of my bag, shook away another surge of tears, kept on walking over the road's uneven shoulder. Ignored the pebble that had somehow worked its way into my boot. I was so tired. So very, very tired. But if I could keep myself going, keep my blood pumping and my feet moving, I'd be fine. I'd be stellar.

If I could hold on long enough to make it home, everything would be okay.

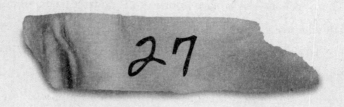

27

IT WASN'T OKAY. GREY'S CAR WAS IN THE DRIVEWAY, and he was on the floor next to the couch, face buried in his drawn-up knees. His phone lay a few feet away, like it had been tossed. I dropped my bag and hurried to him, fear clawing through my chest.

"Oh my God, what happened? Are you all right?" He didn't answer, and a sudden horrible thought blew a hole through my mind. "Is it Skye? Are Skye and Dad all right? Greyson, you have to talk to me."

The sound of his name seemed to rouse him; he shifted and spoke, his voice a blank reflection of his face.

"I got into Duke."

It was the last answer I expected—so completely out of nowhere, it didn't register as a real sentence for several beats. Then it engulfed me, sending a strange burst of joy through the middle of my misery.

"Are you serious? Grey, I'm so proud of you, I—" I paused. He didn't budge. "Shouldn't you be happy?"

"I got into Duke. Then I told Sadie." He lifted his head and stared through me, then at me, then right into my eyes. "And then we broke up."

His words twined around the memory: Sadie in the warehouse lot, disheveled and angry and covered in tears. My heart swooped low, a bird diving too close to rocks.

"You're fucking kidding me."

"I told her I got into Duke," he said again. "My top school. Everything I've been working for since I can remember. And do you know what she said? She said: 'Grey McIntyre, how could you do this to me.'"

"Oh. Wow."

"Yeah, 'wow.' She made it all about her, just like every other thing."

"Well, I'm sure she didn't mean it, Greyson—you know how she is. Once she gets used to the idea—"

"Not this time. She doesn't want to leave Asheville. She wants me to get a local job, and marry her, and never want anything more than that for the rest of my life."

I shrugged, mouth twisting as I looked away.

"I'm sorry. It sucks. But if this is your dream and she won't support you, maybe it's for the best."

"It damn well has to be," he snarled, "because I'm *not* giving up Duke. I'm not waiting for 'we'll see' to turn into permission. And you warned me, right? That we were incompatible, and I always took her shit. You warned me, and I blew it off."

"Yeah, what else is new?" I threw him a mirror image of his own glower. "Look, I love Sadie. She's the sweetest girl in the world. But she's got you so trained."

"She does not."

"Grey, you were too scared to tell her you applied for college until you had your acceptance letter in hand. This might be the first time you ever actually told her no, and look how it ended."

His face was a landslide, anger and sorrow engulfing his remaining dignity. He slumped forward, elbows on knees, hands gripped in his own hair.

"I can't lose her," he howled. "She's my whole life. Why am I doing this, Elaine? Why can't I just be happy with her, like I always was?"

God. He was doing that weird, gulpy, wheezing thing guys do when they're too upset to function——not calm but not exactly crying, every breath a miserable, wet grudge. I wanted to yell at him and hold him and love him so fiercely, he'd never again know what it was to hurt. I wanted to run away, as far and fast as I could go.

Instead, I focused on peeling my boots and socks off my sore feet, rubbing the raw spot left by the pebble. Giving him space until his wheezes turned to sighs.

"If she made you that happy, you wouldn't have looked for more in the first place," I finally said. "Greyson, what did you think would happen? You'd take all your years of studying and put it toward . . . what? Crafting artisan soap, with my dad?

Was Skye going to get you a job at the fucking Biltmore? You're better than that. You're going to be so much more than Sadie can imagine."

He sat up, scrubbing a sleeve over his face. Those eyes, weary and swollen, still beautiful. Still so lost. He took my hand before I knew how to stop him, threaded his fingers through mine and held on tight. The chills were automatic, less a thrill than a shudder. I was so tired.

"Thank you," he finally said. He peered at me, seeing for the first time past his own tears. "You . . . Have you slept, Elaine?"

"I sleep," I said, voice the ghost of a sigh. Not lying by the most technical of technicalities. "I just haven't been sleeping—sleeping well. Lately."

"When was the last time?" I could see him counting backward in his mind, and I looked away before he got to the end of that little equation.

"I'm fine, Greyson. Anyway, you're one to talk."

"I have a medical condition that literally keeps me awake. If I had the choice—hey. What happened to your foot?"

"I had a rock in my shoe. It was . . . a long walk home."

"You *walked* home? Why?" He blinked at me as if I hadn't been sitting there the whole time, took in my clumped lashes and tearstained cheeks. "Have you been crying?"

"Oh." I dropped his hand and rubbed my eyes, fixing them somewhere over his head. "I might have been. Connor—" The name stuck in my throat, blocked by a fresh sob.

"What about Connor?" His eyes bugged. "Did you guys break up? Are you shitting me right now?"

"If you can count it as a breakup. It's not like we were an official couple, right? Just friends, technically speaking."

"Oh, technically whatever. The texting, the spinning wheel. That fucking bracelet. He's been all in for ages."

"Those aren't indicators."

"They are to normal people, Elaine." He shook his head. "Sometimes I forget how cold you can be, how completely devoid of empathy. You're like a goddamn Vulcan."

"I am plenty empathetic, you asshole. I'm sitting here listening to you, aren't I? Trying to be supportive, even though Connor—"

His name shattered under its own weight, breaking into splinters, then dust. Grey's sigh was long and loud, heavy with regret.

"Hey. I'm sorry." He was quiet for a moment, then shifted closer, pulled me into a hug. "Come here."

I braced myself for the expected chills, the incomparable high sparked by his touch. Nothing. A different kind of tremor seized my body, minuscule and unsettling.

If this was love, I damn sure wasn't missing much.

I bit down hard on the inside of my cheek—hard enough that I almost couldn't hide my wince, or the shiver of revulsion at the taste of blood. Every nerve ending crackled, startling me awake with a sickening jolt.

28

"IT HAS TO BE PERFECT, ELAINE. IT HAS TO BE JUST THE thing."

Grey squinted at a bag of gingersnaps, browsed past the mochi and frozen waffles, picked through a row of ice cream cartons. I clutched the handles of the already overflowing shopping basket and leaned over the deep freeze, let the chill seep into my tired eyes. This outing was the official worst of all the bad ideas.

We'd fallen into a weird routine of grief and neutrality, my bleak fatigue a contrast to his burgeoning, skittish elation. Once the initial breakup shock wore off, Grey had embraced his new-found freedom, taking full advantage of all the perks therein. By the time the tears had dried on my face that first night, he'd already busted out the LEGOs; two days later, he'd com-mandeered the living room entirely, building the Millennium Falcon and getting baked as shit, while *Mad Max: Fury Road* played on a loop in the background. It was a good one for wakefulness, at least—I'd sat through it at least five times, and would gladly repeat as an alternative to sleep. Or to watching my stoned stepbrother sift through the entirety of Trader Joe's on a random Wednesday night.

"I am so hiding your stash when we get home," I told him as he chucked a bag of sesame sticks in my direction. "You'll never smoke another bowl as long as we live."

"I make no such promises. Would Paul still hook you up, do you think? I might have overestimated my supply."

"I'm not even asking." I winced at the mention of Paul, and all the implied proximities. "Can we please go? Before you blow Skye's quinoa budget on chips?"

"One second. I need something sweet. But what? That is the question." His brow furrowed, voice dropping to a mutter. "That is, indeed, the question. And—oh, hell yes. Elaine, check it out."

"Cookie butter? You're officially disgusting." I held out the basket, but he hugged the jar to his chest, pawed at the lid like a clumsy toddler. "Greyson, you are not eating that in here."

"Oh, I am *so* eating this in here. Won't even need a spoon."

"Gross." I set the basket at his feet, pressed my palms to my temples, massaged them in slow circles over my weeping eyes. If I did actually wear makeup, my face would be an utter shitshow. "I'm getting a coffee sample."

"I want one too. Extra sugar. Oooo, can we hit Starbucks?"

"Only if you hurry," I called over my shoulder as I reached the end of the aisle. "Put the jar down and pay, so we can—oh, excuse me. I'm—oh."

It was too ridiculous, after the way we'd ended: literally running into him. Blinking Connor Hall into focus against a backdrop of pasta and cereal, surrounded by tins of holiday cookies, bags of tea and coffee and nuts.

Two days had drifted by without him, bleak as a storm-heavy sky. I'd convinced myself it was for the best; our arrangement, begun with what I'd thought was a clear understanding of certain circumstances, overtook itself long ago, echoing a routine I knew all too well: I was a disaster, and he loved me anyway, and now he was gone. The latest in a string of boys and their attachments, and their needs, and their stupid fucking feelings. It hurt, yes, but those things always hurt. At least it was done.

And suddenly there he was in front of me——poison and thorns, face flickering from shock to anger beneath the cheerful overhead lights. A bad idea, fraying at the seams. I couldn't look away.

"Hi." My hand found his arm without a thought, faltered in the air as he stepped out of reach, scowl bleeding to a smear through eyes that burned with more than fatigue. He wouldn't even let me try. "Wait. I——"

"Elaine. Elayyyyyyyne. This lid is, like, cemented on." Grey rounded the corner and smashed into my back, bulldozing me into a display. "Aw, shit. You okay? Oh. Hey, man."

Connor's eyelids didn't close so much as sag. His fingers clenched around the handle of his shopping basket, tensed and whitened, braced for the blare of the voice behind him.

I hadn't seen Sadie in more than passing since the night at

the warehouse. She'd stonewalled me at school, and I'd been a tad too preoccupied to chase her down, what with keeping my eyes open, focusing as well as I could on class and work and the still, dark screen of my phone, which was decidedly not being inundated with texts from Connor. Not that I was reeling from shock over that little factoid—next to metal, bitter silence was his medium of choice.

His sister, not so much.

"I saw you put that soup back, Connor Hall. I told you, I'm paying for those, and whatever else extra you want. You need to eat better, and I don't have nearly the—"

Sadie, decked out in silver sequined boots and a fur-trimmed Santa sweater, nails done in candy cane stripes. Brilliant and brittle as freshly blown glass. Her lips slackened when she saw Grey, then pursed, then flattened to a crimson blade as they landed on me. Connor stalked away without a word.

"Well," she finally sneered, dragging her eyes over my fraying braid and bitten nails, the droop of my overlarge flannel shirt. "Don't *you* look a treat."

"Sadie." I winced away from her snakebite glare. "Is he—"

"You don't get to ask me about my brother. You don't get to ask me anything." Her phone blared "Jingle Bells" from her purse. She dug it out and answered without breaking eye contact. "Where are you? Stay out there, I'll buy the stuff. Don't argue. It's—hey. Hey! Don't you dare follow him, Lane Jamison. Come back here!"

It took me no time at all to pick him out of the crowded parking lot. Sadie's car was parked right near the entrance, haloed in
streetlight glare. Connor paced its length back and forth like a
caged thing as he spoke into his phone.

"Just come get the money, Sadie. No, I'm not all right. I need
the keys, and——"

"Connor."

The phone drifted to his side, Sadie's squawks spilling forgotten from the earpiece. He turned to face me; his eyes snagged
mine, dragged the air from my lungs and the heat from my
cheeks. Sunk like meat hooks into a side of flesh.

"Please talk to me, okay? I'm sorry."

"Lane, I can't. Seeing you here, out of nowhere—*with* him—
it's too fucked up."

His words spun out low, drifted to the ground between us.
He dropped his gaze, as if hoping to watch them land. I stepped
closer, and he flinched; he did do that. But he also sighed. His
eyes closed as I tucked a strand of ever-errant hair behind his ear.
It slid back down as if I'd never touched him.

"Then let's fix it. Let's at least try." Fear welled in my belly at
the unflinching set of his face. I beat it back, my fingers grazing
his cheek as I let my hand fall away. "Connor, I miss you so much.
I'm so——"

"Leave him alone. Haven't you done enough?"

She sailed toward us, proud and furious as a ship's prow, shrill
voice swooping ahead before she was even through the doors. It

pummeled my shoulder blades, raised my hackles as I turned to meet her glare.

"This isn't your business, Sadie."

"You shut up. I told you—I told you he'd fall for you, and you used him anyway. Now he's a mess, and here you still are, making it worse. Why can't you just stay away?"

"I didn't *use* him." I faltered, barely kept my footing on that particular tightrope. "I didn't know he'd—"

"Excuse me, folks. Excuse me? Who all's with this kid?"

The voice slid between us, tilted our heads back toward the entrance door. The store manager leaned halfway out, eyeing our little gathering. Grey stood to her left, clutching the open jar of cookie butter in sheepish, sticky hands.

"He's mine. I mean, I am. He's my brother." I blinked hard, bit a ragged hole through the inside edge of my lower lip. "Step-brother. Is everything okay?"

"Sure will be, once he pays for what he's eating. Can't let him leave until it's settled." She gave us the once-over, lingered on Sadie's fury, Connor's hunched shoulders and downcast eyes. My own bleary, red-threaded stare. "Not drinking out here, I hope?"

"No, ma'am. Grey, go ahead and check out if you're—" I huffed the end off the sentence as he shook his head.

"Forgot my money. Thought I had it, but I don't."

"Really? Really, Greyson? I swear to God."

"Sorry. I'll pay you back as soon as we get home. Promise."

I dug my wallet out of my bag and chucked it at Grey, squeezed my eyes shut as it went sailing past him into a display. The doors closed as he chased after it. I pivoted away from that nonsense and straight into the perfectly painted snarl of Sadie Hall—a glitter bomb of hairspray and eyeliner and candy-apple rage.

"He's 'yours,' is he? That didn't take long."

"Oh, please. I'm tired, okay? I'm fucking tired, and I misspoke, so back off. Now."

"Don't you threaten me. I knew it. I should have anted up, huh? I'd be raking it in, what with all my insider information. But I never thought you actually *would*."

"Sadie, I have literally no idea what you're talking about."

"Oh, really? Well, allow me to inform you. Ever since your parents got married, there've been bets, Lane. Actual wagers, on how long it'll take Grey to get you into bed. And most people don't think it'll take very long at all."

The news scorched my scalp, slid icicle shards through the space behind my eyes. I pressed numb fingers to my temples and tried to speak through the rise of my gorge.

"Who're 'most people'?"

"Hmm, let's see—maybe half the school? There's even a bet on whose room you'll use to do the deed."

"Huh. Interesting. Which one has the higher odds?"

"Excuse me? You think this is *funny*?"

I didn't, but I laughed anyway—a low, mad giggle that ended in a shudder as I drew a hand across my eyes. It came back wet.

"Sadie, what I'm dealing with right now . . . This information means less than nothing. And it's far from the worst they've said about me."

"But is it true?" Her eyes filled, but didn't waver. "Tell me."

"It's bullshit. Believe me or don't—though bullshit and Grey tend to go hand in hand, as I'm sure you're well aware."

Sadie's hands clawed into talons, then doubled into threats that might have sent me fleeing, had I not been delirium in human form, without a fuck left to give in the wide, wide world. It was worse than guilt or resentment, that indifference to the girl who'd been my friend.

"You don't know anything about Grey and me," she spat. "There are things between us that are sacred—that are *ours*. Things a girl like you will *never* know."

"I don't doubt it. But there was plenty he hid from you. Things he wouldn't have had to, if you weren't such a pain in the ass."

It was almost worth the entire mess, the look on her face. Her eyes were wildfire; her mouth a wet blur. Her answer sliced through me, words honed to razors on her dark, bitter drawl.

"Maybe not. But whatever you think of me, Lane, at least I'm not a whore."

"Sadie, stop it."

That voice, low and rough, filed dull along all its usual edges. Those unexpected words, washing me in wary hope. Connor's back was rigid, and his head was down, face hidden by his hair as he spoke.

"Lane isn't the problem. It's me."

"I'm sorry, honey, but I'm only—"

"Trying to help. I know. I appreciate it. Could you unlock the car and go get the stuff?" He finally raised his head, face blank and cold as the wind. "Sadie. Please."

Her mouth pulled sour around the request, gnawed through what must have been a lexicon of angry words. She fumbled her key fob from her purse, tossed it to him, and swept away with her head held high, leaving me alone with a Connor who'd gone fuzzy at the edges. I blinked him back into focus, pressed a jagged fingernail against the ridge of my knucklebone. Swallowed yawn after yawn.

"Are you all right?" he hedged. "You look . . . How are you sleeping?"

"I'm not. Maybe one or two spells a night. Here and there in the daytime. Broken up in between longer periods of not even a little bit, and all of it bad." I shook my head at his creased brow, swiped a hand across my stinging lip. Squinted at the tiny speck of blood on my thumb. "And don't worry—it's the nightmares. I'm not up at all hours getting nailed by my stepbrother, in case you're looking to win a bet."

"Jesus. I don't know anything about all that, okay?" He cleared his throat. "Whatever information Sadie has, she didn't hear it from me."

"There's nothing to hear. And at this point, it doesn't matter anyway."

"No. I guess it doesn't."

The doors opened behind me, ejecting my wallet, Grey, and his grocery bags on a gust of supermarket heat. He sidled up to me, subdued, reeking of cookies and weed. Connor stared at him, then at me, holding my burning, barely open eyes. Let me watch as something crumbled in his, then hardened over.

We'd veered too close to real. He'd field-dressed his heart and scattered the pieces, demanded I match them up with my own in a way that was beyond me, and how else had I really expected it to end? He was right. It *was* too fucked up. But he was also wrong.

He wasn't the problem. I was. Me, with my riddler's heart, every answer leading to no. Our future decided for him long before he'd ever seen my face.

By the time the car door slammed behind him, I'd already turned away.

29

I ROLLED HIS KNIFE OVER AND OVER IN MY HANDS, THE gleam of nightstand light twinkling in tiny starbursts off its edge. That lamp had been on for days—it was too easy, without it, to slide into slumber. Too easy to slide right into that bathroom on a slick, warm-puddled floor. It wasn't much—mostly shadows—still, more than enough to see the blade-shaped dent in the pad of my thumb, as I pressed the two gently together.

It's a fascinating thing, the fragility of human skin—the organ formed specifically to hold in everything that keeps us alive. You'd think we'd be made of something stronger, that didn't give and split and empty so easily; that didn't fail at the scrape of claws or teeth, or bubble away at the slightest lick of flame. And, when left to nature, the return to the earth doesn't take long at all. The rotting starts immediately: limbs stiffen; innards evacuate and wither; even the blood goes bad, whether trapped in the veins or streaked across an otherwise spotless floor. Enough of that hits the air, and you can smell it across the house before you even know it's been spilled.

It's so very, very easy to bleed. A bitten lip during dinner, a careless kneecap nick in the shower, a cutting-board mishap in the kitchen—accidents, relatively painless. Quick to flow, quicker to stanch. Try holding that knife to your thigh, though. Try summoning the will to open your arms to the elbow when you have a shred of self-preservation left in your body. Even Connor didn't get all the way there before backing out, and yet afterward he'd gone one step further, embraced the same sharp edge he'd used against himself. He'd taken a weapon and made it a tool, then turned it back once more by putting it in my hands.

And how easy he'd made it, drawing his blood—like the act itself was poised in my DNA, ready to manifest at the wink of light on steel. I'd barely even argued. It was far, far simpler to make the cut when the resulting pain belonged to someone else.

My eyes drifted shut on the heels of those thoughts; my hands skittered the knife along my thumbnail, flicking a small sliver from the crescent, right down to the quick. I started, shook myself back to waking, blinked until my eyelids buzzed.

I had to move.

I wandered through the house, twirling the X-Acto between my fingers like a tiny baton, tossed it on the kitchen table on my way to the fridge. I needed to sleep, but I didn't want to sleep, and what the fuck else was new. I poked through the shelves, ate a grape, drank straight from Dad's cold-press carafe. Bit a chunk from the block of cheddar and left it unwrapped on the shelf. Left the door open as I shuffled through the cabinet of teas and herbs and essential oils, seeking something to knock me out. Maybe I could at least relax—bliss out on some organic chamomile, or goddamn belladonna, or whatever witchery Skye had stuffed in all the little pots and jars lining the shelves.

The remedies mocked me from their neat, benign rows: lavender and sandalwood, eucalyptus and clove oil. Ginseng capsules. Milk thistle. Rose hips. Echinacea. Ginkgo. Skye's trusty guelder rose. Grey's melatonin and valerian, which clearly didn't help him a single goddamn bit. Enough loose tea to open a shop. Nothing that would actually help. I knew Grey's weed stash was long gone; maybe I'd dig out Dad's from its sad, easily discovered hiding place, get stoned enough to sleep without dreaming for more than five, ten, twenty minutes—maybe even a repeat of the rare hour I'd sometimes manage to snag between bouts of wakeful misery. If I could achieve that, I'd smoke everything in the house and wouldn't even care if he caught me.

I didn't know I was laughing until I choked on my own tears. The tremors started in my hands, spread upward through my arms and shoulders. Slid their madness down the ribbon of my spine.

"Elaine?"

His voice was a crack across the jaw. A double dose of Grey blinked at me from the doorway, then swam back into a single form as my eyes adjusted. He was awake, of course; that I might run into him hadn't even crossed my bleary mind.

"Oh, hi. Insomnia?"

"Yeah." He closed the fridge, zeroing in on the open cabinets at my back, concern and confusion playing tag across his face until his eyes landed on the table. He had the X-Acto in his hand before I could blink.

"What's this?" His voice hissed somewhere between groggy and mad, *S*'s seething around his retainer. "Is this Connor's?"

"Oh. Yeah, I might have taken a souvenir on my way out of the warehouse." I snorted into my hand at his bug-eyed glare. I couldn't help it—everything was silly and hilarious and heart-breakingly imperfect.

"You might have—goddamn it, Elaine. You know I'm not letting you keep this, right?"

"'Letting' me. Like that's a thing." I leaned back on the counter, noting the way his eyes slid up the length of my bare legs. I waited until they made it to my face, then returned fire, let my gaze roam its way from the floor to his flaming cheeks. Gave him a look dirty enough to stain. "So, were you out here hoping for another peep show tonight? Or do you think you'll stick to mansplaining tea bags?"

"What the fuck. I was *not* hoping for—this whole thing—" His face twisted, frustration spattered in fury, at the stream of tiny, insane giggles bubbling over my fingers. "Come on."

"Wherever are you taking me, *Greyson*?" My voice was light and mocking, threaded with delirium. Grey McIntyre had me by the wrist. He wore Stormtrooper pajama pants and was pulling me down the hallway to my very own bedroom, and just a few months earlier I'd have flayed skin from bone myself to make this moment real.

He deposited me through my doorway and ducked into his own room, returning sans both knife and retainer, his tongue working over his teeth. I grinned at him from my perch on the edge of the bed.

"Lane, this has to stop."

"Ooooh, you called me Lane. This must be getting serious, *Grey*."

"Cut the shit. When was the last time you slept?"

"Not sure. How long ago did we party with the dead boy?"

"Holy——that was almost two weeks ago."

"Well, it hasn't been *that* long. December. First. December first was the last."

"Elaine."

"I'm sorry." My eyes fluttered, suddenly wet again, and I crumpled over, forehead to knees. My gasps rolled over themselves; a wild giggle cut through my tears, soaked up one too many, and dwindled to a wet cough. I didn't hold back. I couldn't.

I heard him sigh, then swear again under his breath, then felt the mattress shift as he sat next to me. Felt the warm drag of his hand across my back. It was the porch swing revisited, but it was different——*I* was different. Weaker. Emptier. Bled dry and scabbed over. He gathered me to him, though, held me against his shoulder and let me soak his shirt, same as before.

"You need to sleep," he said, once I'd reduced myself to sniffles. "No more excuses."

"I *can't* sleep. It's too much—every time I sleep, I dream. It feels like I'm dying."

"You'll die if you don't. In reality." His arms tightened around me, stilled the shudder of my frame. "Eventually, your body will revolt and *make* you sleep, whether you want to or not. You don't want it to get that far."

I was too defeated to do anything but nod. I let him take over, let him help me into bed and pull the quilt up to my shoulders. My eyes were closed by the time the light clicked off. I barely registered the dip of the mattress as he settled beside me, leaning against the headboard.

"Go to sleep." His voice swam into my ear, nudged me further from my fading thoughts. "I'm right here."

30

I WOKE CHOKING, HER FLAYED FINGERS TIGHT AROUND my throat.

"Whoa, steady. It's just a dream." Hands caught me as I scrambled up—Grey's hands, gentle and safe, easing me back against the pillows. The light clicked on, pushing the shadows toward the door. He slid down to lie beside me, turned on his side so we were face-to-face, inches apart. "Do you want to talk about it?"

"No." And I didn't. They were horrors best left in a single corner of the world; whispers spun into shadows at the edge of a work-space light. The wrong fingers wiped a stray tear from the bridge of my nose. "Now you see why I can't sleep. You don't have to stay with me, you know. I'll be fine."

"Stop. I said I'll take care of you, and I will." His breath caught, then frayed and shuddered, went jagged all at once as our eyes met. "I'm here—if you need me. However you need me."

Something familiar and horrible snaked fingers around my throat; something pushed those same fingers in between my ribs, worked them into my lungs one at a time. The space between us buzzed and thickened, heavy with need. Hazy with fear.

"Grey?"

"Oh God. I'm sorry. I'm so sorry." He rolled away and sat up, hunched over his drawn-up knees. "I didn't mean that. I swear—I would never—"

"Grey."

His name. A sigh, not a question, slipping like water from my throat. Stopping him cold as he turned to face me.

"This is real, isn't it, Elaine? There's something here."

The words burrowed deep inside me, tearing into that space between logic and dreams. Ripping me open, the way he always had. I sat up as he shifted closer, reached for me, trapped another tear beneath his thumb. His palms slid over my cheekbones, and God help me, I leaned into it. I let myself get lost between his hands.

"Is this okay? If not—" He swallowed the end of his thought, blew it out in a ragged sigh at my nod. "You want this too?"

"Yes." It was an automatic whisper, skirting the edges of a lie. I closed my eyes, like blotting out his face would explain *that* fucking flicker of insight. Of course I wanted him—he'd laid the groundwork for what wanting meant. "But there's so much you don't know. You don't understand—"

"I do. It's the same for me."

His kiss found my cheekbone, then my eyelid, stopping the world again and again. He was longing and memories, and surprisingly chapped lips; the whiff of nighttime retainer breath a slap to my gag reflex, a detail that damn sure had never factored into the old Grey McIntyre seduction fantasy. Not that I was one to judge, what with my stiff shoulders and claw-rigid fingers, my sweaty pajama top, my tangled, unwashed hair. I started as his finger traced my neck, flinched as it found my collarbone. My vision blurred and realigned, refocused on the shadow of his jaw-line stubble, a bit too rough to be inviting.

I was disconnected, so exhausted, so strangely analytical, and sweet *fuck* could I maybe stop scrambling for an exit tucked in the walls of this unreal maze? I'd turned myself inside out, wishing for this——how many nights had I spent consumed by a half-awake need, reaching for him across an empty space? How many times had I lived this moment in someone else's arms?

"Is this okay, Elaine? I——oh. Sorry."

Well, maybe not *this* moment. Maybe not the abrupt meeting of his forehead and my nose, or the clumsy trek of fingers that could have belonged to anyone. Skin he'd never touched broke out in chills, more of a crawl than a shiver, as his hands fumbled across the minefield of my hips. But I'd take the way those hands grew urgent, found the hem of my shirt and slipped beneath it, followed the trail of my spine to my rib cage. Slid carefully over my sides, pausing just at the swell of my breasts. Stirred through my ashes until they sparked.

His gaze found mine, unzipped me, stealing every wisp of air from my lungs. That spark leaped from my skin to his, lightning arcing puddle to puddle, and it was *something* at least. It wasn't solace and secrets, or the warm press of familiar lips. It wasn't the molten silver slide of skin and leather that ended with my senses shattered, never once failing to leave me weak.

But so what if the medium was foreign—it didn't mean we couldn't try. We could sand the edges off all our mismatched bits, rearrange them into brighter patterns; our own kind of mosaic glass, useless until it broke. Maybe we could still make it into something nice.

I knew I looked like death—like fog and shade, threaded through with watery light. His eyes dropped anyway, took me in from lips to legs, then up again, the way they had a million years ago in a moonlit kitchen, and uncountable moments since. The flutter he sent through my heart was weak, but familiar. Routine.

I'd caught him wanting me, so many times.

"You're so beautiful. You're so—"

And then he didn't say anything at all. His words faltered as my hand rose, crept beneath my shirt to cover his; positioned his palm, pressed it to my skin just so—this *would* be what I wanted, if I had to orchestrate it from start to stop. His voice stumbled over syllables, ended in nonsense as I echoed his gasp, moved our hands together, up and over, and together we caught fire.

It was a collision. Rock and ocean, embers and wind, crashing together; falling in a tangle of limbs and longing and fear, and *this*. This, finally, was what I'd craved. Him, undone and dangerous—gentle—rough with need. My hands, guiding his, then falling away, tugging his shirt up and off. The thump of his heart, reaching through his flesh to knot with mine.

"This is okay, right?" His words were soft and low, warm against my parted lips, and if he would only stop asking me that, everything would be perfect.

"Yes," I breathed. "I'll tell you if—ow. That's my hair."

"Oh, sorry. Are you——"

"Still my hair, Greyson." He cringed, burying his face in my neck.

"Sorry. Man, I suck."

"It's fine. Could you maybe stop——"

"Yeah, yeah. Sorry. This was a bad idea."

"No, I mean stop apologizing. If I didn't want this, I'd say so."

"Yeah. Okay." His mumble, muffled against my skin, turned to another softer kiss. He propped himself on his elbows and hovered over me, drew back far enough to see my face.

"God. This is weird. It's weird, isn't it? Us?"

"It's getting there," I muttered, eyes straying to the half-open door. "If we do this——"

He shifted his weight to the side, lay facing me again, but closer. His thumb traced my lower lip, sent an odd chill over my scalp as his fingers slipped through my hair and down my neck. Lost themselves once more beneath my shirt, looping that chill around my rib cage. I blinked at him, then past him, refocusing on the drag of his palms, unscarred and unfamiliar. Softer than I needed.

"No, it's definitely weird. You were supposed to be my sister.

But I moved in, and this whole house—you're everywhere. You're all I think about—this, right now. It's all I want."

He pulled me close again, and there it was: his heart. That was what I knew of him—that sturdy thump, reliable and safe. Separated from mine by bone and veins, and too many years since that first moment I'd leaned against it. Too many moments since then, spent chasing that bliss. And there *he* was, as if I'd finally hit on the right combination of wishes, only to find they were being answered all along.

It rode the edge of every hope and daydream. It was smothering heat and sour flesh, the weird catch of teeth along my jaw—hands that rushed instead of wandered, fumbling over my thighs. It was nowhere near enough.

Still, my body sought his naturally; my arms moved without me, clung to him, pulled him into another kiss as he hitched my knee over his hip, fingers grazing over the prickles of my unshaven thigh.

What. The fuck.

My eyes damn near bugged out of my head. Desire fell away from me like ice calving from a glacier, dropping forever into the frigid sea. He mistook my horrified gasp for passion, though; he swallowed it, returned it, breathed deeply against my suddenly slack mouth. I almost always kept my legs smooth, but the whole mental break thing had back-burnered the hell out of *that* priority. Besides, I had yet to meet the guy who'd slam on the brakes over some stubble when we were otherwise ready to go, so what the fuck, indeed——what the fuck was *wrong* with me, that I was letting it derail the moment, and if this wasn't the biggest failed experiment since the goddamn frog dissection itself. God*damn* it.

I seethed over those thoughts, then worried them, then gave up worrying, all at once too tired and defeated to care. My mind drifted past his lips and out the window, dissipated as it hit the air. Left me compliant and empty, the usual reflexive severing of heart from limbs, and for a single hideous moment I thought this was the best we'd ever be——this predictable, one-sided parody, so taboo it was a joke before it happened. Awkward as two mismatched hands, accidentally tied together.

But what did it matter? It wouldn't be a line crossed so much as a step taken——another shaded square in the pattern. Yet another dropped stitch. He'd be his own brand of distraction, and it made zero difference in the grand scheme of me——here I was, still alone. Still staring at the unchanged, empty road ahead.

And was this really how love looked from the other side? Grey McIntyre, saving me in his own way, over and over. The return to the start——to the heartbeat and voice that soothed my fear; to the safe circle of his arms, inadvertently restraining mine. Life lived in a dreamy bubble of anticipation, every moment without his hands spent waiting for them to find and somehow wake me——as if the press of my skin wasn't the antithesis to our reality. I was supposed to be his sister. It *was* weird.

And it was wrong. It was completely, utterly wrong.

He was only a boy. Not whatever passed for destiny, not the start of something more. Not a copper band, curved to the exact measure of my wrist, and certainly not the hands that shaped it.

Not the boy who'd finally coaxed a glow from somewhere deeper than my heart.

Something caught on the edge of that thought, tugged sharply as Grey breathed my name; tugged me not toward him, but away. Sloughed me off from his Elaine—that devoted, lovesick, irrational girl, forever prodding him into shapes that interlocked with hers and had nothing to do with who he really was.

The girl I used to be. And that was fine.

But it was no longer real.

"Don't call me that."

He started and blinked, drew back slowly.

"What? Are you okay?"

"No. I'm not." I curled my hands over his, moving them gently off my face, and sat up, leaving him behind. "And my name is Lane."

We stared at each other, apprehensive and awkward, his befuddlement turning to realization, then to abject horror.

"Oh my God. Elai—Lane, I'm sorry." He rolled to sitting and leaned away, like I was catching. "I thought you wanted—I read this all wrong, didn't I?"

"No, you read it right. I loved you. For a long, long time." I steeled my courage and sought his eyes. Let myself feel the last flutter of that long-cherished ache. "But that's over now."

He picked over my words, cracked them open and checked for rot. Nodded at the truth he found. Unsurprised. Not even hurt.

"So that's it, then. Wow."

"Believe me, if you'd wanted me before all this happened, I'd have been yours. I'd have done anything in the world for that."

"Now you tell me."

"Grey, you were with Sadie. We barely knew each other. And whatever you're feeling now, for me? I don't think it's real."

"I do love you, though."

God. A part of him meant those quiet words, I could tell. And I wanted to hear them, in every way—tossed casually across a room, or tacked to the end of a laugh; wanted them frustrated, and penitent, and whispered against my skin. I always had.

I just didn't want them from him. Not anymore.

"Not like that, you don't."

He dropped his eyes, then his head. Dragged his fingers through his hair, clasped them at the back of his neck.

"No," he said. "You're right. Not like that."

It was the answer I'd hoped for—sure and clear, utterly final. Devastating.

He wasn't the be-all and end-all I'd imagined. He wasn't my savior, or my salvation. The sun would rise, and this night would be wiped away. However much he wanted me, it was nothing that could last.

And that was okay. Even though it hurt, it really was okay.

"It's for the best," I said, nudging his knee with mine. "I

mean, it's either this or a fully screwed family dynamic."

"You think?" He looked up, mouth pursed, trying so hard to repress a grin. But our eyes met, and neither one of us could take it—we collapsed into laughter that became breathless, hysterical mirth tears.

"Rob would hate me," he gasped. "I'd be forever shunned for corrupting his little girl."

"You wish. Pretty sure I'd be the corrupter in our case."

"Shut up. At least we'd have the whole 'meet the parents' thing out of the way. No need to worry about in-laws getting along when they share a bedroom."

I laughed harder, wiped my face, and when he pulled me into a long hug, it wasn't weird or awkward or heartbreaking at all—it was gentle and soothing, a splash of water on the embers of what we'd almost been. A promise of everything we'd grow to be.

"Whatever happens," I said as we drew apart, "I want us to be family. All of us. Always."

"Same to you, Elaine. Lane. I meant Lane. Sorry." He sat back, rubbing a hand over his tired eyes. "You're still Elaine to me."

"You can call me that, if you want. As long as I get to call you Greyson."

"You and my mother," he sighed, resigned. "No one else."

"Deal. And maybe we can never speak of this again?"

"Never ever. Could you do me a favor, though? Try to sleep, just a little bit more?" He held up a hand at my protest. "I'll be right here, the whole time. I promise."

"Greyson. I don't know."

"Trust me. I'll keep you safe."

And somehow, I knew he would. So, I lay back down and let him slip a hand in mine. Let him settle on the floor next to my bed and stand guard as I gave myself over to the weight of exhaustion.

Somehow, after everything, I trusted him enough to finally close my eyes.

31

WE SAT IN GREY'S CAR IN THE PACKED LOT, STARING through the windshield at the warehouse. I wasn't exactly craving an audience of *artistes* for this particular talk, but life was nothing if not a conveyor belt depository of things I could do without.

I'd finally managed to get some real rest. Not that it had been a peaceful, uninterrupted rest by any means—Grey woke me half a dozen times, pulling me from different versions of the dream. Each time patiently waiting out my tears and gasps, coaxing me back to the pillow. Staying right beside me, until morning shone through the curtains and dragged us both to bleary consciousness.

After a Starbucks run and a busy yet uneventful day at school, most of which we spent actively avoiding Sadie, Grey and I had holed up in the library to study for our upcoming pre-holiday exams. Or, more accurately, he'd studied while I'd stared at reams of pages and notes, wondering how I'd managed to create them without retaining a single scrap of their contents. We hit

Starbucks again, and then he'd bypassed our usual route, took a rogue turn, and headed for the riverfront. I didn't bother to protest—he might as well have read my mind. I'd woken that morning in a buzz of adrenaline, the weight of Grey McIntyre lifted from my heart. Yearning and determination filling the fissure it left behind. It was sooner than my nerves preferred, but it was, truly, what I needed.

I had to see Connor.

It was my fault, how we'd disintegrated. Sadie, for all her hyperbole, was right—I'd known he was falling for me, and instead of facing it or calling things off, I'd shut my eyes and opened my arms, tangled my thoughts up with all the wrong sounds. Doomed us both, long before the run-in at Trader Joe's—which, yes, had been a special train wreck all on its own. Turns out, it's pretty easy to fuck up an important conversation on day five of zero sleep. Who knew?

In the end, it had taken someone else's hands to make me realize his were all I wanted. Now I had to make it right. I had to try.

"Well, I guess I should get this over with." I unbuckled my seat belt and steeled myself, took a few deep, cleansing breaths that didn't do shit. "Come on."

"Nope. Whole lotta nope. Reservation for Nope, party of one." He pulled his Kindle and a can of organic ginger ale out of his bag, then raised an eyebrow at my huff. "What?"

"Wow. Thanks for your support, Greyson."

"Look, he and I were on bad terms *before* I broke his sister's

heart. I'm not about to stroll on in to his lair of knives and fire."
He chuckled at my resigned sigh, popped the tab on his soda as
I climbed from the car into the misty, chilly night. "Good luck."

The party hit me in the face. It was barely seven, but the main
room was packed with people—some familiar, mostly strangers,
all trapped in a dirty bomb of pot smoke, sweat, and overly loud
Nick Cave. I scanned the room for Connor, expecting to find him
holding up a wall with his shoulder, maybe languishing in a fit of
ennui with two or three painters and a tragic sculptor.

I was not prepared in the least to have him see me first.

He was bone and blood, in a sea of crumpled paper. He was
close, only five or so feet away. On the far side of the universe.

"Hi." His jaw clenched, bitter, at the sound of my voice. I
approached him anyway, holding his eyes. I hadn't spent all my
spare time with Connor Hall these past months without learning
how to field a death glare. "Can we talk?"

"Sure, we can talk. You first."

"Can we talk somewhere we can actually hear each other? The
roof? Your room?"

"Paul has guests in our room." He wavered, and for one horrible beat I thought he was on his way out—that he'd saunter
away and leave me to fend for myself against the surge of party-
goers. But his head dropped, and he sighed, and he did walk away,
but he also motioned for me to follow. "Come on."

We snaked through the crowd and out the front door, dropped
into a void of sudden frigid silence as it closed behind us. He'd

left without grabbing a jacket; I watched that fact flicker across his face as his arms crossed over his T-shirt.

"So." The word was a dead thing, cold as the air. "Here you are. And I'm *right* in the middle of a gathering."

"I can see that," I sighed. "I wanted to apologize, for before. I was a mess, and wasn't sleeping, and I took out a lot of my shit on you. You don't deserve that."

"No, I don't."

I waited for him to continue, perhaps even add a thought or two of his own to the conversation. He was pure Connor, though, stubborn as fuck, whittled down by rage. I should have known him making this easy on me wasn't going to be a thing. I'd have to work for every word.

And I knew I would—I'd do anything it took to wipe that look from his eyes. I wanted to cry on him and hug him, wrap him up and let him love me. Talk to him until my words turned to kisses, then turned back to predawn whispers. I wanted nothing so much as to simply hold his hand.

There was no grand epiphany, no pivotal moment, pieced together with frogs and nightmares. He was my friend, and then he was more, and then he'd crept beneath my skin and turned it inside out. I'd ruined everything, of course, but it wasn't too late; it couldn't be. I'd live a lifetime of waking hell if it meant another chance.

If he knew nothing else, I wanted him to know that.

"Okay. I came here to say sorry, and now I have. So." The

twist of his mouth was the only sign I was talking to anything but a wall. "Do you have anything you'd like to add? Or do I not inspire more than random monosyllables?"

"I don't really know," he flatlined. "I mean, what's the best way to say goodbye to the girl you love? You tell me, right?"

"It doesn't have to be goodbye," I whispered, miserable and lost and wildly hopeful. "I never wanted that."

"It doesn't matter. My whole life, it's the same old story: everything would be fine, if only I was someone else—literally, in your case." He shook his head, cutting me off as I drew breath to answer. "No. If you don't love me, it's better to cut me loose."

"I never said I didn't."

It was the last thing I'd meant to say. Not that anything was coming out the way I wanted, but there it was—the shards of something true. Pieces finding their places slowly, so close to being whole. His eyes fell shut as I slid my arms beneath his, felt his thin frame beneath his thinner shirt. Felt his ribs and angles impale me, bleeding out the other side. He stood still for a moment, unresponsive, then crushed me to him all at once, my name sandpaper in his throat.

"Lane. Don't."

"But I do. I—" The words slid to the tip of my tongue, skidding to a stop before they hit the air. I gritted my teeth and barreled ahead, trapped beneath a two-faced truth I barely understood. "This is real, okay? It is, and I don't know how to do this, Connor, but you have to trust me. Please believe me. Please."

For a moment I thought I'd reached him. I thought it would be enough to keep his arms around me, keep his lips pressed to my hair and his hands clenched in my coat. Then he spoke, and undid the last knot of hope in my heart.

"Believe you? You can't even say it. Look, I know you never wanted—any of this, but I can't go halfway with you. Not anymore." He took my wrists and broke my grasp, put my arms gently away from him. "I can't have you sleep in my bed if you wake up wishing it were his."

"It's not like that. Grey and I—he knows everything now. We talked it out, and he kissed me, and it was a complete dis—"

His laugh, thin and sharp as any scalpel, gutted my protest. He raised his eyes over my shoulder, fixated on the car. On Grey, conspicuously absorbed in his Kindle.

"Christ. If you really do love me, spare me the details of your little dream date. I'm past my suicidal phase, but don't think it won't fuck me up but good in its own special way."

I stared at him, mouth forming wrong around everything I had left to say. His laughter settled into a smirk; his quirked eyebrow provided the crowning asshole touch. Anger welled like fevered blood, consuming my guilt. I'd compromised everything for this—set aside years of fear and pride, stuffed down every scrap of dignity until I choked, and he was fucking *grinning*. Did he really think I'd let him stand there and mock me? Did he even have a fuck to give?

"Don't you dare, Connor," I said, low. "You knew how I felt.

You knew it all, and you wanted me anyway—you don't get to blame me now for being honest."

"Oh, trust me, I'm fully aware of my role in all of this." Connor backed away, opened the warehouse door, stepped over the threshold. Turned away from me; my arms; my desperate, overflowing eyes. "Go on back to him. You have a chance to finally get what *you* want. You should take it."

"Goddamn it, will you listen to me? That is not what I—"

The door clanged the end off my sentence.

I heard the click the second I touched the handle. This door hadn't been locked a day since I'd known him, and he'd gone and fucking locked it in my face.

That son of a bitch had locked me out.

"Hey. HEY." I yanked on the handle again, then pounded on the metal until it sang. "CONNOR, OPEN THIS DOOR."

"I doubt he's planning an encore." Grey's words were soft at my back. "I still don't want to go in there, but I can text him for you, if you think it'll help."

"Ugh, no. I appreciate it, but that might be the worst idea you've ever had." I stared at the sliding door another beat, then lashed out at it, my sudden violent kick echoing through the lot. "FUCK YOU, CONNOR. FUCK YOU."

"Okay, Elaine, I think we've done enough. Come on." Grey tugged me away from the door, steered me across the gravel to his waiting car. "Let's go home."

32

"SCORE ONE FOR APARTMENT LIVING, RIGHT?"

I blinked at Grey. He was flushed and breathless, slumped against a tree, rake handle gripped loosely in his tired hand. We'd spent the entire afternoon raking the yard, yet barely made a dent in the ankle-deep leaves. It didn't matter that there were four of us, double that of every year previous, or that the day was sunny and cold and beautiful. It didn't matter that we were all home at once, a rare occurrence made possible only by our school holiday break and the seasonal employee Dad had hired for the business. My back hurt. My knees hurt. My arms and feet and head and heart—everything hurt. All I wanted was to curl under a blanket and be still.

"I love these woods," Grey continued. "I always hated our old apartment, with no yard and no trees. I always wanted a space like this. But leaves in general can kiss my ass."

"Yep. Welcome to the reality of outdoor chores." I ditched my rake and leaned against the tree beside him. Skye and Dad were still soldiering on at the other end of the lot, smiling at each other over a half-full lawn bag. Yard work was shockingly less efficient when forty-five of every sixty seconds were spent gazing into each other's eyes. "Wait until it's time to shovel snow and salt the icy sidewalks."

"I preferred the bulb planting. That was fun. That was the day I really started to feel at home here."

"Yeah, I remember." The bulb planting, Jesus Christ. *That* was a day that could pass without further mention into eternity, a stitch slipping unnoticed from the needle. The starting point of our unraveling.

Not that I wasn't weirdly nostalgic for the simple days of unrequited longing; Grey's constant and oblivious rejection had become routine, a dull, comfortable sting that blended time into itself. It sure was less complicated than the tornado of fucking feelings that now spun through every waking moment.

It had been so much easier, not knowing what I was missing.

Grey plucked a leaf from my hair and began picking it apart, tipped his head back to rest against the bark. Closed his eyes, seeking the sun.

"I heard from Sadie this morning."

"Did you?"

"She wants to get back together. Said she'll wait until I'm done with school, that we can make it work long-distance." His eyes opened, mouth pinched over a sad, sorry frown. "She says she still wants to marry me."

"Oh, Grey." I had to fight to hide my grimace. I of all people knew how it felt to love him, helplessly and hopelessly, and have that love amount to nothing. Poor Sadie. "You told her no, didn't you?"

"I had to. I can't go back to how things were. I can't be what she wants. But I never thought it would come to *this*. I thought she was the one, bizarre as that sounds."

"But how does that work? How can you love her like that and still decide to let her go?"

"One has nothing to do with the other. We broke up because we want opposite things, but she's still Sadie. Of course I love her." He picked the last shreds off the leaf and tossed away the skeleton. "Who knows—maybe she *is* the one. But I need to sort myself out before I can say that for sure. And I need to do it on my own."

"Oh. Well, you'd know better than I would." I pushed myself off the tree trunk and fished my rake out of the leaves. "Fortunately, I've sorted out enough about *my*self to avoid that 'together forever' shit in the first place."

"Well, sure, for now. But don't you want a family, eventually? Don't you want to belong to someone else, and have them belong to you?"

"Yeah, that's a great idea, Greyson. I can barely function as an individual, but let's go ahead and chain another human to my side for the rest of eternity. Where do I sign up?"

"Whatever. You're tolerable enough. And I know at least one human who wouldn't turn down a set of those chains."

I thumped the rake against the ground and turned to face him, mouth set, hackles up. Stomach knotted somewhere around my ankles.

I'd spent years molding the edges of my life into very specific shapes, ones that could never hope to align with my mother's. I'd sliced all the heads off the fucking hydra; detonated every path that led to marriage or children; picked Grey out of thin air to complete the package—the perfect dream guy, unavailable and unattainable. Impossible to connect with at all, much less drag down an aisle of any kind. Now here he was, beautifully human, toe-to-toe with me instead of lashed to a pedestal. And now here *I* was, again, with too many options on the table. Too many paths leading straight to a white-tiled floor.

"Okay, you can stop right there. Not that I can't appreciate the compliment all but fucking shrouded in that statement, but none of what you're saying applies to me, or ever has. Not even hypothetically." I stabbed at the leaf pile a couple more times, then shoved the rake away. Pressed my palms to my aching eyes. "Fuck this. Fuck this entire time of year."

"Hey." He was beside me then, retrieving my rake and taking my hand, closing my fingers around the handle. Covering my grip with his. "It'll be okay."

"No, it won't. You broke Sadie's heart. I broke Connor's. Neither of them will talk to me, and you're going to Duke. I'll be here alone, tripping over our poor lovesick parents every time I turn around. Tripping over my whole fucking flat tire of a life."

"So, change your life. What do you want to be? What do you want to do? Go do that."

"I have no idea. None." How I could think about the future long-term, when life consisted of getting through a week, a day—even an hour at a time? I'd never had a direction beyond "hopefully not backward."

"What about college? There's plenty of time left to apply."

"I'm not you, Greyson. I don't have the grades for a full ride, and I make fucking yarn accessories for a living. What I have in the bank wouldn't even cover books."

"You don't have a college fund?"

"You *do*?"

"Yeah, it's called my father's problem. Court-ordered savings account, in lieu of child support. I get statements every month— trust me when I say I'm set."

"Well, the whole soap-making single dad thing doesn't exactly net untold riches. They used to have some savings, but it got eaten up in funeral expenses and moving out of that house. She had insurance, but it wouldn't pay out for a suicide."

"Oh."

"Yeah, 'oh' just about covers it, huh? Everything circles back, no matter what I do."

He fell silent, studying me. I stared at the tree line, a wash of tears clenched just behind my jaw.

"It seems that way sometimes, Elaine. I know it does. But I promise you, it won't last forever."

"Sure feels like it will. Feels like the whole world is dead, right about now."

"Not for long. It's almost the solstice." He took the rake from my hand and pushed it through the leaves, uncovering a vibrant patch of green. "See? All this life, still hanging in there. It takes more than a few leaves to smother the world."

"I miss him, Greyson."

The words fell to our feet and rolled away, scuttling for cover. We stared after them, Grey's foot moving absently back and forth over the uncovered grass. Skye's laughter trailed after her and Dad as they headed for the house, their yard bags abandoned, nowhere close to full. His hand guided her through the back door, slipped around her hip as the screen swung shut behind them.

My father, so ridiculously content. So effortlessly buoyed by Skye—by her careful hands and level, clear-eyed gaze. The soft, frequent stretch of her smile. Her unscarred arms and effortlessly beating heart.

It must be a relief for him, in so many ways, to share his home with a happy woman.

The kitchen light went on. We watched through the window as Dad opened the refrigerator and bent over, searching the shelves, watched Skye give him a playful swat on the ass. I turned away from that horror in time to see Grey shudder in shared revulsion.

"I know how it feels to miss someone," he said, voice catching. "It sucks to be left behind, wondering why you weren't enough to make a person stick—never really *getting* it. Always looking for that one thing you could have done to make a difference. But it happens to everyone, at some point. And that pain won't last forever either."

"That's what I'm afraid of."

"Yeah," he said, squeezing his eyes shut against a flash of sun dipping sharp and sudden through the naked branches. I watched it play across his face, turning his skin and hair and mouth to flame. "I know exactly what you mean."

We'd barely settled at the table when Dad and Skye ghosted us, retreating to their bedroom with their sandwiches. Grey slumped in his seat, staring at his own food with markedly less enthusiasm than he had the moment previous.

"Don't get me wrong, Elaine. I think Rob's great, and I'm glad my mother found someone who makes her this happy. But holy shit."

"No, I get it. Believe me, I'm suddenly nauseated myself." I sighed, using a corn chip to push a glob of egg salad around the edge of my plate. "At least they're compatible and infatuated and completely in love, even if it is sick-making."

"Very true." His chuckle was almost a sigh. "Mom told me their fate lines are nearly identical. Pretty sure that convinced her on the spot it was meant to be, and that was before he'd even asked her on a date."

"I'm sorry, but what the hell are you talking about? Fate lines?"

"Palmistry. You know, the lines on your hand, and how they speak to your personality and destiny. They compared their hands the first time they met. You know the rest."

"*That's* how they got together? You have got to be fucking kidding me."

"I am one hundred percent serious. Look." He took my right hand, turning it palm up in his. "These lines represent aspects of your character. Their depth and appearance speak to who you are. Foretell your future."

"Oh, Jesus. Here we go."

"Shut up. These are the three major lines: life, head, and heart. And that one right there is the fate line: the one that brought our parents together, leading you and me to this very moment. That one's tied to everything else—anything that happens to you or because of you, within or beyond your control."

"Ah, I see. And which one's the bullshit line?"

He tried so hard to hold in that laugh. He tried so hard I almost felt sorry for him, but one giggle escaped, then another, and soon we were both howling. My forehead was on the table, his was bowed over my still-upturned palm, and there wasn't enough air in the world to help us catch our breath.

"I know," he gasped. "I know it's bullshit. But it's fun, isn't it? To try to guess how life will go? And it's always cool when some little thing comes true. It's like the whole universe is aligning: nature, man, and cosmos—everything linking together. Everything destined to be."

"Yeah, and now you and I are related because our parents' hands sort of match. That goes a bit beyond harmless fun."

"But see, they're perfect for each other. These things happen, and they just *fit*. They *can't* be random. Everything circles back on itself. Everything falls into place."

"And you believe that, after all that's happened."

It wasn't a question so much as a declaration, a defining facet carved on the heart of Grey McIntyre. He *did* believe—it was there in the sure set of his shoulders and in the shadows beneath his tired, tranquil eyes. It was good to see him smile again, to see him slowly recapturing the boy he'd been.

"I do," he said. "These past couple months, my head was in a real bad place—like, the one core tenet of my moral compass is to do no harm, and that basically all went to shit the second I moved in here. Now I have this laundry list of things I fucked up, that I can never take back, and it's killing me. So many things I should have done differently."

"Karma's about to break a piece off your ass," I snickered, taking far too much pleasure in his answering groan.

"That is way too true to be a joke, Elaine. Still, things are turning now. Think of what it took for us to get to this moment, right here, and the infinite number of ways it could have gone differently. I can feel that circle closing, see so many things I thought were permanent dying in front of me, and it's heartbreaking—but at the same time, it's like they're not really endings. They're the jumping-off points for everything that's about to start. And I can't wait to see what—"

His phone howled as he spoke, Sadie's all-too-familiar ringtone blaring through the kitchen. That calmed him fast. He let it go to voice mail, and she immediately called back. Then a third time, and his mouth was a hard pinch.

"Do you need to get that, Greyson?"

"No. I asked her this morning to give me some space, and she agreed. Yet here she is, mere hours later. I'm not even surprised."

He sighed and dropped my hand as the phone shrilled yet again.

"Holy shit, she is not letting up. Hold on."

He barely got more than a syllable out before the world upended. I could hear her nonsensical sobs as if she were right there at the table. Grey frowned at the phone, then looked at me, my concern reflected in his face.

"Hey, are you okay? Sadie—Sadie, I can't—I can't understand you, babe. Calm down. What? They what? Wait there. No, wait there. I'll pick you up. Yes. I know. Don't be sorry. I love you. Of course I do. Sadie, stay calm. I'll be there soon."

"What is it?" I was on his case before he even disconnected the call. He stared at me, his eyes wide and green and horrified. "Greyson, what?"

"It's Connor," he said, kicking the legs out from under my heart.

33

SHE STOOD ON THE CORNER BENEATH A LEAFLESS OAK
tree, barely visible in the streetlight. The sun had set on the drive
to her Biltmore Forest neighborhood—or, more accurately, the
neighborhood three blocks from hers, where she'd told Grey
to pick her up. She hadn't brought a jacket; her shirt was long-
sleeved, but thin. I could see her shivering before we were close
enough to slow down.

Her face changed as Grey pulled up to the curb, closing and
darkening at the sight of me climbing out of the front seat, holding the door for her to take my place. She hesitated, then raised
her head, focusing on some distant point beyond us as she spoke.

"Thanks."

She tried to step around me, but I caught her hand. Her fingers were long shards of ice, stubbornly limp against my palm.
She no longer wore her promise ring.

"What happened, Sadie? Please tell me."

"He called me from the police station. I don't know why he's
there, or if he's okay, or what's going on at all—he only had a

minute to talk. He told me to get hold of Paul, have him come down there. And then I tried to leave, but my dad—he heard me on the phone, and he took my keys, and . . ." She crumbled, coughing out a tiny sob. "I left anyway. I waited until he'd gone out to the kitchen, and I just grabbed my purse and ran out the door. They don't know I'm gone, and he's going to kill me. But I couldn't leave my brother there."

"We won't. I can't leave him either."

"I know. Lord, Lane, I know you can't." Her voice was small and scratchy, jagged with tears, face blurred to a quavering mess as she pulled me into a hug. I saw Grey in profile over her shoulder, head bowed over the steering wheel.

"We need to hurry," she finally said, letting go of me and sliding into the front seat. "I don't know if he's been arrested, or needs bail money, or when they'll let him go, but we need to get there and help him, before my parents realize I'm gone."

I crawled into the back seat and buckled up, rummaged in the seat pocket for a tissue. I found an old Bojangles' napkin, crumpled but clean, and immediately reduced it to soggy shreds. A movement between the front seats caught my eye—his hand, reaching across the console for hers. Her fingers, shuddering, then clenching, then linking with his. His face lit in silhouette as he looked at her, holding her eyes past the point of safety, past the point of rationale, and I saw the stop sign and the other car, was drawing breath to warn him, when he swung his gaze back to the road and tapped the brake casually. Drew us smoothly to a stop in plenty of time to dodge disaster.

* * *

"I just need to know what's happening. Please."

"I understand, miss." The cop barely glanced up from her screen, clearly unmoved by my distress. The station lobby was empty, aside from us, which was probably for the best—she'd acknowledged me through the front desk's glass barrier only long enough to confirm Connor was, in fact, somewhere inside the station. Since then, crickets. "Someone will be with you shortly."

"Look." I leaned against the counter, put my mouth right up to the intercom, earning half a bored glance. "My—friend is back there. His sister has been waiting forever—we all have—and . . . Can you at least tell me if he's okay? Can you tell me ANYTHING AT ALL?"

"*Ma'am.* Have a *seat.*"

A hand curled around my wrist, caught it right before my palm slapped the glass. My stepbrother, stilling my fingers with a gentle warning. He gestured to the row of chairs across the lobby where Sadie huddled, silent and miserable.

"Elaine, come sit with us. I'm sure he's fine."

"You don't know he's fine, Greyson—you can't just *say* that like it's a fact, when you don't *know.*" I yanked my arm from his grip, whirled to face the cop. She'd swiveled her chair during my diatribe, turned her back on us entirely. "He needs *help.* He needs *someone.*"

The station door swung open then, and Paul strode in on a late-autumn gust, as if my words had summoned him from the very heavens. He glanced around the room, brushed a leaf from the shoulder of his trench coat. Took in my livid eyes and frantic, flailing hands; Grey's frustration; Sadie's damp, blotchy cheeks.

"All right, then. Where is he?"

"I DON'T KNOW, PAUL. NO ONE DOES. APPARENTLY, HE ONLY EXISTS AT ALL IN SOME WEIRD, ALTERNATE TIMELINE, BECAUSE NO ONE HERE WILL TELL ME ANYTH—"

"ELAINE."

The word blew through the room. Grey tossed his head, addressed Paul directly as I blinked at his haughty profile. "We don't know exactly what's happening. The details of his situation have not been made available to us at this juncture."

"Right. I'm on it. Sadie, honey, come with me. We'll get it all straightened out, okay?" She all but flew from her chair, disappeared into his massive hug. He nodded at me over her head, gesturing to the door with his chin. "I got this, Laney. Y'all go wait outside."

So, Grey and I waited. Planets spun off their axes and fell into the sun. Stars imploded and winked out of existence. Empires rose and fell, spawned new civilizations; babies were born and grew and bred and died for generations, and still we waited. I paced the tiny parking lot, sat on the curb, paced and circled and paced again, worrying the remains of my napkin. Endlessly worrying, in every way.

"Here they come."

I was halfway across the lot before Grey finished speaking. I saw Paul at the counter, still speaking through the intercom as the door closed behind the Hall siblings. Connor's lean shadow led the way, head down, hands shoved in his jacket pockets. It collided with my feet and stopped him cold.

"What—Lane? You're here."

"Of course I'm here."

There was nothing else to say. Everything lay between us, real and whole, as if time had stopped that day at the warehouse—that hazy, lovely afternoon, right before death rushed in and snuffed my heart. If I'd only told him then—how many, many things it would have changed. How bright and warm the world would be, if I'd tipped my face toward the sun.

Brighter, at least, than the scowl that shadowed his face as his eyes slid from mine and landed on Grey. Leaped from there to his sister's guilty sideways glance.

"Goddamn it, Sadie. You really had to, didn't you."

"Daddy took my keys, Connor. I didn't know who else to call." She faced him in a flare of defiance, met his glare head-on. "What was I going to do, *not* be here for you? I told you, that'll never happen again."

"You shouldn't have bothered them."

"Yes she should've. I'll always help her if she needs me." Grey's voice drew her gaze to his, held her eyes even as they spilled over. "Always, Sadie."

His name spun from her mouth like silk. His shoulder muffled the rest of her words as they wrapped around each other, her hands disappearing into fistfuls of his jacket. They still loved each other so completely, so shamelessly. They always had, and some jealous, ugly part of me had wished that dead—had wanted nothing more for years than to see them split. And now they had.

It wasn't what I wanted at all. Not for them, or for myself.

I felt Connor's eyes on me, caught them before he could look away. They were hollow wastelands, bloodshot and blank.

"Sorry about this," he muttered. "She shouldn't have made it your problem."

"It's not a problem at all. As long as you're okay."

"That remains to be seen." His shoulders quivered; he forced them straight, lifted his chin. Dared me to pity him. "I'm not talking to you guys through bars, so that's something."

"Should I even ask? Were you actually arrested, or . . . ?"

"Picked up for questioning, technically speaking. For verbal assault. 'Communicating threats' is what they called it."

"What? When did you do that?"

"Fucking Bukowski. Paul found out he's the one who's been setting up those parties, hijacking the space with all his tweaker friends. Dealing out of the goddamn bead room. So I banned him last week, and today I get home and there's a fucking squad car waiting for me. They bring me in, and him and his friends were lined up in there, waiting to give formal statements. Said I threatened all of them, that time I kicked Aiden out."

"Oh Lord, no. Do the police think you killed Aiden?" Sadie turned away from Grey, mascara-streaked eyes lit by a sweep of headlights as a car pulled into the lot. "Connor, what's going to happen?"

"Nothing, as things stand now. They know he OD'd. They tried to make me talk, but I wouldn't, and then Bukowski changed his story, and the other guys are in there high off their asses—they're not looking real reliable. But they fucked up bad this time. We won't forget."

"Who, you and Paul?"

"All of us. The street kids, the artists—we handle our own problems. We mind our own business, and we don't talk to the cops. Ever." He blinked hard, stared past me to the lights of downtown. "I should be in the clear. No one gives a shit about a dead junkie, and there's no proof I said anything either way. But—"

"Sadie Lynn Hall, you step away from that boy."

His voice was as loud and skin-crawly as it sounded on the television, his smirk twice as nauseating in person. Connor's entire body snapped around as his father strode across the parking lot toward us.

"What the fuck is he doing here, Sadie?"

"I don't know. I certainly didn't invite him." She was livid, her face red and blotchy and streaked with tear tracks. "Daddy, how did you—"

"Didn't take much detective work to figure out where you'd gone," the reverend drawled. "I hope you enjoyed your outing— those car keys are mine until further notice, and the door to your bedroom has been removed from its hinges until I decide you've earned it back. Are we understood?"

"That's not fair! I didn't do anything wrong. I was trying to help, and I—"

Connor laughed, a single short bark that bordered on madness.

"You took her door, huh? Sounds familiar. Make sure you cut off the breakers in there too, and take her blankets and pillow. She might start thinking she has a right to basic human comfort, and then where would we be?"

"Don't you speak to me, son. I came here to collect your sister, not subject myself to your *innumerable* charms."

"Don't you ever call me 'son.' As far as you're concerned, Sadie is an only child."

"Connor?"

The Mrs. Reverend Hall stood by the car, face a malformed origami of shock and sorrow. Her lips wobbled as she took in his set mouth and proud, furious spine, his hair and his piercings and the shadows of his cheeks. The jut of his collarbone. The wide-open wounds of his eyes.

"Mom." The word came out strangled and small.

"Oh, honey. Oh, look at you. You're so thin. You're so— Sadie, why didn't you tell me he was so thin? What happened to him?"

"You know exactly what happened to me. I hope you're enjoying your—what did they convert it to, Sadie? A sewing room?"

"Quilting room," Sadie whispered, cowed and miserable, tears cutting a steady stream down her cheeks.

"A *quilting* room. *Very* quaint. I assume your husband put the door back on? It gets drafty, otherwise. Wouldn't want you to catch a chill."

The reverend stepped between them, faced off with Connor, and there it was: the haughty chin. The dark, disdainful eyes. The contemptuous smirk, wringing any semblance of joy from those same full lips.

"That's enough, Connor. You will not take that tone with your mother, not while I have a God-given breath left in my body. Sadie, get in the car."

"No, Daddy."

"Young lady, do not make me repeat myself."

Sadie. The sweet, perky, strong-willed Sadie I knew—that girl turned to mist in that parking lot. She threw her arms around her brother, broke into violent, silent sobs as he returned her hug.

"Be strong," I heard him whisper. "Hang on just a few more months, and I'll find a way to get you out. I swear."

She could only nod as he gently unlatched her arms and turned her around, giving her a little nudge away from him. Her feet carried her forward dutifully, automatically, but she looked up as she passed us, sought and found my eyes. Drew back from my outstretched hand.

"Help him," she whispered.

"Babe." Grey was in ruins beside me, a mess of tremors and

ragged breaths. She wouldn't look at him. "Sadie, please."

"Sadie, come home with us," I said, low.

"I can't. Don't worry about me—I'll be fine. Just look out for him, Lane. Please."

"Of course I will."

My words followed her to the car, lingered at her back as she climbed in past the wreck of her mother. Reverend Hall stalked after her, herding them both like cattle.

"Rebecca, time to go."

"He's my son."

"He made his bed. Get in the car."

"He's my *son*, Grady. He's *our* son. Look at him."

"He said it himself—he's no son of mine." He leaned into her face until she shrank away, buckled beneath his words and his gaze and his inky-dark shadow. "Get. In. The. Car."

I didn't bother watching them leave. I ran straight to Connor and caught him up, fit myself to his angles and edges. Released my breath only when I felt his arms enfold me, hesitant, then hard. Felt him collapse from the inside out.

Grey stared at the space where the car had been, then kicked the curb as hard as he could.

"Fuck. That fucking bastard," he spat. "We need to get her out of there."

"We can't." Connor's voice was little more than a whisper. "She's a minor. If she leaves home, they can call her in as a runaway, say she's delinquent. Get her in all kinds of trouble, and us, too, if we help her leave. He won't give a shit about her, or anything that happens, until he loses control."

"Control?" The word fell hard from Grey's mouth, a dire question with too many possible answers. "What the fuck is going on in that house? How could I have not known about this, Connor?"

"Because we Halls are good at hiding our shit. Don't blame yourself, man—there's nothing you could have done. I'm just glad you were there for her as long as you were." He lowered his head to rest against mine, pressed his lips to my temple. I held him tighter. "She knows she has to stick it out and finish school. Get out under her own steam, so she doesn't end up like me. She'll make it. She's tough."

"She shouldn't have to be tough. Goddamn it. There has to be something we can—"

A clamor behind us scared me out of my skin: Bukowski and his friends, making their way toward us, heads down, steps hurried. Paul appeared at the door, gave us a thumbs-up, then motioned for us to go. Connor's arms tightened around me, stealing some of my breath.

"Come on." Grey headed for the car, and I followed, one arm solid around Connor's waist. I thought he'd protest, try to stay and stare down Bukowski. Possibly start some bullshit fight, get arrested for real, or at least get hurt.

But he didn't look back. His head stayed down. His arm stayed locked around my shoulder. His feet followed mine without complaint as we walked away.

34

THE RIDE TO THE RIVERFRONT WAS A STAGE SHOW OF repressed rage, quiet gloom, and unsaid words. Grey coasted through stop signs and barely acknowledged traffic lights. Connor sat beside me in the back seat, kept his hand locked around mine. Stared out the window, so I couldn't see his face.

It didn't take long to reach the warehouse, but we still sat in the lot for a solid minute before he let go of my hand and touched the door handle, hesitating. Grey turned in his seat, nudged Connor's arm with a tentative knuckle.

"You sure you're okay here, man? You can crash at our place, if you want."

"I'll be fine. Thanks for the ride. And for bringing Sadie out."

"No problem. Hey . . ." He paused, then reached into the center console cup holder, coming up with something small and silver. He held it out to Connor with a grim smile. "It doesn't matter what happened with any of us, good or bad, okay? We're your friends. We're here for you."

Connor's shoulders sagged at those words. His hand closed

around the offering; the other clenched and relaxed on the door handle, almost imperceptibly.

"Yeah."

I met Grey's eyes, communicating without words. He held my gaze for a moment, then nodded once and turned back to face the steering wheel. I pressed my hand to Connor's back, felt it tense and quiver through his thin jacket, sending my heart into my throat. My voice slipped out small, but strong. Determined.

"I'll stay with you."

When he didn't do more than sigh in response, I followed him out of the car, slid an arm around his waist, and guided him across the lot.

We weren't even to the door when my phone buzzed. By the time I fumbled it out and read Grey's message, he was halfway down the road.

I'll pick you up in the morning for work. Let me know if you need a ride before then. Good luck.

The front room was empty, the main lights dim. Paul must have cleared the place out before heading to the station, likely guessing Connor would be in no shape to monitor anyone, regardless of how things went with the cops. I waited while he locked the door behind us, then followed him through the shadows to his room.

We stood side by side, staring at his futon. I moved my

hand into his, eyes falling shut as he gripped it tight.

"Do you need anything? Should I order dinner, or make you some tea?" Tea, for fuck's sake. I'd lived with Skye too long.

"Not really hungry. Thanks anyway."

"Okay. If you need to get some work done, I can stay out of your way. Or we can talk. Whatever you want."

He sighed, running a hand through the wreck of his hair. I swallowed my nerves before they burst from my mouth in a rush of words I couldn't unsay.

"I need to sleep," he said. "Sorry. I know it's early, but—well, if you want to stay up, it's fine. I get why."

"I'll try to sleep too. It hasn't been as bad lately."

"Okay." His silence wailed through the room—then he moved abruptly, dropping my hand. Grabbed his bathroom caddy and headed for the door, head down, almost rushing. "I'll go get cleaned up."

Alone, I fidgeted and shifted, removed my boots, curled up cross-legged on the futon. Pulled my sleeves down to cover my hands, then pushed them back up again to my wrists. Unwound my hair elastic and unwound my braid, finger-combed the waves from the bottom up, wishing I'd thought to grab my messenger bag on the way out the door.

I hemorrhaged confidence by the liter waiting for him, every second that passed another second spent wondering why I was there. Why I'd thought he wanted me to stay in the first place, and whether I'd be doing him a favor if I disappeared before he returned, instead of hanging around casting shadows. My indecision stalled my action, though. When I looked up, it was too late.

He stood in the doorway in sweats and socks and glasses, face scrubbed, eyes sad. They moved along my shoulder and neck, down the curve of my arm and the length of my hair. Trailed back up my body to search my face. I wanted so badly to gather his splinters in the cup of my palm, to put them all back in the right order until he was whole and unbroken and everything worked again.

"Is this still okay, that I'm here? I don't have anything to change into."

"You can wear my stuff. The pants might be too long, but—"

"Just a shirt is fine."

I looked away as he pulled a clean shirt from one of his clothing totes and handed it to me. I turned it over in my hands, forbidding myself from actually bringing it to my nose.

"My caddy's on the sink. I kept your toothbrush. I mean—I hadn't—wow, that sounds psychotic." He rubbed a hand over his face, slipping his fingers beneath his glasses to press against his eye. "I should have thrown it out, but I . . . didn't. So, it's still there."

"Okay. I'll go get ready."

He still had my toothbrush. It was where I'd left it, mixed in with his cologne and shaving cream, his contact lens solution and four kinds of soap. I focused on that single fact, that piece of me he hadn't been able to throw away. It steeled me against the memory of slack-dead jaws and unblinking eyes, chased the shadows into the hallway: I was back in the warehouse, and it was just a bathroom. Aiden had died right there in the space next to my feet, and it was just a bathroom. Connor wanted me to stay, and he'd kept my toothbrush, and it was just a bathroom.

I had to be stronger than this.

I brushed my teeth and shed my clothes, used his comb to smooth my hair. Washed my face and dried it on the clean towel he'd left for me, then lost myself in an oversize T-shirt that smelled like him and made my eyes burn with longing. By the time I made my way back to the room, my breathing was almost normal. Connor sat on the edge of the futon, elbows resting on his knees. He raised his head at my footsteps, watched as I stowed his caddy in its place and set my clothes on the drafting table next to my purse. His hands worried a small object, turning it over and over between his fingers.

"What do you have there?" I hedged, witty and brilliant, and not at all an awkward human travesty.

"Not sure. Grey gave it to me in the car."

My breath caught as he opened his hand. A silver trinity knot glinted in his outstretched palm.

"That's his triquetra. Wow." I smiled at the uncomprehending arch of Connor's eyebrow. "It has a few different meanings across cultures, but to Grey, it's a symbol of protection—his way of ensuring your safety. I know it doesn't seem like much, but for him to give that to you—"

"I get it. This . . . means a lot, after everything." It disappeared into his grip as he looked up to meet my eyes. "Are you okay? With being in that bathroom, and all?"

He'd been through hell that day, and it showed on his face. Still, he worried over me, even as his world listed out of orbit.

"I'm fine. Are you?"

"Yeah. Lane, I'm sorry. The way I spoke to you, that day we broke—that day I told you to leave? That was shitty. It's how I was raised, and it's not who I want to be. I'm trying to do better. Constantly."

"It's okay. I mean, don't ever do it again, or whatever, but. You know."

"I won't. So." He broke off, coughed out the end of a sigh. "About tonight."

My eyes found the floor in the silence that followed. I felt tiny in his shirt, awkward and uncertain. Very self-conscious and very dumb, thinking I could somehow swoop in and save him, when we were a matching set of disasters.

"I'm sorry," I whispered. "I shouldn't have assumed you needed—someone here. Anyone here. Me. If you want me gone, I can text Grey. It's no problem. I—"

"Stop. I'm glad you stayed. But—I don't know. I want you here, but if you're not comfortable—"

"Hey. We don't have to deal with any of that tonight. I stayed to be here for you, not to drag out all our issues." I swallowed hard and stepped toward him, slid my hands along his jaw and into his hair. Tilted his face until his eyes found mine. "I just need you to know, okay? I should have said it back."

My words stole the air between us, turned it to bitter dust. His face fell, even as his arms wound around my hips. Even as he leaned into me, resting his head against my belly.

"God. Please don't do this. I love you, but I can't have this talk right now."

"But I thought you wanted . . ." I swallowed the lump in my throat, sending the words back down with it as I knelt to his level. "Connor, I've been awful and selfish, and I'm so, so sorry. I wish I'd been strong enough to tell you then."

"It was never about the words. If we're going to work—*really* work, not just go back to how we were, semantics is the least of our worries. And after this shit tonight—the cops, my sister, my fucking parents—Lane, I'm a mess. And look at you." His voice lost its edge, fingertips brushing my cheekbone, tracing the ever-present shadows beneath my eyes, and if I couldn't put his needs before mine even one single goddamn time, I didn't deserve him in any capacity. "Neither one of us has the energy."

"Okay. Later."

"Thank you." The relief in his voice was a skittish, living thing, scratching at me with guilt-tipped claws. If he'd laughed in my face, it couldn't have cut deeper. "Lane, I—"

"It's fine. Just rest."

He nodded, too defeated to do anything but pull away. He set his glasses and the triquetra on his worktable, flicked the switch on his lamp, and curled around himself, facing the wall. I pulled the blanket over us both, fit myself against his body, slipped my arms beneath his. Pressed my cheek to his back and whispered my love, silently, into the curve of his shoulder.

Eventually his breathing slowed, and his fingers found mine. My eyes drifted shut, blinked open, shut again with the rise and fall of his chest, until they fell one last time, and for once I didn't dream. And if we woke in the night, and forgot we no longer had any claim on each other—if we set aside that minor detail for some secret, unspecific stretch of time—well, that was nobody's business but our own. It certainly didn't carry over to the morning, when instead of waking him as I used to do by trailing my fingernails along his neck, I slipped from his bed and left him sleeping, with nothing more than a short text.

Gone to work. Let me know if you need me.

P.S. This is Lane.

Or maybe it did carry over. Because even though I didn't hear a word from him in return that day, not even his usual reassurance that he'd realized it was me without my postscript, my phone buzzed in my bag on Tuesday, with a message that left me slumped against the back wall of the market booth, forehead pressed to my knees, tears running down my face. Everything else swelling loud and desperate and scary behind my ribs.

I do.

35

MY FAMILY WAITED UNTIL CHRISTMAS EVE TO PUT UP the Yule tree, just like always, our celebration lining up with the federal holiday based solely on Dad's last-minute vendor discount at the market. I hated rushing it all at the zero hour—every year was a stressful, disorganized race against midnight, the opposite of festive, and of course I never said a word. That Dad always tried so hard, in his own way, only made me feel worse when I caught myself grinning through gritted teeth, wishing his own way was just a little more focused—a little more right. A little less utterly subpar.

This year, though, felt different. Maybe it was Skye's upbeat attitude, or Dad's markedly enhanced enthusiasm. Maybe it was Grey's childlike awe at the sight of an actual full-size tree in the house, a luxury their tiny apartment had never afforded.

"It smells so good," he kept saying, as if he'd never seen an evergreen before, and he fell victim over and over to the needles, fingers heedless and excited and dripping with ornaments and anticipation. He was still a bright spot on the bleak face of everything—that hadn't changed. He was still all the things I'd wanted, before the things I wanted took on a different, darker form.

We were a family now, all of us. It wasn't just Dad and his earnest delusions, trying so hard to drag a smile from my eyes. It wasn't just me wearing one of my thousand unperturbed faces, each one a small piece of a bigger lie. We were mother and father, brother and sister, and the house felt crowded in the best kind of way, as if ready to overflow.

Once the tree was done, Grey settled in front of the *A Christmas Story* marathon, while Skye and Dad prepped the weird, partially vegetarian spread for our holiday dinner. I wandered through the house, restless and anxious, knowing exactly what I wanted but unsure how to go about getting it.

I'd heard from Connor once since his last text, stumbled my way through a conversation too short and far too loaded to settle things one way or the other.

Your blanket project is still here. Do you plan to finish it, or . . . ?

I'd like to at some point. I can come get it if it's in your way.

It's never been in the way, Lane. I'll hang on to it until you're ready to start working again.

I'm ready when you are, Connor.

He'd dropped off the face of the earth since then, as had Sadie. I'd been more than a little surprised when Grey told me they hadn't reconciled; after the way they'd clung to each other in that parking lot, I figured it was only a matter of time. Whether her silence stemmed from anger or embarrassment, I didn't know, but he'd finally given up after she'd refused to acknowledge any of his many texts. I'd reached out to her myself, on his behalf, and gotten a prompt reply:

GO AWAY

It might have stung more, had Sadie not routinely texted in all caps, regardless of her actual mood. Still, her message was loud and clear.

So that was that.

And now it was Christmas Eve, and I missed them both. I'd paced the hallway countless times, turning thoughts of Connor over in my mind. Turning his bracelet over on my wrist, running my fingers along the stones and edges——his feelings, strangely and fearfully wrought. Beauty, forged and shaped from thoughts of me.

Finally, I drifted into my room, shut the door, and sat cross-legged on the bed, phone clutched tight in my determined hands.

Hi, it's Lane.

I know it's you, Lane. You're still stored in my phone.

Just making sure. Are you alone?

Well, that's a refreshingly direct inquiry. What are YOU wearing?

My laugh drifted into a sigh. I could live my whole life waiting for an emotionally neutral interaction with Connor Hall, and be in my grave long before it occurred to him to have one.

Shut up. I meant are you alone for Christmas. What are you up to tonight and tomorrow?

Oh. The usual, I guess. Art and etc. tonight. Volunteering with Sadie tomorrow, once she's done with church. Might get drunk after, haven't decided.

You're welcome here, you know. If you want.

The phone was silent for about a decade, as the little ellipsis that indicated a response in progress appeared and disappeared, then appeared again. I was formulating the right message to give him a graceful out, when the ellipsis turned to words.

I appreciate it, but probably not a good idea. Nothing personal—just too awkward for everyone involved.

I understand. Let me know if you change your mind. You're not alone if you don't want to be.

Thank you. It means a lot that you're even asking.

I wouldn't ask if I didn't mean it.

Another eternal pause, then:

I know you wouldn't. Hope you have a good Xmas. I love you.

I immediately pressed the call button, hoping against everything that he'd answer so I could say it back. That he wouldn't be a total Connor and let it go to voice mail after a text like that.

He did, though. No surprise there.

My phone fell from my hands. I don't know how long I sat there, shaking and gulping and struggling toward calm, but finally I dried my eyes, collected myself long enough to send back a single word.

Same.

* * *

"Hey. Are you okay?"

Grey hovered in the doorway, peering in at my tear-streaked face and briar-patch hair emerging from the cocoon of quilts and pillows.

"I don't know. Did you need something?"

"They're making tea and hot chocolate. Rob said to ask if you want any. Also, the movie is about to restart." He hesitated, then crossed to the bed, perched gingerly on its edge. "Can I help?"

Grey McIntyre. Once my wildest dream, so suddenly and completely dead to me in that way—yet still protecting me. Still putting himself between me and the things that hurt, whether I needed him to or not. So accustomed to seeking solutions, he'd never even realized he was the problem.

"I doubt it. Thanks anyway."

"Me confronting him is still on the table." He smiled at my sudden guarded blink. "Like it's not obvious. Did he call you?"

"I texted him. Here."

He studied the text log, a small, wistful smile creeping over his face.

"Yeah, that's Connor for you. I'll take you over there now, if you're up to it. I mean, if you want to see him, after everything."

"Well, you know. Gotta regain access to that art space some-how."

He nearly swallowed his own tongue. I watched his eyes bug as he processed my words, reached backward in time to their origin. They spread across his face and neck in a red tide splash of shame.

"Sorry." I retrieved the phone from his frozen hand, listlessly glancing at the unchanged screen. "That was uncalled for."

"No. I actually really deserved it. But you didn't." He stared past my head, addressed my batik wall hanging like it had a face and a fuck to give. "I wanted you, and it made me feel like shit, and I went straight to the place I knew for sure would bring you down with me. My mother would kick my ass if she knew what I said."

"Oooo, blackmail material," I deadpanned. "Happy Yuletide to me."

"Dude, don't even joke about that." He peeled his eyes off the wall hanging and resettled them on mine. They were sad and beautiful, and so familiar. So weird, how my heart didn't so much as hiccup. "I don't have an excuse, Elaine—I'm just so fucking sorry. And I'll make it up to you. I'm on your side now, whatever happens."

"I appreciate it." I eyed the nervous fidget of his fingers, raised an eyebrow at the still-fading flush of his cheeks, wondering if we were even capable of engaging in normal, non-awkward conversation. I hadn't heard him jerking it through the wall lately, so that was something. "I know you and Connor aren't exactly getting along right now."

"Our issues are myriad, yes—but I get where he's coming from. What Sadie pulled with me was the same stuff that drove him away from that whole family." He shook his head, a deep, sorry sadness twisting his face. "It's not even her fault. You saw her dad—she's being who she was taught to be. That kind of stuff tends to stick."

"I think there's hope for Sadie. She just needs to grow up. Get out of that house, figure out who she is. And if it turns out she's still a control freak, well—"

"Bullet dodged. I know. It still sucks." He cleared his throat and squinted at the ceiling. I focused on my hands, gave him a moment to collect himself. "Don't give up, okay? If he really does love you, he'll find his way back."

"And if he doesn't?"

"Then you go on. You make your own plans. You do your own thing. You become Lane."

"Yeah, I'll get right on that. I'm sure she's a real piece of work."

He ruffled my hair, dodged my attempts at retaliation. Blocked the incoming throw-pillow missiles with one of my slippers. Slid off the bed in a heap of laughter and offered me a hand as Skye's teakettle whistled, inviting us to the kitchen.

"I'm sure she's amazing. And want to know the best part of all of this? With or without him, you get to find out."

36

"SKYE, CAN WE—TALK?"

My stepmother blinked up at me from the kitchen chair, distracted by the task of pulling a knee-high boot over her dark green leggings and thick wool socks. Her coat was buttoned to the throat, snug around the merino blend scarf I'd made her for Christmas. She'd worn it constantly in the two days since, thrilled by the way the autumnal hues picked up the darker red glints of her hair.

"Sure, Elaine. I have to leave for work, but I have a moment or two to spare." She straightened up and rested her elbows on the table, taking in my pale, troubled face as I slid into the chair across from hers. "What's wrong?"

How to begin—how to even start with that fucking list. My sleep had improved, but the nightmares were far from fading. I missed Connor with a ferocity that left me weak, every thought and memory a thorn-sharp sting. I was alone; I was lonely. It ached in unfamiliar ways, like the pinch of too-small shoes, ruining every step. It swallowed me deeper, every day.

It was hard enough to ask for her help in the first place. Dad was wonderful but useless, too close and too Dad-like to bear any of my burdens without unraveling. As for Grey, I'd heard every last damn word he had to say on the subject—not that he could really sell himself as an expert on healthy emotions at this point.

Skye was neutral, though. Skye was approachable. Skye was the closest thing I had to a mother.

After so many years spent getting by on my own, I really, really wanted my mom.

"Lots of things." I shrugged, staring down at my hands. At the neglected edges of my fingernails, pressing into my palms. "Emotions. Stuff like that."

"You haven't spent much time at the warehouse lately, I noticed." When I didn't answer, she nodded, reached across the table to pat my arm. "I'm sorry. Breakups are never easy."

"We want different things. Or, we did. And it hurt him too much, and we fought, and—by the time I realized I—I don't know." So frustrating, how I still couldn't fucking say it, even when he was miles away. "It's all fucked up. Sorry."

"No problem. We're all adults here, right?" She grinned at my reluctant nod. "So, is it something you can fix? What do you think you'll do next?"

"I don't know. I don't have much of a choice, do I? The communication hasn't been great."

"If you think there's still a chance, you could always reach out. But what do you *want*? Not necessarily from Connor—in general.

In a partner. The checklist and the deal breakers, if that makes sense."

"No. I understand." If there ever was a minefield, Jesus Christ. How best to explain it all to Skye, when a scant few months ago, I'd been pining for her son? Skipping over that little detail was a given. "I guess I thought I knew, and then . . ."

"What you thought no longer fit what was real," she finished, smiling. "One of life's favorite little tricks."

"What if you don't even *know* what's real?"

It burst from my mouth, startling us both. Skye drew breath to answer, but I was in it now—I could feel the rest of the thought surging to the forefront, questions I'd never been able to articulate, all suddenly clamoring to be asked.

"Everyone else knows what they want—Sadie would be married right now, if she had her way. I know Greyson wants a family someday, and the whole eternal life mate thing. And Connor—" I choked on his name. "They're all so *sure*, and I'm just *not*—and no one understands. What if love, for me, doesn't fit with all that? Am I the problem? Am I doing everything all wrong?"

"Elaine, no. There is no 'wrong' way—you're young. You have plenty of time to figure it all out. Or maybe you figured it out already, and want something different. Something safer."

"Safer? What do you mean?"

"It all depends." She moved into the chair next to mine, placed her cool palm over my fist. "Having a family can be a wonderful, fulfilling journey. But it also means putting the needs of your children before your own, unconditionally and always—and often, the needs of your partner. Most people don't realize their capacity for that one way or the other until it's too late."

"Wow. Yeah, I can totally see the appeal."

"They forget to tell you that part," she sighed. "It's certainly not for everybody, as some of us learned the hard way."

"Oh." I watched her closely, didn't miss the way her mouth tightened at the edges. Skye wore motherhood like a second, silken skin. That she might regret her choices had never crossed my mind. "That must have been rough for you."

"For me? Oh no, Elaine——Greyson is my light. I wouldn't give him up for the world. But his father . . . I was optimistic. I spent a long, long time trying to fit who he was into who I thought he was. It took waking up one day to find him gone to make me face the truth of him. And even then it was years before I found any kind of peace."

Her words scooped a tiny hole in my chest, forced a wispy image into sharper focus: little Grey with morning-heavy eyes, still blinking his way out of sleep. Unaware he was about to face his first day of forever without a dad. No wonder he hadn't slept properly since.

Skye was right——you can't take a hit like that and expect to recover on a standard timeline. Grey was practically a grown man, and he still hadn't ironed out the finer points of restful slumber. As if he was still afraid to close his eyes, in case the people he loved disappeared while he was dreaming.

I could pretty well fucking relate.

"It was for the best, though," Skye continued. "It hurt like nothing else, to realize how wrong I was about something that had felt right. But there was a relief in it, believe it or not—realizing my child and I deserved more. No amount of sunshine can fix a man who doesn't want to grow."

"Keep expectations realistically low," I joked, cheeks aching through a hideous grin. "Got it."

"I'm not saying *that*," she chuckled. "But people will ultimately be who they are. When your heart muddles everything else, you have to trust your eyes." She checked her phone and stood, pulled her gloves on one by one. "I can't stay longer, or I'll be late. Will you be okay? I can drop you off at the market, if you need your dad. And we can always talk more, when I get home."

"I'll be fine. Thanks, Skye."

"We're in all of this together, hon. Whatever you need, we're here."

"Was it really palmistry?" I blurted, stopping her hand on the doorknob. Cringing at the bewilderment twisting her face. "How you and Dad met. Greyson said your hands aligned, or—your fates. Something. And then you decided to get married?"

"Oh. *Oh.* Honey, no." Her laughter rang like wind chimes, lovely and bell-clear. "Rob was delivering soaps to the shop, and he scraped his hand on one of the shelves. I offered him our first aid kit, and he made a joke about ruining his fate line and how the cut may have just remapped his destiny. Just a tiny, silly moment, but it made me laugh. That was the icebreaker, and the rest is . . . now."

"I can . . . *totally* see that. I can picture it happening, like I was there." Dad and his shy grin, his cheesy jokes and easy manner. Remapping his destiny for real with an offhand remark. "Grey made it sound like you got together based solely on your palm prints."

"Greyson may have gotten a couple wires crossed in the retelling. In the end, it was our hearts that matched." She paused, regarding me with her head to one side. "Elaine, no one can be everything you need—but the right person will never stop trying to understand exactly what that is."

She smiled her way out the door, left me staring after her, my face frozen in an automatic, answering grin. It faded in less than a minute.

Unlike Sadie's, my dreams for the future were murky at best. All of Skye's wisdom about needs and wants and expectations— how could any of those exist for a girl who breathed moment to moment, with barely time to form a thought, much less a plan? I couldn't foist that life on someone else, no matter how long they followed me with open arms.

I'd made the day-to-day work on my own so far. I would be fine.

But what if things had gone too far? What if day-to-day was no longer enough?

I shook that one out of my head, pressed my fingers to my aching eyes. There *was* no "what if." My mother had made that choice for me. Drawn a crimson line in every shade of sand, when she pulled her own literal cut-and-run.

Most days, I was too much like her to even wish for more. How powerful a wish it would have to be, to overcome that legacy—was I supposed to risk one for the other, knowing my choice might one day run out warm around the toes of my own child? How could I even consider it?

I couldn't. And I won't.

I'll never force anyone to scrub away my blood.

37

~~How to Be Me~~

~~Who Is Lane Ja~~

~~Defining My Future Self~~

Things I Know about Me

Hair: Long, dark, straight, same as always. Eyes: Brown.

Face/Body: No third-party complaints thus far. ~~Sideboob apparently nice enough to almost immortalize WHY. WHY WHY WHY DID I WRITE THAT. UGH.~~

Personality: Quiet. ~~Mostly nice.~~ Probably used to be better. ←Need to work on that.

Relationship Status: I hate this question.

Life Goals: ????? Something with knitting/yarnwork? Fiber "artist"? Note: Get own wheel someday. Ask ~~Connor~~ PAUL, ASK PAUL for details on warehouse wheel. Also, form ACTUAL life goals at some point. ← (Priorities, much?)

Likes: Fiber art. Gardening. Caffeine. Yoga. Netflix. Reading, sometimes. ~~Is this really it? How is this everything? Why. Why why why~~

Dislikes: Sleeping. Sadness. Too many things. This list.

I Am: Rob's daughter. Annie's daughter. Skye's ~~step~~daughter. Grey's ~~sister.~~

~~Stepsister~~

Sister

I want: my mother ~~out of my head~~

~~To go gently into that good~~ finally be at peace

I want: to finally be at peace

~~But maybe not in exactly the same way, or do I wow, this went to the dark place all at once, did it not~~

I want: to be happier. However I can.

I want: Sadie to forgive me.

I want: Connor ~~to call me~~

~~apologize come back to me stay with me love me~~

~~Him. I just want him.~~

Why.

~~I don't~~

~~I don't know~~

I don't know

That night—or the next morning, really, four a.m., found me at the kitchen table, sorting through what it meant to become Lane. The checklist and the deal breakers. Making a goddamn archive of my life's minutiae, as if committing things to paper was the key to the girl I was. As if the right combination of words would unlock the gates and set that stranger free. So far it was nothing but garden-variety bullshit: yarn and flowers and general fiber art. Books and yoga. Bitter coffee. A quiet mouth, set in a bare, blank face. Oh, and Netflix. Can't forget that.

All surface shine and crossed-out gibberish, her girlish shadow swallowed by a longer, darker form.

Lane herself was a gutted building—a hollow shell, home to vermin and empty spaces and things not worth the trouble of hauling off. Long ago robbed of everything worth anything. Still, even on the worst days, I didn't want to die.

So I stood up. I placed my feet, one by one, ahead of each other. I did what I had to do to go on, even as every step forward left a scar on my heart.

The dream had been different—somehow better, somehow worse. My mother lay on the floor, sprawled and still, eyelids, lips, and cheeks washed the same watercolor blue. Sadie stood in the corner, nose to the wall. Her back was straight and proud, her hair a colorful riot of tiny satin ribbons, silky and inviting. Ribbons that snagged on my fingers, melding into the flesh, unraveling like stitches in a frogged scarf and taking her head with them. It thumped across the floor, stopping faceup at my feet. Her mouth dissolved and bled away like sand beneath eyes that turned from blue to brown, and suddenly the face was Connor's.

That had been the end of sleepy time.

The X-Acto waited in my nightstand drawer, an alternate ending to any fucked-up story. What I wouldn't give for the simplicity of a cut, or the sudden snap of bone—to feel the thrill of a moment as it happened, instead of constantly reaching backward. My whole life spent bending and breaking, weaving memory wisps into patterns that clashed with reality. Hell, look what I'd done to Grey.

My brother. An idea I'd had a long time ago——the promise of another story, beautifully bound and waiting to be written. I'd fallen over myself to fill the pages, scattered them with grand ideas, stitched its seams with delusional thread. Formed him around my concept of love: a safety net, stretched over a bottomless pit. So brilliant and bright, it'd had no trouble eclipsing the real thing.

I'd had it. It had been right there, yet I'd gone ahead and fucked that up too. Ignored the drag of the blade for the phantom ache of a long-missing limb, and for all I knew, it *was* too late. My hands might never be steady enough to close that wound.

None of that mattered, though. Not really.

Because it wasn't about Grey, or Connor, or which one of them I loved; it wasn't about saving someone, or being saved, or finding myself enveloped in the strangest, most unexpected corners of another person's heart.

It wasn't about them at all, and never had been.

She'd loved me fiercely. I knew it with a certainty that couldn't be moved, and yet I still couldn't fault her for clawing her way out of the world——for wanting nothing so much as the *relief* of nothing, regardless of the mess it made. It was love itself that took her to that place, opened her heart to rivers of endless, overwhelming grief. Better to cut it out entirely than to welcome even one more drop.

I understood my mother. Even though she'd left me, I didn't blame or doubt or hate her.

Trouble is, I also didn't remember her.

I knew her face, of course; it smiled at me from assorted frames, in every room of the house. It stared back at me from every mirror. But I knew nothing of her hands or voice, nothing of her laugh or the swing of her hair. What I knew was a nightly reel of blood and agony—an endless cycle of hell, choked with the stink of death. That last image—that drained body in that white bathroom—that was all I truly had of Annie Jamison. That was the beginning, and that was the end. That was my mother, wrapped around eternity.

Water and rock. If I lost the dreams, I lost her, too.

Who *was* I, without her blood drying, tar-sticky, on the tiles? Who was I without that final atrocity unspooling over and over at my feet? Was the memory itself the key to that destiny, or was it the only thing holding me back?

And if I did forget—if I could so easily let go of the single, defining thing that made me Lane, what was the point of it in the first place?

What was the point of anything, if it all slipped down the drain?

"Elaine."

His sleep-heavy voice cracked the silence, jolting through my veins like ice. He stood in the doorway, rumpled and blurred and soft around the edges.

"Oh. Greyson." I brought my hand to my face, slid my fingers along alarmingly wet cheeks. "Oh. Oh God. I'm sorry. I didn't—"

"I'm getting Rob."

"No, I'm fine. I'm—"

"I'm. Getting. Rob." And he was gone.

I gave myself over to exhaustion, let myself sink low in my chair. Rested my forehead against the table, too drained to do anything but breathe.

"Elaine, honey, sit up." Dad's hand was gentle on mine as he knelt beside my chair. Skye crouched on my other side, her hand steady on my shoulder. Grey hovered in the doorway, then moved to the stove, gathered jars and infusers, filled the kettle and set it to boil. "What happened? Are you sick?"

"No. It was—" I gulped and shuddered, the thought alone enough to cut. "It was the dream again. But different. Horrible."

"The dream?" Skye looked at Dad, who'd gone still at my words, his face a reflection of everything cold in my gut as he took the chair next to mine.

"You told me they stopped," he whispered. "You said you were fine—you had me take you out of therapy. Why?"

"I didn't want to go anymore. I was starting to forget her, and I knew if I kept healing . . ." My bravado crumbled, falling to the table to mix with my tears. "Oh, Dad. I can't do this anymore. I can't do any of it."

"How can I help you, honey? Tell me how to help you."

He was getting earnest and agitated, his natural reaction to conflict and crisis both. Dad was an amazing and wonderful person, and he loved me, but his own fragile heart bore bruises enough. When it came to stuff like this, he was just another set of shaking hands.

"You can't help me. I'll be fine. You should go back to bed."

"But you're not. You're not fine. You sound like——oh, Elaine. You sound exactly like your mother."

I raised my eyes——*her* eyes, her same shape and color and blank, listless sheen, to find his had already overflowed. My father wept in front of me, too unsurprised.

"When you were a baby," he said, low, "you wanted to be held every minute of the day. Annie would rock you to sleep, and the second she tried to put you down, whether in your crib or the swing or the bassinet, you'd wake up shrieking. She had to wear you in a sling just to get anything done at all. You still need that——you still need someone to wrap you up and keep you safe."

"I don't. I never asked anyone to carry me."

"No, you didn't ask. But not asking isn't the same as not needing. And it's my fault."

"This isn't your fault, Dad."

"It is. Your mother needed help. She needed far more help than I could give her, but she was so stubborn——she wanted to deal with it on her own, and I let her. We both thought love would be enough to get us through. And we loved each other, and we still had you. And she loved you so much." His voice cracked on the last word. "She said she was fine, that she was getting better every day. I wanted to believe her, so I shut my eyes to anything that told me different. And in the end, I failed her. I failed her, and I'm failing you, and I will never ever forgive myself."

Dad's head dropped to the table, and I lowered mine to rest beside it, cooling my cheek against the wood. That he could bleed so easily—that was something. That he felt his wounds, acute and painful, painfully real—that he let them leak into the world, unchecked. It was more than I could do, most days.

My brother appeared in front of me, a mug in each hand. He had no idea what to do with any of this mess, so he just stood there with his tea until Skye took the mugs and placed them on the table.

"Lane, honey, I'd like to ask you something," she began. "Please tell me if I overstep, okay?"

"Okay."

"As a mother, I can't imagine losing a child. It's not a thing that can be overcome by sheer will. From everything I've heard, your mother was a beautiful person, inside and out. But she was broken beyond comprehension. Far more than even your father knew."

"Obviously." It came out harsher than I meant it. Dad gave a thin wail. "Fuck. Sorry, Dad. Skye. Sorry."

"Don't apologize, sweetheart. Are you sure this isn't too much to hear?" I nodded, and she continued. "Likewise, I can't possibly know the pain of losing a mother, especially as young as you were, in such a brutal, violent way. We're here for you, all three of us are—but you need more than we have to offer. Will you let me find someone to treat you? Someone who can really help you begin a healing process?"

A part of me, the stubborn, frightened, sharp-clawed recluse, screamed from the corners of my mind. I was tired, that was all. Once my brain had a chance to rest and recover, I'd get back to the busywork—restock my knit items, crank out some more jewelry. Get myself a spinning wheel and learn how to dye fiber, maybe start my own line of homespun yarn cakes. My art would save me, like it always did—it had gotten me this far, and it would carry me through. I needed sleep, not therapy.

If I could just clear my head, I'd be fine.

But she'd stayed busy too. My mother, smile in place, soothing my father's worries with reassurances and gentle words, cleaning her bathroom until it gleamed. Moving through the days until her feet wore through, and still she walked, balancing on nothing but bone. Sure, she'd kept going—she strode straight down her path without stopping, ignoring the pebbles in her shoes. Ignoring the offered hands and gathering shadows both as she waded into quicksand, and by the time the mud reached her eyes, it was too late.

In the end, she'd drowned alone.

Still, some part of me didn't want to heal—it wanted the wounds and blood and memories, and the unending, unparalleled fear that, so far, had kept me going. That part opened my mouth, prepared to fight. What actually came out was as much a surprise to me as anyone.

"I don't want to die. I don't. But I can't handle living if it feels like *this*."

"Don't say that. Please don't say that," Dad keened. "My baby. My baby girl."

He practically dissolved onto the tabletop. His hands curled around mine and held on tight. Skye's covered his, containing and soothing us both.

"Elaine, I have a dear friend who specializes in trauma and grief counseling," she said. "She's a wonderful doctor and a very kind, sympathetic person. I'll call first thing in the morning, if you're willing to see her."

"Maybe. There's so much, though. I don't know if there's enough help in the world for how I'm feeling."

Dad came back to life beside me, wrapped his arms around my shoulders. He'd likely have pulled me all the way into his lap if he didn't think I'd tip him over.

"Please do this, Elaine. Please. We'll do whatever it takes to make it happen. Whatever you need. I couldn't save Annie, but I won't give up on you. I won't lose you, too."

I rested my face against his hair, felt his tremors all the way to my bones. I met Grey's eyes across the table. His smile tugged its twin from my mouth, sparked a blur of tears in my tired eyes. They ran warm down my face, a relief for once, rather than a defeat.

I could cry, and it would be okay. I could stop—not forever, but long enough to shake out my own pebbles. Long enough to pause and collect myself, make sure everything worked before pressing on. I was Lane, not Annie—and I wasn't alone.

I would never be alone again.

"You won't lose me, Dad," I said, more sure than I'd been in a long, long while. More sure of me than I'd been in years. "I'm not going anywhere."

38

AND THAT'S HOW I ENDED UP IN THE SQUISHY CHAIR ON the second-to-last day of the year, watching pale sunlight struggle its way through the clouds to light the windowsill. The office was the upper story of an old Victorian, cozy with fireplaces and bookshelves and ludicrously overstuffed furniture. I'd have been perfectly happy moving right in had I been able to ignore the reason I was there in the first place.

The world no longer swayed beneath my feet or fuzzed at the edges through the trippy lens of sleep starvation. I felt better. I felt like me—a stronger, more purposeful version, less confused, more optimistic. Familiar even, as if this version of Lane had been a true thing all along, buried beneath the surface mess. Like still-green grass beneath a scatter of autumn leaves.

I'd do what I could to clear it all away. Anything and everything, to keep her safe.

Dr. Hamilton was shorter than me, yet infinitely radiant, warm and bright in a way that made everything else fade to watercolor. Her voice was a friendly lilt that matched her face, smooth and dark and angular beneath a frenzy of curls, and wide, kind eyes that made you smile back. She bustled around the room, straightening cushions, rehanging an escaped shawl on the wrought-iron coatrack. By the time she settled across from me, notepad balanced on her thighs, I'd become one with the squishy chair. I curled my legs under me and rested sideways against the arm, practically fetal.

"Are you comfortable, Lane? Some people are intimidated by those cushions—they want something firmer, a little more solid."

"I love it. It's like a little nest."

"I agree completely. I prefer my chairs as soft as they can get. Feels like I'm being wrapped in a hug every time I sit down. So." She linked her fingers beneath her chin. "We can begin whenever you're ready. Everything that happens here will happen at your preferred speed. Let me know if you feel overwhelmed, and we can take a break, okay? Whatever you need."

"Thank you. I'm glad you're here. I mean . . ." I swallowed, feeling awkward and dumb. "We weren't sure you'd be available to see me, so close to Christmas."

"I don't take off around the holidays, darlin'. This is the time of year I'm needed most." Her lips parted in a smile, friendly and sweet around crooked front teeth. "It's perfectly normal to feel nervous for the first few sessions. We can do some breathing exercises, if you like."

"I'm not exactly nervous." I focused on a swirl of drifting

leaves, watched them pile against the window frame before scattering on a breath of wind. "I feel so stupid, though. Like I barely have a right to be sad at all, when so many people have it worse."

"Nonsense. Pain is a universal affliction—no one in this world is spared. As for you feeling 'stupid,' well—that's one of those words we should try to leave at the door whenever we can."

"I'm sorry. I didn't mean—"

"It's fine, honey. But try not to be so hard on yourself. Kindness—forgiveness—love—these things cost nothing to practice. And you deserve them all." Her hands steepled beneath her chin as she regarded me, head to one side. "That seems like as good a place as any to kick off our session, don't you think?"

"Okay," I whispered, her words seeping in and taking root. Budding already, like all they'd been waiting for was a flash of sun. "I'm just not really sure where to start."

She settled back in her chair, crossed one knee over the other, and set her notepad aside with an easy nonchalance. Her frank gaze invited anything, demanded nothing.

"Why don't you start at the beginning?"

And so, I did.

39

THE SECOND DAY OF THE NEW YEAR WAS DRY AND frigid, cold enough to repurpose December's muddy remains into a brand-new front-yard skating rink. I slid carefully over the fragile ice, balanced a bin of hand-knit items against Grey's car as I fumbled for the keys.

"He said he'd leave it unlocked."

Her voice so close nearly scared me off my feet. Sadie grabbed my arm with one hand and the bin with the other, steadying us both.

"I didn't know you were coming over." I glanced at her car. It was parked haphazardly, one tire resting on the curb. "Got your keys back?"

"For errands only. I texted Grey last night, figured I'd get the rest of my things while I was out and about. He said he'd leave them in the car." Her eyes snuck past me to the house, seeking Grey's bedroom window and its dark, still curtains. "I guess he's still asleep."

"I'm sorry it ended this way, Sadie. I know he never wanted to hurt you."

"Honey, there was no avoiding it." She stuck the bin in the back seat, grabbed an already packed tote bag of her stuff from the floorboard, then straightened up, exhaling the tension in her shoulders. "I'd like to say I'd do things differently now, but I have a sinner's heart, same as anyone. I'd probably screw it up the same way all over again."

"Maybe not. But Duke is his dream. That decision wasn't yours to make, no matter what you'd planned."

Her face changed, split open along the seams. Trembled at the edge of breaking.

"It wasn't just me, Lane. He always talked about how we would build a life together, take our best assets and combine them into a single powerful force. Like Voltron." Her smile was a weak reply to mine, closer to a grimace. "Those plans were *ours*—*I* was his dream. He told me. And I believed him."

"I think you were." I glanced back at Grey's window. The curtains were still closed, but the light was on. He could burst through the door at any moment, skid toward us on a sheet of ice and indignation. "Maybe you still are. But he needs to follow this one before he figures out the rest."

"As long as he's happy. That's all I want for him. I only wish he'd have let me know when it all turned to lies." She shook her head and continued, barreling on as she tended to do. "And then there was the whole matter of you."

Ah yes. That. Sadie's eyes were clear but guarded, simmering with that low-grade ire. Connor's words surged out of nowhere: *He's a good kid, but come on—he's no saint.*

For all his secrets, no one knew Grey better than Sadie did. She'd seen how he'd looked at me long before they broke up. She'd known the whole time.

But that was done. I'd pined, sure; I'd fucked up, certainly. But I hadn't betrayed her, and I hadn't made him leave. Whatever had happened once the world fell down—that only mattered if I let it.

Still, though.

"Yes, there was that. And I . . . Sadie, you have to know it wasn't about you. I loved him for years, before any of this." I blundered ahead, cheeks roasting, eyes pleading with her to understand. Hoping she'd hear me, with all my heart. "I know—you're like, 'what the fuck, Lane,' right? But there's this super-convoluted origin story on my end, and he had no idea, and then he was just *there*, in my house—and I should have dealt with it right then. Whatever he felt, I could have drawn a boundary and stuck to it, and I didn't. And it ruined so many things. But I promise you, it's not an issue now."

I watched her face, which somehow hadn't changed—she blinked at me, perfectly plucked brows arched over neutral eyes. Not even a little bit shocked.

"Well, that'll be a story and a half for the grandkids, I'm sure. But I have a few more things to say about it, Lane, issue or not."

I eyed the still-quiet house, wondering how long it would take Grey to get his happy ass outside if she decided to start swinging, and whether I could make it back to the porch over the icy lawn without sliding straight into a broken leg. I braced myself for nastiness—a slap or a shove. Maybe angry words. Instead, a soft sigh misted out through her plum-frosted lips.

"I don't know what all went on between you two," she said, holding up a hand. Stopping my reply before I'd thought to start one. "But it doesn't matter. Me and Jesus, we've had a talk or ten these last couple weeks—and whatever you did, Lane, it's no excuse. None of it justifies my sins."

"Your—what?" I scrolled through her role in the shitstorm of the past few months, wondering if the whole mess had also gone down on an alternate timeline. One in which Sadie had emerged with anything but the short ends of all the sticks. "What did *you* do?"

"Lord, honey, what didn't I do? I forgot the Word of God. I was jealous; I was self-righteous and arrogant and mean, and I said and did some real nasty, unchristian things. Especially to you." She stepped forward and stared me straight in the eye, her gaze bright and glistening. Unwavering. "I shouldn't have called you names, Lane, or put myself above you. I shouldn't have judged you in the first place. We girls need to stick together, whatever our differences."

"Yeah," I whispered, moved to sheer bewilderment. It was the very last thing I'd expected to hear—which said more about me than it did about Sadie. "Well, thank you. I guess."

"Don't thank me. Just forgive me, if you can. And if you can't, at least know how sorry I am for all of it."

"Of course I forgive you. I'm sorry too—for everything. The last thing I wanted was to see you hurt."

"Thank you, honey." She was quiet for a moment, turning something over in her mind. "I'm having lunch with Connor after my errands. I can tell him to call you, if you want. Or even that you just say hi."

"Oh." All of my breath caught on the word. The idea of opening that door—of welcoming Connor over the threshold and into my post-breakdown world—crackled like heat lightning across my skin. "I don't know. I don't think he really wants to see me."

"Don't be ridiculous. He's been a mopey mess all week because he thinks *you* don't want to see *him*."

"I've been kind of busy," I muttered. "Anyway, I haven't heard from him since he turned down my invitation for Christmas."

"You haven't heard from him because he's had his stubborn behind holed up in that warehouse, working his hands bloody so he won't have to admit he was wrong—and you're as impossible as he is. You two had your arrangement, and your total honesty thing, and that worked when it was all you wanted. But if you want more than that, you have to *try* for more. That's what matters, you know—that you never stop giving it your best, even when it hurts." She shook her head, offered me a small, sad smile. "Next time I see a wishing star, I'll send a special one up to Heaven for you both."

She fell silent as my eyes spilled over. I pressed my palms to my face, catching the tears before they could go cold on my chilly skin.

I hadn't wished on stars since I was eight years old.

It never made sense. The sky is full of specks that only twinkle from the past—pinpoints of long-dead light, reaching us through space years after ceasing to burn. Half the time you're staking your hope on an empty space.

I'd try it, though, futile or not. I'd wish on every star that ever was, if it would bring him back.

Sadie's blurry hand appeared, offering me a Kleenex printed with red and green snowflakes. I reduced three of them to a less-than-festive state before I found my voice.

"Tell him I miss him," I finally whispered, fixing my gaze on our feet: my battered Docs with mismatched laces, shifting nervously next to her hot pink Uggs. "Tell him I'm not with Grey, and I never was, and I don't want to be. Not now, not ever."

"Is all that true? I'm not going to lie for you."

"You won't be lying. Just—tell him I need him too."

The Uggs moved toward me in a single giant step. Sadie, solid and strong and bighearted, a burst of strawberry shampoo and vanilla perfume. I hugged her in return, hard as I could through her overstuffed jacket.

"I was going to do that anyway." She smiled as she released me, tired and sad, sweet as she ever was. That mischievous glint in her eye, anticipating her role as matchmaker. "You and my brother have ten years, from this moment, to get right with each other before I start nagging. I call maid of honor. And

I'm not standing next to Grey in the pictures. Do you think Connor would cut his hair? It's a special occasion, after all."

"Wow. Okay. Can we maybe ascertain if he's speaking to me first?"

"You just leave that to me, honey—I'll get him all straightened out, and everything'll be perfect. We'll be sisters for real, one way or another. As long as I can wear pink." She bounced in for another hug and bounced right back out again, sliding away from me to her car before I could gather my wits to retort. "It's destined to be, Lane Jamison. Every last bit of it."

She dropped a wink out the window as she pulled away from the curb, maneuvering over her own tire tracks, and then she was gone.

Harvest season had come and gone, taking with it the spicy vibe of autumn. Christmas was a dead thing too, packed back into taped-up boxes. We'd swept the place of holiday cheer, bid farewell to the market bustle of busy hands, the overflow of hot cider and pumpkin bread; cleared the tables once heavy with squash and bright with holly and garlands and rows of shiny apples. The slow season was officially upon us, and the outdoors held zero appeal—nothing but wind and teeth and bitter steel clouds, winter stalking us through every crack.

Grey tried, at first. He wasted a good part of the morning prodding me toward busywork and neutral conversation before settling back in the chair with his physics homework. Helping the few customers we had, when he realized how useless I was in the capacity of speaking to other people.

It was beyond slow. I passed the time fussing over the display: rearranging the hats, fanning out the gloves, stacking bars of soap like bricks before sweeping everything aside and starting over, unable to focus. Incapable of setting things exactly right.

I was contemplating the perfect way to twist a length of scarf when I felt his foot nudge my calf.

"Elaine. *Elaine.* Oh, for—wake up, will you? *ELAINE.*"

The words barely made it to my brain. He caught my eye and lifted his chin, gesturing behind me. I blinked at him, then turned, and my insides went still. Connor stood at the market entrance, stomping ice off his boots. The winter air had smacked his cheeks, left claw marks across the bridge of his nose. His head was bare, his ears bitten raw, hands shoved in the pockets of his oversize peacoat.

Something pulled at my heart, directed my hands to grab the nearest, warmest hat from the table: a stocking cap, dark brown and chunky-knit. I gathered my own hat and gloves, shrugged into my coat, slung my messenger bag strap across my body.

"I'll be right back," I said to Grey's raised eyebrow. "Okay, maybe not. I don't know. You're in charge."

"Go on," he said. "I've got this."

I didn't look back. He'd be fine without me.

Connor raised his head as I approached, making my way

across the country mile of market to where he stood, blowing on his hands. His palms were red and chapped, the left one marred by an angry-looking scab.

"What happened there?"

He smiled at my question and flexed his fingers, tugged the edge of his coat sleeve loose from his wrist cuff. I glimpsed the shine of the triquetra, anchored to the leather through the pinnacle of each lobe, as he tucked his hands back in his pockets.

"Sometimes inspiration strikes. Sometimes it strikes for a six-hour stretch when you haven't slept in two days and decide a metalworking marathon should be a thing."

"Well. It must have been some kind of end result."

"It's everything I wanted it to be. For that, I'll take the scar every time."

"Can you wear a glove over it? I have mittens in the booth." He shook his head, the corner of his mouth twisting upward. "Connor, it's freezing. One mitten for your good hand, at the very least."

"I'm not going around like an asshole in one mitten, Lane. I'm either all in with the cold hands, or not at all."

"Stubborn. Take this hat, at least. You know you can't resist my fiber art."

His laugh was short but soft, edged with a nostalgia too acute to be wistful.

"My one true weakness. Thank you." He turned the hat over in his hands, smiled as he pulled it down over his glowing ears. Lifted that smile to mirror mine as he shrugged out of his backpack and fumbled with the zipper. "Speaking of."

"You didn't. Since when do you knit?"

"Taught myself last month. I had to——this was sitting there in that bag, unfinished, taking up all my space. Absolutely in the way. Someone had to do *something*."

"Shut up. I told you I'd get it whenever you were——oh. Oh, Connor."

It was a swatch of midnight, begun with my hands, ended with his. Knit with yarn we'd spun together, a million years ago. My blanket, expertly finished, silver beads scattered in tiny, glittering bursts throughout the final third of the pattern.

"I used the beading technique you taught me, that day with the necklace," he said, staring at the floor. "It's beautiful work, but it needed an extra touch. Nothing flashy, just a few——"

"Stars." There it was: the open sky and mountain air. His hands, pulling me through the window into another world.

"Yeah. I should say something like it symbolizes eternity or the infinite depth of our potential as humans. But really, it just reminds me of you. Fuck, I'm terrible at this." He drew a breath and met my eyes, cracked a smile at what he saw. "Walk with me?"

"Yes," I said, before the question mark found its way out of his mouth. "Yes."

I tucked the blanket carefully in my bag and followed him outside, blinking at the bright, cold day. We didn't go far, because there wasn't really anywhere *to* go—the parking lot was an impending hospital bill, the roads beyond it slick and treacherous. We picked our way to the median, away from the buildings and cars and the worst of the ice. Stood facing each other, unsure how to frame what came next.

"So. Pink? Really?"

"Oh my God." My burst of laughter trailed off into a sigh. "Your sister, your problem. At least we have a decade to talk her into a tolerable shade."

"A decade?" He hung his head in defeat. "Goddamn it, Sadie. She gave me five years, tops, then spent the past two hours nagging me to get over myself before it's too late." He echoed my quiet laugh, then took my hand in both of his. I added my other hand to the stack, his so cold I felt them through my gloves. "So, on that note, is this a good time for Total Honesty Mode?"

"Any time is a good time for Total Honesty Mode."

"Yeah. It is." He sighed. "I am so sorry. I started this, knowing where you stood. It wasn't fair of me to ask for more. And I should never have put that whole thing with Grey on you, when you were so messed up."

"It wasn't even about Grey—it was my whole life, and everything I've ruined. Everyone I've pushed away, because I couldn't fix myself, or let go of things that hurt me. It was like I had to sabotage my whole future, to make sure it never matched my mother's."

"That's another thing," he muttered. "I knew you were struggling. I saw you suffering, and tweaking out, not sleeping, and I didn't do a goddamn thing. I told myself you were strong enough—that you could tough it out if I gave you the space you needed, and you'd let me know when you wanted to try again. I left it all up to you, instead of meeting halfway—then, when I didn't hear from you after Christmas, I figured I'd fucked it up for good."

"I can explain all that," I broke in. "It's been . . . a rough road, these past weeks. I had to focus on my health, which meant taking a step back from everything else. I'm sorry."

"Lane, don't you ever say sorry for that. I should have been there, helping you—maybe then it wouldn't have hit you so hard." He looked away, blinked hard at the swell of distant mountains. "I should have been the one pulling you out of it."

"It's not your fault. This was always going to be what broke me." I braced myself against a gust. Connor stepped closer, put himself in the path of the wind. "I'm trying, though. I'm getting help, but I don't know when I'll be back to normal—or if there *is* a normal version of me. 'Normal' may just mean less screwed up than now, for all I know."

"That's all any of us are, I think—more or less screwed up, at any given moment. It's all chaos." His hands gripped mine even harder. "What the hell, though, right? I know I'm a wreck, but I love you. I'll take any number of scars, if we can make this work."

He caught me in those eyes and scooped me up, held me close and broke me open. It wasn't about belonging to him, or owning him, or surrendering the best parts of myself so we could be together. It was about belonging *with* each other. About both of us bringing those best parts to the forefront and loving each other fiercely, even on the days that "best" seemed hardest to find. Loving each other even more those days, when everything else came crashing down.

"Total Honesty Mode?" I whispered.

"My very favorite mode."

"I want that too. Scars and blood and chaos, and everything else. Completely."

"Lane." My name was a sigh, barely misting the air between us. "Please say you mean it."

"Of course I mean it." I reached out and touched his face, held him still in the cradle of my palm. "You and your near-empty glass."

"Whatever. You love my cynicism."

"I love *you*, actually. No one else."

"Yeah, well. Same difference."

The catch in his voice negated the joke, and he tucked me against his chest, wrapping his coat so it engulfed us both. I rested my ear against his heartbeat, relaxed at the pressure of his lips against my hair. Said it again and again into his shirt as the sun struggled loose from the clouds. It lit the world and all its stains and blights and near-blinding beauty, sniffed out all the secret shadows and chased them deep into the woods. Glinted off the ice like classroom lights off the curve of a scalpel—like a bathroom vanity, off a razor edge.

All those things, tucked away behind my heart; disorganized and overlapping, scrabbling relentlessly beneath my skin. All of them, bleeding out on my steady pulse, leaving me lighter every passing day.

Leaving me, still standing, at the end of every heartbeat.

My name again, a whisper followed by a kiss, both left in the hollow of my temple. I raised my face to meet his smile, and no winter sun had ever shone so bright.

RESOURCES

24-7 support for people in crisis or emotional distress:
- suicidepreventionlifeline.org
- National Suicide Prevention Lifeline: 1-800-273-8255

Grief and bereavement support for all ages, including kids, teens, and young adults:
- dougy.org/grief-resources

Resources for runaway and homeless youth:
- nationalsafeplace.org/homeless-youth
- For immediate help, text the word "safe" and your current location (address/city/state) to 4HELP (44357).

Resources for young people in abusive households, relationships, or situations:
- nrcdv.org/rhydvtoolkit/teens
- National Domestic Violence Hotline: 1-800-799-7233

ACKNOWLEDGMENTS

As anyone who has read my early drafts knows, I've never had a shortage of things to say. And yet, when I sit down to write these acknowledgments—when I try to tally these feelings in black and white—I realize that even I could never find enough words to express my love and appreciation for the people who made this book a reality.

To my extraordinary editor, Liesa Abrams—every trick of magic, science, and alchemy, in this or any other timeline, could not have produced a better set of hands with which to shape this story. For your insight and understanding, your advocacy and encouragement—for appreciating my roots and urging me to dig even deeper, without fear of judgment or repression. Thank you for seeing, for connecting, and for giving my words a platform and a voice. Working with you has been the privilege of a lifetime.

To my utterly wonderful agent, Christa Heschke, for not only embracing my dark and gritty content but reveling in it—for your belief in my vision and my work, your confidence in the story I wanted to tell, and your persistence in finding it the perfect home. I will never forget that you didn't waver, even when I had my doubts. I look forward to many more years of creativity, collaboration, and lyrically written murder—all our usual stuff. Thank you, so much, for everything.

Unending gratitude to Mara Anastas, Chriscynethia Floyd, Rebecca Vitkus, Caitlin Sweeny, Anna Jarzab, Emily Ritter, Nicole Russo, Christina Pecorale, Victor Iannone, and Jen Strada. I am proud to have been given a place at Simon Pulse, and thank each and every one of you for your feedback, support, and enthusiasm for this book.

Thank you to Laura Eckes, for a cover beyond any of my expectations. You pulled details and references, bits and pieces, from my story and made them into art. In a million years, I couldn't be happier with the final result.

Daniele Hunter, even if this story had fizzled out entirely and ended up in the publishing equivalent of a dead-letter office, your feedback alone would have made it all worthwhile. Thank you for your support, your fangirling, your enthusiasm, and for cheering me on.

Shannon Powers, my sister in angst, I'm so glad I got to share this one with you. You helped me iron out so many things in those early drafts—thank you for *getting* this book and working with me to make it so much more. Please know I stand ready to return the favor at any time.

Cynthia Thornton, the cornerstone of my Asheville artist life, thank you—for my first ever piece of fan art; for the encouragement and brainstorming, the market trips and crocheting sessions and fact-checking; the riverfront "research" and late nights in the studio that helped me breathe the details into this story and steer it where I wanted it to go. I've stood in awe of your beautiful work for so many years—to have you love mine in return is an incomparable honor. I am beyond proud to call you my friend.

To my most beloved EWC—even at the height of my verbosity, I could talk until the thesaurus ran out and never say enough. This book, or any of my work, really, would not exist without either one of you. Ron Walters, you've been a voice of reason and encouragement for so long, through so many hundreds of thousands of words, both necessary and not so much. You've pushed me to write past my comfort zone, talked me down from the highest pinnacles of my ridiculousness, checked me on "guy" stuff, and never let me go halfway on anything. Jill Corddry, you are a rare prize among humans—one of the kindest, most generous, most supportive friends I've ever known. You are the first I go to when I'm excited or frustrated, inspired or stuck, need a chat or laugh, or am just in the mood for a good old-fashioned Winchester gif session. Your unabashed enthusiasm and never-ending willingness to yank me out of my own head and solve my wordy messes have made all the difference in everything I write. You were my first true fangirl, and I can never fully express my thanks. (Really, I can only hope you will someday forgive me for killing off . . . well, you know. And the other. And yes, that one too.) Thank you both, from the very fiber of my heart.

To my fellow #roaring20sdebut authors, especially Jennifer Moffett, Nora Shalaway Carpenter, and Liz Lawson, for the early reads and reviews, and for being generally awesome. I am proud to be counted among a group of such kind, enthusiastic, and talented writers.

Special thanks to the #WIPmo crowd, circa 2015—you kept me showing up, night after night, on that roughest of rough first drafts. Knowing I wasn't just typing into a lonely void means the world.

Susan Capozza, when I was on the verge of setting aside my words for good, you were there to take me back to the start—to remind me of the notebooks and stories, the poetry and plays, and all the ideas. You encouraged me to try again. You brought me back to writing. My first critique partner, my eternal friend; who else could I text from a Target bathroom, so regularly and so devoid of shame? Who else could ever be my cabbage? Thank you, for a lifetime of support and love. I love you.

Mom and Dad, for stacking books on top of other books and letting me dive in and read every last one that caught my eye; for never taking a book from my hands or underestimating my thoughts and curiosity. For teaching me to question everything, yet never stifling or censoring who I tried to be; for loving me for me, and never withholding praise or encouragement. Your sincere respect for me, as a daughter and an individual, has been a gift beyond riches. I love you so much (yes—more than sugar).

To my siblings, for putting up with all my weird big-sister stuff—Emily, Erika, David, Patrick, and John, I love you all. And to Brad, to whom I must seem even weirder, for the support and encouragement all the way back to the Florida days. Thank you.

Brandon, the best person I know—to list in detail all you've made possible for me, from this dream, to everything else, I'd need an entire other book of pages. You saw me right from the start—you encouraged me to write and create and succeed and achieve; to push myself past what I thought was my best, and to never give up on myself or on us. You've stood by my side through the best and worst of everything. I love you so very, very much, and am so proud to share my life with you. :<>

Henry and Cora, you are my whole life and my whole heart. You are the reason I stand and the strength behind every step forward. I will never stop trying to grow and learn and teach, to listen and help and understand. I will never stop trying, every day. I love you.

And last—but never ever least—for Gini. You always knew I could.

Turn the page for a sneak peek
at *Where Secrets Lie*.

SUMMER 2019

They weren't there.

I let the storm door close at my back, shutting out the river-soaked fever of the afternoon. My eyes adjusted to the dim indoor light, taking in the frown of the grandfather clock in the corner and the spatter of color on its polished face—broken sunbeams twisting their way to rainbows through the cluster of antique prisms in the entryway window. The air was cool and dry, sweet with almond oil and the soft flora of my grandmother's perfume. Fat to bursting with the tension of unsaid words.

I hadn't made it past the foyer, and the summer was already ruined.

"They haven't been by?" I asked, hating the panicked twist of my own voice. Hating the glimmer of hope I'd let bloom into flame. "You're absolutely sure?"

"No, sweetheart, they haven't." Grandma's eyes slid from me to my mother and back to me again, her brow furrowed. "Teddy finished up early today and went on home. Didn't say a thing about coming around this evening. As for Benny, he's been a bit of a pill these past several months. Your aunt Madeleine called earlier, said he won't leave his room, and—well, she wouldn't repeat his exact words. You know how he gets."

"They must be down at the cove already. I'll go see if they're waiting for me."

"Amy. They're not." She sighed, distressed as always by unpleasant conversation. "I'm sorry, dear. Let's go out to the kitchen, have a talk. It'll be okay, I just know—"

I was already gone.

Mom's anger was narrow, a thin, fine needle piercing the back of my head as I fled up the curved staircase. Louder in its silence than my shoe soles on the polished oak, or the worried lilt of Grandma's voice trailing at my heels. I focused on my retreat to the heavy bedroom door and its solid lock—my mother's old room, a child's room, yellow and pink and tucked under an eave. They put me there every year, as if they hadn't noticed that the short, slight girl who'd once squeezed her tiny body into all the hidden recesses of this big Victorian fun house had spent the past few summers bumping her head on the stupid slanted ceiling of that room. Sixteen years old and looking down at the world.

I dropped my stuff on the frilly duvet and crossed to the window, stared out at the empty trailhead. Tamped down the tears crowding the back of my throat.

For the first time since I could remember, the boys weren't waiting for me.

There was no point in texting Ben. River Run was too goddamn backwoods for its own cell tower, the property too removed to access what little coverage managed to straggle over from the nearest one. Even if it did, he probably wouldn't answer—Ben with a grudge was Ben at peak asshole, eclipsed in magnitude only by Teddy and his injured pride. I should have known better than to hope they'd show.

It was simple math that screwed us, really: We were an odd number—a prime number, divisible only by itself. Impossible to split into two equal parts. This natural discrepancy was one we gladly overlooked when the distance between us was literal, remedied by a first-class plane ticket, the end of the school year, the start of my parents' clockwork season abroad. And once together, it never mattered anyway—it was easy as anything to ignore the subsurface shifts and tectonic pressure, bound to end in cracks.

A blur of memories clamored for space in my head, so many summers rushing back at once, and *this* was how they wanted things to end? Fuck the phone. Fuck them, too—if they wanted to play cold shoulder, they'd damn sure picked the wrong opponent. I'd dissolve into mist before I'd let them see me beg.

The doorknob's rattle shook me from my thoughts. The lock clicked and gave; she was in the room before I'd even turned around.

"The door was locked for a reason, Mother."

"As if I don't know the trick to this old door. Freshen up and change your blouse. Grandma's got dinner planned, and . . ." She paused, studied my wet, red eyes and quivering chin. Her mouth tucked itself into a delicate sneer. "You shouldn't cry. It's showing."

"I don't care. Tell them it's allergies."

"You look miserable, Amy. Hold still." She crossed to the bed, pulled my Chanel compact from my purse. My vision sharpened to a surreal collection of shapes as her face neared mine and I shut down, withdrawing into the pocket of my mind—the noiseless, empty safe space that let me endure the blotting and blending as she coaxed me back to unblotched perfection. "I'm sorry he disappointed you, but it's no big shock, is it? Typical River Run boys."

Her words were venom-tipped darts designed to sting. What little I'd said on the subject last fall had still been too much. It was all I deserved, trusting that she'd give a fuck about my emotions apart from the impact they had on my art. Her fingers tightened on my chin as I tried to turn away.

"I'm not discussing him with you, Mom."

"He's never *been* up for discussion. Your focus is your work and your future, not a dead-end summer fling—if you can't uncouple one from the other, he's better off at arm's length. I can only guess at the real reason you came home empty-handed last year."

"Seriously? I told you I lost my satchel, along with my sketch-book and everything else in it. And I made up the work, remember?"

"I remember that's what you *said* happened. Not that careless-ness is an excuse. Don't forget these trips abroad are for your benefit as well—everything about my life, every extra moment beyond the bare minimum spent with your father—all of it is to ensure your success. All so you'll never be chained to this place, or anyone in it."

"Whatever. If you hate River Run so much, maybe you shouldn't drop me off here for months at a time."

"Watch your tone, young lady. Your grandparents love you, and I make allowances for that. What I won't do is nod and smile while you throw away the world." She brushed a final swipe of powder over my skin, turned me to face the vanity. "There. Much better."

She had indeed worked magic. My face was blank and lovely around smoke-lined, arctic blue eyes; the pale, tousled mess of my hair skimmed a perfectly blended jawline. My mother stood behind me in darker shades of everything, smile cold as the teeth of winter. I only had to look at her for one more day.

It would be easier once she was a literal world away. My parents would have a whole overseas flight to repress their marital issues, then they'd trek through the world behind a united front—through Johannesburg, Budapest, Jerusalem, wherever—my mother's eyes glued to the camera, every image another staggering paycheck when paired with my father's words. Jake and Eleanor Larsen, the husband-and-wife photojournalist powerhouse duo whose political and humanitarian projects overrode their forever-impending divorce. Those summers abroad kept me in the top private schools, hired the most prestigious art instructors to shape my future, kept my mother's closet overflowing with Kate Spade, and kept my father's Tesla Roadster in the garage of our enormous Great Falls home, for the few weeks a year he bothered showing up to park it there.

My father. A snow-washed glacier who'd much prefer to sink into the sea alone than endure even the idea of footprints. Mom's coldest cold shoulders were desert sands compared to his indifference. I'd learned *that* little trick from the best, to be sure—I'd never been a daddy's girl, but I was certainly his daughter, down to my frost-studded core.

It wasn't that he'd left us, gradually and without any sort of official verbal indicator—I of all people understood the undeniable urge to flee my mother at all costs. He was his own special brand of uninhabitable, who gifted his feelings to pages rather than people. Still, it was that he'd left *me,* young and defenseless, alone with her in a too-quiet house. A house where even a four-year-old was subject to her hovering hands and frantic voice, and rabid, relentless standards.

It hadn't taken her long at all to turn an exceptional preschool art project into a vicarious set of goals—to swap crayons for pastels, then pencils, then charcoals and ink, all before I'd learned to write my name. My childhood bled into an endless blur of figure study and cramping fingers, color wheels and still lifes and thumbnail sketches, all framed by the edges of my mother's shadow. She monitored the progress of the hands I'd inherited from her as if she wasn't the inspiration behind my desire to redraw the world. As if my hands couldn't just be my own, no matter what their shape. Now, my talent had surpassed even her most far-fetched hopes, opened doors neither of us expected—doors that triggered my own personal countdown, once I realized I could walk through any one of them without her, then slam it in her face when she tried to follow.

Twelve years and hundreds of miles from the first spark, that flame still burned. It fed on the grind of pencil lines and brushstrokes; on my apprenticeship and private tutelage. On my acceptance into an elite high school for the arts, where I joined the cutthroat seethe of students, all aspiring to unmatched greatness. We worked side by side and neck and neck, rivalries bleeding into resentments, the nature of our shared ambitions superseding personal connections— and that was before adding in our parents and their vicarious hopes, their personal issues and social aspirations, that culminated in more private lessons and hours of practice, leaving no time for sleepovers or shopping trips or, until recently, boy-shaped distractions.

That last one—well, that was a situation best left on the Eastern Seaboard, folded down into a memory and tucked safely in the pocket of his fucking sweater-vest. None of it had meant a thing beyond the first resentful impulses.

It had made Mom happy, though. Holy shit, had it ever—that old-money, furnace-eyed prospect, with his sharp cheekbones, his own credit card, his actual pressed slacks. A musician, of all things—a seventeen-year-old piano prodigy, who'd supported my goals, sympathized with the constant practice and constraints on my time, which very closely mirrored his own. He'd existed in smudges of skeletal branches and winter frost; in the twinkle of holiday lights on white DC marble. He'd whirled me through a season of gilt-edged, upscale recklessness and melted away in time for spring.

She'd taken that breakup harder than he had, my mother. Not that I gave a flying shit concerning her thoughts on the matter, but he'd made for a good cover story while it lasted. Much easier to hide behind her rules and expectations when his very presence canceled out her deepest fears. Easier to let the prodigy escort me through tree lightings and gallery openings, let him kiss me on New Year's Eve over glasses of vintage champagne he didn't have to pay for and, later, pretend he hadn't meant to feel that far up my skirt. Better to select and disconnect than deal with the day-to-day disgruntled gloom of various rejected art boys, or the fallout of random flirtations, unsolicited feelings, and the inevitable disintegration of both. As far as my heart was concerned, he'd barely existed.

There had only ever been three friends who mattered to me, who let me breathe and feel and be myself; who loved that self beyond the measure of my hands. Who exploded from the woods each summer in a frenzy of shrieks and laughter and open arms, eager to sweep me up and make us all whole again.

There had only ever been one boy.

And as I followed my mother down the carved oak staircase, properly freshened and powdered back to blank, I set about draining my nerves to match. The hollow inside me filled with sleet as that last day clawed its way to the surface, no longer willing to sleep.

The table was polished to its glossiest cherry shine, set with Grandma's embroidered linen runner and silver charger plates beneath the nice company china. A step down from formal, but more than the usual day-to-day comfort of the kitchen table. They almost never used the dining room.

It had to be a family dinner. Fuck my life.

"That was Madeleine on the phone, dear," Grandma chirped, bustling in from the kitchen, drying her hands on a rooster-red dish towel. The downstairs rooms were warm and bright, as if waiting to welcome me in every way. "They're having a bit of trouble getting Benny in the car. He's not feeling much up to a visit, she says."

"Good," I answered, slouching against the wall. "I can do without a visit from *Benny*."

"You'll be happy enough to see each other once the smoke clears," Grandpa said, taking half the entire summer to navigate his frail frame around the intricate dining chair arms. "A year's time enough for whatever's eating at you two to die down. In the meantime, we can do some eating of our own."

"God, can anyone just listen to me for once? I don't want to see Ben, okay? I don't. I won't."

"Well, okay, then." Grandpa shuffled back and forth, finally settled into the seat, poured a glass of sun tea from the pitcher next to his place setting. "If it's that big a deal, you can fix a plate for upstairs, and wait till you both cool off some. Maybe in a day or so—"

"No." My mother's voice was a sharpened ax, chopping off his words like a limb. Stilling the helpless fidget of my grandmother's hands. "We will all eat together, like any normal family. You will sit with us and say your hellos, and you and your cousin will act right, or so help me, Amy. I will not tolerate tantrums at your age, especially in your grandparents' home. Am I clear?"

"Yes, Mom." My breath was the edge of a whisper, the words filtered through a haze of cotton batting.

"Yes, *ma'am*."

"Yes, ma'am."

"Thank you, honey." Grandma crossed to me, voice soothing the cuts left by my mother's. Her fingers reached to smooth a strand of my hair, a soft, affectionate gesture ending in the same gentle tug one would give a dog's leash. I waited, but she held tight until I looked up. "It's for the good of the family. This is what we do."

His blurred reflection leaped across the windowpane, scarring my view of the yard—the crooked trees and jagged rocks, our path a hole in the familiar, looming thicket. Our childhood playground, backlit by a flash of sun. I cast a glare over my shoulder, met its twin in the bitter angles of his face.

My cousin leaned against the parlor doorframe, his whole demeanor honed slick and sharp. The boy version of me, staring back from hardened eyes.

He looked older than last year, startlingly so. His hair, though shorter, was still long for River Run. Still white-blond and impeccable, blunt cut right below his cheekbones and slicked back from his face. His hands were larger, his limbs longer, and he was finally as tall as me, grown into the broad, arrogant slope of his father's shoulders. A sudden ache sliced through my throat—a bone-deep longing for us, the way we'd always been: the three of us bound as one, inseparable until that final, awful day.

"Seriously?" I spat as Ben dragged his sneer from my hair to my shoes. "I thought you'd stay home."

"I was the first one in the door," he drawled. "Wanted to see if you had the sack to show your face."

"Because I'm the fuckup in this scenario? Benjamin. Please."

"Please whatever. You're the one who said we were done. And that's without mentioning the elephant in the room—or, more accurately, the elephant who is decidedly *not* in this particular room."

"I'm aware of the elephant."

"Good, then you'll recall the elephant was also a huge asshole, right? Or did you totally block out his part in this?"

"I 'recall' everything—and as I *recall,* you started it. You're the one who ruined us."

I turned back to the window, stared through our reflected faces, focused on the empty mouth of the path. Winced at the involuntary catch in my voice. He'd sense that weakness and fall upon it like a jackal, lock his jaws the second he hit bone. He always did.

"You started it," he mimicked. "Like I'm letting either one of you put this on me."

"It was your fault, Ben."

"Not all of it. I know I fucked up, but so did he. And you sure did do your part, Ames, so fucking own it. Don't hole away upstairs, or hide out in the sitting room, crying at the trees."

"I'm not crying." I whipped back around to face him, smeared a fist across my stinging eyes. Officially undid my mother's attempt at makeup repair. Pathetic. "*Or* hiding."

"Oh really? Guess that's for the best. Far as I can tell, nobody's trying too hard to seek."

His grin widened at my gasp, flexed open and bit down, feeding on my pain. His laughter followed me as I stalked past him, steeling myself to face our family.

ABOUT THE AUTHOR

Eva V. Gibson is the author of *Together We Caught Fire* and *Where Secrets Lie*. A bookworm since early childhood, she has routinely gravitated to the dark and gritty, reading, then writing, stories with grim themes and flawed, complicated characters. She lives in Northern Virginia with her family and spends most of her time brooding, baking, creating, and parenting, awaiting the day her kids read her books with equal parts excitement and trepidation.

BELIEVE IN YOUR SHELF

Visit RivetedLit.com & connect with us on social to:

DISCOVER NEW YA READS

READ BOOKS FOR FREE

DISCUSS YOUR FAVORITES

SHARE YOUR IDEAS

ENTER SWEEPSTAKES FOR THE CHANCE TO WIN BOOKS

Follow @SimonTeen on

to stay up to date with all things Riveted!

Can you fall in love with someone without the
humiliating weirdness of having to actually see them?
Ask Sam and Penny.

How much can you really tell about a person just by looking at them?

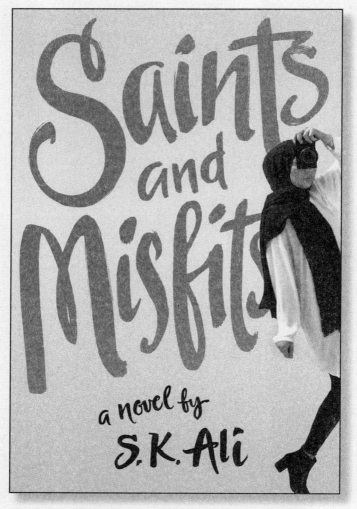

Saints and Misfits

a novel by

S. K. Ali